RACE TO NOVUS

R.A. CLARKE

For the three most important people in my life, Steve, Eithan, and Austin... You are muses, my cherished support, the owners of my heart, and treasures of my world.

FREE LAND - THE GREAT RACE TO NOVUS - FREE LAND

EVER DREAMT OF TRAVELLING TO WILD AND VIBRANT PLACES? TO OWN A SLICE OF GALAXIUM WHERE YOU CAN RAISE A FAMILY AND LIVE OFF THE LAND? THEN 2450 COULD BE YOUR LUCKY YEAR!

JOURNEY TO JOYA, OUR NEWLY COLONIZED PLANET. RACE THROUGH AN UNCHARTED FOREST, AND EXPERIENCE A WORLD UNLIKE ANY OTHER. THE FIRST 50 TO FINISH WILL WIN A PARCEL OF LAND SURROUNDING OUR NEW SETTLEMENT, NOVUS. DON'T MISS THE CHANCE OF A LIFETIME! THESE PARCELS ARE FREE, WITH ONLY A TINY PERCENTAGE OF ANNUAL PROFIT PAID TO GOVERNUS CORPORATION. SOUND LIKE AN OPPORTUNITY YOU'VE BEEN WAITING FOR? GET DOWN TO THE START LINE! A DEDICATED JOYAN TRANSPORT DEPARTS FROM THE PLANET HOBS IN EXACTLY <u>0</u> DAYS.

<u>ADVISORY</u>: RACE AT YOUR OWN RISK. THE ROUTE IS UNMANNED AND SPANS SEVERAL DAYS. NO ADDITIONAL SUPPLIES WILL BE PROVIDED. ONE PERSON PER FAMILY IS PERMITTED. ENTRANTS MUST BE OF LEGAL AGE ON THEIR HOME PLANET. GROUND CONVEYANCES ONLY. NO AIR TRAVEL IS PERMITTED. ENHANCED FUEL IS PROHIBITED. ALL VEHICLES ARE SUBJECT TO INSPECTION. RACERS SHALL RECEIVE A MANDATORY OCULAR IMPLANT. GOVERNUS IS NOT LIABLE FOR ANY DAMAGES OR INJURIES INCURRED BEFORE, DURING, OR AFTER THE EVENT. RULES ARE NON-NEGOTIABLE; JUDGES' DECISIONS ARE FINAL. READ THE RULES AND PRIZE INCLUSIONS IN THEIR ENTIRETY <u>HERE</u>.

CHAPTER 1

The transport ship quaked as it descended through the remnants of an asteroid belt surrounding Joya. Fragments of icy geodes bounced off the hull shields. I shifted the gear slung across my back as I hurried toward the live cargo hold, landmarking along the corridor to keep my balance. Poor Herc wouldn't be impressed by all the jostling. Hopefully, he didn't lose his footing and hit his head or pull a muscle. An injury was the last thing we needed right now.

I breezed through the viewing deck, catching a hand wave in my peripheral. A group of racers had gathered to watch as we approached the newly discovered planet. Two competitors I'd befriended during our four-week trip from Hobs were in the mix. I also caught a glimpse of the top half of Joya beyond, and I couldn't help but veer towards the portal to sneak a quick peek.

"Hey." I slid in next to Sarah and Griggs who'd made space for me. "I only have a second. Gotta check on Herc. So, that's it—Joya…" Peering through the portal, the planet came into full view. Vast open spaces of grasslands and hills covered most of Joya's visible terrain, broken up by river threads and countless dense winding strains of forest scattered about in no apparent pattern. Those must be what the race rules called 'Sweeps'. The way they appeared curled and stretched reminded me of earthworms stranded on a sidewalk after a rainstorm.

"The one and only," Griggs drawled.

"No lakes or oceans." Sarah tilted her head in a *huh* kind of way.

I shrugged. "Maybe it has aquifers instead?" The ship trembled again, spurring me into action. "Oop—gotta go. I'll see you guys on the start line."

Sarah offered a fist bump before I could back away. "Make sure you oil your horse's legs." She was a year older than me at twenty-five, and was half-human, half-Crimeon—reptilian genes which bestowed a slight alligator texture to her skin.

I chuckled. "Oh, he's greased up and ready. If only a little oil'd clear up *my* nerves."

Sarah patted my shoulder. "Don't worry. Once we're moving, our jitters will fuck off." As a repurposer by trade, she made her wage transforming outdated tech into usable tools. Being accustomed to dealing with brash roughneck types on the regular, and not one to show weakness, it was a kindness she'd included the word 'our' in her reassurance.

Backing away, I smiled. "Thanks."

"Save us a spot if you get there first, will ya?" Griggs gave a lazy salute, his five-o-clock shadow doing little to hide his dimples. He'd grown up on Earth like me, but moved to Mars at a young age. He never elaborated on the why of things, and despite my curiosity, I didn't pry.

"Right back atcha." I waved, then hurried off down an adjacent corridor.

The cargo hold wasn't much farther. Good thing, because my gear was feeling heavy.

The ship rattled less and less as I went, and by the time I rounded the final corner and entered the room, the tremors were negligible. But how had Herc weathered the worst of them?

I rushed to his enclosure and set down my things. "Hey, buddy. Are you okay?" I swiped my digicuff over a security pad while catching my breath. It flicked from red to green. Blue light from Herc's ocular implant reflected off the metallic walls within, giving his stall a cyan glow. All sixteen-hands of him rippled with eagerness—his ears alert and muzzle already reaching through the gate's bars for a snack he expected to be in my pocket.

Yeah, he seemed just fine.

Stacks of heavy-duty crates tethered by cargo netting lined the wall opposite the row of live cargo stalls. Fans pumped fresh air through meshed vents overhead, while simulated sunlight filtered down through the chamber. All hard lines and metal panels, the hold was not an overly welcoming environment, but after adding a cozy layer of bedding, it had served its purpose. The adjoined exercise space had enabled me to ride Herc during the trip, too. A lifesaver. Even though his prosthetic legs didn't require a workout, the rest of him still did.

I swung open the steel gate and Herc was right there, voraciously nuzzling at my pockets. Shuffling my way into what had been his home-away-from-home, I let out a chuckle.

"C'mon now. Let me at least get in the door." Finally, I was inside far enough to shut the gate behind me. But me turning away didn't deter Herc in the slightest. "Alright, alright. Here you go." I pulled the carrot from my pocket and he gobbled it out of my palm. No use torturing the horse. I bought a fresh bag yesterday in preparation for our arrival on Joya—well, not exactly fresh. This transport ship had replicated food. No hydroponic gardens to be found.

"We'll be landing soon." Herc nudged me and I gave his smooth black coat a pat. "Yeah, I'm eager to get off this ship too. We need sunshine and solid ground beneath us again, hey?"

I put his bridle on, then laid his custom saddle atop his back. "Hopefully soon, we'll be setting up our own place here. A spot we can be proud of—where nobody knows anything about my past and we're free to do whatever we want. A true fresh start."

Workable land wasn't easy to come by these days, no matter where you hailed from in the Galaxium. Affordable land, even less so. And free land? Yeah, right! That's what made this race impossible to pass up. It not only offered land prizes, but in the fine print it also specified each winner received a 100,000-credit start-up loan for the purpose of launching a homestead. I'd been mulling over the possibilities a lot these past weeks. Assuming cows didn't already exist on Joya, I aimed to bring them here and earn a steady income supplying colonies with quality beef.

It felt good to stand on my own two feet… something I'd never really done before.

It was actually quite embarrassing to admit, being twenty-four-years-old, but most of my life's choices had been influenced by men. I grew up under my father's thumb, fulfilling all of my family's expectations, and then—well, I got messed up in a regrettable debacle that tethered me to the ranch for the past three years. A very *long* three years.

I gave Herc's neck a stroke. "Listen, if we win this thing, I'll pay off every last credit I owe, then maybe I can finally get you a girlfriend. Whaddya think of that?" Herc let out a timely whinny and I laughed. "Yeah, I thought so." Cattle aside, I also dreamed of breeding horses with Herc as my prize stud. Being a Friesian, he had an incredible mixture of intelligence and power.

I'd won him in a drunken game of pocket poker—aptly named for its tendency to fill or empty said pockets—three years ago on one of Earth's colonized planets, Helix II. I'd been there with my ex, and only dumb luck saved me from losing all of my family's crop money as it passed through my gullible fingers. At first, I was pissed at receiving an almost three-year-old colt in place of the much-needed credits I was due, but soon realized I'd actually been paid quite well. Probably better than my opponent realized in his deeply inebriated state. Herc was pure—unrefined.

Genetically refining Earth-born beasts of burden became mandatory back in the early 2200's. The process, which minimized breed deficiencies, nearly wiped out pure-blooded horses. *Nearly.* A fringe group of breeders happened to preserve some of them as rare collectibles.

Turned out, the precious warhorse descendent I'd won was worth a small fortune.

His pedigree didn't keep my family from despising me though...

I cleared my throat, pushing away an influx of intrusive thoughts. Using my hands, I inspected Herc's four bio-linked leg prosthetics, each made of burnished, diamond-hard metal and interlocking components that formed exceedingly efficient limbs. I finished cinching his saddle next, then packed the remainder of his food stores. There wasn't much left of the real stuff I'd originally stockpiled—my transport rations working out exactly as planned. Carrying mounds of excess food during a race wasn't exactly feasible. So, once that ran out, we'd dive into the Meal Preserve Packets I snuck from the storm cellar back home. Neither human nor equine MMP's were particularly appetizing, but they'd provide nutrition to keep us going.

Once I secured my bedroll and swollen saddlebags—packed with my food, changes of clothes, a toiletry kit, med kit, our breathers, and a couple of items my mother gifted to me—I sheathed my pulse rifle in its scabbard and tied a rope around the saddle horn. Straightening my shoulders, I perched both hands on my hips and took a deep breath. We were ready.

A musical chime blared over the ship-wide comms. "*Attention all travellers of starship Vetera. Welcome to planet Joya. Ensure your quarters are clear of personal effects, then proceed to a designated exit and disembark in an orderly fashion. We hope you enjoyed your trip.*"

"About time." I reached for the tan cowboy hat hanging between my shoulder blades and pressed it atop my head. Four weeks was plenty long enough to spend aboard a transport. The sooner Governus got Transport Conduit Gates constructed enroute to Joya, the better. Not only would TCG's cut the monthlong trek exponentially, but they'd surely boost tourism, too.

"Looks like we're finally clear to get the hell outta here. Are you ready, big guy? Feeling good? Feeling strong?" Herc let out a soft nicker, his real eye staring into mine. I took that as a yes. Opening the gate, I led him out just as a stocky racer named Jorgep rushed into the hold to collect his mount. He looked frazzled, his thick legs moving fast. The wispy spread of feelers lining his jaw stood out like he'd just touched a ship security officer's shock baton.

We exchanged smiles and nods, having become familiar over the weeks. He was an odd fellow, but friendly, and had joined into an alliance with Sarah, Griggs, and I. Since he and I were the only two racers aboard who'd dared to bring non-mechanical conveyances, we'd had this quiet space mostly to ourselves and bonded over it. His mount was a Bleenad named Keemi, an intense-looking creature—tall, thick-bodied and scaly, with gnarled overlapping teeth and three eyes descending each side of her rounded face. The creature looked likely to rip a man's arm off, but from what Jorgep said, she was quite the sweetheart.

"Finally, it's the big day," I called out as we headed toward the riser, eager to get outside. "Meet you at the start line, okay?"

"Yes. I shall see you there, Miss Finn." He smiled, gave a crisp wave, then returned to his rushed preparations. I wanted to tell him—yet again—to drop the 'Miss', but A) he was pretty busy, and B) I knew doing so was futile. The guy hailed from a planet that put a major emphasis on respect. Politeness was just Jorgep's way, ingrained from birth.

Scanning my digicuff across the log pad, I signed Herc out, then pressed the ground level button. My unruly russet-coloured braid fell over my shoulder as I donned a well-worn pair of leather gloves. The riser doors slid open seconds later, and we entered.

Herc's hooves clopped against the crosshatched metal floor, the sound echoing as the doors closed behind us. The riser descended, eliciting that familiar floating stomach feeling.

My thoughts swirled with unknowns during our short ride to the surface. Would the land Governus offered be as fertile as described? What would we encounter in this so-called Sweep? I, like the other racers, had taken a gamble travelling to Joya without seeing a full participation contract first. We knew nothing beyond what the rules section stated in the ad. But the fact it was Governus putting it on—a respected corporation whose humanitarian projects offered housing for many overpopulated planets—counted for something in my mind. Sure, there were rumours saying they'd used cut-throat tactics, but what corporations didn't? Big business ruled the three amalgamated galaxies forming the Galaxium. Right now, I only hoped I hadn't wasted a month of my life and my meagre savings to get here.

The riser doors opened. A wave of brilliant violet light washed over me and I blinked several times to adjust to the foreign hue. I didn't bother to engage my breather since I'd been assured the atmosphere was safe on Joya. Interestingly, the air seemed denser here. When I took a deep breath it tickled my throat a bit, but not uncomfortably so.

I led Herc out. The smell of hot metal, dust, and exhaust permeated the air as we strode down the ramp onto the docking pad. Other racers disembarked from several exit doors spaced across the length of our robust transport vessel, filtering into the fray below.

Here we go.

CHAPTER 2

p ahead, at the entrance to a pathway leading into the settlement, stood four sharply dressed individuals I assumed to be Governus representatives. A crowd had gathered behind and around them, comprising a mixture of racers and Egan residents—colony folk. Broad smiles of welcome split the local's faces. Tipping my cowboy hat, I smiled back. A bottleneck had formed up ahead where participants stopped to provide their own customary greetings to the organizers. Layered voices and engines of all kinds hummed and growled to life as the procession slowly moved along. Herc's ears flicked in all directions while he surveyed our chaotic surroundings.

As we walked, the odd individual got a little too close, jostling for position and crowding in on Herc. Most of the time, he tolerated it, even though his ocular implant shone green. An understandable reaction. But, whenever his eye turned red, nostrils flaring, I spoke up.

"You better back off unless you wanna get kicked," I warned one such racer who'd squeezed in on Herc's right, my tone as flat as the Manitoba prairie.

The bulbous fellow with greasy hair covering most of his body scoffed and flashed two crossed fingers at me. Historically, the gesture indicated a desire for good luck back on Earth, but Galaxium-wide, it was better known as a tell-off. A harsh one. The guy pushed forward, roughly shoving Herc's hind end in order to squeeze his slender solar cycle past.

"Hey!" My protective instinct kicked in. "Don't touch my—"

Herc's neck bumped into my shoulder as one of his powerful rear legs shot out, kicking the guy's cycle right out from under him. The bike clattered to the ground, banging against another vehicle, and the guy toppled onto an unimpressed racer—a tall man wearing an ornately embroidered green hooded cloak—who promptly swore and shoved him off. Popping back up to his thick webbed feet, Mr. Hairy-Pants checked the damage, seeing a hoof-shaped dent in the side panel of his vehicle. He scowled at me, spitting a few choice words.

"Warned you." I shrugged, leading Herc right on past. I stared straight ahead, worried he might escalate things, but he didn't, and I tried my best not to let on that I'd been nervous. It was imperative not to appear weak in this competitive and uncertain atmosphere. Calling bluffs in certain black-market casinos had taught me that. *Stand tall, Finn. Fake it til' you make it.* Most folks gave us a respectfully wide berth after that, which was a relief. But to make things easier, I manoeuvred Herc to the outskirts of the throng and kept moving forward. No use making waves.

Several minutes later, we reached the back end of the clustered bottleneck.

A group of colony children caught my eye on the left. They jumped up and down like they had springs for feet, pointing fingers at Herc with wide eyes. *They've probably never seen a horse before.* Flashing an amused grin, I gave a signal for Herc to prance. In his agitated state, my highly trained horse responded slower than usual, but within a few seconds his neck arched and his knees lifted high—hooves bouncing. The brief action sent the kids into a flurry of excited whispers, and to my surprise, a collection of adult colonists clapped at the display, too.

Oddly, I felt like one of those pageant queens I'd seen in reels at the humanity museum. On display for everyone's viewing pleasure. "Hopefully there won't be a swimsuit portion," I muttered to Herc, whose eye still glowed a tell-tale shade of green. Somewhere nearby, an engine backfired and his well-muscled body jolted to the side. I held firm to the reins, hoping he didn't decide to bolt—I'd never be able to hold him if he did. His legs were too powerful. But thankfully, he let me pull him back in close. I patted his neck. "Easy now. Everything's alright."

Competitors sized each other up as they made their way down the makeshift aisle. There was a real mixed bag of species. Many I'd encountered before on space stations or during my past gambling excursions, but others were truly new to me—perhaps hailing from more remote parts of the Galaxium. Some eyes were friendly, some curious, others calculating. Not everyone I'd met on board had been friendly, that's for sure. Not a shock given the nature of the race.

Taking my turn, I stopped before the Governus reps and presented a hand to shake amidst the chorus of chatter surrounding us. A bearded man—an advisor—with a nest of horns twisting atop his head shook my hand first. After him came a grey-skinned and well-muscled male whose entire lower half was bionic. His name tag said Steel—a CEO. He presented a grin that didn't quite reach his eyes, and I took a mental note. Next down the line stood a tall woman with similar grey skin. Another CEO. Khana. She wore a black bowler hat with a sleek striped pant suit, perfectly streamlined to her shapely form.

The woman grasped my hand, shaking firmly. "Welcome to Egan." Khana's voice sounded husky yet powerful. A wide smile graced her face, her striking ice-blue eyes exuding incredible warmth. "I must say your mode of travel is most... interesting." She seemed a pinch curious, or perhaps mystified. Maybe both.

"Happy to be here, ma'am. And yes, this is Hercules, my horse. Ever seen one before?" Herc stomped his hoof, ears twitching.

"I haven't. You've given me a first today." Khana nodded regally, before waving me onward. "The race begins at noon. Please make your way to the start line to register and receive your implant." She pointed down the dirt road leading through the settlement. "Good luck."

"Thank you, ma'am." I smiled, then moved on to shake the final Governus advisor's tentacle-like hand. After sharing a final nod, I notched a boot into a stirrup, and swung onto Herc's back. With reins in hand, I squeezed my heels and we took off at an easy lope.

Riding through town, we slowed to a walk and I took in the rows of buildings lining the street. Sheets of metal were bolted together in various angular constructions. Some had been slathered with colourful paint, which I assumed was an attempt to make it feel homier. The odd storefront was intermixed between homes, each one offering a variety of basic goods and services. Shopkeepers stood at the ready watching the procession go by, eagerly awaiting the business this influx of travellers might bring.

A pair of three-wheeled off-roaders kicked up dust as they sped toward the crowd gathering up ahead. I watched it swirl and found myself smiling. Growing up on a cattle ranch, I'd been exposed to a slew of historical movies called "westerns". I was kind of like one of those cowgirls right now. Riding into a new town seeking to make a fresh start. If it weren't for all the commotion these high-tech conveyances caused, I'd half expect a tumbleweed to roll by.

When we finally reached the end of the settlement, the buildings halted abruptly, with nothing but grassy hills and sky existing beyond them... except for the hazy smudge stretched across the horizon. That had to be the Sweep—the uncharted wilderness we'd be racing through. The new settlement of Novus and free land parcels awaited racers on the other side.

It seemed a bit odd that it remained unmapped or explored, especially given the scanning technology that existed today. I was surprised a powerful company like Governus hadn't done that first thing before sinking any resources into colonization. But I pushed the wayward thought aside as we arrived at the line-up. The notion of an uncharted Sweep wasn't outlandish enough to outweigh the reward of free land. It was time to focus. Getting through that forest and securing my land was all that mattered right now.

Competitors filed forward to sign in with the registrar and we followed suit. I was dying to know how many racers there were. Two fifty? Two seventy-five, maybe? My stomach grew heavy thinking about it, like I'd just gorged myself on a bowl of my mom's fireside beans—which I realized I might never taste again. I cleared the sudden lump in my throat, then told myself it could be worse. A less risky race would've attracted way more competition. I wiped a band of moisture from my brow and replaced my hat. As the sun climbed higher in the sky, the air warmed with it. Two hours to wait. I swung a leg over the saddle and dropped to the ground. Best give Herc a break before go time.

Thirty minutes later, we finally reached the front of our line and the race administrator recorded my details on his sign-up sheet. The portly fellow handed me a roughly drawn map and an information sheet, then transferred the contract to my wrist cuff.

"So… Finnley Rucker. Read it, sign it. Don't forget to hit submit. No signed contract, no race. Once you do that, you head into *that* building—" He pointed to the last structure on the far side of the street. "Get your monitoring implant and you'll be good to go. No implant, no race. Got it? Good luck."

"Yes, thank you, sir," I said. "Can I ask—" But he was already waving the next competitor forward.

Alrighty then.

I led Herc into the shade of a nearby building, and gave him a chunk of carrot while I reviewed the contract. From what I could tell, everything seemed on the level. An injury and indemnity waiver added to the rules I'd already read. No strange provisos or overworded clauses meant to confuse. Simply race at your own risk for a chance at free land. Well… almost free. If I won, ten percent of my homestead's annual earnings would be due to Governus in perpetuity. A living tax, essentially—and not excessive. I could handle that.

For good measure, I saved a copy of the file to my cuff's internal storage. Then I digitally signed it and hit *submit* before turning off the projected 2D digiscreen. Turning to Herc, I ran my hand over the star etched into the polished metal that covered most of his forehead and right cheek. A real star used to be there before the accident. I blinked away images of his body laying broken on the rocks, still as vivid as if it happened yesterday.

"There's no turning back now, Herc," I whispered, leading him toward the implant location. "We're in it to win it." He blew a warm breath of air in my face, his fuzzy whiskers tickling my cheek as I tied him to a post several feet from the door. Racers were scattered about all over the place, killing time by reading, chatting, gambling, arguing, or even napping. I eyed the closest individuals warily, not particularly keen on leaving Herc here unattended.

After removing my pulse rifle from its scabbard, I energized the reins and engaged the built-in shock lock feature on the leather saddle bags straddling Herc's back. If anybody tried to untie him or break into my bags, an alarm would notify me while simultaneously sending a solid jolt into the offender's system. A standard feature these days. Couldn't be too careful.

I slipped inside the building to obtain my mandatory implant. "Will this take long?" I asked the nurse who led me into a small operating room.

She gave a soothing smile. "The procedure takes ten minutes, tops."

"Thanks." *Good. I don't want to leave Herc for too long.*

The multi-limbed doc strode in moments later and explained the procedure. "I will numb the area, then affix this appliance to your temple." He held up a metallic button-sized retinal monitor. "The implant's needle houses bio connectors designed to patch into the host's visual cortex—your visual cortex—allowing viewers to see through your eyes."

"Right… got it." I nodded slowly. "But, what about privacy? And permanency?"

The doctor tapped his clipboard. "I assure you the implant is fully removable post-race, and it has an auto-sensor to protect you. It has no audio, and no sensitive body parts will be visible at any time."

I remained leery. Not having had any enhancements done to myself beyond a synth tattoo on my hip, I wasn't keen on getting an implant. But I also wanted a shot at winning that land. Realistically, retinal implants were pretty common. *Suck it up, Finn.*

"Listen." The doc must've sensed my hesitancy, because he hooked the implant up to a screen and handed it to me, pointing to its pinhole exterior capture lens. "Point this at whatever sensitive bits you like and watch what happens on screen." He turned away. "Go ahead."

"This is just bizarre…" I mumbled, but grudgingly did what he said—had to. How else would I know for sure? Flashing the pinhole down my shirt, I snuck a peek at the screen with one squinty eye. Nothing but indistinguishable blurs showed up. I smiled, relaxing. *Okay, this is doable. No embarrassing bathroom episodes.*

"Good?" The doctor's tone hinted at impatience.

"Yeah, good."

About ten minutes later, I walked back outside. A bit groggy, I winced in the sunlight and tenderly rubbed the circular disc on my temple. The doc had warned lethargy and nausea were common side effects of the relaxation shot I was given. "It will pass soon," he'd said.

It better. I need to be alert for this race.

Herc nickered a greeting as I re-joined him. To my relief, his eye glowed blue again—a positive sign. Clearly, nobody had messed with him while I was away, and he was finally getting used to our new surroundings. Too bad I couldn't warn him it was about to get a lot crazier.

Another forty-five minutes passed before an announcement called all racers to the start line. I led Herc over, my grogginess long gone, and stopped at a heavy-looking steel desk where a floppy-eared guy was organizing things.

"Here's your number," he said. "It corresponds to a space on the start line. Head over there now. Oh, and there's two-hundred of you racers here, so keep things calm and orderly."

Two hundred racers had turned out for the race. Well now, that number was less than my original guesstimate. "And just to confirm, there's only fifty parcels up for grabs, right?"

Floppy-ears gave a bored smile. "Yes, fifty. Move along. Good luck."

I clucked my tongue as we claimed our designated space on the line. *Two hundred racers...* So, that meant I had a twenty-five percent shot at a piece of land. Those odds still weren't as good as I'd like them to be, but they were good enough to keep my hope alive.

CHAPTER 3

early an hour later, most racers had been registered, implanted, and pointed toward their designated spaces along a sprawling red start line. Ol' floppy ears had walked by several minutes ago, announcing the race would begin as soon as everybody was in place. Craning my neck, I spied the last competitors making their way to their spots.

Any time now.

While Herc topped up on water I'd poured from an outdoor tap, I surveyed the competition. What a collection of individuals. Lifeforms of all shapes, sizes, colours and consistencies were on display. There were the slender and ever-grumpy Ganglians, the statuesque Pembru, Zebords like Jorgep, slippery-faced Tumcah, and spotted Feedo. I also spied eight-limbed Monam, spike-backed Lashee's, and translucent skinned Neersoo, among countless other species of alien residing within a month's travel of Hobs. Not many humans, though. Sarah, Griggs, and I were among the few. Well, Sarah was half-human anyway. Her other half was a reviled reptilian species, but thankfully, she hadn't inherited many Crimeon features. The faint texture to her skin gave her enough trouble as it was. Her lineage didn't bother me at all, though. To me, Sarah was good people until proven otherwise. I was happy the three of us connected on board the ship during our four-week journey to Joya. Despite being fully prepared to race alone, the idea of forming an alliance had grown on me.

The majority of the racers kept busy tinkering with their machines or sizing each other up. Not counting Jorgep and myself, the field consisted of mechanical vehicles propelled by all manner of wheels, skids, or tracks. I'd seen a few hover ships earlier in the day, but sadly, none made the cut during inspection. I'd witnessed one such rejection up close en route to our spot.

"Flak off you slaggers!" a Sessiyon had shouted, slamming his fist onto the Governus inspector's table. He had pale grey skin and striking eyes, just like the two Governus representatives I'd met earlier.

In response, the Governus inspector stood tall, crossing his arms. "A hovercraft does not have wheels, therefore it travels by air. Air travel is not permissible. It said so clearly in the rules. You shouldn't have brought it." He swept a clawed hand toward the Sweep. "If you wish to race on foot, be my guest. If not, kindly remove yourself from this line. My decision is final."

"Nobody on the transport told me it would be rejected!" the Sessiyon growled.

"The transport is just that. A *transport*. It's not their race to govern."

The livid racer thrust two crossed fingers into the inspector's face.

"The transport ship departs for Hobs tomorrow." The inspector calmly held up a credit wand. "Here, please have a drink on Governus for your trouble. Just hold up your wrist cuff."

"A drink? A drink!" The Sessiyon swung a fist at the inspector, who skillfully dodged it before pushing the man's back to send him flying. Two Governus guards swooped in from nearby and captured the offender's arms, dragging him backward.

The inspector held up a hand and the guards paused.

"No, I insist." He approached and tapped his credit wand to the seething racer's cuff. "Safe travels home." Then the inspector waved him away.

What a gut punch that must've been.

Ousted racers aside, the general mood on the line was a mix of cheerfulness and impatience, with a few token faces looking like they just gulped some sour milk. Some racers interacted, while others kept to themselves. Arguments or fights broke out now and then. One Tumcah dude down the row even sang to pass the time, his less than melodic opera earning him several requests to shut up. But the guy just laughed, his generous gelatinous belly jiggling as he belted it out. Jorgep wasn't far away, and seemed to get a real kick out of the crooner's infectious cheeriness. His unmistakable guffaws sliced through the din with ease. But many, like me, stared ahead, contemplating the raw alien expanse of forest that laid before us. The Sweep.

Herc finished his water and I collapsed the container, tucking it into a saddlebag. Wiping the sweat from my brow, I clipped the edge of my retinal monitor, wincing as a twinge shot through my temple. The doctor had said it would take a few hours to get used to the implant. At first it had tingled, which I didn't mind. But now it felt like a nasty sunburn, mixed with the odd needle poke. I wasn't overly keen about having Governus in my head, either. But at least the reasoning they gave made some sense. With all the action of a race, external cameras could be lost or broken too easily. In order to thoroughly monitor and respond to medical emergencies, the cameras had to be reliable.

I caught eyes with Sarah down the line on my right and waved. She'd brought a bright orange and yellow bio-mech suit. It was capable of tripling an athletic human's natural speed—a sport model, though all mech's were still bulky. At least it would do most of the hard work for her.

I noticed the same tall, green-cloaked racer from earlier claiming his designated spot five down to my right. The hood hid his facial features well, yet he looked up enough once for me to see he was a Ganglian. That explained the height. He caught my curious glance and glared back.

Averting my gaze, I focused on Griggs, a few bodies away in the opposite direction. He shot me a quick smile, dimples on display. Ignoring the faintest tingle that caused, I tipped my hat in return. Being an ex-military guy, I thought he'd be driving some huge beast of a machine, but no. He rode a sleek chrome covered spyro cycle, designed to travel light and low to the ground. Its hybrid engine was powered by both the driver's foot rotations and fuel.

"You ready to rock?" he asked, quoting one of his favourite slang terms from the 21st century. Griggs had quite the obsession with pre-contact earth culture. Some of the things that interested him were just bizarre—like the internet, muscle cars, or rap music.

I scoured my brain, then replied, "You got it, dood."

"Nice! A late 20th century catch phrase. You've been paying attention." He flashed me a thumbs up, then pulled on his helmet. Reclining in the seat of his cycle, he stretched his feet to the pedals. Then, reaching forward, he pulled down the handle bars— ready to go.

"What about you, bud? Are you *ready to rock?*" I smirked at Herc, rubbing his muzzle. He bobbed his head and stomped, as if impatient for the race to start. I heard the faintest hum as his robotic eye scanned left and right. It shone blue again, a good sign he was settling into the near constant engine revving and cacophony of voices surrounding us. I tightened the braids woven into his mane, then gave the saddle a once-over for good measure.

There was nothing to do now but wait.

Questions niggled in my brain as I admired the rolling plain. Long emerald, blueberry, and straw-coloured grasses rippled rhythmically to a melody the wind created. Roughly a mile up ahead, the sweeping expanse disappeared into the mysterious forest, which stretched on for an indeterminable distance. What existed there remained completely unknown. Questions snuck into my mind. *Was I right to take the gamble and come here? Isn't gambling exactly what I've been trying to atone for the last three years? Am I even strong enough to do this?*

"Hey, human!" a throaty voice boomed from my right. The Ganglian, who'd seemingly taken a shine to glaring at me, motioned for my attention with a flick of his wrist. He stood tall beside his robust motorcycle-looking rig with thick pipes sticking out the sides like stubby wings, the whole thing covered in hand-painted symbols. His slender sinewy form looked odd next to that beast of a machine. Like a full-grown bull rubbing up on a flagpole.

Several sets of curious eyes swung my way.

"The name's Finn," I clarified with a nod, forcing a smile.

"Yeah, whatever." He let his hood fall to his shoulders as he strode closer, passing the other machines between us. He looked Hercules up and down. Fleshy scale-like protrusions covering his skin twitched as his thin lips curled in amusement. "You really expect to compete with *this?*" Laughing, he slowed to a halt a few feet away.

"Most certainly," I replied evenly, already sensing how this interaction was likely to proceed. Typical Ganglian with a mightier-than-thou attitude. Ever since the trade accord was signed, allowing them to do business with green-listed planets, they'd been a barely-tolerated presence within the civilized Galaxium. If not for the vast mineral resources and innovative technology Ganglia produced, nobody would give them the time of day.

A surprised reaction was understandable, though, since there weren't many horses in these parts. Not yet anyway—I aimed to change that. However, I didn't get the feeling he was merely surprised. I didn't like the way he was sneering at my horse.

"This is an Earth *horse,* correct? A flesh and blood creature." He scoffed, reaching a lanky arm to poke one of Hercules's metallic front legs. "Well, mostly."

"Hey, no touching." I moved between the Ganglian and my mount. Herc sidestepped, snorting behind me, and the unsavoury fellow backed off. But only slightly. "Can I help you with something specific, mister…?"

Twisting his narrow features into a sneer, he answered, "Raker." Then he glanced around, raising his voice. "And help from a *human*? Never."

A few snickers filtered into my ears.

There was obviously more than one Earth hater in this lineup, a fact which only reinforced the need to watch my back. Humans were nearly as despised as Crimeons by a select minority. When humans first achieved sustainable long-range space travel and encountered life on other planets, they'd been viewed as rudimentary at first—like cute little babies that knew nothing. It was true in a way. Humanity had barely begun their quest for the stars. Yet, over time, being nothing if not determined, humans worked hard to harness more advanced tech and forged peaceful relations with other species. Then, about 100 years ago, Earth played a large role in creating transport conduits that regulated and allowed efficient travel for all treatied planets within the Galaxium. Humans claimed a place in the upper echelon of civilized cultures.

However, regulating the trade routes pissed off a lot of folks—especially the black-market planets with their beyond-the-law business ventures—and the lingering bad blood never seemed to scrub out of the carpet.

"Yeah, alright." I tipped my hat in a curt gesture, opting to disengage. "Well, since we have no business with each other, you best get back to your spot, then."

"Oh, don't mind my curiosity…" Raker continued exaggeratedly, adding a faux polite nod. "I couldn't contain myself. I simply *had* to come see this slothenly creature up close." He took a step back, eyes lingering a second too long on Herc's saddle packs.

"Slothenly," I replied flatly, doing a poor job at hiding my irritation. I'd had just about enough of this guy. Clearly, he'd deemed anything Earthly as less-than. If I let it slide, I'd only add fuel to his misguided beliefs…but I didn't want a confrontation either. So, I opted for the competitive answer. "Well, I guess we'll see, won't we?"

Raker's eyes narrowed. "Yes. We will, indeed."

Murmurs rippled through the crowd, breaking our stand-off.

The Governus representatives strode past the start line into the field, a league of underlings in tow. They called for quiet from both the racers and the colonists who'd gathered to watch the proceedings. Excitement quashed the impatience previously on everyone's faces.

The dapper-looking leaders held their heads high, showcasing the polite disinterest typical of a big corporation. Like other such businesses, buying up new planets had made them powerful, their operations expanding and turning profit from mining ore and other precious materials wherever they laid claim—or took a claim from a lesser company. Perhaps that's why I'd been surprised by the race advertisement at first, wondering why such a prominent company would give away free land. It seemed odd, but they were also huge on colonising, and that equalled money too. They must've had a clear strategy fuelling their decision.

The Governus representatives' reserved expressions broke into gregarious smiles. The woman with grey skin and those startling blue eyes took a step forward, her arms spread wide.

"Greetings! I am a CEO of Governus, Khana Leenayt. This is my business partner, Steel—" She motioned to the half-bionic man beside her. "And we'd like to officially welcome you all to our newest, and very beautiful planet, Joya." A metallic insignia of three triangles framing a planet glinted in the sun on each of their bowler hats.

Raker shot me one last glare then strode back to his own space.

Ignoring him, I focused on the CEO. *Here we go.*

"Governus is currently celebrating our 150th year in business! To commemorate that amazing milestone, we planned this race as a way to give back and pay our prosperity forward." Khana paused for applause before continuing, her voice echoing from the loudspeakers erected along the start line. "Now, I trust you've all signed the contract, read the rules, and are aware of the dangers. Each of you has been outfitted with an implant that allows us to visually monitor the race and provide updates to the residents here, who will be eagerly cheering you on. Since we're dealing with uncharted lands, monitoring was a prudent safety protocol to implement. I'm sure you understand."

She pressed her palms together in front of her chest, then swung one arm out toward the trees in the distance. "Beyond the Sweep lies Novus, a fledgling settlement, and fifty free parcels of fertile land. But you won't just find land there… you'll find dreams, too. The kind that come true!" A few hoots erupted from the crowd, and the CEO smiled—her lips wide, yet tight.

She motioned with her hands for silence. "If you're among the first fifty racers to reach Novus, you'll join us as a valued member of Joyan society henceforth. I guarantee you will fall in love with our communities, and trust me when I say, we can't wait to meet the lucky winners. So—race hard, be safe, and we shall see you on the other side."

The crowd clapped, whistling and cheering. The CEO signalled her colleagues and all of the representatives engaged their boot thrusters. In a synchronised motion, the group rose into the sky. Khana deferred her spotlight to Steel. The metal-legged rep who wore an ornate suit jacket with tails, and held up a strange wide-barrelled gun, moved forward.

"One last reminder. If anybody has medical or vehicle troubles, we *will* see it and arrange to get you as soon as is feasible. We will also see any kind of aggression, so ensure you play nice." His tone deepened for those last pointed words, hard as quenched Damascus, but then brightened again. "We wish you the best of luck as you venture forth to grasp your destiny. The race will begin when this gun fires." He raised the weapon, finger hovering over the trigger.

Chaos erupted from the competitors. Engines roared to life, drowning out the already boisterous spectators. Energized yips and hollers sliced the air as racers psyched themselves up.

I ran a soothing hand down Herc's neck when he startled, prancing and shaking his head. Grabbing the suede saddle horn, I planted a foot into the stirrup and swung into the saddle. Herc reared and I compensated, whispering, "Shh, big guy. I know it's a lot, but I'm right here with you. Shh…" His heavy front hooves thumped back to the ground. "That's a good boy. We can do this, you and me. Let's crush this race and build our dream ranch. I'll do the human stuff; you do the horse stuff. Deal?"

Herc's prancing lessened, but I could tell he was still nervous. His mood-ring eye never lied. Knowing Herc, he just needed to get running and everything would be fine.

Adrenaline coursed through my veins, activating and invigorating my senses. The breeze felt crisper against my skin; my vision clearer; hearing sharper. *This is it.*

The Governus rep, shouted, "Ready?"

Engines revved. Gripping the reins, I leaned forward, heels down.

"Set!"

A hush descended over the crowd.

Bang!

CHAPTER 4

The reverberating crack of the pistol echoed through the air. I gave Herc a kick with my heels and we were in motion, surging forward in a gallop. Within seconds a cloud of dust arose, swirling and mingling with the pale violet sky as frenzied take offs exploded all around me. Engines roared and jagged treads tore into the dirt, voracious for traction. Clashing metal rang out as racers bumped and jostled for position, cutting their way through the grassland. I pulled back on the reins and cut hard to the right, narrowly avoiding two racers who'd crashed up ahead. Each of the riders scrambled to right their machines and get back in the race.

We'd lost some ground, falling behind the pack. The tall grasses whipped against my feet, while the dry earth it sprouted from got torn up something fierce. I pulled up the bandana around my neck to cover my nose, coughing from the dust these vehicles kicked up. Being in the rear wasn't exactly where I wanted to be, yet finding a way through that wall of grinding metal didn't seem like a challenge worth undertaking. It wasn't worth Herc getting hurt.

Besides, my alliance members and I had a plan.

I noticed Sarah working her way towards me from the right. Griggs did the same from the left, keeping pace with me. A minority of others showed similar patience, probably having the same idea. It made perfect sense to conserve energy and wait for more aggressive engines to surge ahead—let them break trail and do the heavy lifting, then we'd use our stored energy to overtake them on the back end. In a distance race, endurance counted just as much as speed.

But where was Jorgep? Had he decided to go it alone?

The muscles in my hands were feeling the strain of holding Herc back. It wasn't easy. The horse's nostrils flared, catching wind as his heavy metal hooves pounded into the ground. Neck arching, Herc fought the bridle, wanting me to let him fly. The faintest whirring of his mechanics reached my ears as I glanced over my shoulder. The gathered settlers roared with cheers and applause, kids bouncing up and down with excitement. With a grin, I snatched the hat off my head and gave it a wave for the crowd.

It took effort, but I slowed Herc even more, lagging far behind. I glanced up at two waning moons hovering behind a layer of wispy clouds, one slightly smaller than the other. It was beautiful. Halfway across the field, the fact I might soon call this place *home* fully sunk in.

Griggs flung an arm out in question, clearly wondering what the hell I was doing.

Bringing myself back on task, I leaned forward. "You wanna have some fun and give em' a show? Let's run! Haw!" I gave slack on the reins and opened him up. After being cooped up in that ship for weeks, ol' Herc deserved to stretch his legs and *really* run before we hit the forest. He responded instantly, his metallic limbs reflecting refracted shards of sunshine as they surged rhythmically. With his ears pinned and tail waving in the breeze, we gained ground on Griggs and Sarah at an impressive rate. My hips rolled with Herc's powerful strides—the saddle's compensation mode on to offset his rapid gait.

"They think we're slow?" I laughed between adrenaline-infused breaths, remembering Raker's sneer at my *slothenly* horse.

Nobody had a clue what this particular Friesian was capable of. Letting loose a carefree hoot, I kicked with my heels. "Hell no, we ain't slow!"

Herc found his third gear, boost thrusters in his hooves fully engaged. The colours of the grasses blurred together as his enhanced legs propelled us faster than nature ever could. I'd only ever clocked him once and it had been impressive, with top speeds between 100-120km/hr. Though I couldn't see my friend's faces, I felt confident their brows would be raised.

The crowd's cheering flared in our wake and within several seconds we'd caught up to Griggs and Sarah. I pulled back on the reins. Herc didn't care for that much, but followed instruction. His breath puffed heavily, and my alliance members settled in beside us to cross the final few hundred feet. The layered thicket of trees looming ahead stood taller than I imagined they'd be, creating a towering canopy. And darker too—but not green. Was it purple?

Griggs gave an enthusiastic fist pump, face obscured by his helmet's visor.

"Damn, that horse can really move!" Sarah shouted, her husky voice projected from a speaker beside her mech suit's octagonal torso shield. She'd at least brightened the glare settings so I could see her face, which had a girl-power kind of smile plastered across it.

"He sure can!" I shouted back, a little breathless, then glanced over my shoulder. The throng hadn't thinned at all. Many colonists watched, soaking in every last second of action. All four Governus reps still hovered in the sky, holding binoculars to their eyes to get a good look.

The first racers disappeared into the forest looming up ahead. They crashed into the flora like waves, their forms merging within the shadows. Countless pathways were created before our eyes.

Just ahead, a robust rover with six wheels and a hefty grill on the front bulldozed its way in, flattening thinner trees in its path.

As if reading my mind, Griggs thrust his chin towards the rover. "Follow that guy!"

I agreed, then glanced both ways. "Where the hell is Jorgep?"

Griggs waved an arm. "He must've got caught up. I lost track of him."

Dammit. Hopefully we'll meet up inside somehow. I liked Jorgep—a quirky guy, but I could tell had a good heart. The way he cared for his bleenad spoke volumes for his character.

"I'll take the lead!" Sarah shouted, surging ahead. She didn't have wheels to worry about, her mech suit the most agile in rough terrain. Griggs and I followed close behind.

Shadows swiftly overtook us as we entered. A world woven with deep violet leaves swallowed us whole. I'd been right about the colour. Even the bark of the trees appeared a woody shade of mauve. Trunks varied between thick and thin, gnarly and smooth. Some had sweeping branches while scraggly vines hung from others. A low-lying leafy undergrowth coated the ground in intermittent patches.

We followed the field at a brisk pace, avoiding deadfall, protruding rocks, and other hazards. Lucky for us, that bulldozer of a rover had ploughed a trail through most of it. Herc had no trouble keeping up. The run had him feeling happy again, which boded well for our journey. His ears were alert, eye glowing blue, and showing no signs of distress.

Alien insects whizzed past, and from the corner of my eye, I spotted one blood red lizard-like creature perched on a rock. Birds flitted in the branches, flustered from the sudden disruption. The ones I could get a good look at had odd upside-down beaks, wings that fluttered like hummingbirds, with feathers of cyan and lemon yellow.

"Wow…" I mumbled to myself. This place was incredible. I hadn't felt the thrill of adventure like this in a long time. I'd gallivanted to other planets and mixed myself up in all kinds of exciting experiences—and trouble—back in my gambling days, but all of that felt like ages ago now. I shook my head, burying the thoughts. I had a race to focus on.

"If it's like this the whole way, this'll be a nice ride," I said to Herc. His ears twitched toward my voice and he whinnied. I stroked his shoulder, feeling muscle ripple beneath my palm. His coat was already moist with sweat around the saddle pad. Not a shock, given how warm it was outside. Living on this planet would be a tropical vacation every day. I didn't mind that at all, but I hadn't factored it into our racing strategy. Frequent water stops would be integral. More than I'd originally planned on.

Griggs swivelled in his seat ahead of me, his visor retracted. "It'll be a *great* ride!" Clearly he overheard my last comment. He grinned, eyes twinkling. The man had such an easy way about him, his countenance both laid back and energized at the same time. It seemed an impossible mixture, yet somehow, it worked. One night on the transport when the others turned in early, we'd stayed up late reminiscing about Earth. He'd made me belly laugh with all of his classic trivia, and our world views aligned more than I thought they would. He'd shifted closer on the bench, one arm brushing mine without thinking. The memory sent warmth cascading up my neck and into my cheeks. Worried he'd notice the blush painting a masterpiece on my skin, I quickly smiled back, grasping the collar of my shirt and fanning it out in an exaggerated manner.

"Would be even better if it wasn't so damn hot!" I let out a low whistle.

He laughed. "Yeah, we might be a stinky bunch by the time we reach Novus."

"It's looking that way."

Griggs turned back around and my smile fell away, nose scrunching. *Get it together. Romance has not worked well for you. You're here for land and to square your debts.*

Grinding gears and growling engines echoed from up ahead as treads ripped across the forest floor. The harsh sounds reverberated off the trees, while majestic sunshine filtered through the leaves above, each beam saturated by sparkling fireflies of dust churned up by the chaos.

"How far do you think we'll get before nightfall? When does that even happen?" Sarah called out, slowing down and sidestepping trees so she could travel beside us a moment.

"Someone said daylight this time of year lasts from about eight to ten—that's fourteen hours," Griggs said, then shrugged. "We'll get as far as we can, I guess."

"We can keep up a good pace until dusk, then set up camp. That should give us plenty of time to button up for the night." In my mind, finding a good spot to hunker down was important in unknown territory. "I need to take regular breaks to water my horse, though."

"No worries, we'll all need breaks. Quick ones, though. For our plan to work, we need to keep up." Sarah glanced between Griggs and I. "Worst case, we could travel through the night and make up ground." She ducked beneath a thick horizontal branch.

"It's an option, though I can't imagine many folks will slog through this terrain in the dark. I'll need to rest Herc at night—no way around it. But, of course, I won't be upset if ya'll want to press on." I certainly didn't relish the idea of losing them, but if they chose that, I'd understand and carry forth. I'd prepared to do this thing alone from the get-go, after all.

Griggs vehemently shook his head. "Making camp is fine by me. This terrain would definitely be brutal to trek at night. Plus I have a feeling this will be an endurance race. Sleep is important." He checked the compass function on his digicuff.

"Sleep is good in my books too," Sarah said, then added, "Are you guys okay with picking up the pace a bit? The ground isn't too rocky. Finn, you think Herc can handle it?"

"No problem." I waved us onward. Herc's hooves had been treaded specifically for off-road travel, but too many rocks could still trip him up. It just meant we'd have to trek cautiously.

Sarah smiled and ran ahead, leading the way again. "I'll slow down if it gets too rough," she shouted over her shoulder. It was nice of her to think of Herc like that. She came off gruff sometimes—a bit of a smart ass, too—but in moments like this, I saw the heart beneath.

While we were all voracious to get our hands on free land, so far, our individual goals hadn't gotten in the way of basic decency. I hoped it stayed that way. But these days I was nothing if not a realist. At some point in this race, it would be every person for themselves.

And I'd be ready.

CHAPTER 5

"Day one is nearly complete," Khana said, pouring a glass of whisky for her brother and fellow Governus CEO, Steel. She poured another for herself before raising it in the air between them. "Cheers to a successful race. May it be filled with adventure, and ripe with *discovery.*"

Steel grinned, raising his glass to clink against hers. "Discovery indeed. Cheers."

***

We travelled deeper, the ground sloping down ever so slightly. I wondered if the Sweep was actually a huge valley. If so, then there might also be a water source running through it. Before the race, Governus staff had announced water in the Sweep should be as safe as Egan. I hoped they were right, as we'd need to replenish our supply eventually.

My mind sunk into brainstorming ways to cross a body of water. If it was shallow, walking to the other side wouldn't be a problem. At least not for Herc and Sarah. Griggs might have issues getting his cycle across, though. If the water was deep, we'd all have problems.

Herc wasn't exactly buoyant.

As the light faded around us, we looked for good places to make camp. Sarah spotted what looked like a rocky ledge up ahead, so we headed for it. The jut of layered stone and boulders was piled up maybe ten or fifteen feet high. Since the ground was relatively flat, and we could keep our backs against the rocks for protection, we dropped our gear.

Griggs and Sarah spread out to collect firewood, while I searched my saddlebags. My fingers dug around, seeking the auto-enclosure my mother had given me. It was strange knowing I wouldn't see her again for a long time, if ever. My folks likely wouldn't venture so far to visit, especially not after I absconded with Herc like I did. A scoffing laugh escaped my throat. Once my father finished raging, he probably poured a drink to celebrate I was gone.

"Ah ha! Found it," I muttered, more to myself than anybody else. Pulling it out, I attached the auto enclosure's magnetic remote to my cuff, then stabbed the pointy ends of all four, 10-inch-long cylindrical stakes into the ground. I butted two of them against the rock face about thirty feet apart to allow enough living space, then stuck the remaining two fifteen paces straight out from there, creating a rectangle. Satisfied, I stood back and pressed *activate*.

Chunking noises rang out like tiny jackhammers pounding against a slippery metal surface as each cylinder extended upward section by section until they'd transformed into eight-foot-tall posts. A hairline golden laser connected each post at the top, then a fine crosshatched netting of beams shot out to thread across the enclosure's ceiling and walls.

Herc eyed the forcefield warily, but didn't freak out. I'd set it up once on the transport ship to get him used to it, and also so I'd have a clue how to use it. I pressed *deactivate,* and the web vanished. Smiling at Herc, I clapped my hands as if brushing dirt from them. "That works well, hey? Should keep us safe for the night."

Herc blinked his good eye and gave a snort.

I pointed to the far side of the enclosure. "I'll rope off a cozy pen for you over there."

His shoulder muscle twitched as he looked away—the horse equivalent of a shrug.

Chuckling, I led him into his designated area, tying him to a slender tree growing alongside the outcropping. I set up the pen and removed his tack. After that I put some feed down and filled a container of water for him. Then finally, I fished out a carrot. He'd done good today—he deserved a treat. But before the morsel reached his lips, his ears perked, ocular implant flicking from blue to red.

Something snapped in the forest.

I spun, hand flying to my pistol, eyes scanning left and right. Staring down the sights, I swept the gun in a slow arc across the darkening forest, searching for any sign of movement.

Another snap rang out, this time accompanied by crunching footfalls and muffled voices. Familiar laughter wafted in the air. I holstered the pistol, releasing a heavy breath and ran a soothing hand down Herc's neck. "It's alright boy. It's just Griggs and Sarah."

Herc's eye flipped to green, before it faded back to blue.

The pair appeared from a narrow trail in the brush and I gave them a wave. Griggs had a generous armload of broken deadfall, while Sarah hefted triple the load with her mech suit.

"Should be plenty enough to get us through the night," Griggs said. "Where should we drop it?"

I pointed near the edge of the enclosure, drawing lines in the dirt to show where the protective field would be once activated. "There is fine. Just make sure it doesn't interfere with the enclosure." I set to work placing stones for the fire pit.

"Righto," he said with a nod.

Once Sarah's wood was stacked, the clear octagonal shield covering most of her torso swung open to reveal her true form.

She sat her suit down with a *thunk* against the boulder beside the enclosure since there wasn't enough room within.

"Want me to make the enclosure bigger?"

Sarah waved a hand. "My suit's equipped with shock skins. I can't see anyone messing with it." She mimicked receiving an electric jolt, then laughed. Pulling her arms out of the mech, she disconnected two corded bio-tethers from dedicated ports in each of her forearms. The jacks functioned similarly to the ones our digicuffs were plugged into. Once free, she loosened her jet-black locks from their ponytail. Sweaty strands of shoulder-length hair fell to cover her previously visible undercut as she jumped out of the suit.

"Ah, that's better. Was starting to get a headache." She pulled a whiffer out of a narrow tin and grabbed a portable torch from her suit's maintenance hatch. After lighting it, she took a deep inhale and strode over to the enclosure. Thick grey tendrils wafted out of her mouth as she sat down beside my makeshift fire pit, and helped me place twigs into a tee-pee shape. I immediately acknowledged why folks called them *whiffers*. No matter where you stood, a person couldn't help but get a big whiff of that pungent smoke. Like burnt tires and bananas.

"Those things stink," I mumbled. Eons ago, a new plant was genetically engineered on Earth, spawning the cigarette-like rollies. Not only was it more efficient to cultivate, but it was also less harsh on the lungs, and twice the relaxant that weed was, sans the apathetic after effects. It promptly kicked cigarettes and marijuana out of circulation.

Sarah shrugged, unbothered. "But they taste great."

Griggs stood off to the side busting long sticks into easy to manage pieces. He slammed a thicker one three times over his thigh before it cracked in half.

"Doesn't that hurt?" I asked, wincing.

"Naw," he replied, then puffed out his chest. "These are man's legs."

"Yeah, okay," Sarah scoffed and I rolled my eyes. Griggs laughed.

Within a few minutes, Sarah coaxed a flame into existence. Just in time, too, as daylight was nearly gone. Time to settle in. After making sure everyone and their belongings were inside the auto enclosure boundary, I pressed *activate*. The enclosures' laser-like netting illuminated, rippling in a glowing wave from one end to the other. The dim golden glow of the forcefield illuminated wherever our firelight didn't quite reach—a perfect night light.

"Nice," Sarah said, admiring the enclosure. "I'll have to build me one of these babies when I go back home. It'll keep me safe while I'm tinkering in the shop into the wee hours."

What I wouldn't give to have her technological knowhow.

"No," I corrected. "I fully expect *us all* to be neighbours *here* on Joya after this."

"Touché." She raised a flaming twig in a mock toast and we exchanged a grin.

I left the fire to check on Herc and finish getting him ready for night. He seemed content in his pen. I was glad I'd brought rope to keep him from wandering off, since the enclosure didn't really help with that part. If I changed its settings, it would keep him in, but then he'd also get shocks whenever he touched it. Bounty hunters used these kinds of shields to hold prisoners for delivery. But, Herc wasn't a prisoner, and I certainly didn't want him getting any shocks.

Echoes of laughter and miscellaneous camp noise filtered through the trees, and I wondered what the other camps were set up like. With so many racers, they had to be spread out all over the place. How did they feel about spending their first night in the Sweep? A few engines still revved, so clearly some had opted to press on.

The non-negotiable need for rest was the main drawback I faced bringing a horse instead of a vehicle. I couldn't just hit the gas and carry onward… but I was okay with that. We'd make do. I gave Herc's coat a good brushing, and when his good eye twinkled at me in the firelight, I knew he was thankful. A few pats later, I whispered, "Get a good nights' sleep, okay?"

His head bobbed and he breathed against my face, the fuzzy whiskers covering his muzzle tickling my cheek. Smiling, I gave it a rub, then left him to relax. It had been a long day and we all needed to recoup.

I carried my saddle closer to the fire and placed it at the head of my bedroll. It wouldn't be a perfect pillow, but it'd be a lot better than nothing. Next, I pulled out a travel pot from a saddlebag and a pouch of dehydrated bean stew. *Just add water.* Doing exactly that, I set it on a somewhat flat rock at the edge of the fire to warm. Griggs was already gnawing on something crunchy, stirring something else he'd poured in a cup.

I coughed, feeling a burn in my throat. Too much smoke from the fire maybe. I shifted my bed over a little farther. It didn't help though. Coughing again, I glanced around. "What the…?" The air within the enclosure seemed to be growing cloudier by the second. Griggs waved his arms to dissipate the haze.

"The smoke's not escaping. Finn, I think your fancy do-hickey is defective." Sarah coughed, joining Griggs in his vigorous arm waving. "Turn the thing off before we all die of smoke inhalation, will ya?"

I tossed a pebble against the shield and it bounced off with a spark of light. "Shit, it's on the wrong setting. Nothing can get out." I growled, pressing buttons on the tiny remote.

"Any time now," Sarah muttered, covering her lower face with the collar of her shirt.

"Yeah, I'm trying," I shot back. "Here." I finally pressed the right button and the enclosure flashed. A smokey plume instantly found freedom, wafting lazily into the sky. After taking several deep breaths of fresh air, and exchanging relieved glances with my campmates, I chuckled. "Well, I won't make *that* mistake again."

Griggs laughed, uncovering his face. "No kidding. So, are we protected from the outside now?"

I scrunched my nose and stood. "Should be. But maybe let's double check."

"Why not—just to be sure." Griggs touched the shield and his hand passed through it.

"Yeah, I won't sleep so well if I need to keep one eye open," Sarah said.

I cocked an eyebrow, levelling my gaze at the both of them. "Well, now aren't you two just *lucky* to have me and my auto-enclosure along then. How *ever* would you have survived?"

Sarah grinned playfully. "Anybody with an auto enclosure is a friend of mine."

Laughing, Griggs volunteered as tribute to test the shield from the outside. He walked through the glowing netting without any issues and picked up the nearest rock. Giving it a toss, the rock rebounded just like the other one had.

"Perfect." I squinted in the dim light to identify the proper setting on the remote. "I'll switch settings now so you can come in. Hang on a sec."

Sarah waved a hand as she stirred the concoction of food bubbling in her cooking pot. "Ah, let him sweat out there for a little bit, Finn. Let's see if Griggs is afraid of the dark."

Griggs shot her a glare and the two exchanged steely looks of bravado.

He crossed his arms. "Come on, let me in."

I made a show of hovering my finger over the remote. "Should we, Sarah? I don't know. Maybe this should be a girl's only club."

Sarah shot me a wink. "Hey, you know I'm *always* down for a girl's only club."

Griggs growled, dropping his arms. "Just let me in already. I'm hungry." When Sarah and I only laughed, he bounced another rock off the shield. "Seriously, c'mon!"

Not willing to risk a blow up, I gave in, pressing the button. As soon as the setting changed, Griggs walked in, making a point of glowering at us both.

"Really funny, guys. Now, what if some alien creature had snatched me up out there? Huh?" His words sounded ruffled, but his actions belied his true disposition. Griggs sat down on a log he'd propped near the fire, stretching his legs out with a lopsided smirk. The more I got to know the guy, the more I believed it would take *a lot* to truly upset him.

Sarah slapped her leg. "Awe, so our brave little Griggs really *is* afraid of the dark."

"Alright, alright." He set to cooking his supper. "And I'm not little, thank you very much."

We laughed, but he wasn't lying. Griggs wasn't little. He was tall and broad shouldered, with an army tattoo on one side of his neck, and a defined line of muscle just barely visible beneath his unbuttoned collar. When I realized my eyes had strayed lower, I averted my gaze.

By now, the noisiness of two-hundred racers sharing a forest had mostly died down. Chatting idly with my alliance members, I watched as my stew came to a boil. Digging in, I thought about what tomorrow would hold. Hopefully, we'd come across a stream. The jugs I brought held enough to last us another day, then water pills would keep us hydrated another few in a pinch. But I really didn't want to dig into those if I didn't need to.

As Sarah and Griggs debated the efficiency of boot thrusters versus thrust jackets, I zoned out, my attention drifting to the forest. Within the firelight's dim illumination, the dark violet foliage only lightened to a maroon tone. Layers of trees faded away until they vanished completely, swallowed by a sucking black abyss of the unknown. I listened as faint buzzing and chirping noises swirled in the air, presumably bugs coming to life as cooler air moved in.

But what else lived here? What thrived in the night? Nobody knew.

For the briefest moment, my skin tingled, as if goosebumps might rise from a chill, yet they didn't. I couldn't pinpoint why, but I had this feeling something was amiss. The idea niggled in the back of my mind, refusing to let go. My eyes searched the inky expanse, but other than the faint hint of a breeze ruffling leaves, and the odd pitter patter of tiny feet—some critter scurrying about—I heard nothing that should raise alarm bells. I glanced at Herc, whose eye remained blue.

Maybe it was the bizarreness of knowing Governus was in my head, seeing through my eyes, that elicited the creepy feeling of being watched.

"You okay, Finn?" Griggs asked.

Jolted from my thoughts, I met his curious gaze. "Yeah, all good. Why do you ask?" I took another bite of my stew.

He shrugged. "You looked pretty deep in thought there. Wondered if something might be bugging you. Just checking." Firelight danced across his features, highlighting the fine layer of stubble covering his chin and painting his dishevelled umber hair with rusty tones.

I flashed a quick smile. *He's perceptive.* "Thanks. I'm fine." Sarah listened quietly, looking back and forth between the two of us with tired eyes. I took another bite of stew, looking down. But when I glanced up again, Griggs hadn't looked away. Warmth crept beneath the collar of my button-down overshirt, and I felt the immediate need to fill the silence. "I don't know why, but I had this feeling like we're being watched."

"Oh really? Why?" Sarah asked, perking up.

"I just said I don't know why." Shaking my head, I added, "I'm assuming it's race nerves working their way out of my system. You know, a little jittery, being in uncharted lands and all."

Griggs and Sarah both looked out into the black, inspecting the shadows for signs of trouble. I groaned internally. I hadn't wanted to spook anybody. Capturing my companion's attention again, I explained, "Listen, when in doubt, just look at Herc. If the eye is blue, that means he's calm and happy. If danger gets close, he should sense it pretty quick. His eye will change colour."

A wide smile spread on Sarah's face. She snapped her fingers. "See, I just love that. Your horse not only has a mood-ring eye, but he's an early warning system too. No wonder you brought him along." She leaned in, folding her hands together. "So, what are his different eye colours and what do they mean? Ocular implants can have a ton."

"I've been curious about that myself." Griggs' attention returned to the fire.

Swallowing the last bite of my somewhat unsatisfying supper, I settled back against my saddle with a chuckle. "You probably know more about his implant than I do, Sarah." She was the tech-savvy, mechanical genius of our little group.

She nodded, conceding her knowledge, but waved for me to continue anyway.

"Alright. Well, Herc only has four colours. Couldn't afford any more than that. I think it works well, though. Blue is for happy, like I said before. Green means he's uneasy. Red is for danger, or if he's angry, and it'll turn white if he's scared or in pain."

"That's fuckin' perfect. Four is all you need, really." Sarah tossed a couple thick logs onto the fire and settled deeper into her blankets. The bags hanging beneath her eyes likely mirrored my own. It wouldn't be long before she passed out and I didn't plan on being too far behind.

Griggs moved off his makeshift seat and stretched out on his sleeping mat. "If you had any more options, it might just get confusing."

"Exactly. I thought the same. Like, pink is for arousal—why would I need to know that? Besides, when the eye doesn't tell me what I need to know, his body language fills in the gaps." I grinned. "He's a pretty good communicator."

"Do you ever wonder what he'd say if he could speak?"

My brows shot up. "Yes. All the time! But I definitely can't afford that fancy upgrade." Chuckles rippled around the fire and I added quickly, "I mean, he'd probably just ask for carrots or apples incessantly."

Griggs flashed those dimples. "Who knows? Maybe he'd surprise you—Herc might be a scholar and a poet."

I covered a yawn. "Gosh, that would be something else."

"Are bionic horses the new craze on Earth these days? It's been so long since I've lived there, I feel out of touch." Griggs poked the coals with a stick.

"Goodness no. Herc's one of a kind as far as I know," I replied. "How old were you when you moved to Mars?"

"Ten. I didn't have any other living family on Earth, so when my mom died, I had to move in with my grandma until I got old enough to join the military. She lived in one of the old dome colonies. The experience was—interesting." He stirred more coals. The fire crackled softly beneath the pitch-dark canopy, a few stars visible if the wind blew the leaves just right.

"Oh? How so?" I glanced over at Sarah, who had stopped contributing to the conversation, her eyes flying at half-mast. She'd pass out soon.

Griggs waved a hand. "Ah, it's a boring story for another time. Anyway, maybe you'll be a trendsetter once word gets out about

Herc. He's pretty amazing. You think, Sarah?" Griggs looked her way, but the woman was out colder than an airlock.

We shared a smile, leaving her be.

"He is pretty great. As for trend setting—not likely, but who knows?" I slid further down until only my head rested against the bottom edge of the saddle. Pulling the blanket over my shoulders, I let out another yawn. "Well, I'm following Sarah's lead. See you in the morning."

With a nod, Griggs closed his eyes. "Have a good sleep."

***

The morning came quicker than I liked, an upswing of chirping birds stirring me from slumber. They flew about in a flurry, as if aggravated by something. I pushed myself up to sit, feeling utterly exhausted—likely the result of waking in the middle of the night yesterday when the transport arrived in Egan, where the day was already in full swing. Quite the shift.

Herc was up and alert, ears pointed as he scanned the forest. Following suit, I strained my eyes to see anything out of place. Using my binoculars, I zoomed in and swept across the space, yet spied nothing concerning. A scan for signs of life failed, so I switched to infrared mode. But sadly, the air was humid enough that the typically contrasted visuals came out somewhat muddy. Unreliable. Giving the binoculars the ol' tap and shake treatment didn't change anything either.

At that moment, I recalled something I'd overheard that floppy-eared Governus guy saying to an inquisitive racer before the event began. He had explained there was no point using scanners, because they wouldn't work. Then he'd added with a touch of attitude, "If we could scan it, why would the Sweep still be uncharted?"

So, something in here blocked scanning technology. What could cause such a thing? *Curious.* The grumblings of hunger quickly over ran my curiosity, though. I needed breakfast in my belly, and coffee, too, before my brain could manage complex thought. Wiping my eyes, I stretched the stiffness from my sluggish arms. The birds had settled down and Herc returned to nibbling on remnants of his feed from last night.

My eyes settled on the metallic breast strap attached to Herc's saddle and my mind wandered to thoughts of home, to my last night there. The horse barn materialized in my mind with such crisp clarity I could almost smell the time-worn wood, hay, and that welcoming equine scent. It was pin drop quiet, and purposefully too early for anyone to be up for morning chores, for I couldn't risk Dad seeing and keeping me from Herc. I'd just finished getting him packed up and was fretting about whether I could hack it out in the world alone, when Herc turned his head to eye me warily, as though he were unsure about the plan.

"Oh, c'mon, don't look at me that way…" I had whispered. "We *need* to go. Who knows what might happen to you if they sell you. Besides, I can't keep subjecting myself to this—" I waved my arms in a broad circle, searching for the right word to describe the emotional Finn bashing I'd faced in our tight-knit ranching community. Even my so-called friends had faded away after word of my transgression spread, as if I might soil their family names, too.

"This what?" The stern and distinctly feminine voice had stopped me cold.

I turned slowly.

My mother stood inside the doorway; a plaid terry cloth robe tied closed about her slightly plump form. Silver streaks within her russet hair glinted citrine beneath the lights, the same light that highlighted the threaded muscles along her crossed arms from years of tough ranch work. Physically, I saw a lot of myself in her.

Same colour hair, height, and slightly freckled oval face. Same muscle.

"Somehow I knew you'd be here." She walked forward, the look in her emerald eyes solemn while her head shook. Funny, how that green seemed to be the only thing I didn't get from her. My eyes mirrored my dad's—blue like sapphire.

I stepped away from Herc, extending my arms out front. "Mom, look, I was just—"

"Stealing Herc. Running away. Yeah, I know." She strode towards me with purpose, then continued right on past. "I saw an advertisement you left open on your digipad the other day. You're off to that crazy race, I presume?"

Confused, I followed her down the corridor, struggling to come up with something to say. "I can't expect you to understand, but Herc's my best friend. Without him, there's nothing left for me here…"

She'd paused in the dark doorway of the tack room and looked at me, a twinge of hurt glistening in her eyes. "Nothing?"

I'd lowered my head. "I'm sorry. Of course, not *nothing*—I mean, I have you. You've been the only one in this family who seems to give a shit about me since my fuck up. I'm thankful for that." I looked back up, my teeth clenched. "But you don't know how hard it's been. I–I just feel so broken—and embarrassed, and trapped—*all the time*. I messed up and betrayed you guys, I own that… but I was a victim too. I got manipulated and used. Now, all I want is to feel normal again."

She flicked on the light in the windowless room and squared her shoulders. "You think I don't understand. But I was young once, too, you know. Rebelled. Made mistakes. Loved the wrong man… I picked myself up from that, just like I've seen you doing. Your dad knows, too. He just can't see past his hurt yet. What you did hurt him badly. Hurt all of us."

My gaze lowered. "And again, I'll say I'm sorry." I looked up. "But how many times can I say I'm sorry? What more can I do to prove I've changed? I've worked my ass off for three years to make amends, yet I keep getting shit on. That's why I can't stay here. I just can't—"

"Shh." Mom pressed a pointer finger to my lips, the look in her eyes softening. "I know." Without another word, she walked to a locked storage cabinet and keyed in a code. The light flicked from red to green. Opening the doors, she pulled out a thick metallic breast strap for a saddle, one I'd never seen before.

"Your father and I used to go on riding excursions back when we were newlyweds. Before we had kids, and time was more our own." She smiled wistfully. "We'd go on long trips through the wilderness and explore all kinds of territory. Find romantic waterfalls. Spend nights under the stars. Roast coffee over the fire at sunrise, then keep riding." She passed the strap into my hands. "In some places, the days got pretty hot—far worse than cattle drives. These cooling breast straps came in handy for the horses, so you should take one to keep Herc comfortable."

I'm sure my eyes bugged out of my head. Words stuck in my throat, coming out as awkward stuttering. "T-take it?"

Mom nodded, her expression even, as though what she'd said meant nothing at all. She moved to another locked cabinet and opened it, her hands retrieving two smaller items.

She held out a white bottle the size of her fist. "These are emergency water-replacement tablets. They only need a few drops to expand into gallons and they'll help keep you hydrated in a pinch. Who knows what you might encounter out there." Then she held out a bundle of four ten-inch-long metal posts, clasped with a two-inch square digipad remote. "And this is an auto enclosure. Your father and I never slept without it. It'll keep you safe at night."

She'd swept out of the room, leaving me staring dumbfounded in her wake. I raked a hand through my hair, then jolted into motion, following her back down the corridor. "Mom?"

Ignoring me, she came to a stop beside Herc, giving him a smooth pat. "I assume you have supplies for his care packed? Brushes, his prosthetic maintenance kit—oh, and spare rope?"

"Uh, yeah. I have everything I'll need. I think." I set down the breast strap and rested a hand on her shoulder. "Mom?"

She finally turned, her eyes glistening. "I'm going to miss you." Mom crushed me in a hug then, her arms powerful yet tender around me. Once the initial shock ebbed, I closed my eyes and hugged her back, leaned into her warmth. Tears squeezed out, slipping down my cheeks to dot the fabric of her robe.

"He's going to hate me even more…"

"Your father can be a hard man to love sometimes, but there *is* a heart beneath it all. I'll deal with him." Mom pulled back, her gaze locking on mine. "I need you to know I'm sorry, too. I should never have let it get this far. I should've stepped in to mend the rifts tearing this family apart—be the voice of reason—and I failed. That's on me. So, I want you to go. Run your race."

Not knowing what to say, I picked up the strap and connected one end to the saddle. It synched immediately. Mom secured the other end in place, then gave Herc another pat. Despite her tightly controlled expression, a quiver shook her lower lip. But only for a second. "Take care of each other." She turned and walked back down the corridor to the entrance.

I swallowed hard and called after her. "I *will* pay you guys back. I promise."

My mother paused on the threshold and returned a solemn nod. Though the words hadn't been spoken, I think we both knew at that moment that it was goodbye, perhaps for good. "Just spread your wings and fly, my girl."

With that she was gone.

Moments later, so was I.

In the not-too-far distance, an engine rumbled to life, the grating sound jarring me from the memory. I wiped away a hint of moisture that had collected in my eyes and cleared my throat. Our fire had dwindled to coals in the wee hours, so I put more wood on, blowing on the coals to entice a breakfast-cooking flame. Sarah didn't even flinch, but the noise woke Griggs.

He sat up with a groan, stretching his arms and back. When his eyes settled on mine, he smiled brightly. Almost perky. "Ready for day two?"

"Ugh, you're a morning person, aren't you?" I groaned, searching the cryo-storage in my saddle bag for one of the squished muffins I'd packed for breakfast. He was far more cheerful than anybody should be at this time of day. The sun was barely up for goodness sakes.

More engines fired up one after the other, the sound filtering through the trees.

Griggs and I shared a look, then we both gave Sarah a nudge.

"Rise and shine. We need to get moving."

CHAPTER 6

We shoved whatever food didn't require cooking into our mouths and packed up camp in a whirlwind, using dirt to extinguish the fire. More and more vehicles revved, and we didn't want to be the last ones on the move. Any kind of head start we could carve out now, might help us in the end. I fed Herc in a rush, then got him saddled and ready to go while Sarah hooked into her suit. Once her bio-connectors were engaged, she stood and closed the torso shield.

"Ready to roll," she said, clapping her heavy metallic hands together.

I took a moment to run my hands over Herc's leg prosthetics, happy the shafts and knee joints all looked good. Aside from needing grease now and then, the bionic prosthetics were relatively self-sufficient. Connected to his body and patched into his brain via similar bio-tethers that Sarah's suit utilized, they functioned just like real limbs. I checked his ocular implant and facial prosthetics, too. Both looked fine. The structural metal had been moulded to keep him looking like a horse should, while the eye appeared distinctly robotic.

On spec, he could see twice as far with that eye. Back home, Herc used to spot me coming with food way before I ever saw him in the fields, rushing to the gate before the other horses even took a step.

I swung up onto Herc's back. Griggs revved his spyro-cycle and put his helmet on, leaving his visor setting on transparent, since a sun shield wasn't really needed beneath the thick forest canopy. His brows furrowed as his vehicle sputtered a few times, then held steady. With a wave of an arm, like a soldier charging into battle, he spurred us into motion for the day. As a trio we took off at a good clip, picking back up on the same bulldozed rover track we'd followed yesterday. Since it was headed in the right direction, we'd take advantage of it for as long as we could. Most of the deadfall had been cleared, thankfully, but the mud and rocks remained obstacles to navigate.

We travelled at a brisk trot, breaking into a lope whenever it was feasible. I visually scanned the forest at intervals, still feeling that nagging sense something might be watching. There was no reason to believe there was… yet, it sat in my mind like an unwanted passenger.

As time wore on, the sun moved across the sky, and its rays sliced through the foliage at a sharp angle, dappling our surroundings with warm light. Though the air was already hot enough, the brightness was certainly welcomed. All I could hear in the distance was continuous crashing and roaring engines. It made me wonder how Jorgep was making out. Was there still a chance we'd meet up with him yet? It seemed doubtful—a sad thought.

I veered Herc around protruding rocks impeding the path, simultaneously ducking under hanging branches that snaked every which way. Several minutes later, Griggs had trouble getting his cycle through a muddy patch, and we tethered him to Herc, who made easy work of pulling him free.

We passed broken-down racers now and then. One was bogged down in mud, buried right up to the seat. Another's engine was smoking, and the most recent victim was a three-wheeler, which simply put, sat dead.

"What happened to your trike?" Griggs asked, but we rode on by when the frazzled racer was in no mood to chat. If she ever stopped swearing, I assumed she might continue on foot—either toward Novus, or back to Egan. Either way would be a long walk. I didn't know how wide this Sweep was exactly, but they all looked a fair size from space.

I pondered what I might do in that situation. Would I keep trying or concede the loss? I liked to think I'd carry on, but with so much ground to cover, the chances of winning—or even surviving—would plummet on foot. Thankfully, in the case of emergency, Governus said they'd send in help. Otherwise, it would really depend *where* you broke down, and without a detailed map, it was impossible to know. The racers we passed were only one day in, so it made more sense to turn back to Egan. But if a person broke down half way through, or more? Well, that changed everything. One might as well move toward the finish line at that point whether you stood a chance to win a parcel or not.

"Is it getting muggier, or am I just imagining things?" Sarah shouted.

"No, you're not imagining things," I flapped my collar to circulate some air. The sun blazed hot overhead, the shade from the trees the only solace.

Griggs swept an arm in an arc. "It's looking less like a forest, and more like a jungle the farther we go. Might also explain the shift in climate."

I eyed several exotic plants as we passed—each showcasing shredded-looking leaves that sprouted from bouquets of woody stalks. "The flowers look more tropical, too. Like those spikey ones over there." I pointed.

Sarah chimed in, "And more vines."

Griggs' arm snaked out to pluck a pink flower with tiny feathery sprigs that splayed from its core. He turned in his seat. "We've been going downhill this whole time. Not a drastic decline, but still—this is definitely a valley. But, what's at the bottom of it?" His tone held an ominous note, even if he didn't mean to.

I nodded. "I've been wondering that too."

Sarah turned to run sideways, one brow arching. "What kind of crazy shit do you think we'll have to cross? River? Canyon? Bottomless fucking pit?"

I failed to suppress a snort of laughter over her bluntness. "Why don't you tell us how you *really* feel, Sarah?"

Griggs grinned. "Nothing beats the unknowns of an uncharted alien landscape. Never a dull moment in the Sweep." His finger shot into the air. "I should put that on a t-shirt."

I raised a hand. "I'll take one!"

"Done deal." He laughed, glancing at the ground beside his spyro.

"You guys are hilarious." Sarah rolled her eyes before turning forward again.

Griggs slowed down. "Hey guys, stop for a minute."

Something about the alertness in his tone captured my attention. I stopped Herc, dropping off his back and tying him to a tree branch as Griggs waved us both over.

Sarah halted, turning with her arms splayed. "What?"

He pointed to the ground, rubbing his neck. "What do you make of these prints?"

Sarah and I leaned forward to see his discovery.

"Uh…" Sarah's eyes widened.

I straightened, planting my hands on my hips. "Now, that's interesting."

Griggs clucked with his tongue. "My thoughts exactly."

It was an animal track of some kind. At least I assumed so. The imprint was depressed into the mud, broad and somewhat oval in shape, with four sharp points giving the top a distinct crown-like appearance. I bent down to take a closer look, almost able to fit both of my hands inside the track. "What do you think might've made this? Any guesses?"

"No clue," Griggs said, flatly. He rubbed his chin, then flicked a finger to the ground beside the track. "And look at that vein of blue dirt. I haven't seen that until now. Have you?"

The dirt was shockingly vibrant—royal blue in colour—and narrow, like a thin lightning bolt running vertically in the same direction we were headed. The underbrush and ground debris limited my ability to see if there were more similar veins close by.

"No. That's new, too," Sarah dug her mech fingers into the vein, unearthing moist chunks. They fell apart in her fingers when she squeezed, dissipating into fine granules. "Weird."

I instinctively glanced back at Herc, relaxing my shoulders when he showed no sign of distress. But sweat darkened the coat around his saddle. He needed a drink. I walked back and poured a portion of water into his container, gave him a carrot, and grabbed some smushed bread to pop into my mouth. Could the creature that created these pawprints have been in the woods near our camp last night? *Maybe that's why I kept feeling like something was watching.*

"Whatever it is, it's fairly big. The Joyan equivalent of a bear maybe? I mean, we haven't seen any large game yet. It would only make sense there'd be predators living in a forest like this." Using my cowboy hat to fan my face, I wished I had Herc's cooling breast strap.

Sarah stood, surveying the forest. "Well, blue dirt aside, I don't like the idea of possible predators hanging around. We better keep an extra keen eye from now on."

I nodded, raising a hand. "No complaints from me."

"Agreed," Griggs ripped into a strip of jerky he'd grabbed, jaw flexing as he chewed.

Sarah bent at the waist, hovering her mech chest over the animal track. As she did, a faint click rang out—like the auto-focus on my parents' ancient hand-held camera.

"What are you doing?"

Sarah smiled. "Recording." She tapped a small black disk inset into her suits' chest plate. "I turned on my suit's auto-record function before the race started, so I could show people back home what the experience was like. A make-shift diary, too. I'm documenting *everything*."

"Thats a great idea." Returning Sarah's smile, I put my hand down next to the print. "Here. To show scale."

"Thanks." She zoomed in.

"No prob. I wonder if Governus is also recording what they see through our retinal monitors? Maybe I can request a copy of mine after. It would be neat to keep as a memory."

Sarah straightened. "You never know. I can get you my footage too, if nothing else."

Before I could reply, Griggs held up a finger. "Sorry to butt in, ladies, but maybe we should keep moving. Daylight's wasting. Plus, I'd rather avoid crossing paths with this bear-thing, in case it decides to come back."

Nobody argued, and in minutes, our group was on the move again.

As the day wore on, the humidity grew merciless, sapping much needed energy from my body. I could only imagine what Herc must be feeling, yet he didn't falter. We kept up a good pace, with minimal obstructions to slow us down. Griggs cycle got hung up a few more times, but on each occasion Herc and Sarah were able to push or pull him through. If the ground got any rougher, though, Griggs might have trouble carrying on. The thought of that didn't sit well with me. I mean, yes, every racer knew the risks when they signed up, and at the end of the day, it was every person for themselves. But now knowing sizeable creatures roamed about, it wouldn't feel right leaving him behind. What if something happened to him?

Herc's saddle *did* have a built-in auto-cart… I could carry him.

Don't be ridiculous, I chided, pushing the thought down—refusing to let it take root in my mind. This was a race I needed to win. If Griggs or anybody else had to drop out, so be it. Besides, who knew what kind of man he truly was outside of these very specific circumstances? I'd been fooled by a handsome, charming man before. *I need to protect myself.*

We passed a few more vehicles that had fallen prey to the Sweep, each racer angry and left to fend for themselves. Of course, we made sure to warn everyone about the pawprints we'd seen, so they'd be aware, but most were too frustrated to care.

"Yeah, yeah. So what? I'll blast em' like I'm about to blast this hunk of junk!" One particularly irate racer shouted, the words emitting from dual mouths on either side of his face.

Sarah's reaction was immediate. "Fuck, whatever. We're just trying to be helpful."

"You'd be *more* helpful if you gave me a new ride. That mech looks nice." The racer's eyes flashed, then he drew a gun—training it on her.

Griggs had his pistols up within the space of a twitch. I drew mine a breath after.

A chunky looking gun slid out of a panel in one of Sarah's mech arms, while a deadly blade slid from the other. "You sure you wanna play it that way?"

His eyes flicked between the three of us, clearly weighing his chances of success. Then he lowered his weapon and brandished two crossed fingers, barking, "Just drive on!"

Without hesitation, we moved past, keeping our weapons trained on him until he'd disappeared from view.

I let out a heavy breath and holstered my pistols, trying to hide the slight tremble in my hands from the scuffle we'd nearly just had. "Well now, he seemed lovely."

Griggs replied dryly, "A real peach."

The further we travelled, the more blue veins streaked through the dirt. There were more of those animal prints, too. They popped up wherever the ground was soft, yet compact enough to retain the unique shape. I wondered if the tracks were made by the same creature, or a family of creatures. Roaming animals on Earth could cover vast amounts of territory in a day.

"Slow down, guys!" Sarah yelled over her shoulder, raising a hand.

From my higher vantage point, I saw movement through the vine-laden trees up ahead. It looked like multiple racers, and there was lots of chatter.

"What's all the commotion about?" Griggs asked.

"Can't tell yet."

We moved in closer. Three conveyances had parked haphazardly around an object barely visible within the leafy underbrush along the edge of the path. Light reflected off a metallic edge poking out at an angle. Too curious not to see what the fuss was about, I swung down from the saddle and tied Herc to a tree. Griggs removed his helmet and got off his cycle, walking forward with me. Sarah approached the attraction first, peering intently down through the leaves.

The three racers turned to look at us. Two were dismissive, while one, an incredibly tall olive-skinned Neersoo fellow, flashed a friendly smile.

"Whatcha got there?" Griggs asked.

The Neersoo man pointed. "A downed drone."

Griggs and I shared a surprised glance. *A drone?*

Sarah nodded—her eyes sharp. "Looks like a Governus drone."

The second racer, a stalky one with an extra pair of hands growing from his chest piped up. "Likely a charting drone. They would've flown it over to get a look at this place when they first claimed the planet. No shock that it's here."

The Neersoo guy chirped, "A mission that obviously failed."

"Yes, it's a charting drone." Sarah motioned for everyone to give her hefty metallic body some space. "Let me have a closer look at it. I want to run a diagnostic to see why it went down."

The third racer—sour-faced, with gelatinous skin that looked like it might slide right off—grumbled, "What does it matter? The thing malfunctioned. Enough said. Besides, you can't run scans in this place." He turned on his heels, sniping scathing looks at me and Griggs as he mounted his double wheeled off-road bike. "I got a race to run and this *Earth stink* is poisoning my air."

Earth hater. I bit back a groan of frustration.

Sarah's distinct alligator-like skin texture didn't save her the heat of his glare either, and she returned a very enthusiastic middle finger. Mister sour-face ripped around the blockade, bouncing over a couple fallen logs in the bush before speeding off down the trail.

"Someone should tell him he doesn't smell so hot either," I scrunched my nose, having been crop-dusted by his wafting trail of body odour.

Griggs ran a hand through his hair. "Ahh, gotta love dealing with that crap."

Sarah grumbled as she knelt beside the drone. "Earth stink. Fucking idiot—deserves a punch in the face. Saggy skin bastard." She opened a dirty, half-rusted panel on top of the drone, and patched a cord from her forearm into the machine. A muted beep signalled her diagnostics were processing. "Hope I see *him* again soon. I haven't had a good fight in a while."

The Neersoo racer chuckled. "Well, he would deserve whatever he got."

Sarah smiled, craning her neck upward. "Damn straight… uh, what's your name?"

"Vernon."

"Nice to meet you, Vernon." She returned to her work, running her arm over the full length of the drone. "Saying that was just uncalled for. I mean, what's done is done, right? He's obviously from a planet who's still crying over spilled milk."

Griggs held a hand out. "Alright, alright. Out of sight, out of mind. The guy's gone."

The racer with the chest-hands curtly bid his farewell and carried on, clearly not interested in choosing sides on the divisive issue. The transport conduit gates had balanced a Galaxium that some believed didn't need balancing. To some, humans were troublemakers. To others, innovators.

Only Vernon remained.

I kneeled across from Sarah, shoving a bushy plant out of my way. Her eyes were busy reviewing the read-out on her forearm. The drone had definitely been sitting there for a while. Its compact manta-ray shaped body was covered in a layer of dirt, rust, and other debris. But, aside from being filthy, it looked perfect. Not a scratch on it. Like it had just fallen right out of the sky.

"So?" I tapped the drone's shell with my fingers.

Sarah sat back on her heels. "It's perfectly functional. It should fly, but just—won't. The engine cut out. It stalled mid-air. My scan suggests some kind of local interference that affects engines or any devices that don't self-regulate."

Griggs squatted beside me, his knee rubbing against mine. "The same interference that's jamming scans? But scan stations run without being monitored… Isn't that self-regulated?"

Sarah shook her head. "It's about the power source. A scanning station still requires electricity to run. Engines need fuel, or a mix of fuel and solar energy—like the drone or your spyro.

Rechargeable batteries, solar, or hydro power, same issue. Without input, there's no output. Hell, even kinetic energy gains power from a source." She glanced around with a contemplative expression. "But what in the world could cause this kind of interference?"

CHAPTER 7

Vernon shook his head. "It makes sense now why Governus didn't allow flying vehicles to race. I bet it really bugged them not being able to scan this place for resources." The corners of his mouth tugged upward into curls, causing the pair of thin, tubular breathing apparatuses built into his cheeks to twitch. "My family has built a similar enterprise over the generations, so I have some experience with developing new planets. I find it humorous we could be walking on a goldmine and not even know it."

"Geez, if only we had time to dig." Griggs tossed a pebble into the forest. "Now I know why my spyro's been fritzing. It's the interference." His brows furrowed.

Sarah stood up, giving a slow nod. "Seems like."

I looked at Vernon. "Is your ride running okay?"

"So far."

"Hmm. Different vehicles have different tech—that has to be the reason why some have died while others haven't. Maybe the interference is at the heart of the Sweep and we're getting closer to it." Sarah's face was bright and energized from deciphering the mystery.

Griggs nose scrunched. "If that's true, then it'll only get worse."

Everyone looked at each other, quiet.

"If their drones dropped out of the sky, why would Governus send vehicles in here? What's the point of a race, if all the vehicles die a certain distance in? And what about Herc?" I blurted, my cheeks warming. "If I'd known *all* mechanical things would be affected, I never would have brought Herc. Why not give racers this information up front, so we know what we're getting into?" I stalked away, stifling a growl.

"It does seem odd they didn't divulge that information," Griggs acknowledged.

"No, not just odd. It's careless." I pointed at my innocent horse lounging in the shade. His eye had turned green listening to me talk, keen to my negative mood. "My damn horse is part machine. This is *very* concerning. Herc's not a bunch of nuts and bolts I can up and leave behind—he lives and breathes, and feels. I can't put him at risk."

Vernon raised his hands. "It is still possible Governus doesn't know as much as we do now. If they *only* sent in drones and *didn't* send a team in, as they've stated, then they only knew flight was impossible—hence the restriction they made." He spoke in a very logical manner.

I planted my hands on my hips, mulling over his words. "Yeah, true."

Sarah walked over and laid a bulky mech hand on my shoulder as gently as possible. "Hey, I have my suit rigged to report if *anything* in the slightest affects it, and there's been nothing. That's a good sign. Herc's upgrades are bionically linked to him just like my suit is to me. Neither of us require external power to operate. Based on the scan, I'm confident bio-tech shouldn't be affected." She smiled reassuringly; the usual brashness washed from her expression.

While her mechanical expertise was reassuring, worry still lingered.

"Listen, I'm happy to stay up front. I'll stop if *anything* weird happens."

Griggs strode forward and wrapped a strong arm around my shoulders, squeezing in a rough, *I'm your best bud* kind of way. "She's right, Finn. There's no evidence to suggest Herc will be negatively affected."

Vernon hesitantly interjected, motioning to Herc. "He certainly is a fine animal… *Finn*, is it? It is clear you care deeply for him. May I pose a question?" When nobody argued, he continued. "If Herc could speak, do you think he would want you to give up?" He dipped his head slightly as three sets of eyes stared at him. "Perhaps it is not my place to speak—not knowing any of you very well. I mean no offence."

Griggs smiled at Vernon. "The man's got a point. It might eat you up inside if you turn back now—if you don't at least try. I get the feeling Herc's an adventurous dude. I bet he'd want to keep going for as long as it's safe." He leaned in closer. "Plus, if you leave now, I'll be all alone with the sassy one over here…" He thrust a thumb toward Sarah, who huffed. "You wouldn't do that to me, would you?"

Sarah grabbed Griggs by the lapels and lifted him a foot off the ground. "Sassy?"

Unfazed, Griggs nodded, grasping the metal hands holding him aloft.

Sarah's eyes narrowed as she considered his words. Then she dropped him and shrugged. "Yeah, I suppose I am."

I couldn't help but smile as Griggs straightened his shirt. They acted just like siblings, always poking at each other. But it was Vernon's words that had really pulled me out of my funk. The guy didn't have to say anything—most folks probably wouldn't have—yet he'd risked pissing me off to give encouragement. He had a point, too. In my heart, I didn't believe Herc would give up unless it was absolutely warranted. I smiled at Vernon. There was something about him that felt comforting, familiar even, though I'd never met him before. Maybe it was the way his eyes held a twinkle. My father's had that too, back when I was still his little girl.

Before I grew up and disgraced him.

I kept looking at Herc, who didn't seem distressed in the slightest, thinking about what life could be like here. I'd promised him a nice Friesian mare to keep him company. *Bio-tech is different…* Taking a deep breath, I approached Herc, stuck a boot into a stirrup, and swung up into the saddle. "I have to look out for his health first and foremost. Since he seems okay right now, and with Sarah running checks regularly, I think it's safe to push on and see what happens."

Griggs stepped closer and patted Herc. "We got Herc's back."

Vernon tipped his head like a proud father, then started his sleek three-wheeled vehicle. "Well, I'm off. It was nice to meet you. Good luck to you all." He manoeuvred past us, then pinned it once he was clear.

Griggs promptly jumped onto his cycle, revving it back to life. "Yeah, we better get moving, or else all of this will be for nothing anyway."

I swept my arm in a grand arc, signalling Sarah to take the lead.

"Fuckin' right. Here we go." She took off at a swift jog.

Applying heel pressure, Herc and I caught up to Sarah, with Griggs close behind. Up ahead, Vernon remained within sight as the trail wound deeper into the increasingly jungle-like valley. At least until we hit a major mud bog—the first of many. Since Vernon's vehicle had wider tires than Griggs' spyro, he peeled through and disappeared.

It took a minute, but Sarah and Herc's well-treaded feet managed the sludge okay, working quickly together to pull the Spyro-cycle through.

Once past the mud, Griggs cycled hard, then jerked back and forth as his engine faltered. He slammed a hand against the handlebars, growling between gritted teeth, "Damn spyro!" As if offended and determined to prove its worth, the vehicle surged back to full strength.

By late afternoon, everyone felt the strain of the trip. We stopped for a quick break to drink water and put some sustenance in our guts. Herc drank his water and devoured every morsel of feed in record time, clearly needing it. His smooth black coat was moist, the hair stuck together forming upside down teardrop shapes all over his body. Though he had to be getting tired, he wasn't showing it. His implant shone blue; his natural eye bright.

I stroked his neck, whispering, "We just need to push a little farther, then we'll stop and get a good sleep. You can do this. But if it's too much, show me somehow, okay?"

Onward we trekked.

Griggs' machine chugged increasingly at random intervals, the strength of his engine flickering like an archaic light bulb nearing the end of its lifespan. I could tell by the near-constant scowl on his face that he was fed up. He had to be worrying he might be hoofing it at any minute. Who wouldn't? In the back of my mind, I considered whether Herc was strong enough to carry him the rest of the way. Based on leg capacity alone, I couldn't see why not. But what about the extra strain on his endurance?

Once again, I shook wayward thoughts from my mind. Instead I whistled a cheerful tune, which only turned my thoughts to Jorgep. He adored music. I hoped he was okay. He'd shared once that he was the son of an overbearing business owner now seeking to carve his own mark, and I empathized with that. But, despite his quirks, he did seem like the capable sort. Plus, he had a Bleenad. He wouldn't have to worry about Joyan bears with Keemi around.

I hoped we'd see him again at the finish line.

After a long and sweaty day, the sun finally waned in the sky. We were all eager to set up camp—preferably on higher ground to avoid sleeping in mud.

"What about over there?" I pointed toward a natural clearing, where a stubby fallen tree led into a cliff face of jagged boulders. We stopped to look. "I'm not seeing much else. That might be our best bet." My rear end was sore from the saddle. *I can't wait to rest.*

Griggs got off his cycle and walked to inspect the spot in question. A minute later, he tapped the ground with his foot. "Seems dry enough. Maybe as dry as we'll get. I'm game."

"Fine by me," Sarah said.

I joined them, dismounted, and dug through my saddle bags in search of the auto-enclosure. The noise pollution of racers crashing through the forest had faded into a mild rumble this late in the day. A few raucous belly laughs rang out from up ahead. Not far, either.

"Hey, there's another camp." Griggs pointed, adding in hushed tones, "Right through there. See the flickers of light through the trees?" Sarah and I both looked.

"Oh yeah." Well, that explained why the laughter sounded close.

Griggs tilted his head. "Think we should move to be safe?"

I held up the auto enclosure posts. "I think we're okay. We've got decent protection from any troublemakers with this. Besides, it's getting dark fast."

Griggs nodded. "Fair enough."

"Uh, Finn?" Sarah said, pointing behind me.

"What's up?" I glanced over my shoulder. Herc's eye shone red, casting an eerie glow into the growing shadows. I drew my firearms, following his line of sight into the bush. Griggs stepped forward, pulling dual pearl-handled pistols from the holsters slung across his shoulders.

"Think it's a bear?" Sarah joined us.

Leaves rustled and something sloshed in the mud up ahead. Footsteps.

"Who's there?" I engaged the flashlight built into my pulse pistol, illuminating nothing but trees. But when I swung the beam sideways, it landed on a raised hand. Then a familiar face.

"Hello again, friends!" Vernon called out, smiling. "I mean no harm. When I heard the sounds of others stopping so close, I wondered if it might be you. I made camp just ahead."

Griggs frowned, lowering his guns. "Geez, you nearly got yourself shot. Thought you were a damn bear. You ever hear the saying curiosity killed the cat?"

"I have not. Seems implausible." Vernon shifted to survey the forest behind him as he came to a stop in front of us. "Bear? You've seen such a creature here?" His hand hovered over the angular ectro-cannon strapped to his waist.

"Not in the flesh. We found tracks in the mud, though. Fair sized ones." Sarah pulled up the image she'd saved and presented it on the inset screen in her Mech's forearm. "See?"

Vernon snuck a glance at the picture, his thick eyebrows raising. "Interesting."

Griggs rubbed a hand over his jaw. "We thought so, too."

"Well, should we encounter it, the meat will make several good meals." Vernon smiled.

Sarah let out a dry chuckle, shooting the Neersoo man a sideways glance. "Sure, as long as we can put it down. You sure are a glass-half-full kinda guy, aren't ya?"

Vernon looked at her quizzically, seeming to consider her words, before answering matter-of-factly. "My people traditionally don't use glass containers to drink our water, full or otherwise."

Sarah started as if to speak, then waved a hand, leaving it alone.

I bit back a grin. The more I got to know Vernon, the more I liked him.

Herc still stared into the forest beyond where Vernon had appeared, so I went to comfort him, whispering, "It was just Vernon. You're okay." But his eye stayed red. I listened for any strange sounds, unable to pick up anything out of the ordinary. Just buzzing bugs, chirping birds, a distant din of racer noise, and us.

Herc's eye flipped to green.

"Oh, there we go." My shoulders relaxed. I looked into his natural eye, rubbing his muzzle. "You good now, boy?" He nudged my shoulder.

Another round of belly laughs filtered through the trees.

Vernon pointed toward the firelight. "I stumbled upon that camp earlier, and after chatting a while, they invited me to stay. Everyone is welcome as long as no race strategy is discussed." He paused, raising his brows. "I thought I might offer you the option to take a competitive break and socialize."

Could it really be so simple?

Something inside told me to trust him—don't ask what. But could I truly rely on my own instincts? I'd been manipulated before, which is what landed me in all kinds of debt. *Just go with it, but keep your eyes open.* I looked at my alliance members. "I'm game. We can still set up my auto enclosure."

Sarah hemmed and hawed, then nodded. "Fine. I'm tired and grumpy, but I guess I can play nice for a bit. Plus, we have power in numbers if shit goes sideways."

"And Herc—our trusty threat detector." Griggs flipped a thumbs up. "Why the hell not."

Vernon returned a stiff looking thumbs up, clearly not accustomed to using the timeless Earth gesture. His mouth formed into one of those curly smiles. "Excellent. Follow me."

Sarah clapped her hefty hands together. "Let's do it."

CHAPTER 8

We broke through the thicket of trees separating us from the neighbouring fire about a hundred feet ahead. The light created a silhouetted effect on the twisting trunks as we walked, highlighting low hanging leaves with slivers of amber. Numerous vehicles sat parked outside an auto enclosure similar to my own. The raucous voices we'd heard earlier quietened as our ragtag alliance approached. A few of the racers even drew their weapons.

Vernon called out, "All is well! It's me, Vernon."

The guns lowered. Eight racers in total sat by the fire. They stood to greet us in the failing light, their faces an understandable mixture of welcome and wariness. Collectively, we raised our hands in greeting. Then I bit back a groan as I laid eyes on Raker, that snide Ganglian from the start line. The severe contour of his narrow angular face, and slim, tall frame was unmistakable.

Of course, he has to be here.

Sarah lowered her face shield and leaned in to mutter, "Damn, the idiot we saw earlier isn't here. Too bad." Her sour face suggested she'd been itching to go a second round with him, but I still couldn't nail down whether she was all talk or not.

"No, *he's* not." Covering my mouth in a faux-yawn, I whispered, "But there's still a hater in the mix—the guy I had a run in with on the start line. I don't know if I should join." I gave Herc a pat as he walked on my other side.

"What? Because of one dickbag?" Sarah whispered back. "Fuck that. We're going to have an enjoyable evening. Griggs and I got your back." She winked and nudged me with her mech arm, nearly knocking me off my feet. "Oop, sorry. Didn't mean to do that."

I gave a mock angry glare, then sighed. "Okay, fine, I'll stay. Maybe he'll be nicer..." Doubtful, but a girl could hope.

Sarah stopped herself from asking a question since we were now within earshot, and keyed a word into the digicuff built into her mech, quickly flashing it at me. *WHO?*

Keeping it casual, I typed in a response and presented my cuff nonchalantly, pretending to fiddle with Herc's reins. *GANGLIAN DUDE.*

Sarah nodded, the *oh, I see* kind, before returning her attention to the meet n' greet.

The group of racers gathered around the fire sat back down and continued with whatever card game they'd been playing. A lean and muscular-looking Pembru woman with a smooth, heart-shaped face stepped forward to meet us, passing through the auto-enclosure wall.

"Hello! My name is Tatara. It's nice to see more friendly faces. Until now, I've only seen other racers after they break down—so, not in the best of moods. I guess tonight people got tired of being alone. I'm happy for the company." The startlingly attractive woman extended a hand to shake—another dated Earth custom that inexplicably caught on like wildfire throughout the Galaxium.

"Yeah, why not make friends along the way? I'm Finn." I smiled and shook Tatara's hand. Her grip was firm. Not some noodle-wristed shake like they're scared to catch your germs.

Sarah touched her chest. "Sarah." Tatara offered her a handshake, then Griggs.

"A pleasure. I'm Griggs. Funny how, in a high stakes race like this, the notion of friendship seems like a luxury." His charming smile won a grin from the camp's spokeswoman. "We understand you're agreeable to us joining in?"

Tatara glanced at the others sitting behind her, then to Vernon. Tipping her chin toward the fire, she said, "Vernon says you're a friendly bunch, so, welcome! We've been playing galactic poker. It's quite the icebreaker." Her oversized almond-shaped eyes sparkled flirtatiously, giving Griggs her full attention.

Griggs nodded. "I bet it is."

The woman rocked on her heels. "Well, feel free to set up camp and join us by the fire any time." She beamed, a second translucent set of eyelids blinking like sliding doors across her irises. Then her smile vanished. "A friendly warning, though... This is my fire. All I ask is that everybody avoids race talk to keep things happy. I don't want any trouble." Then, like a switch flipping, her face brightened again.

Griggs' even keeled countenance never wavered. "Makes sense. We'll set up over here." He pointed to a somewhat flat area several feet away. "Thanks."

I dismounted and dug out my auto-enclosure again. While Sarah parked her mech-suit beside Griggs' spyro, I drove the first post into the ground.

Tatara took notice and approached me with an entrancing smile. "You have an auto-enclosure, too! Best purchase I ever made. If you want, we can probably sync them up and cover a larger area. Easier for moving around." She raised her hands. "No pressure, of course."

"Thanks. I'll let you know," I replied, feeling somewhat intimidated by her. I knew, from the few fleeting glances I'd stolen of myself in my tiny travel mirror, I wasn't exactly looking radiant right now. Yet, whatever grime she'd collected so far didn't mar her visage one bit. Had Griggs noticed how pretty she was?

Resisting the urge to smooth my wrinkled shirt and secure the wayward hairs hanging in my undoubtedly dirt-smeared face, I fanned my shirt collar for airflow instead.

Tatara noticed my movement. "It's hot on this planet, isn't it?"

I gave a self-deprecating chuckle. "Yeah, it's turned me into a sweaty mess, not gonna lie." I paced about fifteen feet and stabbed the next post into the ground.

She followed. "I can't imagine what that must be like. Pembru don't sweat."

"Ah." I nodded, my smile plastered in place. *That makes sense.* "Lucky you."

She shrugged. "Luck to some—curse for others, right? Well, I'll let you finish setting up." Tatara cast her eyes back to Griggs, who'd already busied himself collecting wood. Resting a hand on one hip, she called out to him, "Griggs… right?" When he acknowledged, her smile took on a sultry vibe. "Can I interest *you* in a game of poker?"

He clucked his tongue. "I'm not much of a gambler, but I'd be willing to give it a go." He looked around at the faces in our small alliance, settling on mine. "Anyone else?"

"Oh yes, of course! Anyone's welcome to join," Tatara quickly added.

"I'll play a hand or two," Sarah said.

Vernon shook his head as he headed back over to the fire. "I prefer to watch."

Uncomfortable with the idea of gambling after spending three years trying to avoid it, ignoring the fact I'd technically gambled by entering this race, I politely declined. I planted the last two enclosure stakes into the ground, then led Herc into an area I roped off as his pen.

Once everyone was inside, I engaged the auto-enclosure. I'd also made an executive decision about syncing it up, and I thought it best to smooth that over with Tatara. I waved her over. "Hey, thanks for the offer to sync our enclosures, but I think we'll just do our own thing. Makes it easier come morning, too." I didn't mention the fact I didn't want to share sleeping space with Raker. Nor did I mention I didn't necessarily want her having easy access to Griggs.

She smiled, showing no sign of having any qualms. "No trouble at all. I totally understand. Oh, and I like your name by the way. I met another Finn once on an Earth space station—he was a grouchy trader. It's such a unique name for a female." Her friendly smile seemed genuine, though her words touched a nerve. The Pembru species as a whole were known to be forthright, sometimes to a fault.

"Thanks." I buried my irritation for the sake of maintaining good relations. "But just so you know, the name Finn is actually unisex."

"Ah, I see. Well, I do think it's lovely. It suits you. See you at the fire whenever you're ready." She flashed another brilliant smile, then walked back to her enclosure.

Suits me. So, does she think I'm man-ish? I knew I didn't exactly smell linen fresh; my hair was probably a rat's nest of horror hidden beneath a cowboy hat, and I was certainly dressed for function over fashion, but... *man-ish?* I gave in to the urge to smooth my wrinkled shirt, then promptly dismissed myself to care for Herc. He deserved some much-needed saddle-free time.

I put feed down and set out his water container, yet the whole time I couldn't get Tatara's comment out of my mind. Did Griggs find me man-ish, too? A powerful wave of curiosity swelled. I discreetly pulled out the tiny travel mirror from my saddlebag. Nobody was paying any attention to me, so I flipped it open. I'd chewed a tooth cleansing tablet each morning, so they looked relatively fine. Taking the tie out of my hair, I loosened the braid and ran my fingers through the dishevelled russet mess. Now that the sun had set and the air temperature had cooled by a fraction, it was the best time to let it breathe. My nose crinkled in reaction to the dusting of dirt clinging to my face and neck—proof of a sweat-soaked and action-packed day.

I'm definitely dirty, but not man-ish…

Though I'd been trying not to waste water, a thorough face washing was imperative at this point. I poured the clear liquid into my hands and scrubbed, relieved to see the dirt gone when I checked my reflection again. The quick fix wouldn't resolve body odour, but at least I wasn't the only stinky one in the bunch. Vernon was especially ripe. What was the old saying… misery loves company?

"You're brave. I'm *way* too scared to look in the mirror," a voice said over my shoulder.

Snapping the mirror shut, I glanced back to see Griggs smirking as he double checked one of the knots I'd tied in Herc's rope pen. Stuffing the compact back into my saddle bag, I stood. "Um, that's probably for the best actually." I feigned a look of horror and disgust, then circled a slow finger in the general direction of his face.

He laughed, walking to my side. "Need help with anything?"

I didn't, but I didn't mind him hanging around either. "Sure, do you want to uncinch Herc's saddle while I take his bridle off?" I pointed to the buckle he'd need to work on.

Griggs rubbed his hands together. "On it." He approached Herc's side and flipped the stirrup up over the seat. "So just undo the buckle here? That's it?"

"Pretty much. Oh, and you'll need to unclasp the coolant breast strap too." I slid the bridle down over Herc's ears and off his nose. Most folks had kept up with the times, using fancy pressure banded bridles that reacted intelligently to digital rein control. But my family still believed a good old-fashioned hackemore worked as well as anything else. Something about holding real reins in your hands just made the act of riding sweeter. My dad was stubborn that way—a stickler for tradition. That might be one of the only things he and I actually agreed on. Why fix something that ain't broke?

Hooking the bridle over a stubby branch, I showed Griggs where he could set the saddle down for the time being. I also triple checked the shock locks were activated, since we were around unknown company for the night. I recalled how Raker had eyed my saddlebags before the race even began, though I had no clue why. The guy clearly hated humans, but it's not like I was a noteworthy one. If I were some celebrity or corporate hob-knob, such attention would make more sense. But I was just plain ol' *me*. A nobody.

"You look good, by the way." Griggs pulled a leaf off a vine, his eyes cast downward as he picked at it. Violet fibres fell from his fingers. He glanced up, then focused on the leaf again.

I swallowed, the action more difficult than normal. Did he just say I looked good? No, he had to be talking about something else. "Um, yeah, *the pen* is in pretty good shape. Herc should be nice and comfy for the night." I nodded.

One corner of his mouth lifted, wrinkling the skin beneath the eye on that side. "Naw, I meant you. I don't know, it seemed like maybe you might've needed to hear that. It's definitely true. Just saying."

My brows raised as Griggs' words sunk in. Then he shrugged, his posture straightening as though he'd been caught doing something he shouldn't have. With a wave of the hand, he added in a much gruffer tone, "No need to make a big deal about it. I'll see you at the fire."

I returned a tight smile before he spun and walked away. Conflicting emotions took up arms and jousted within me. My greater instincts had me scoffing at the thought he might look at me as anything other than a race buddy, but a tiny sliver battled back with bashful glee. Giving Herc a carrot, I took a brush to his coat to distract myself. It wouldn't be an intensive grooming like he deserved, but it would definitely help him feel more comfortable.

"What do you make of what just happened?" I whispered. My companion turned his broad head and nudged my shoulder, stomping a feathered hoof. His non-glowing eye blinked at me. "Yeah… you're probably right. He's just being nice—trying to keep morale high. I mean, that's gotta be it. Right?" Herc let out a soft nicker and I rubbed the non-metal spot between his ears. "Thanks, buddy."

My stomach growled. I needed to get food cooking on that fire sooner rather than later. The odd engine still lingered in the distance, but the night air had calmed substantially. Standing in the relative quiet felt nice. Moments like these made me realize just how peaceful life was back on the ranch. Sheltered from the hubbub of society. No chaotic vehicles revving in your ears, or strangers to put on a good face for. I pulled another carrot from my pocket, grinning when Herc gobbled it up. Comfort food. I gave the big guy another pat, then left him to relax.

Time for food and rest. The constant mental alertness, and heat of the day had taken it out of me. Way more than I expected. And I found my legs were a touch achy from being wrapped around Herc's solid midsection all day. Pulling out a stew pouch, I glanced at the collection of racers around the fire. Sarah and Vernon had claimed their spots, already munching on supper. Griggs had finished laying out his bedroll, joining the fireside chat. Tatara's face lit up as she waved him over, shifting to make space for him.

Slapping on a smile, I approached. A muscular fellow named Dino, who had what looked like dinosaur spikes running down the length of his neck and spine, inched over enough on his log so I could sit down. On my other side sat a quiet guy with inkblotlike markings covering his skin. Vernon, Tatara, Sarah, Griggs, and five others spread around the pit, including Raker who sat across from me. I could feel the heat of his stare, but refused to acknowledge him. So far everyone seemed to be getting along and I hoped that continued. A calm evening suited me fine.

Griggs waved an arm to get my attention. "You sure you don't want in on the poker game?" Tatara and a few others glanced my way.

Though a buried piece of me was tempted, I shook my head. "No, I'm good, thanks."

"So, you come from Mars?" Tatara turned to ask Griggs. Her body shifted closer. Too close. Barely twenty percent of species in the civilized Galaxium were compatible with humans in the physical sense, and Pembru happened to be one of them. Crimeons, like Sarah's mother, and Neersoo, like Vernon, were also on that list.

Griggs nodded, not seeming to notice her nearness. "Yeah, I moved there when I was ten. Grew up there, but I haven't been back for years. I just pop in to visit every now and then."

"Oh, you must tell me what it's like…"

The pair carried on chatting, but I looked away, swallowing a groan. I didn't need to see the flirt fest. I caught Sarah's eyes across the fire. She raised her brows at me—a knowing smile crossing her lips. I raised mine in challenge, as if to say *what?* Her gaze flicked to Griggs in a meaningful way. I rolled my eyes, mouthing the word *No.*

She nodded sceptically and bit into her nutrient bar.

I typed a message into my digicuff and sent it to her. *SO YES, GRIGGS IS ATTRACTIVE. BUT THAT'S AS FAR AS IT GOES.* First and foremost, I wasn't brave enough to risk heartbreak again. Second, I didn't want to ruin our dynamic. Third, this was a race, not a singles star cruise.

Sarah responded. *DO WHATEVER YOU LIKE. GET IT GIRL.*

Not helpful. I looked away, focusing on other conversations. Though interesting, I struggled to settle into any one of them—feeling anti-social. Perhaps the excitement of the last couple of days was catching up to me? Still, I listened politely, despite being in no mood to compare vehicles, discuss the nicest Vanaxillo moon to vacation to, or the latest news about conduit routes to be built. Transport conduit gates—or TCG's could be a contentious point, depending on who discussed the matter. The vast majority of folks supported the gate system, which had been the brainchild of Earth, because it benefited so many. But select planets still despised the invention, and all who created it.

I simply focused on satiating my hunger, digging into some freshly warmed stew. But then the unmistakable voice of Raker carried above the crackle and pop of toasting logs.

"So, Finn…"

CHAPTER 9

"**H**ow's the horse holding up?" He asked. "You were lagging behind pretty badly off the start line. Of course, I saw this from my place at the *front of the pack.*"

I forced myself to meet his gaze. *Show strength.* Shadows loomed beneath the severe line of his brow, the contrast at odds with the warm firelight reflecting in his snakish eyes. My mouth pressed into a tight line, but I made it lift at the edges. "He's doing just fine, thanks for asking. Obviously, we didn't lag *too* far behind. You know, since we're here and all."

Sarah looked between Raker and I, straightening in her seat. A few other sets of eyes swung our way, too. I was fairly certain the tension was palpable.

Vernon spoke up. "How do you two know each other?"

"We met briefly on the start line," Raker replied. His eyes returned to mine. "I'd never seen a horse in person before and simply had to go see the rudimentary creature up close."

The chatter quietened on all sides.

I set my bowl down, knitting my fingers together. "You're entitled to your opinions. But respectfully, horses are not rudimentary creatures. They're intelligent, hard-working, and loyal." Holding my expression in a neutral position, I was proud of myself for being so diplomatic.

A low rumble escaped Raker's throat as he leaned forward. "Yes, but my opinion holds far more weight than a humans' does.

After neutering enterprising planets the way you have, you don't deserve to win free land." A myriad of grumbles rolled around the circle, calling for calm.

"Hey now—" Griggs started.

"*But*," Raker emphasized loudly. "I will appease Tatara's wishes, will remain a gentleman and tolerate your presence here." His smile was a thinly veiled sneer.

That sure took a turn. I bit my tongue and held my head high, eyes boring into his. *Fake it til' you make it.* As much as I wanted to bark back—and I *really* wanted to—I refused to stoop to his level. Ganglia was still widely considered a black-market planet. Sure, they'd cleaned up their act about a decade ago and joined the Galaxium Trade Union, or GTU, but everyone knew they still conducted underhanded "business" on the side.

Sarah didn't care about stooping. She scoffed; her words clipped. "Geez, you must be buddies with the asshole we met earlier today. I didn't pop him one when I should've—" She raised a clenched fist. "Maybe I'll get a second chance with you."

Raker laughed and Sarah's strong hand flexed. The murmurs grew louder, folks talking over one another. A few racers including Dino muttered for Raker to shut his mouth, a supportive sentiment I appreciated. Another racer supported Raker, while the rest merely watched. Tatara motioned with her hands for folks to calm down, though her efforts proved futile.

Raker's sharp eyes swept from one face to the next. "What's everybody getting upset about? I'm just saying what we're all thinking about humans, even if nobody will admit it."

"That's enough. Keep it civil," Tatara warned.

Deep down I worried he was right… but the majority around the fire didn't seem to support his take. I considered returning to my auto-enclosure to avoid further confrontation, but I didn't want to give Raker the satisfaction. Taking a steadying breath, I spoke in a firm tone. "Listen, Raker, we've all had a long day, and quite frankly, I'm not in the mood for this kind of bullshit." The Ganglian's eyes flashed, but I continued. "I won't insult you or your planet, if you don't insult me and my planet. Fair enough?"

He shrugged; eyes cold as he glanced at Tatara briefly. "For tonight, I will agree."

"Perfect." I picked up my bowl of stew again, wanting to finish the last few bites before it cooled. Griggs cast me an approving look, his normally green irises obscured by vibrant amber firelight. Many furtive glances flicked my way and I gritted my teeth, studying my spoonful to avoid the attention. I couldn't figure why this guy had such issues with me specifically. He clearly painted all humans with the same brush, and yet, seemed to hone in on me more than the others present. Did I remind him of someone he hates in some way? Maybe a woman who broke his heart once?

A tiny glimmer of happiness sparked inside at the notion of a woman breaking his heart. That warm thought seasoned the last few mouthfuls of my stew.

People resurrected their cheerful dispositions as the evening carried on, and after a while, eyelids started drooping. It wouldn't be long before folks turned in for the night. Vernon sized up the available space around Tatara's fire, which wasn't much, and politely asked me if he could sleep around our fire. I discreetly messaged Griggs and Sarah, and neither had any issue with it.

"Sure, no problem." I smiled.

"Thank you. These old bones require rest. Shall I start a fire over there for you?"

"Go for it." That was mighty kind. With him over there alone, though, I'd keep a closer eye on Herc to be safe. Vernon ambled away and I considered doing the same. Sleep sounded amazing, and frankly, I had zero desire to spend any extra time in Raker's airspace.

He'd struck up a conversation with his one supporter—a thick-bodied racer. Their chat started with Joya, guessing why Governus bothered to pay the fee to claim it as their own. Raker had done some research, said full planetary scans had shown no significant life or resources. From there, the conversation morphed, and they delved into deep discussion about the uptake in planetary colonization and corporate takeovers. I eavesdropped quietly, staring into the fire. Raker seemed to know a lot about the subject—how big money players ruled the Galaxium, snapped up all the land, and created monopolies.

"Especially after what happened on Zorpo-Bexa, every corporation in operation has been clamouring to get in on that kind of action. The mineral market is the ultimate high-stakes lottery," Raker said.

"Yeah, but how likely is a new planet to yield ore like Zorpo-Bexa did?" the robust racer retorted, and I didn't disagree. That rare aggregate strengthened any existing metal compound three-fold. The substance was desired… and thus, that corporation made an absolute killing.

"Unlikely, but not impossible," Raker replied. "If it *does* happen again, I doubt anyone will know until the product goes to market. Too many corporations are out for blood now."

The other racer shrugged. "You're probably right about that."

I didn't follow big business news, but I'd overheard my father discuss it before. He told our neighbour Wes once, "It's wild. If big companies show any sign of weakness these days, they'll find themselves the victim of a hostile takeover, forced off-planet, their assets usurped."

The elderly man had replied with his trademark drawl, "Yeah, the Interplanetary Magistrate and Gala-Rights Commission seems fine with letting corporations figure things out amongst themselves, as long as takeovers are executed clean—meaning, no civilian collateral damage. The GTU only gives a shit when unfair transactions of goods and services are reported."

My dad just shook his head. "I reckon, their blind eyes are bought and paid for."

If I owned such a business, and I was thankful I didn't, I'd hate knowing that at any given moment, a posse of hard-knuckled competitors might show up to shove a gun in my face and try to force me out. Not to mention, having to forever ferret out spies and look over my shoulder. It was all a little too wild-west for my tastes. No thanks.

As I watched flames dance an intricate tango across the charred wood, my eyelids grew heavier. The steady crackling of the logs lulled me into a state of warm relaxation and I leaned forward, resting my cheek in the palm of my hand. Voices surrounding me slipped in and out.

"Finn," Griggs' voice broke through my daze. He'd sat down beside me and I hadn't even noticed. I straightened, looking around. Dino, who previously sat beside me, was now busy pulling out a bedroll from his pack. Tatara shoved her log seat out of the way and settled onto her bed. The Quiet Guy, whom I hadn't heard utter a single word all night, was already asleep, snoring like a buzzsaw, while Raker and his new friend still chatted in hushed tones.

"You, okay?"

I gave my head a shake, yawning. "Yeah, fine. Just zoned out for a minute there."

"Looks like everyone's packing it in for the night. Ready to head over to our fire?" He stood, motioning with his head toward where Vernon already slept. Sarah waited behind us.

"Oh, yep. Sounds good. I'm wiped." I slapped my thighs and pushed to stand.

"Yes, get a good sleep little Finn. All of you." Raker commented dryly. His eyes raked over the three of us. "Your fragile human bodies will most certainly need it." His resultant throaty chuckle sent a heat hotter than embers straight into my cheeks. I wanted to tell him off so bad, but I wavered and Griggs beat me to it.

"Shut your face Razor, or whatever the hell your name is." He stepped forward; bicep flexed as a finger pointed at our adversary. "So much for civility, hey? You don't know a single thing about us, and I'm sick of you haters tarring all humans with the same brush. Nobody *here* had anything to do with those gates getting made."

He'd taken the words right out of my mouth. I almost felt jealous he got to say them. This guy needed to hear it, though I doubted he'd take it to heart. *Damn conduit gates.*

Raker stepped forward to meet Griggs, their steely glares clashing.

"Oh, and another thing," Griggs said, not backing down. "If your planet wasn't doing shit they shouldn't be, you wouldn't have trouble, now would ya?"

Uh oh.

Raker roared, and I instinctively rushed forward, sandwiching my body between the two raging bulls before fists could fly. "Whoa now, let's all just settle down." My hands thrust up between them. Tension permeated the air, the commotion capturing everyone's attention.

I pressed my arms outward to encourage peaceful separation, but the instant my flat palm connected with Raker's chest, the racer reacted like I'd scalded him with a branding iron. His hand lashed out like a rattlesnake, his bony grip catching my wrist and twisting. I winced, dropped my shoulder to lessen the pressure as he pulled me in tight to his body. His eyes seared into mine. Pain jolted through my wrist and up my arm.

Griggs and Sarah exploded behind me, voices shouting and feet shuffling.

Raker's grip tightened, his horrid breath assaulting my nose as he growled in my face. It was at that moment, I felt something shift inside—like a barrier giving way. Rage stained my vision red. I coat-tailed his swift motion with my own, my free hand whipping at my hip.

His eyes widened; snarl fading. Everything went quiet.

My brows lifted in defiance as I shifted to reveal the smooth muzzle of my pistol now dug into the tender flesh beneath Raker's chin. My glare burned as hot as the fire. Spoken between gritted-teeth, I offered a hard-line challenge. "I suggest you kindly release my wrist *now* if you fancy keeping your head intact today."

Raker's new friend whipped out his gun, training it on me. Then, faster than Herc could snatch a carrot, everyone's guns were up. With competitive tension already fierce, nobody was taking any chances. The sound of energised weapons hummed to life all around me. Polished metal and synthetic guns pointed in all directions, glinting with flickering citrine reflections. Racers eyed each other up—all temporary pleasantries of the evening lost like wafting smoke into the night air. Despite the ominous atmosphere, my focus remained locked on Raker.

"*Whew*, now it's a party!" Sarah chirped; her gun trained on Raker's buddy.

"Let her go," Griggs ordered, standing just beyond my peripheral vision.

Raker's eyebrow twitched, and I could tell he was contemplating his options.

"Stop acting like idiots and put your damn guns down!" Tatara shouted; her voice icy.

"Nope," Griggs snipped back. "My gun stays up until *he* comes to his senses. If he doesn't, that just means I'll have one less racer to beat." His tone told me everything I needed to know. He meant business. Despite his military background, I never fathomed him capable of such intensity—he'd always been so easy going. Then again, before now, I didn't think I had this kind of grit in me either.

I pressed the muzzle deeper into Raker's throat. "So, what's it going to be?"

Raker's flat nose crinkled, then he released his grip, taking a step back.

The urge to rub my tender wrist was strong, but I resisted, unwilling to show he'd hurt me in any way. I holstered my weapon, and slowly, everyone else followed suit.

"For fuck sakes, what did I say about not wanting any trouble?" Tatara barked, clearly not impressed. Her brows scrunched so tight together, I worried she might pull a muscle. "You guys—" She singled out my alliance. "Go to your enclosure and sleep it off, or get the hell out. Those are your options. And all of you here—especially *you*—" she pointed at Raker. "Settle down and keep to yourself."

"Fine by me," I muttered. Without a second glance, I spun on my heels and happily returned to my waiting bedroll. Griggs and Sarah followed close behind, all three of us promptly claiming spots beside our fire. I looked over at Herc. Satisfied he was doing fine in his pen, I leaned back against my saddle and let the fire entrance me once more.

"Holy fuck. Vernon slept through that," Sarah mumbled with a low chuckle.

"Heavy sleeper," Griggs said dryly. "Remind me never to let him babysit my kids overnight. He wouldn't hear shit."

"You have kids?" I couldn't help but ask.

He smirked, shaking his head. "My *future* kids."

Sarah laughed, tossing logs onto the fire. The smoke must've tickled her nose because she let fly the most forceful sneeze I'd ever heard in my life.

Vernon shot straight up, his eyes darting about. "What's going on? What was that noise?"

"Really? *Now* you wake up?" I said, incredulous.

A baffled Vernon lifted his hands in question while the rest of us locked eyes and burst out laughing. We reeled ourselves back in pretty quick though, quietening down so as not to disturb our already on-edge neighbours.

Vernon raised his brows. "Did something happen?"

"I'll take this one." Sarah flopped down on her side. "We just had a huge showdown over there. Finn got grabbed by some colossal dickbag with a human complex. Then she nearly shot said dickbag in the throat. And you—dear sweet Vernon, didn't even flinch. Not until I *sneezed* just now. Apparently, a sneeze is where you draw the line."

"Oh…" His face morphed in groggy surprise. "Gracious! Is everyone okay?"

I waved a hand, deciding to take it easy on the older racer. "We're fine. It's all good."

"I see." Vernon slumped back into his prone position. "Well, I'm glad everyone survived. See you in the morning." His eyes slammed shut; passed out again in record time. I was jealous.

"And on that note. Night guys." Sarah burrowed beneath her blanket across the fire, then abruptly raised her head once more, displaying a wicked grin. "Oh, and by the way, Finn—that gun-to-throat manoeuvre was amazing. I bow to your brilliance."

I chuckled. "Thanks."

Sarah disappeared again, leaving only Griggs and I still awake. For the life of me, I didn't know why, though. I needed sleep, especially after that encounter. Now that the adrenaline was wearing off, my hands had developed a tremble. I pulled my blanket over my arms to cover it, then yawned loud and long.

But, before I could say goodnight to my freshly knighted protector, he spoke.

CHAPTER 10

"That *was* pretty impressive." Griggs glanced at the other enclosure, lowering his voice even further. "The guy one-hundred percent deserved it. He shouldn't have touched you like that." Lying down, he rolled to his side to look at me, his body resting only a few feet away. Too close, yet at the same time, not close enough. Protectiveness had been a good look on him. The spark of attraction I'd been trying to snuff out ignited into flame. *Dammit Finn.* Thankful for the dim light hiding a flush spreading to my cheeks, I forced the most platonic smile I could manage.

"I'm just happy it worked out… thanks for standing up for me back there." The heat in my cheeks intensified, spreading elsewhere as his eyes locked on mine, and I resorted to one of my father's old sayings. "Yep, you're a good egg."

His brows raised. "A good *egg?*"

"It's a real saying!" I hastily defended my words. "It means you're a good person." Griggs scrunched his nose and I tossed a few fallen leaves at him.

He shook his head, amused. "I've never heard that before in my life."

"Oh, right, I forgot you grew up on Mars. What would you say there instead?"

He smirked. "Not *you're a good egg,* that's for sure."

Raking a hand through my hair, I huffed in mock indignation. "Whatever."

Griggs poked my arm, then tucked his hands beneath his jaw—like a child curled up with a blankie. I wondered if that's how he normally slept. "Good thing I love eggs. And you're very welcome—you know, about the Raker thing. Nobody messes with my friends."

Friends. Okay, good to know where he stands. Now I could eviscerate any ridiculous notions running through my mind about him. I blinked hard a few times, my eyes feeling like they'd been dipped in sand. I needed sleep, yet couldn't keep myself from asking, "What was life like growing up on Mars, anyway? Take me through a day in the life of Griggs—is Griggs even your real name?" There was still so much I didn't know about him.

"Questions, questions. I'll tell you what. I'll answer any two questions if you'll answer two of mine. Deal?" He extended a hand, waiting patiently.

Slapping my palm into his, I shook it. "Deal."

Griggs' fingers were slow to slip away, skin brushing against mine.

I cleared my throat. "So?"

A weird groan-like sound escaped him. "I never tell anybody my real name. Like *never.* But I shook on it, so…" His mouth opened dramatically to spill the secret, which I was now quite excited to hear. "But you need to swear you won't tell anybody."

I matched his tone. "I won't. Now, what is it?"

Griggs shrugged. "Fine. Okay—here goes…"

"Oh my gosh, spit it out already!" I whisper-shouted.

He cringed. "It's Gregory."

"Oh." *Well, that was anti-climactic.* "Um, that's a nice name. What's wrong with it?"

He scrunched his nose. "Nothing, but there's more. My middle name is *Ignacias.*" He rubbed a hand over his face. "I'm not overly fond of Gregory. It's so bland. No character to it. But I absolutely detest my middle name. *Hate it.* In school I got called Iggy."

"Oooh, yeah… that's rough." I stifled a giggle over his exaggeratedly forlorn expression. "Wait—so, you're not only a good egg, but a good Igg, too?"

Grigg tossed leaves at me this time. "See this is why I never tell anyone."

"Sorry I couldn't resist. You know I'm just teasing." More leaves cascaded over my face and he chuckled, which was a relief. I worried I'd actually offended him for a second.

"I'll let it slide. *So, anyway…* I eventually combined the two— and voila! Griggs."

I smiled. "I like that. Makes perfect sense to me. Now, what about Mars?"

Griggs shook his head. "Naw, naw, we're taking turns. I get to ask you a question now."

The man's chipper enthusiasm in the face of exhaustion was infectious. I nodded.

"Great. Okay, hmm…" He tapped his chin for a moment, pondering. "How did Herc come into your life, and how did he become bionic?"

I made a tsk tsk sound. "That's two questions. Which one do you want first?"

Griggs' irises flamed like a prairie sunset in the golden firelight. He promptly rephrased both into one single question. "Can you please tell me the origin story of Herc?"

Rolling onto my side, I faced Griggs full on. "Well played. Okay, so it's kind of a long story. I'll try to give the simplest version—I'd like to get to bed sometime this century."

Griggs laughed. "Sorry, I'm keeping you awake. We can chat another time, too…"

I regretted saying anything. Despite being tired, I was enjoying myself. "No, it's all good. Really. Two questions each, then sleepy time. So, I got Herc three years ago. He was young—a colt, just shy of three years old. I actually won him in a game of pocket poker. See, he's a Friesian, a rare "collectible" breed." I framed the word in finger quotes.

Griggs cocked his head. "Collectible. That's interesting."

"Right? He's a descendant of original stock—has unrefined DNA. Friesians nearly went extinct, along with Thoroughbreds, Clydesdales, and Arabians… but thankfully, a few *very-rich* horse-lovers preserved them. The rarity makes breeding very lucrative, and that's what I aim to capitalize on with Herc if I can win us some land."

Griggs smiled. "So, you'll have a bunch of min-Herc's running around. Nice. What other plans do you have? Maybe settle down—start a family?"

"Hey, no freebies. Is that your second question?"

"Nope." He twisted an imaginary key into his lips, sealing them shut.

A grin slid across my face. "Anyway, the guy I won Herc from didn't have the credits, so he gave me Herc instead. The whole ordeal caused a bunch of trouble with my family. My dad pretty much hates me—" I stopped myself, not particularly wanting to dive into that aspect of things. "But, that's all in the past now. I have Herc and that's all that matters." I shrugged.

Griggs' eyes shone with understanding. "I can relate with family issues. Mine's not sunshine and roses either." He continued to stare at me for several more moments. "And…?"

"And what?"

He cleared his throat loudly. "Aren't you missing something? You forgot to explain how he got his bionic legs. That's part of his origin story."

"Right." I tucked the hair behind my ears and took a deep breath. "When he was still green broke Herc had been out in the fields with the other horses and somehow managed to get through a fence. He wandered too close to a cliff edge—not a huge one, maybe a six or seven-foot height—but when the rock gave way, the drop was enough to do damage. He fell, broke all four legs and bashed one side of his face on a rock." My jaw clenched as vivid memories flooded back to me. "I found him lying there in pain. It was horrible."

I heard Grigg's sharp intake of breath, but he said nothing. Just listened.

"A lot of folks wonder why I bothered saving a horse in such poor condition, especially since his tech ain't cheap. I guess the answer is twofold. Um… the money I used to win Herc belonged to my family. My boyfriend at the time manipulated me into helping him cheat, but that's no excuse. Anyway, our livelihoods kind of hinged on *Herc's* livelihood after that. My father had wanted to sell him, but my mother convinced him not to based on his future value. If Herc had died, the money I gambled away would've been lost for good. That was the *only* reason my father scrounged the credits for his surgery. Yeah, it's a whole messy saga of events I won't bore you with. Simply put, I made some *unfortunate* errors in judgement that I've learned a lot from." I grimaced, remembering the turmoil of that time. Why was I even saying this much? Hearing all of this certainly wouldn't improve his impression of me. Yet for some reason I couldn't explain, opening up to Griggs felt comfortable. Safe.

Griggs nodded, his face solemn. "We all make mistakes, Finn. The fact that we learn from them is the big thing. And you're not boring me. Not at all." He twisted a leaf in his hand. "Sounds like if Herc hadn't been so rare, and you hadn't fought for him, he wouldn't be here today. No wonder you're so protective. He's lucky to have you." I couldn't get a good read on his expression in the dim lighting, but his tone was warm.

"We're lucky to have each other. That horse helped turn my life around. Gave me a new dream." I exhaled heavily. Vulnerability swelled and I hid it with an awkward laugh. "Sorry for rambling on. Geez, you're getting my whole life's story for the bargain price of two questions."

Griggs waved a hand. "I'll have to step up my game now. It's only fair you get a bargain too." We laughed together, but once it ebbed, he added, "Seriously though, I'm happy you shared. It's good to get to know you better—what makes you tick." He leaned up on one elbow, the light catching more of his face. His expression was soft, sincere.

I smiled. "Same."

Griggs covered his mouth, letting out a lengthy yawn. "Maybe we should save the last two questions for another time? We've got an early morning and another full day ahead of us."

"Yeah…" I mumbled, surprised by my disappointment. "However, we might get busy and forget all about this. Why don't we power through? Answer quickly and then we're done."

Yawning again, Griggs agreed, signalling with a rolling wrist for me to carry on.

"Okay, so, Mars. Go." I couldn't get over how easy he was to talk to. I suppose I had a rough idea. On the transport ship en-route to Joya, Griggs, Sarah, Jorgep, and I had hung out a fair bit. The conversation always flowed easy between the four of us, despite our wildly different personalities. However, despite the fact Griggs and I did share drinks alone in the bar once, we hadn't really gotten into personal stuff—like, the real personal stuff. Sarah being the exception, I hadn't delved much deeper than surface level with anyone.

"I lived on Earth until I was ten. Those years were rough, but having good friends in school made it tolerable. My mom got into some bad stuff—using synth gels and you don't want to know what else. She barely kept enough food in the fridge. Then she pawned me off on her estranged mother—my grandmother—shortly before she OD'd. My grandmother took me in out of pity, but she wasn't happy about it."

A part of me deflated inside. "I'm so sorry. That must've been hard."

Griggs stared into the sky. "Yeah, the whole thing kinda messed me up, I guess. Going from Earth to a Mars colony was a shock to the system. Everything's red and dusty. You can't just bugger off and escape your troubles when a dome's holding you in. I fell in with a bad crowd—did all the wrong things. My grandma kept me alive and all that, but she was *not* the maternal type. The woman had impossible standards and let's just say she was *heavy handed.*" Griggs let out a heavy breath. "As soon as I was old enough, I joined the Martian military. The structure and comradery helped me get my head on straight again. Gave me a sense of purpose. People actually gave a shit about me. It filled some holes inside, you know?" He glanced my way with a resigned smile. "I've got some nightmares and a bum knee out of the deal, but life goes on. Like my old commander said, striving means thriving. And that's why I'm racing."

"Wow, I can't even imagine what all of that must've been like… I do understand rejection though. My father can hardly stand being in the same room as me. Not all families are healthy." *Why did I just say that? Now he's definitely going to think I'm a horrible person.*

Griggs shook his head. "I don't know everything that's happened in your life, but I can tell you have a big heart. I bet your dad will come to his senses eventually… And if he won't, you'll have me." His nose scrunched adorably as he smiled, sending a flutter into my stomach. Then he quickly added more seriously, "And the rest of the crew, too. You know."

"Thanks." I resisted the urge to reach out for his hand.

Griggs cleared his throat. "Looks like I shared *my* whole life story, too!"

I gave a smug grin. "I got my bargain after all. Now we're even."

A horrific noise exploded into the night.

Griggs and I shot straight up, heads swivelling as our hands reached for weapons. We identified the source at the same time. I blew out a relieved breath and Griggs shoulders relaxed. A very loudly snoring Vernon laid across the fire. It sounded like he'd swallowed a pig and his 3-wheeler at the same time. Sarah didn't even flinch. We looked at each other, stifling laughter.

Griggs laid back down. "Alright, here's my last question."

Leaning back against my saddle, I gave the go ahead, the promise of sleep tugging at my eyelids. With each passing moment, it grew harder to hold them open.

"After hearing your story, I'm curious about something. You looked uncomfortable when Tatara asked us to play poker earlier, then you declined to play later, too—and you just shared you won Herc playing poker. Are you anti-gambling now?"

I nodded. "Gambling has caused me a world of trouble. That and the fact I stupidly dated a guy who sucked me into his schemes. He was so smooth when he wanted to be—really made me feel special. I realized too late he was bad news." I picked a twig off the ground, turned it in my fingers, and tossed it. "Now I'm just trying to make it right, and *never* be that person again."

He bowed his head. "Sorry. Your ex sounds like a real piece of work. Hearing that, it makes sense now, why you didn't seem too keen on the idea of settling down earlier."

"It's not that I don't *want* that. I do. It's just I—I don't know. It's complicated."

Griggs' lips pursed. "Maybe you just need to meet the right guy…"

"Who knows? Maybe." I shrugged, self-conscious. "Anyway, this was good. It was nice to chat." Sliding lower on the saddle, I stretched my arms out. "But, now it's bedtime."

"Indeed." Griggs tossed another log on the fire. "Good night, Finn."

"Night." I rolled over. Save for the sounds of crackling wood and Vernon's intermittent barrages of snoring, the world went quiet. Like an assassin in the night, sleep came quickly.

***

A snort roused me from my slumber. And something else I couldn't quite quantify—like the tail end of a cry. A shrill tone, yet muted as though it had originated far in the distance. Was that a scream? My eyes popped open, glancing around the fire at my still sleeping companions. I looked at Tatara's enclosure, worried Raker might be up to no good, but there was zero sign of movement.

My gaze settled on Herc.

His eye glowed a brilliant white, nostrils flaring as he shifted from hoof to hoof.

"What is it, buddy?" I sat up, mumbling more to myself than to him. He didn't appear injured or labouring in any way. So, what was causing such a severe reaction?

I followed his line of sight into the forest. It was black as pitch out there, only the closest trees dimly illuminated by the dwindling firelight. I engaged the flashlight on my pistol, using it to scour the darkness. My ears strained to hear something—anything that might explain Herc's white eye. But there was nothing.

Maybe a Joyan bear is nearby. We'll have to keep an eye out tomorrow.

"It's okay, boy," I said a little louder, turning off my light. His ears twitched towards me, yet his focus didn't leave the trees. "We're protected in here. Everything's fine."

I tossed a couple of logs on the fire to stoke the flame. Then, blinking heavily, laid down. As I pulled the thin wool blanket back up over my shoulders, a strange light in the periphery of my vision caught my attention. I turned my head and looked into the dark once more, this time seeing two round and very reflective orbs suspended in the inky gel of night. *What the...?*

They blinked.

I shot up, breath hitched in my throat. But the mystery orbs had vanished.

After several minutes of searching, they never returned, and my stiff posture relaxed. I could hardly keep my eyes open, and my head ached slightly. I started to question whether I'd seen anything there at all. Was my mind playing tricks on me? Perhaps my exhausted—and likely dehydrated—brain decided to manifest an alien creature for this uncharted landscape. And yet, I had definitely thought about being watched by something enough during the daytime.

Glancing back at Herc, it was a relief to see his eye had returned to green. Not blue quite yet, but it was a good sign. Laying my head back down, I let my eyes flutter closed once more.

Whatever it was—if anything—must have moved on.

CHAPTER 11

Khana strode into the monitoring room. She surveyed the wall filled with screens that switched between live feeds of approximately two hundred competitors. Two desks sat before the screens. She nodded to a sandy-haired employee named Jareth—one of her top officers—who diligently monitored a complex panel of controls. At the other table sat her right-hand man, with his bionic legs resting atop the ebony desktop. Steel leaned back in his chair and Khana placed an ash-skinned hand on his broad shoulder. "How is the race progressing?"

Jareth flicked a switch and Steel pointed to one of many screens. The video showed a group of racers, including that crazy one who chose to ride a horse, of all things, inspecting a downed drone. The timestamp showed it was from earlier in the day.

"A few of our drones have been found now." Steel indicated the other video feeds in question. He looked over his shoulder at his fellow CEO. "That means by tomorrow, the field will have travelled as far as we've ever gone. And you know what that means."

"Good. Keep me apprised." Khana turned to Jareth. "And you, get me the daily broadcast edit within the hour. The colonists are clamouring to see more footage and get updates on the race—some are even betting on potential winners. They're having fun with this and I'd like to keep them appeased."

A smile crossed Jareth's face. "Sure thing, boss."

Khana nodded and turned for the door.

"Oh, sister?" Steel drawled, stopping her.

Khana turned with brows raised. "Yes?"

Steel dropped his feet off the table, swivelling his chair to face her. His eyes were hard, true to the name he'd been given. "This race better work out as planned. Otherwise, we'll have gained nothing from this convoluted venture of yours. As our *oh-so-noble* brother Garido said, it seems like a lot of rigamarole for a less-than-assured payoff."

Khana motioned to Jareth with a crisp head nod toward the door. Without hesitation, the man stood and exited the room, closing the door behind him.

Smoothing the black argyle patterned pants suit hugging her body, she walked back towards Steel. "There are two hundred racers scouring that Sweep—which means free labour and zero casualties for us. Would you prefer to waste more of our own resources? The nature of our business dictates a certain level of finesse and subtlety sometimes. We need to figure out what we're dealing with, first and foremost."

Khana smiled sweetly, bending at the waist until they were eye to eye. His orange irises contrasted with her blue ones. His inky black hair the yang to her near white locks. Truly, they looked nothing alike, aside from their shared grey skin tone. A by-product of experimental genetic alterations their parents so graciously bestowed upon them in utero. "And *don't* rehash anything Garido says. It makes you sound as dumb as he is, and I don't believe that of you."

Steel's brows pinched together, gaze cool.

She ran a hand down the side of his face. The hard line of his jaw flexed ever so slightly, then Khana sharply slapped his cheek. "You will respect the calls I've made, brother. Don't forget that this colonization project is mine. Let me do the thinking, okay?"

Steel's eyes flared with rage; fists clenching, but he made no move towards her.

Khana turned, calling over her shoulder, "Tell me the moment things get interesting."

*****

Roaring engines woke me from my sleep. Loud. Close. The forest still appeared a dull grey, the sun barely kissing the morning sky. Coals smouldered in the firepit as the smell of woodsmoke seasoned the air. Was somebody from camp on the move already? I stretched my arms and rolled over, meeting Griggs eyes as he stirred. After flashing a quick smile, I averted my gaze. Something about our chat last night made me feel closer to him. Like a connection—a more substantial one than before—had been forged. But I had no clue if he felt the same way.

Maybe I shouldn't know. This was still a race, after all, and he was still a guy I might never see again once it was over. Call it old fashioned, but even if I wanted to, I wasn't keen on romantic flings, regardless of how tempting. I couldn't trust myself to stay detached, and the fear of getting hurt again was too strong. If there wasn't a real chance Griggs could be more than a situational friend, it would be foolhardy for me to invest time in that.

The engines revved obnoxiously, followed by metallic clinking noises and a throaty cackle. A quick check showed nobody in my alliance was missing. Who was leaving?

I looked where all the vehicles were parked just in time to see Raker's rear wheel spinning in the moist dirt, stuttering until the tread finally found purchase. A second later he tore off down the path, disappearing beyond trees that appeared to swallow him whole. He wasn't alone, either. The sneer-faced asshole who'd pointed his gun at me last night, rode behind him.

The sound of Raker's devilish laughter wafted back to my ears on the faint breeze. "Guess they're determined to get an early start." I shrugged. Fine by me. The less I saw of that Ganglian the better. Breakfast would be much improved without his toxic presence.

His campmates woke from the racket, too. Dino, the big guy with the dinosaur spikes running the length of his back, walked out to his triple treaded dura-track with a suspicious twist to his expression. His machine was aggressive looking, with bold red and yellow flames painted down the sides.

I pulled my hair into a ponytail, watched him key in his unlock code and hit the ignition. The engine cranked, then died. He pressed the button again with similar results. He swore, and pressed it three more times. Nothing changed.

"Tatara, check your vehicle." Dino opened his hood panel.

"Why?" Tatara asked, disengaging her auto-enclosure.

"Just do it." He waved at the others. "Everyone. Check your rides."

Griggs and Vernon exchanged concerned glances, immediately leaving our enclosure to inspect their own conveyances. I looked at Herc, who seemed well, aside from the fact his eye glowed green. I wondered what made him uneasy. The unnerving dream from last night flickered in my memory. The darkness. The blinking eyes. Yet, in dreams I'd had before, details were typically inconsistent and hazy. This was different. Even now, those cat-like orbs glowed crisp and vivid in my mind. Was it possible I actually woke up last night?

Sarah dragged her sleepy form off the bedroll and checked her mech suit, keying in a code on her wrist cuff. The bulky rig hummed to life, and the thin, pink lumen strips outlining the tangerine-toned musculature of the suit glowed like normal. "My suit works fine… But it was shock locked."

Vernon spoke up. "Well, mine's dead."

"Shit, my spyro won't start either." Griggs kicked at a pile of leafy debris with his foot.

A chorus of frustrated growls rang out as the rest of the racers tried and failed to start their vehicles. Then the shouting started.

A wiry female racer named Cala barked, "Did anyone know about this?"

"If any of us were in on it, do you think we'd still be here?" Dino retorted.

Someone snipped, "With that Raker guy's attitude, why'd you let him join the fire?"

"He should've been kicked out, and then *this* happens! Convenient…" said another.

Tatara certainly didn't take kindly to that insinuation. "Just because it was my fire, don't you accuse me of being in cahoots with those weasels. Last time I checked, my vehicle got hit too." Tatara glared at anybody brave enough to make eye contact with her. Nobody dared to argue her point—who could? She was right. We were all in the same boat.

"That *yeeptak!*" Tatara's beautiful face contorted with rage as the Pembru insult rolled off her tongue—a slang word the universal translators didn't recognize.

Quiet Guy, whom I still hadn't heard utter a single word—picked up the biggest rock he could lift and hurled it into the nearest tree trunk. Every muscle in his two-toned body flexed as he took a deep cleansing breath. Then he pulled out a tool kit and set to work on his off-roader.

Sarah had remained quiet, which was surprising. I figured she'd have some choice words to share as well. But instead, she slipped over to Griggs's machine. "Can I open the hood panel and take a peek?"

Griggs waved a hand. "Go ahead." He stared at the foliage-obscured sky with a sour look on his face, jaw clenched tight.

Given my history with Raker, I opted to keep my mouth shut and my face neutral, though inside I felt like screaming *I knew he couldn't be trusted!* The guy had given me bad vibes from minute one. I was just thankful he hadn't tried to sabotage Herc. Then again, if he'd been stupid enough to try that, I might've caught him before he got to the rest of the vehicles.

Vernon, who'd remained bizarrely calm, waved his hands in the air. Walking into clear view of everyone, the eldest racer pointed in the direction Raker and his minion fled. "Everybody, please try to calm down. I'm certain this is exactly what that undesirable fellow wanted. To get under our skin. To—"

"To get under our skin? He sabotaged us!" Cala roared. "If we can't fix whatever he did, we're done. We've lost this race."

Vernon seemed unfazed by the sharp rebuttal. "Yes, I realize that. Believe me, I understand your frustration. My 3-wheeler is shut down too. All I am trying to say is that fighting amongst ourselves won't solve our problem."

"He's right," Griggs chimed in. "We couldn't have predicted any of this. But now he's shown his true colours—we won't make the mistake of trusting him again."

"*If* we can get our vehicles running. You're forgetting the *if…*" Tatara said.

"That's a big *if*," Cala grumbled, clearly not impressed as she tossed her thick braid of fleshy locs over her shoulder. Teensy and Lootas, the other two racers I hadn't spoken to much around the fire, both seemed to share her disgruntled sentiment, their expressions sour.

Vernon pressed his oblong palms together. "We all seem like smart individuals here. I'm sure if we put our heads together, we can figure it out."

Sarah stood up, blew the fallen hair out of her eyes, and grinned. "Hey Griggs." When he looked, she pressed the engage button on his spyro cycle and it flared to life. It sputtered briefly like it did yesterday, but otherwise ran perfectly normal. She casually tossed him a wrench.

"What the—well done, Sarah!" Griggs beamed, practically falling into the seat and revving the engine. "You really are a mechanical genius. What was the problem?"

"*You really are a mechanical genius*—what, did you doubt me?" She cast a wry glance, then continued. "Your energy regulator chip was triggered. It's a tiny part that almost never fails, so it gets buried in hard-to-reach places. Just needs resetting. Without it though, the engine won't function." She brushed dirt off of her hands, giving the hood a firm tap. "I accessed yours by shifting a connecting panel that secures your steering column—an impossible find for anyone who doesn't know what they're looking for. That Raisin guy knew what he was doing."

I smirked. "His name is Raker."

"Whatever." She shrugged, turning to the next closest vehicle, which was Tatara's. "Do you mind if I check to see if your rig has a similar problem?"

"By all means, check away. Thank you." Tatara's smile was as bright as her eyes as she invited Sarah over with a graceful arm flourish.

Griggs held up the golden wrench Sarah threw to him. "What's the deal with this?"

Sarah knelt beside Tatara's vehicle. "I found it in the grass beneath your ride. Our saboteur must've been in a rush and dropped it. Unless it's yours?"

Griggs shook his head.

Dino spoke up, "I saw Raker using golden tools when he was tinkering last night."

"Mystery solved… not that there was much of a mystery." Sarcasm infused my words.

Our resident technological wonder muttered, "I'm kind of sad that douchebag never tried to mess around with my mech suit.

I've got shock skins installed. We would've known pretty quickly what he was up to." Shock skins utilized similar technology to the shock locks protecting Herc's reins and saddlebags. They sent a generous jolt into whoever tried to tamper with or break in, while simultaneously sending an alarm to the owner.

Tatara chuckled, leaning to rest her forearms on her tracker bike's handlebars. "I'm also sad that didn't happen. That suit is quite amazing, by the way. I've been admiring your colour choice—pink and orange."

"Seeing him yip from a shock would've been stellar." Sarah swept her hair away again and glanced up with that cheeky grin of hers. "And, thank you." Her attention lingered on Tatara's face a moment longer than was necessary, which Tatara didn't seem to mind at all. *Hmm, interesting…* No, better than interesting. That meant Tatara's eyes weren't only for Griggs. Inwardly, I cheered, then in the next breath, chided myself. *Griggs can hook up with whoever he wants. Get your shit together, Finn. This is getting pathetic.*

Ten minutes later, Sarah successfully restarted Tatara's bike. Since her vehicle used different propulsion tech, Sarah connected diagnostic cables to scan for the error. Tatara purred with excitement when it worked. Sarah's smile seemed brighter than I'd ever seen it, a hint of rose on her cheeks. I really couldn't blame her for noticing Tatara. She was gorgeous.

I got Herc saddled, fed, and watered while Sarah continued helping anybody who needed it, though Cala and Quiet Guy chose to do it themselves. Within the hour, everyone was up and running again. Folks packed their gear and scarfed a quick breakfast. Cala took off as soon as she was able, skipping food entirely, which made me wonder what her deal was.

"It could've been much worse." Sarah climbed into her suit. "Thank fuck nothing Raker did was unfixable, because there isn't exactly a parts shop around here."

Tatara chuckled at Sarah's colourful verbiage, then straddled the ribbed seat of her tracker bike. "Who needs a shop when we have you." She winked, making Sarah grin.

Shaking my head at the pair's blatant flirtation, I swung onto Herc's back and gave his neck a pat. "You're thankful? I was seriously starting to worry how Herc and I were going to schlep all of you around." Letting out a laugh, I settled into the saddle and gripped the reins. "I mean, I have an auto-cart installed, but there's no way it's big enough."

"Auto-cart. Does it work similar to your auto-enclosure?" Sarah asked.

My brows raised, surprised she didn't know. "Yeah, same concept."

Sarah tilted her head, her tone dry, "Look, I repurpose old tech, vehicles, and do a little hacking on the side. But I haven't exactly kept up on the latest cart tech."

"Duly noted." We shared a chuckle, then took off down the path. Our caravan had swelled with the addition of several more racers. Tatara, Dino, Quiet Guy, Teensy, and Lootas—whom we knew the least—had all decided to travel with our alliance. Supposedly we seemed like good folk, and power in numbers and all that. I had a sneaking suspicion that keeping Sarah close by in case their vehicles experienced more trouble was the true goal, but since none of them managed to piss me off last night, I was okay with them joining.

My mind wandered back to the mysterious eyes in the forest as we travelled. Were they real? If yes, who or what did they belong to? Herc's ocular implant hadn't been blue ever since, and he seemed perpetually agitated, swinging his head from side to side often—like he was on the lookout. I found myself mirroring his actions. Was our theory correct and some kind of Joyan bear was nearby? Or something more worrisome? I pondered whether

I should tell the others. With Herc acting so nervous, it grew harder for me to believe it was all a dream.

And what about Raker? That guy deserved a beating for what he did. Admittedly, I wasn't shocked there'd be some shady characters lurking amidst this melting pot of racers. Someone was bound to stoop to such a low—it was just unfortunate it impacted us. We were a solid hour behind the rest of the field now because of him.

A teeny part of me wanted to see him one more time so I could give him a piece of my mind. But the larger part hoped I never saw that despicable man's face ever again. All I wanted was to get to the finish line with as little drama as possible. Preferably near the front of the pack so I could get my pick of the land parcels.

I slipped my hat off my head, letting it dangle by its string down my back. The ground's downward slope increased by a few degrees, leaving little doubt we were approaching the heart of the ravine. The foliage seemed denser through this section, the canopy tightly knitting itself to enclose us in a shadowy cocoon. I wiped sweat from my brow, wishing there was more of a breeze. Each breath felt harder, heavier—the viscosity of the air itself growing thicker with humidity. Herc's cooling chest strap worked overtime to keep him regulated.

Extra water breaks would be integral.

I fanned the collar of my overshirt, sweaty and gross all over. If it got any hotter, I'd have to strip down to the tank top I wore beneath it and risk branches scratching my bare arms.

A few hours into the day, we came upon that big rover sporting the heavy grill and scoop blade affixed to the front. The one who'd unknowingly cleared a path for us the entire way thus far. His vehicle, like so many we'd been passing, was down for the count. Keeping a cautious hand on my pistol grip, I called out, "You doing alright?" The racer barely registered my words, giving a sluggish nod. In truth, he looked a little dazed. Maybe the heat had gotten to him.

"You have enough water?" I asked out of courtesy. He nodded again.

Griggs gave a crisp wave on the way by. "Alright then, good luck."

With the Rover out of commission, it was up to us to traverse the uneven forest floor.

Sarah stayed out front, like always—though, we had to explain why to the others. Not everyone had seen the felled drone. So far, her mech suit and Herc both remained unaffected by whatever interference existed here. Aside from his constant green eye, and the extra work he did carrying my ass around in this heat, Herc appeared to be doing fine. A blessing.

However, Grigg's cycle wasn't faring as well. It now chugged on a regular basis—the engine's power stuttering. Worry marred his features whenever it happened. And he wasn't alone. Everybody's vehicles were acting up. I feared it wouldn't be long before they all simply shut down. What a cluster fuck that would be.

I followed right behind Sarah for this leg of the journey. Every now and then she called back warnings about obstructions like rocky sections, fallen logs, or mud holes. Griggs and Vernon rode next in line, then Tatara and the others brought up the rear. The strange blue veins running in the ground grew a little thicker the further we travelled. Thorny vines and swooping branches protruded everywhere. Thankfully, due to the matted canopy overhead, the leafy underbrush grew low and sparse. Trees weren't grouped together as tight through this section of the forest, either. Every now and then, we crossed tracks left by other racers who'd ventured this way. Not many, though. The fact that two hundred racers could spread so thin only highlighted how vast the Sweep really was.

"What's up with Herc?" Sarah asked over her shoulder. "His eye's been green all day."

I briefly debated whether to say anything, then quickly decided it was best to be open about it. If I were in her shoes, I'd want to know, too. "Something spooked him last night. He's been wary ever since. I was pretty groggy when it happened, and I honestly thought it was all a dream this morning. But Herc hasn't settled down, which is weird, and since what I saw in the forest was so vivid—now I'm thinking it might've been real."

Sarah did a double take. "You saw something? What?"

"I don't really know what it was for sure. I think eyes." Herc shifted sideways beneath me as his hooves found their way through a rocky patch.

One of Sarah's brows arched. "Eyes? Okay, start from the beginning and tell me what happened. Actually—" Sarah lifted a closed fist and the caravan came to a stop. She waved at everyone, bidding them to come listen. "Everyone should hear this."

I took a deep breath, wiping my slick brow again. "So, last night I woke up to a weird shrieking-type sound and Herc's snorting. Everything looked calm, but Herc's eye was white which caught my attention pretty quick."

"White means fear." Griggs explained for the new racers' benefit.

I nodded. "Or pain. But he wasn't injured. He was watching something in the forest. Yet, when I looked, I couldn't see anything."

"Hmm…" Sarah said, her voice the slightest bit tinny as it transmitted through her suit's speaker. "Maybe the bear-thing was close by?"

"I wondered that, too." I didn't want to freak anybody out, but I had to tell the rest of the story. "But when I tried to go back to sleep, I saw two orbs in the dark. Really round, kind of like cat eyes—but not. They looked at me, blinked once, then disappeared." A cold shiver tingled, raising goosebumps on my arms, the sensation a stark contrast with the Sweep's perpetual heat.

Murmurs rolled through the group.

"Eyes." Sarah let out a low whistle. "Shit. Could you tell what they belonged to?"

I shook my head. "No. It was too dark. And remember, it might just be a dream…"

Dino spoke up in his gruff voice. "We should assume it's real for now."

"He's right. It's best to err on the side of caution," Vernon agreed. "Thank you for sharing that information, Finn. I suggest we all keep our eyes open. Now, we should really keep moving. Thanks to that Raker fellow, we've lost enough time in the day."

Nobody argued and the caravan carried on.

Twenty minutes hadn't even passed before ragged chugging noises stole everyone's attention. Dino jerked back and forth inside his narrow dura track buggy. The vehicle bucked in revolt, as though fighting a debilitating seizure. Then the engine cut out completely.

Dino swore a litany of unfamiliar curses as he jumped out, slamming the door shut. Growling from the back of his throat, he kicked the front fender. The caravan came to a stop.

Sarah sighed. "I guess, I was ready for a break anyway."

CHAPTER 12

The majority of our short break was spent swallowing food, guzzling water, and discussing new developments. While Dino battled to get his buggy running, we sat on logs and vehicles seats placed in a haphazard circle. Conversation inevitably circled back to the eyes in the dark. Sarah showed images of the animal tracks she'd documented to anyone unaware.

"There are animals in every environment," Vernon said logically.

Lootas, a jittery fellow, piped up quickly. "Yes, and some are *dangerous*."

Tatara nodded enthusiastically. "Like deadly dangerous. Example—desert Gratcons on Hobs—hello. They're blood sucking lizards who camouflage with sand and shoot venom."

Vernon capitulated. "That is true."

"But there's no reason to assume *this* animal is deadly." Griggs chewed a snack he'd pulled from his pack. "It could simply be curious. Remember, we're foreigners here."

Teensy stood and flexed the quadruple pectoral muscles on his bare chest. "Well, I've been hunting my whole life, and to me, shooting a predator that big is a fun challenge." He brandished his pulse rifle as though it were made of gold, saying, "If it's mean, bring it on."

"Sit down," Lootas muttered and Teensy laughed, a cackling sound.

I had a hard time looking at poor Dino. Sarah hadn't been able to fix his vehicle—another of the Sweep's mechanical casualties. It looked like he'd be stuck here while the rest of us carried on. But the determined guy just wouldn't accept it.

"So, who can I hop on with?" Dino blurted, glancing around the group.

An awkward silence set in. Eyes flicked in all directions, nobody thrusting a hand up to volunteer. The competition was fierce for this land, so why would anyone help someone else succeed? Nobody knew each other well here. There was no implicit trust or deep connection.

Well, except for the growing bond I'd formed with my core crew.

He shifted in his seat. "Look, I get it. But if we cross the finish line *together*, I can't *beat you*, right?" His palms were up, imploring with his eyes, and still nobody replied. Again, I felt sorry for the guy, but it was one of the risks in this race. We signed up, knowing there could be troubles. The terrain could've been impassable to any of these vehicles, including Sarah's suit or Herc, and we might've been in the same boat. It was a crappy reality, but a reality nonetheless.

Griggs finally broke the silence. "Sorry, but my cycle is running like shit as it is. I don't want any extra weight bogging it down."

At least he was honest. In my heart, I knew I'd try to help Sarah, or Griggs… maybe even Vernon, now that I'd gotten to know him better. But I didn't know Dino from a hole in the ground. And I didn't want to put more strain on Herc in this heat unless I absolutely needed to.

A stream of similar let downs followed from the rest of the racers present.

Dino knit his fingers together, sighing. "Okay, what do I need to pay? A trade? Is there some kind of deal we can cut? Back home

I'm barely scraping by. My wife and kids are relying on me. I need this land." He appealed to us again, searching people's eyes. "Anyone?"

A few eyebrows rose in response, but the silence grew even more uncomfortable as people considered the proposition. Nonchalantly, I fingered the butt end of my pulse pistol as a different realization dawned. If nobody agreed to take him on, how would he handle it? As we'd witnessed before, desperate people could do unexpected things sometimes. Dino had several working vehicles right here at his disposal.

Finally, Vernon said, "I may have space. What are you offering?"

Dino's eyes lit with hope. "Uh, I can give you 500 credits."

Tatara scoffed at the lowball offer.

The racer raised his hands, skin wrinkling between his nubbed brows. "I know I don't have a lot, but if you help me get the land, I'll give you the 500 and then another 1000 when it yields profit. I'll sign something on your digicuff if you want. All you need to do is drag my ass across the finish line." He extended his open hand. "Deal?"

Vernon stroked his angular chin as everybody watched with rapt attention, our eyes flicking back and forth between the two men.

"Oh, alright. But only because you pulled me out of a mudhole today." Vernon slapped his palm into Dino's. As they shook, a collective breath of relief released around the circle.

Dino beamed with a happiness he couldn't hide. "Thanks so much. You have no idea."

Vernon, proving to be a thorough man, pulled up a translucent screen via his digicuff. He punched in a couple quick sentences to log the contract, and had Dino sign.

I smiled. "Glad that worked out."

Tatara stood, looking into the sky. The sun blazed overhead, hazy slices of light penetrating the web of leaves overhead. "Break over. Now that Dino's sorted, let's go."

Dino grabbed his pack and hopped on the back of Vernon's vehicle. I mounted Herc once more, and seconds later, our caravan continued down a less-than-ideal path. We tried to keep moving forward in the same general direction, weaving around rocks and roots, and veering at times to try and find the smoothest route. Now and then we crossed more broken down vehicles, whose owners had continued on foot—pressing forward towards the finish line.

Wow, the numbers are really dropping.

"How's everybody doing back there?" I called out from behind Sarah.

A myriad of responses reached my ears—from "alright" and "good", to Tatara's cheeky "are we there yet?" Herc's breathing sounded a little heavier than normal, and I wondered if the heat was taking its toll. He'd done so well this whole time, but that coolant chest strap could only compensate so much. Or it could simply be because the air was so dense. I found it harder to breathe, too. It wasn't burning my lungs or anything—it didn't seem toxic.

Sarah used her internal filters to scan for signs of any contaminant. That yielded negative results. It was safe, just humid and *thick*, like the air was slowly turning to gelatin.

Flashes of movement glinted up ahead.

Guns went up immediately, our contingent poised to blast anything dangerous that might jump out at us. We approached with caution, but as we pushed past the underbrush blocking our view, the threat level immediately eased. It was just a racer walking. Obviously an owner of one of the abandoned vehicles we'd passed. I holstered my weapon.

The hairless figure wore a pink shirt and gun belt—clearly a Flexsion, due to their characteristically bulbous forms and pale, gooseflesh skin—didn't look back at the sound of us coming. She stumbled over a log, righting herself with all the grace of a drunken ship steward. I wondered if the loss of her vehicle had hit hard enough for her to start day-drinking. I'd seen Dino swig from a flask he had stashed somewhere. Raker had, too. It seemed like an odd choice to get sloshed in the middle of a strange forest, but who was I to judge? I'd had a few good benders in my day.

We cut around the figure, and she remained dismissive of our presence.

"Hello there!" Griggs waved.

The Flexsion glanced over with unfocused eyes. She waved back, then pointed at Herc, a silly grin splitting her face. "Funniest looking bike I've ever seen!" She broke into giggles.

Curious whispers flew, and I exchanged a bewildered glance with Griggs and Sarah.

"I'll check it out," Sarah muttered. She let us pass by, then stepped closer to the wobbly individual. "Hey you, are you feeling alright?"

She nodded sloppily. "Just great! A fine day for some exxxccercise!"

"Um… alright." Sarah swivelled to look at us with raised brows. Shrugging, she stepped back. "Listen, you better lay off whatever you've been drinking. We've seen creature tracks in the mud, and you don't want to be caught—" she fumbled for the right word. "Unprepared."

"No, no, I'm good. Feeling great. This place is so happy."

"…right." Sarah turned and rejoined the caravan. As she passed me to regain the lead position, her mech hand formed an "C" shape. She tipped it to her lips a few times.

I smirked. Glancing back over my shoulder, I saw the smile still lingering on the Flexsion's face as she lumbered forward. "Well, I hope she gets on okay."

Griggs jerked as his spyro chugged. "I'm sure it'll be fine."

It felt weird leaving a person behind in that condition, but what else could be done? Our group was already running heavy with faltering vehicles, and that racer was far from svelte. Nobody else had raised a hand to take on that challenge either. Sure, this racer seemed like a happy drunk for now, but that could change in an instant. I focused on moving forward.

A new sound reached my ears. It came with each faint breeze, patchy like intermittent static playing on an antique radio set at low volume. I tilted my head. "Do you hear that?"

Sarah swivelled. "Yeah, I hear it."

"I'd say there's a river up ahead!" Vernon shouted from behind.

A round of fatigued chatter erupted immediately, everyone excited to douse their heads and fill canteens—providing the water was potable. I silently daydreamed of a sandy stream with shallow pools to temper any swirling currents. My goodness, wading into cool water, as long as it was safe, would feel like absolute heaven right about now. But more than anything, I hoped it was easily passable. There'd be a lineup of disgruntled racers if it wasn't.

"Question," Tatara blurted randomly from three vehicles back. "Has anybody wondered why Governus didn't send their own charting mission into the Sweep?"

"What makes you ask, Tatara?" Vernon replied.

She bumped over a jagged log, jostling in her seat. "Just curious to hear theories."

I turned at the waist to make eye contact. "This race is to celebrate their anniversary and attract new colonists. Maybe they find watching this kind of thing thrilling? Historically, with old Earth television, the more risk the higher the viewer ratings."

Griggs smirked. "Hey, they've made us wear these retinal monitors. Who knows? Maybe they're taking bets on winners and watching the race with popcorn in hand."

Tatara's head tilted. "Hmm… I don't know what television is, or popcorn, but that's an interesting theory."

Sarah spun to run backwards. "Whaa? You've never had *popcorn*? It's so good." She rubbed her belly, then in what seemed like an afterthought, added, "So, what's *your* theory?"

Tatara pursed her lips. "I've been wondering if this race is pulling double duty—not just about a celebration, but about getting us to do the dirty work of charting it for them."

Sarah shrugged behind her octagonal torso shield. "Well, I'm sure that has to be a happy bonus." Her nose scrunched before flashing a hem-and-haw smile. "That would be pretty shitty of them, if that was the case. And a hard call without proof. Governus could've purposefully delayed charting the Sweep in order to make the race more interesting. Who knows?"

Tatara swerved to avoid a decomposing stump. "I hope that's all it is."

"Me too," I said. "The alternative seems so devious. Why would anyone do that?"

Tatara's face grew serious. "Exactly." Then she brightened again. "Well, anyway…" She let the words fade and silence ensued.

But Sarah was quick to lighten the mood again. "Just remember, we could be stepping on all kinds of priceless shit *right now,* and Governus has no clue." She made a show of glancing beneath her feet the next few strides. "Watch for anything bright and shiny!"

Tatara's face split into a smile. "You're too much, you know that?"

Sarah winked back. "Better too much than too little."

I rolled my eyes.

The path grew rockier and we angled our trajectory to the right to avoid the worst of it. Herc's treaded hooves were holding up thus far, maintaining their grip. Several times, he had to tow vehicles over a sizable deadfall when it crossed our path. It would've taken far too long to cut or move the logs off the trail. He still breathed heavier than I'd like, but seemed to be functioning okay. I asked Sarah to check her suit's internal scanners again.

"Perfectly fine," she confirmed.

As I reeled in the rope from our latest pull, the edges of my vision went blurry. Blinking hard, I gave my head a little shake to snap out of it. The blurriness ebbed, but a lightheaded sensation crept in to replace it. *I must be getting dehydrated. I need to drink more water.*

Griggs spoke up before I had the chance. "You guys' mind if we take a quick water break? My head's swimming a little bit in all this heat."

"Absolutely, I'm parched as well," Vernon agreed, as did the others.

I swung off of Herc's back, holding onto the stirrup when my balance faltered. Several seconds passed before the unsteadiness ebbed, then I retrieved our water from the saddlebags. I opted to use one of the water tablets my mother had given me, tossing it into Herc's container and pouring several droplets onto it from my canister. It fizzed to life, its mass gurgling and expanding, until a bucket full of liquid stared back at me. I had absolutely no clue how the science worked, but these tablets were incredible. Herc drank without hesitation.

Griggs nodded, equally impressed by the magic act I'd just performed.

"Just add water." I smiled and guzzled my fill, but reminded myself I could *not* let my canister run out completely. Without those few precious drops, my handy tablets were useless.

One of the racers at the back spoke up, though not loudly. "I'm really starting to hate this humidity." It was Quiet Guy, of all people—with a surprisingly deep voice for his lean frame. It was the first time I'd ever heard it. He wiped sweat off his face with such vigour I thought he might erase the Rorschach-like markings framing his eyes, nose, and mouth on both sides.

Vernon chuckled. "Not me. I am loving this, my friend." When everyone turned to look at him, incredulous, he laughed louder. "Neersoo are built for tropical climates. My home world is equally hot. If not more so."

Quiet Guy looked appalled. "Remind me never to vacation on your planet."

I giggled, then screwed the stopper back onto my water canister. *Quiet Guy is funny.* "You know, this is the first time I've actually heard you speak. What's your name anyway?"

Quiet Guy's eyes brightened a shade. "I suppose I prefer not to speak. On my home planet we communicate with our minds. Words are immaterial, though we learn them for commerce." He smiled then, creasing the inky patterns on his cheeks. "I am Enek."

Ah ha, that makes more sense now. "Enek. Nice to officially meet you."

He bowed his head to me. "You as well."

I went to collect Herc's container, pleased to see it empty. "You made quick work of that water. Good job. You needed that." Rubbing his neck, I wished his eye would turn blue again.

A distant shrieking noise echoed.

Herc whinnied in response. I stiffened, a hand moving to my pulse rifle. The cry reverberated through the trees, the faint sound shrill yet raspy—and familiar. It came from too far away to pinpoint an accurate direction, though.

"What the hell was that?" Griggs pulled out one of his pistols.

"It didn't sound like a person's scream," Vernon said.

Tatara spun in a slow circle, her eyes scouring the forest. "No. It sure didn't."

Griggs donned his helmet. "Whatever it was sounded far away."

"Think that's the owner of those pawprints?" Dino swigged from his flask.

Sarah, Griggs, Teensy, and Vernon all shrugged in tandem.

A heaviness settled into my stomach. "I've heard that before." All eyes swung to me. "Last night, when I saw the eyes in the dark, I vaguely recall hearing a noise just like that when I woke up. I think that's what Herc snorted at—maybe what made his eye turn white."

Nobody appeared thrilled with that information. Hell, I wasn't keen on hearing creepy cries in a strange forest, either. Eager to get moving again, I swung into my saddle, but the motion caused my head to swim again. I gripped the horn.

"You okay, Finn?" Griggs' brows furrowed.

"Yeah. All good. Let's get moving."

CHAPTER 13

We hadn't travelled far before we came across a welcome sight—a certain stocky racer with fleshy feelers dangling beneath his chin sat atop an unmistakably robust creature.

I surged ahead of the group, a huge smile erupting on my face. "Jorgep!"

Sarah waved a mech hand at our lost alliance member. "Holy shit! There he is! Man, we thought we'd lost you!"

Our friend's bleenad Keemi, walked in lazy circles and stomped on something beneath her feet. I wondered if she'd cornered some rodent-like creature to make a quick snack of. Or perhaps, like a dog circles before squatting, she was looking for a place to relieve herself. Jorgep appeared unconcerned, giggling as he watched his mount do whatever she was doing.

He didn't look up as I neared. "Jorgep?" I waved enthusiastically to get his attention, but had no luck. "Hey, Earth to Jorgep. It's me, Finn! I'm so happy we found you. Sarah and Griggs are here too." He finally glanced over with glazed eyes and my excitement slipped a little. "Are you okay?"

Jorgep smiled, almost sleepily, his chin feelers rippling like a cutesy finger wave. Being the perpetually polite guy he was, he said, "Oh, hello there, Miss Finn. Fancy meeting you here." The bleenad's broad head raised, letting out a gruff grunt before returning to her ground search.

My brows furrowed. Slowing Herc to a stop maybe twenty feet away, I strained to see what she was intent upon. There was nothing there—unless it was too tiny to see.

Something isn't right…

The others caught up to me.

"You know this guy?" Tatara asked.

Griggs got off his cycle. "Yeah, he was with us at the beginning but we got separated when the race started. Thought we'd lost him for good." He turned back to Jorgep with a beaming smile, hands planted on his hips. "Eh, Jorgep? Boy, I was hoping we'd catch up with you somewhere down the line."

Jorgep lurched in his metallic saddle as his bleenad hopped after something. He lost himself to giggles, completely ignoring Griggs. I got off of Herc and tied him to the nearest tree. The motion blurred my vision again, lasting longer than before. I paused, leaning on Herc, and breathing deep for a few seconds.

Griggs walked up to me, his hand touching my shoulder. "You sure you're okay?"

"Yeah, fine." I forced a smile, not actually certain I was. "This humidity is really affecting me, I think. I've been feeling lightheaded." Grabbing my water canister, I took several ravenous gulps.

"I've been feeling off myself," he muttered. "And what's up with Jorgep?"

Tatara strode up. "He's clearly drunk on something, just like that other racer we saw."

Sarah, who'd been eyeing our possibly inebriated friend, shook her head. "No, I don't think that's it. I mean, look at Keemi. The thing is just as looped as Jorgep, chasing an imaginary friend around." She levelled her gaze on us. "I highly doubt they were doing shooters together."

"Hallucinations?" I asked.

"From something he breathed in, or food poisoning, maybe?" Sarah glanced around. "There *are* wild berries around. Jorgep and the others could have eaten the same fruit."

I tapped my chin. "That would make sense."

Dino piped up from the back. "Seriously, who'd be dumb enough to eat alien fruit?"

All eyes swivelled to Jorgep who was currently staring bashfully at Tatara, giggling as he tipped his flat-brimmed hat. Then something invisible flying through the air caught his attention. His head twisted furiously atop his neck trying to keep track of it—whatever it was. He thrust his hands out over and over like a cat trying to catch a butterfly.

"Okay… so what do we do? We have to help him," I said. No way could I leave him behind in this state. A stab of guilt twisted knowing I'd left the other racers… but I forced myself to shake it off. I wasn't aware of this issue then. Plus, it was unreasonable to take responsibility for random people I didn't even know. *This situation is different. Jorgep is my friend.*

I noticed the newest caravan members step back, clearly not wanting to get involved. Everyone but Dino and Tatara, which pleasantly surprised me. Vernon joined our circle too. He never seemed to back away from a challenge—and so far, had been unfailingly supportive.

I coughed, a tickle in my throat.

Griggs walked towards Jorgep. "I'm going to see if I can get through to him. Try to figure out what he ate, or if it's something else affecting him."

"While you're there, get him to put on his breather. Can't hurt to cover all our bases at this point." I opened my saddlebags and dug for my med kit. There were anti-toxin pills in there, but who knows if any of them would work for Joyan substances.

"Will do!" Griggs approached casually, raising a hand to our friend. "Hey Jorgep, what did you eat today?"

The bleenad's head snapped up, eyes darkening as she let out a terrifying bellow. The sound was gravelly, consisting of several reverberating tones in different octaves. Keemi stumbled forward, baring a mouth full of jagged teeth.

Griggs jumped back, stumbling over his feet to get clear.

I dropped the med kit I'd been inspecting. "Whoa! Get your ass back here!" He didn't need my encouragement to do that, though. Griggs zipped back in short order. Keemi's face calmed quickly, and she lumbered away again, her owner happy to go along for the ride.

Griggs leaned on his cycle's handlebars, breathing heavily. "So, *that* didn't work."

Vernon chuckled. "You still got all your important parts, right?"

"Thankfully, yes. Damn, that thing's got some big teeth."

Relieved he was okay, I picked up the med kit I dropped and packed it back into my saddlebag. I grabbed my rope off of the saddle horn instead. "She's usually really sweet. Whatever's affecting her is making her extra protective." Giving Herc a pat, I untied him and mounted up. "I have a new plan."

Tatara's brows raised. "Oh? And what do you have in mind?"

I flashed a grin, tightened the strap holding my cowboy hat in place, then pulled out a worn pair of leather gloves from my back pocket. "I aim to do a little bleenad roping."

Vernon and Dino laughed. Griggs grinned.

Tatara didn't seem quite as amused. "You're going to try to rope that thing?"

I nodded, pulling my gloves on. "Absolutely." Prepping the rope for the lasso, I stretched my neck and shoulders. "We can't help him while he's in that saddle—she won't let us get close. If I can get Keemi's head under control, then you guys can pull Jorgep down. Um... I'll tie her off on that tree over there." I pointed.

Tatara scoffed. "You're crazy."

I raised my brows in challenge. "You got a better idea?"

She remained silent.

Sarah lifted a mechanical hand to give me a high five. "Finn, I love this plan."

"Good, because you're going to be my rodeo clown. Your suit's strong enough to withstand a few bites if things go south."

"Rodeo clown, sure." Her grin morphed into one of confusion. "And what's that now?"

A nostalgic smile crossed my face. "Rodeos were big for country folk in the 21st century. Not so much, anymore. But people in my home community still get together once a year to hold our own version. Calf roping, barrel racing, bull riding—the whole shebang. A rodeo clown distracts the raging bulls so they don't trample cowboys after they get bucked off."

Sarah's eyes lit up. "Oh, so, distraction—done deal."

Griggs looked at the handful of racers hanging back. "You guys want in on the action?"

Teensy and Lootas politely declined.

Quiet Guy—er, *Enek,* stepped forward. "I'll help. But if I get chomped, you all better sleep with one eye open." He seemed serious with one spotted brow arched at a severe angle. Silence fell, nobody knowing what to say to that. Then he broke into a wry grin. "I'm jesting."

Chuckles rumbled around our tight circle, intensifying like a slow clap. *Funny again. Who knew the man had such a sense of humour?*

"Alright, you're in. Operation catch-a-bleenad is officially a GO." I squeezed my heels and moved Herc forward, weaving around boulders protruding from the moist earth. Sarah kept up beside me. My co-conspirators followed on foot, ready to strike once the coast was clear.

I whispered to Herc, "Alright bud, let's rope us a big-ass steer."

Keemi had stopped again, pawing and snapping at the ground. Giving her a wide berth, we manoeuvred beside her and I swung the rope in circles above my shoulder.

Jorgep looked over with that silly smile. "Oh, it's you again. Have you seen the dancing korklenap? He's surprisingly agile for such a round fellow."

I had no clue what to say to that, but Keemi reacted to the sound of her owner's voice, head snapping up. Her rusty lizard-like eyes narrowed on me as her lips parted to reveal teeth. Ridges of jagged wrinkles formed around her mouth, stretching up her thick snout. Her skin twitched as she poised for attack.

"Cue the rodeo clown!" I commanded, but Sarah was already in motion.

She bounded in to steal Keemi's attention. "Here kitty, kitty!" Sarah lunged out of the way as the bleenad bit at her, then twirled in front. Narrowly avoiding another snap, she danced her way to the opposite side. "Who's a good bleenad?"

Keemi snarled and snapped, following after her.

Perfect. I brought Herc around in a circle, swinging my arm over my head as the others crept up behind Keemi.

Sarah leapt side to side like a poorly trained ballerina, the dome of her face shield visible every few seconds above the bleenad's back. "Any time now!" she shouted.

I threw the rope, which skidded off Keemi's angled neck, landing in a stubby bush below. "Shit." Her blocky head swung my way as I furiously reeled the cordage in. She lumbered after me. "Retreat!" I called to the others and spun Herc around to avoid catching a bite.

My faithful rodeo clown went to work, tickling Keemi with a leafy branch.

Laughter rang out from where our vehicles were parked, Lootas and Teensy clearly getting a kick out of watching this play out.

"Come on you big beautiful beasty!" Sarah challenged.

I let out a snort of laughter, bringing Herc around for another attempt. Poor Jorgep was hanging on for dear life with all the jostling back and forth, yet his smile never faltered. He even hooted, like he was enjoying a thrill-ride at Carnival Rush Space Station.

My arm circled in the air again, sweat trickling down my neck. I let the rope fly, and this time, it circled the target's head. "Yes!" I pulled the loop tight. Keemi roared, thrashing and hopping to free herself. Jorgep almost went flying, which would've been perfect. Alas, fate wasn't that kind. I reined Herc into a sharp turn, and we rushed toward the tree. Keemi charged, trying unsuccessfully to bite through my metal-meshed rope.

We executed a tight turn around the trunk, tied off in a hurry, then galloped away again. We halted at the end of our rope and Keemi sprinted straight past the tree. My asshole puckered as I questioned whether my rope calculations were correct. Was my end truly longer than hers?

Barely five feet away, Jorgep's mount jerked backward like she'd hit an invisible wall.

A relieved breath rushed from my mouth as Herc pranced in place. As Keemi fought, frothing at the mouth in her rage, the team moved in. Tatara joined Sarah in distracting Keemi, while Griggs, Vernon, and Enek yanked on Jorgep's foot. The heavy racer didn't budge.

Jorgep sagged to the side, wailing, "Bugs are attacking my feet!"

Keemi swung her mighty head, slammed it right into Griggs, and sent his body crashing through a heavy thicket with a pained grunt.

"Griggs!" I stared at the spot he'd vanished, waiting for him to push through the foliage and say he's okay. But that didn't happen. "Hurry up!" I shouted at the others.

"Fuck this." Sarah lunged forward. One metal arm snaked around Keemi's neck, hooking under her jaw. Clamping her hands together, she had the bleenad trapped in a headlock. Keemi thrashed, her teeth skidding off Sarah's face shield. "Get him down *now!*"

Tatara and Enek launched themselves at the impaired racer, dethroning him and crashing to the ground. Vernon grabbed Jorgep's collar and unceremoniously dragged him away.

Jorgep flailed, screaming, "The bugs, the bugs!"

Sarah let out a battle cry and shoved Keemi's head in order to dart away. Once out of snapping range, she punched the air in victory. "Fuckin' right! Like a boss!"

Cheers rose from our audience, but I felt like flipping them the middle finger. Not much help they'd been. I couldn't be *too* mad, though. They didn't know Jorgep. Honestly, I was surprised they'd even stuck around to watch.

I slumped in my seat, relieved. Vernon slapped a breather on Jorgep and Enek sloppily stumbled back to the vehicles to retrieve a med kit. As I glanced furtively to Grigg's last known location, my peripheral vision went fuzzy again. Images of other stumbling racers flipped through my mind. Was it just adrenaline affecting Enek now, or something else? I hoped the toxin tester revealed some vital clues.

"Sarah, can you hold this rope? I need to check on Griggs."

"Shit, right!" She jerked into motion, taking the tether.

Another one of those haunting shrieks echoed in the distance again.

Cheering from the vehicle area ceased immediately. Then someone started laughing hysterically. *Really?* I sliced a glare in that direction, seeing Teensy, Lootas, and Enek doubled over, shoulders shaking. Not only could somebody be injured, but there was also a mysterious creature lurking about. It was one thing to celebrate, but another thing to be a jerk.

Pushing that aside, I dismounted. "Griggs? Are you alive in there?" My legs wobbled as I ran toward the thicket. Somewhere behind me, Dino started cackling. I heard Sarah tell the gigglers to shut the fuck up. *What the hell is going on? This isn't normal.*

"I'm alright! I'm good," came Griggs' laboured reply. He pushed through the willowy thicket and I skidded to a halt. He held his ribs with one hand, but waved with the other, shooting a lopsided smile my way.

"Sorry, I got the wind knocked out of me pretty good. Hit something on the way down. I'll be sore, but I'm fine." Griggs stumbled enough to topple, then clumsily righted himself.

"Are you sure?" I replied, ready to help him walk if he needed it.

"Yep, I'm sure." He let out a girlish giggle. Stopping abruptly, he gave his head a quick shake. "That was weird. Anyway, you guys should come see what I found over here."

Sarah shouted, "Spill it. What did you find?"

"Well, I didn't technically *find* it. It was more like I *landed on it.*" He let out another high-pitched laugh as he ran a hand through his twig-infested hair. The simple action resulted in a pained grimace. He must've noticed my concern, because he locked eyes with me. "I'm good. Just deal with Jorgep, then get back here— it's best you see it rather than me trying to explain."

Dread tightened the knots in my stomach.

Geez, what now?

CHAPTER 14

I think he's coming out of it!" Vernon shouted, kneeling beside Jorgep.

Oh good… However, laughter still emanated from the racers waiting by our vehicles. Enek hadn't returned with the med kit, either.

Glaring, I muttered, "What's so damn funny?" But even as I said it, an odd sensation washed over me. The knot in my stomach untangled itself—that heavy feeling easing. The blurriness seeped into my central vision and swirled like a gust of wind kicking up a dirt devil. I turned back to Griggs, eager to show him the whorls, but he gawked at the sky in a daze.

His hair shifted on his head, twitching like it had a life of its own. *What the…?*

A pair of white rabbit ears pushed through his dark wavy hair, curling at the tips.

Slapping a hand over my mouth, I swallowed my laughter. "Griggs…" I bit my lip. He wasn't paying attention to me, so I poked him in the shoulder. "Griggs. What's with the ears?" I reached out to touch them, feeling the baby soft hairs beneath my fingertips. *So soft…*

Griggs finally lowered his eyes to mine, inspecting my arms as they stretched over his head. He ran his hands along them, mouth open in awe. "Your arms, Finn… they're like porcelain." He inched forward, pressed his cheek against my right bicep, then ran his stubbled jaw up and down. The tingles I felt sparkled before my eyes, spreading outward in pink and purple streams until glistening colour covered my entire body.

"Oh my God, I'm beautiful!" I cried, giggling with glee. "Look at me!" I stepped back, spinning a circle for him, my feet catching on something and nearly falling over.

Griggs caught me in his strong bunny arms and his eyes widened. "You really are. You're so smooth—and shiny, like the sun before it touches the horizon." He started giggling like a child high on sugar. "Stop twirling like that, though. You're making me dizzy."

"I'm not twirling, silly." A snowman walked up behind Griggs's shoulder, smiling as he offered me his corn cob pipe. Coughing from the smoke, I politely declined. Then, with a friendly wave, the frosty being meandered his way into the distance. I looked back at Griggs, laughing. "What a friendly snowman. How has he not melted in this heat?"

"What?" Griggs tittered, which only made me laugh harder.

Somewhere in the back of my consciousness, I heard somebody shouting. The words were so faint and far away— clearly not meant for me. I pinched the bunny nose that sprouted on Grigg's face. "Oh, my goodness, you're adorable. How have you not told me you're part rabbit?"

He didn't answer, too entranced watching his hands as they ran up and down the sides of my body. Then he knocked his knuckles against my shoulder like a door. "Your skin is so glassy. Beautiful… I promise I won't break you."

My sparkles changed colours with each of his words, painting my flesh anew. Then his lips were on mine, the kiss soft, yet urgent at the same time. He pulled me closer, and I melted into him. He felt so warm—the snow-white fur covering his flesh silken beneath my touch. Waves of sparkling rainbows exploded from me, slathering the world with colour.

Griggs hands squeezed my buttocks, sliding to grasp beneath my thighs. He hoisted me in one powerful motion, and my legs wrapped around his waist.

"Fruit flavoured porcelain—damn, you taste so good. Like strawberries and ice cream," Griggs muttered against my mouth.

I giggled with pleasure, soaking him in. *I wonder what will happen if I mate with a rabbit? Will I have babies or bunnies, or will they be hybrids?* The distant voices spoke again, but closer this time. Though they were muffled, I could make out the words. The familiar female voice said, "OH shit, oh shit, oh shit... hey, guys? Um... guys?"

Footsteps rushed closer.

I didn't care if she was talking to us or not. The voice was irritating like a crackling loudspeaker I couldn't shut off. Griggs lips slanted over mine as he lowered us to the ground. Straddling his lap, I wrapped my arms around him and he breathed heavily against my mouth.

"Seriously guys! Cut it out!" the voice grated again.

A hand grabbed my arm, the firm touch instantly tainting all of my beautiful sparkles. I shrugged it away, letting instinct take over as I moved against my furry bunny.

"Vernon! I need breathers, stat!"

A male voice shouted back from far away, "I have my hands full with Dino and that quiet fellow right now! Jorgep, are the others under control? Can you find their breathers?"

"After I tackle Miss Tatara. She's trying to go streaking!" came the reply.

"Well, hurry!" the annoying woman shouted, gripping my arm again.

Griggs's paws were everywhere. I raked my fingers through his hair, caressing his long fuzzy ears. Then my mouth was abruptly dragged away from his. I straightened, twisting to give this infuriating offender a piece of my mind—but broke into hysterics instead.

"Sarah? Is that you?" She was out of her mech suit, and dressed like a pirate—complete with a curved brim hat, a black eye patch, and wooden peg leg. A green and red parrot even squawked on her shoulder. I tried pushing her away, but her fingers were unmovable. Griggs caressed my waist and thighs, which still draped over his legs. He kissed a line across my collarbone and I sighed, rainbows bursting from my mouth.

"Back off, Griggs." Sarah's free arm, which now wiggled like a noodle, pushed Griggs back. I tried to wriggle free, to send her away, but Sarah's fingers dug in.

"Ow! Hey now, that's not fair. We're just having some fun." Changing tactics, I gave her my best puppy dog eyes, even batted my eyelashes. I wished I had crackers to bribe the parrot.

"Believe me, Finn. You'll thank me later."

"Oooh, grumpy pirate." I huffed.

Heavier footsteps approached. "Here!" That voice… I knew that voice—wasn't that Jorgep? But I didn't see Jorgep. Instead, a huge goldfish wearing a tuxedo toss something shiny to Sarah. *Oh God, did Jorgep turn into a goldfish? How will he survive outside the water?*

Something cold pinched my nose and chin.

"What's stuck on my chin?" Griggs bellowed. I glanced at him, seeing a coral-coloured starfish affixed to his lower face. He rubbed at it, but Sarah promptly slapped his paws away.

"It's a starfish, silly. I have one, too!" Crossing my eyes, I looked down my nose.

Griggs' fear evaporated and we erupted into laughter. Then he murmured something about wanting to taste more strawberries. His paws reached out for me again, and I leaned in, titillated by the very thought. However, our attempts to pick up where we'd left off failed miserably. Pirate Sarah pushed Griggs again, and kept me imprisoned in her iron grasp.

"Just—don't fucking touch each other," Sarah barked.

Griggs groaned and tried pawing at his starfish again.

Sarah growled. "Don't touch your breathers, either."

"Ahem, they're starfishes. I think you're hallucinating!" I fell forward, doubling over with giggles so light and fluffy, they filled my whole body with clouds. The buoyant cumulus lifted my arms up, and I wondered if I might float away.

"*Riiiiight…*" Pirate Sarah's lips twitched in the corners. "Well, don't touch the starfish then. Got it?"

I saluted. "Aye, Aye, Captain!"

***

Standing in a semi-circle twenty minutes later, the whole group stared at the discovery Griggs brought to our attention. The awkwardness was as thick as the air we inhaled—despite the breathers we now sported. Arms crossed uncomfortably. Nobody smiled. Glancing up, my eyes darted furtively between faces. But when Griggs looked, my eyes snapped back down.

Jorgep chuckled, a dumbfounded look crossing his face. "Goodness, I've never experienced such insanity in my life. Truly, you all should've seen—"

I sliced a hand through the air. "Let's not talk about it."

Jorgep raised a finger. "But—"

"NOPE."

Jorgep lowered his finger.

Sarah's eyes were trained on me, and I could sense amusement oozing off of her. If she hadn't just saved me from… *myself,* I'd be tempted to smack that look off her face. But, taking a deep breath, I tempered my desire—something I sorely wished I'd could've done twenty minutes earlier. *What an idiot you are, Finn.*

My face hadn't stopped burning since I came to my senses and leapt off of Griggs' lap. Though I tried not to think about it, I could still feel Griggs' lips on mine. The gentle touch of his hands. His very unfurry muscles beneath my fingertips.

From what Sarah said, it only took a couple of minutes for the breathers to kick in and detoxify our system, clearing whatever had tainted the air. Once back in reality, group members found themselves caught in a variety of bizarre situations, and full memory of what they'd done. Tatara had stripped to her underwear. Enek thought he was a piece of grass. Dino believed he was some invisible flying creature. It might've been funny if it weren't so embarrassing.

Jorgep obviously still found it humorous, though. Once the fog had cleared from his brain, he'd thanked Vernon who'd helped him, then tackled the task of putting a breather on his bleenad. He'd also attached an equine breather on Herc, before chasing after Tatara—a kindness I appreciated. Though Herc hadn't been acting up, his heavy breathing did ease up after the breather went on. So maybe more than humidity had been bugging him after all.

Sarah theorized that since the interference seemed to be strengthening the deeper we travelled into the Sweep, and now the air was changing too, she was willing to bet that the cause of both was likely the same. Since her suit filtered the air for her, she'd remained unaffected. Vernon had remained clear of mind, too, thanks to his built-in breather. Lucky.

I cleared my throat, pointing at the focus of our attention. "So, a hoverbike." The sleek machine sat useless; its pointed front end nosed into the ground after having hit hard. One of the angular panels mounted beneath it had been snapped off. Covered in a layer of debris and grime, just like the drone, I could tell it had been sitting here a while. But unlike the drone, this machine wasn't in working condition. Its grey hood and side panels held dents and gouges.

"A *wrecked* hoverbike," Sarah qualified.

"A *Governus* hoverbike," Griggs finished, pointing out the familiar golden insignia imprinted below the machine's cracked windshield. "I landed on it when Keemi tossed me, before everyone—you know—went loopy." His words hung awkwardly in the air.

Then Dino threw a hand up. "What the hell? They said they didn't chart this place. So, what, they just lied?"

I lifted my eyes, disgusted by this discovery. "Yeah, they lied, Dino."

Vernon stepped closer to the bike, inspecting the damage. "Yes. But the larger question at play here is, *why?*" He ran his lengthy fingers along three jagged, one centimetre-wide clefts in the metal. Three perfectly parallel slices nearly two feet long. "Something big did this."

"No way, ya think?" Lootas chirped snarkily.

Vernon cast an unappreciative glare his way. "Watch your tongue young man. We're all in the same boat together, and there's no need for cutting remarks."

The chided racer huffed, then looked down, mumbling, "Sorry."

Letting out a sigh, Vernon, the oldest racer present, smoothed the frown from his face, returning to his inspection. His implanted breather, which consisted of two curved protrusions that stuck out an inch on either side of his mouth, shifted slightly as his fingers stroked his chin. Compared to his, standard-usage breathers like everyone else had were low-tech. No bio-links or auto-filter screens—just transparent diamond-shaped coverings that clipped over the mouth and nose, housing two pen-lid sized filter cartridges.

Sarah, knelt beside the hoverbike to patch into its interface. She ran the same scans she'd completed on the prior drone. However, after a minute passed, she sat back and shook her head. "No dice, it's too damaged. I can't get any residual readings from it."

As the group continued discussing, I wandered off, looking for any other signs of struggle. The ground was too compact to show any tracks. Where was the rider of this machine? If the hoverbike was attacked by something with claws, a bloody outcome seemed likely. Surely there must be remnants of a body lying in the vicinity. But there was nothing visible.

I pushed my way past a stubborn swath of willow-like brush, and a gleam caught my eye. The corner of something metallic glinted beneath dappled sunshine—another panel perhaps.

Rushing over to it, I yanked the branches back.

"Guys, I found another bike," I called over my shoulder, the revelation sitting heavy. "Same thing. Wrecked. We should fan out and look for more. The seat on this hoverbike, similar to something one might see on a human-made 20th century snowmobile, was slashed. Bits of foam padding littered the mud beneath the vehicle. But that's not what caught my eye.

Others spread out through the trees, as I bent over to grasp what looked like swaths of weathered gray cloth wedged beneath the bike. With a hard yank, I pulled them free. Turning each one over in my hands, I spied dark red-tinged stains on each one. Not grease or oil. Looking closer, my throat went dry. That had to be blood. I laid them on the ground.

"What did you find?" Griggs appeared beside me with a tentative smile.

Startled, I jerked back, glaring at him. An image of me caressing his fuzzy rabbit ears flashed through my mind, and a searing heat burned my cheeks anew. I looked down, focusing on the grimy smoke-coloured fabric. "I found pieces of a uniform. A bloody shirt, I think. Look—" I pointed to where the three pieces fit together perfectly. "What do you see?"

"Three claw slashes, just like the ones on the bikes." Griggs clucked his tongue.

I nodded. "Uh huh."

Tatara called out, "We found two more hoverbikes a little deeper in. There's also an empty metal canister over here. From the markings on the side, it looks like poison!"

"Poison? Were they trying to kill these things?" Griggs said.

I slapped the seat. "Whatever they were doing, they didn't make it out."

Another haunting shriek echoed from afar. Griggs and I tilted our heads to the sky, alert and listening. Despite the lingering awkwardness, our eyes locked together.

Two rounds of blaster fire cracked somewhere up ahead, the sound eliciting a collective gasp from the group.

"Who's shooting?" asked Teensy.

Dino clenched his fists. "Agh, what the hell is happening?"

"Let's get the fuck out of here!" Lootas blurted.

Griggs jolted into action, striding to meet the others. I followed right behind, watching him stuff the shirt fragments into a cargo pocket. He caught me watching and muttered, "Evidence." Then he addressed everyone. "We need to keep moving. The faster, the better."

"Agreed." Sarah immediately turned to leave the thicket.

A shadow crossed Vernon's eyes. "Yes, I believe we have worn out our welcome."

Herc! I'd left him tethered to a tree in the clearing. Sprinting flat out, I burst through the edge of the thicket—the same ones Griggs had been thrown through a short time ago. My eyes scoured the trees as I went, seeing no movement. Herc was fine with his equine breather still in place, standing beside Jorgep's sizeable bleenad. Thankfully, the two shared an amicable companionship, both used to each other after weeks spent en-route to Joya.

Everybody rushed back to their vehicles as Jorgep and I swung into our saddles.

"Governus, you pieces of shit!" Griggs hopped off his cycle, boot kicking the side of it.

With a heel squeeze, I reined Herc his way. "What's up?"

"It's dead," he growled, jamming his finger onto the engage button over and over. The spyro barely sputtered once each time. "Shit, shit, shit!"

A curse exploded from Tatara's mouth. "Mine too. Dead."

Sarah wasted no time inspecting the vehicles, but couldn't resuscitate any. The Sweep's interference had claimed them. Once again, everybody looked at each other uncomfortably.

I dug through a leather compartment nestled opposite my rifle scabbard. "I'd let someone ride with me, but with all my gear, the term *saddle sores* would take on a whole new meaning." I pulled out a three-inch wide circular plate and clicked it into a matching depression behind my saddle seat. Next, I swung down to the ground and attached a pair of thick rings to connection points on the lower rear edges of the saddle.

I nodded at Griggs. "I use this baby all the time on the ranch. Brought it along in case of an emergency." With a crisp click, my fingers pressed the circular activation pad. The auto-cart hummed to life. "I'd say this qualifies."

A glowing net of light expanded from the rings to form a holographic cart, built with a singular design to carry heavy loads. Yellow cross-hatched beams outlined the cart's dimensions as it hovered in the air horizontally behind Herc's flank.

I flashed a tense smile. "It's not spacious, but it'll hold you. Get your stuff and get on."

"Are you sure?" Griggs eyes widened with a mix of shock and gratitude.

"Well, what else are you going to do?" *I'm not about to leave you behind.*

Wordlessly, he rushed to unstrap his gear pack from the rear of his cycle.

Tatara promptly appealed to the group. "There's something out here with us—c'mon guys. It wouldn't be right to leave anyone behind." Unfortunately, nobody had space on their streamlined vehicles, I'd already snatched up my chosen cargo, and Vernon already had Dino.

That only left Jorgep. All eyes swung to him.

Contrary to what little I'd learned of her personality, the usual confidence in Tatara's captivating gaze was now shrouded with worry. Jorgep's robust saddle boasted ornate metal embellishments, and the deep seat formed a stubby "U" shape. One side of the U rested between his legs, the other created a perfect backrest for a passenger. Currently a pack was tied behind him, but if he strapped those belongings behind the seat, Tatara would fit.

With hands raised, words toppled from Tatara's mouth. "I'll strike the exact same deal as Dino if you'll take me on."

Jorgep's feelers curled beneath his jaw. "Deal? What deal? I feel like I've missed something important."

A hushed scream sliced the air—a person's scream.

Herc let out a snort, his hooves shifting in agitation.

Tatara's hands steepled in front of her chest. "Right, you weren't with us then. Listen, I'll pay you 1500 credits to carry me to the finish line." More frantic screams rang out. Not close, but everyone surveyed our surroundings for threats anyway.

"Whatever's out there is hurting people. We need to move!" Lootas wailed.

"Then go! Nobody is holding you here!" Tatara snapped. The racer fell silent, his lack of forward motion telling. She swallowed hard, staring straight into Jorgep's soul. "2000. Please?"

Jorgep's face twisted in confusion—bordering on shock. "Goodness Miss Tatara, what kind of gentleman would I be if I accepted payment in your time of need? I'd be happy to give you a ride." He shifted and resecured his gear.

"Thank you! I'll be back!" Tatara beamed, racing to collect her things from her vehicle.

I flashed a smile at Jorgep, impressed he'd proven exactly the kind of man I believed him to be. It was nice to see chivalry—regardless of where it hailed from—was not dead. Though I wondered if Vernon was irked by Jorgep's gentleman comment. If he was, he didn't show it.

Tatara rushed back to Jorgep, then hesitated. "That thing's not going to bite me, will it?"

Jorgep laughed heartily. "No, no, Keemi is a big softy—that is, until she gets high on hallucinogens." He leaned forward and scratched his mount's solid neck. "No more drugs for *you*." Pulling Tatara up by the hand, Jorgep helped her get settled behind him.

"Thank you again. And I'll still pay you."

He waved a meaty green-skinned hand. "It's my pleasure, Miss Tatara." A grin brightened his round face, the fleshy feelers beneath his chin rippling like a wave. "It will be nice to share a ride with such a beautiful woman." He looked as proud as a kid who'd just won a lifetime supply of chocolate. "And please, don't be afraid to hold on."

Tatara chuckled, but sliced an uncomfortable glance at me and Sarah.

I smiled back, motioning for her not to worry about it. Sarah mouthed the words, *he's harmless*. More screams echoed through the air, accompanied by several haunting shrieks.

Griggs hoisted his bag and his body into the bucket of my auto-cart.

The caravan took off at a crisp pace, delving back into thicker forest. I was sad to leave that clearing, as I much preferred the open sightlines it afforded. Griggs jostled back and forth in a rhythmic fashion behind me, the auto-cart swaying with the motion of Herc's gait. He leaned back against his pack awkwardly, with his legs half hanging out of the cart, and an I-don't-know-what-to-do-with-myself look on his face.

"You alright back there?" I asked.

"Yeah." He held on tight to the glowing edges of the cart. "This definitely isn't how I pictured finishing this race, but I'm rolling with it. Thanks again."

I nodded. "Now we just need to cross the finish line."

CHAPTER 15

A reverberating shriek split the air, closer this time.

After keeping up the pace for half an hour we hit a section of thick undergrowth that forced us to weave a tight path between rocks and violet-clad trees, which spurred feelings of claustrophobia. Not only was I on extra high alert for hazards given that Herc now toted an auto-cart, but I also had to keep my eyes peeled for whatever creature taunted us from beyond. More and more, shrieks or screams, or both, rang out. We hadn't been able to pinpoint which direction they came from before, but as the minutes ticked by as the sounds grew louder, it became clear we were moving towards it. Worrisome. What was happening out there?

Sarah extended the blade from her mech arm, chopping vines and slender trees to pave a way for the caravan to roll on. Nobody spoke to each other, all eleven of us focused on slogging through the rough terrain while straining to hear signs of impending danger. Vehicles chugged along. Sticks, mud, and saturated leaves covered the forest floor, spliced with mossy patches that made the ground compress like a sponge beneath us.

"Okay, at this point it's worth asking—do we keep moving forward?" Sarah shouted.

"You want to turn around and forfeit the race?" Dino asked from behind Vernon.

Sarah scowled over her shoulder. "No, I don't *want* to. But vehicles are dying and clear danger sits between us and the finish line. We could still turn back."

I glanced down at Herc. Was winning a piece of land worth his life or mine?

Lootas shouted from the back of the pack. "I'd be willing to retreat."

"Of course *you* would," Teensy snarked, receiving a glare in return. "I'm not giving up. I came to win a race, and I don't mind blasting a few beasties to do it."

As if on cue, a shriek filtered through the jungle behind us and we all craned our necks.

"Shit," Tatara muttered. "Sounds like our escape route is officially closed."

Jorgep nodded. "Yes, it seems we're destined to meet the local fauna, regardless."

Sarah increased the pace. "Might as well keep moving towards the finish line then. By now, it's likely closer than turning back to Egan anyway. If anyone wants to turn back though, feel free. Nobody—" she cut Teensy a pointed glare. "—will judge you for it."

But not even Lootas chose to strike out on their own.

Within the hour, all functioning conveyances in our caravan sputtered badly, which didn't bode well. Come to think of it, it had been a while since I'd heard engines revving or wheels screeching from the myriad of offroad vehicles up ahead. Were no others still running?

When the last of our last vehicles died, what would we do? Herc could maybe carry one more body in the auto-cart—squeezing tight with Griggs. We'd be short on seats no matter what... Someone would be left behind. I couldn't in good conscience leave anyone vulnerable like that, not when faced with this new and uncertain threat. Passing by walking racers during a competitive race was one thing. It was easy to trust they'd be okay, especially since Governus would come in an emergency. But our current situation had grown into a whole new beast.

It was beyond a simple race now.

Yet, regardless of how I felt, there might be little choice.

Pulse and blaster fire cracked, mixing intermittently with frenzied shouts and screams. Sounds of war. They kept increasing in both intensity and volume, leaving racers uneasy.

"Shit is seriously hitting the fan somewhere. I don't like this—not one bit," Griggs said.

I nodded, my lip sore from biting it. "Yeah, I'm kinda starting to regret not turning around before. It's way louder up ahead than behind us." *Why do I always mess things up?*

Griggs hit me with a reassuring look. "Hey, we're a resourceful bunch. It'll be fine."

Everyone had their guns at the ready. I'd pulled out my pulse rifle, leaning the barrel against my shoulder while reining Herc one handed. Griggs gripped a pistol in each palm.

The trees opened up some, improving our line of sight on one side. But only slightly. Growing up, my father took me hunting with him sometimes, and I'd learned the clearer a view the better. Navigating away from the thicker bush on our left, we moved as fast as was safe. Thankfully, there was more moss than rocks on the trail now. Herc broke into an lope, keeping his head up and uneasy eyes on his surroundings. His snorts rang out over and over.

He was hearing things I couldn't. An eerie sense of dread settled over me.

Just then, a clanking chug signalled the death throes of Quiet Guy's vehicle.

"Hop on!" I said, halting beside him. He blinked, then scrambled to grab his duffel bag and jump into my cart. Griggs shimmied over, squeezing tight to one side as the younger racer wedged himself in. Neither seemed impressed by the fact their legs and arms had to touch, but nobody complained. They'd survive.

"Keep going!" I called out to Sarah at the front of the caravan. Herc's take off was a touch slower than normal. Towing the extra weight would take more out of him cardiovascularly, but at least his enhanced legs absorbed most of the direct bodily strain. Thank goodness for that. I murmured a quick "good boy" to him, giving his neck a stroke.

A barrage of gun blasts splintered the air ahead, echoing from two sides.

Herc whinnied, startling, his neck arching as he sidestepped. I whispered calming words as I corrected and squeezed with my heels, trying to keep him moving forward. His head swung to the side—his ocular implant glowing a brilliant red. *Oh no…* Knots already in my stomach quadrupled in size. "I know it's scary, big guy. But we gotta keep going. We *need* to keep going."

"Herc's eye is red!" Griggs' voice wobbled with each bump the cart encountered.

I grit my teeth, firing back, "I'm well aware." My fingers tightened on the reins.

Another volley of shots. I instinctually cringed. The sounds were much louder, from somewhere off to our left—near enough that I could make out a fearful scream… *"Run!"*

"Shit, they're close!" Griggs yelled. He and Enek aimed into the trees on the left.

Another shriek ripped behind us.

"Too damn close!" Tatara promptly used Jorgep as leverage and turned herself around in their perch atop Keemi's back. Once sitting back-to-back with Jorgep, she swept her sights across the caravan's rear flank. "Be ready for anything!"

Lootas let out a strained whimper, his eyes wide with fear. He waved a hand in front of his vision. "Governus, can you hear me? Governus, we're in trouble. We need help! Send help!"

Dino called out to the trembling racer, voice bitter. "Knowing what we know now, how do you think they're gonna get to us before these things do? We're on our own."

Lootas stubbornly shook his head. "No, I don't believe that. They'll come."

"Suit yourself." Dino looked away.

Metal slid against metal as a second blade descended from Sarah's other mech arm. Now, with blasters in hand and a knife arming each blocky wrist, she was lethal at any range.

More gunfire. More screams. We surged through a jungle layered with flora.

"My 3-wheeler is dying!" Vernon's words were laced with urgency.

A quick glance over my shoulder confirmed his machine jerked to a sudden stop. Lootas and Teensy weren't faring any better, their vehicles slowing, sputtering more than they ran.

The caravan ground to a halt.

Shrill animalistic screeches haunted the air as shots reverberated like jackhammers busting cement. The sound of rustling leaves and snapping twigs reached my awareness, adding a new layer of trepidation. Pulling on the reins, I laboured to keep Herc from rearing up. Fear swelled, cold and insistent, permeating every fibre of my sweaty body, but I couldn't let it take control. Not now. *What do I do, what do I do?* The rustling steadily intensified, as though the Sweep itself were coming alive. Hands trembling, I gripped my pulse rifle with white knuckles. The guys jostled in the cart as Herc's hooves danced, his eye now a brilliant white.

A shriek split the air—loud and throaty. The rapid patter of feet accompanied it.

"Whatever it is, it's coming!" Dino shouted.

Vernon abandoned his rig and furiously stuffed items from his storage compartment into a satchel, slinging it over his shoulders in record time. Teensy and Lootas mirrored his efforts. Dino kept watch with his gun up, prepared to run with the other vehicle-less racers.

As I flinched at every new shriek, an idea slammed into my head.

"My auto-enclosure!" I slid off of Herc's back, and yanked out the cylindrical posts. Griggs and Enek were by my side within seconds, each grabbing one and darting away.

"Quick, give me one!" Tatara dropped down from the bleenad. I tossed the last post to her and she stabbed it into the ground somewhere behind Keemi.

"Everyone, get inside the perimeter!" I thrust Herc's reins into Vernon's hand and raced several yards ahead. Lining myself up with Griggs, I sunk my post into the ground. Whoever wasn't placing posts had guns up in search of a target. "Enek is your post in?"

The rustling sharpened in the bushes, something coming in quick from the left.

"I can't see shit. The bush is too thick!' Dino spat.

Enek shouted from behind Keemi, "Mine's in!"

"Extending now!" Only three of the four posts shot up at my command. Mine didn't budge. "Shit!" I pressed the button again, but still nothing happened.

Teensy fired a round into the bush. "Saw something! It's fast—don't know if I hit it!"

"Please hurry!" Lootas warbled.

Hitting the button was useless. "The stupid thing won't extend!" A streaking strobe of shadow slipped across gaps in the foliage to our left and a gasp ripped from my lips. I blinked furiously as sweat stung my eyes. Jorgep fired two rounds at another shadow, then everyone fired.

Herc whinnied, fighting Vernon's hold.

"Easy, boy!" I mustered the calmest voice I could. *Please don't get loose.*

Sarah turned her back to the whipping shadows to come help me, but barely made it a step before a hulking sinewy body launched out of the trees onto her back.

"Fuck!" She twisted violently to shake it off.

Amidst a chorus of gasps, guns took aim, but couldn't fire, lest they hit Sarah.

The monster was big, its leathery body showcasing a texture reminiscent of a monitor lizard, while moving with the agility of a predatory cat. Its heft was similar to a tigers'. Its hide had a striped pattern, too, starting from the neck and fading into its haunches. Though its stripes weren't black, but an orange tone. The creature clutched Sarah's shoulders, its torso and hind legs running the length of her seven-foot-tall mech. Three-inch-long talons scratched as gnarled shark-like teeth snapped, skidding off the backside of her face shield.

"Shit, shit, shit…" I hissed. Yanking the post out of the ground, I inspected it for dents or anything that might keep it from extending. Nothing. I removed the top laser cap and blew into the open end. Grit spit back at me. I blew again, harder.

Sarah stabbed over her shoulder with her machete-like blades, eliciting a cry from the creature as one of her thrusts connected. She spun around, trying to shake it off.

Keemi snarled and snapped, fighting against Jorgep's control.

I slammed my post back into the ground and hammered the button. It surged upward, completing the haphazard rectangle. "Yes, it's up! Get that thing off of her, and get inside the enclosure!"

Sarah stabbed again and it shrieked, but didn't release.

Griggs rushed forward. "Turn around!" He took careful aim, his expression steeled by the focus it took. "Turn!" The minute she spun, he fired two quick shots into the side of the beast's chest. Loosing a scream of pain, it shuddered and fell to the ground. In the space of a breath, Sarah and Griggs rushed inside the perimeter, and I hit engage. The auto-enclosure burst to life, its glowing walls rippling and knitting together.

Two more creatures surged from the trees, hurling themselves at the shrinking gap in our crosshatched barrier. Our guns blazed, knocking the closest one down. The second beast rushed in just as the gap disappeared. Its thick body slammed into the protective wall, then rebounded from the jolt of electricity the enclosure applied. It fell hard onto its side, but quickly scrambled to right itself. Its jaw seemed to unhinge as it shrieked, clearly pissed it missed out on a meal. It stared with piercing orb-like eyes, a thin slit splitting the centre of each generous golden iris.

The eyes from the dark...

"Let your ammo recharge. We're safe for now," Vernon said.

Weapons hesitantly lowered amidst a chorus of heavy breathing.

Several more creatures appeared, circling us. The shield flickered.

Griggs looked up. "Are we? Is this enclosure even going to hold?"

Mentally drained, I raised my arms and let them drop to my sides. "I sure hope so."

"Me too." Griggs nodded. "Good job getting it up, by the way. Quick thinking."

Similar murmurs of thanks reached my ears from the other group members. My fellow racers seemed to deflate watching the irritable creatures pace back and forth beyond our safe space. Everyone's sweaty faces looked pale from the shock of what just happened. I took off my hat and brushed strands of wet hair off my face, sucking in deep breaths to collect my composure.

"Well, that was unexpected," Sarah quipped dryly, breaking the silence as she inspected her lightly scratched face shield. She'd opened it to let some fresh air in, took two deep breaths, then clipped her portable breather on. She didn't climb out, though—likely to ensure she was ready at a moment's notice. I didn't blame her for that line of thinking.

"No fucking kidding," Tatara grumbled.

"Are you okay?" I asked Sarah.

She nodded. "Yeah, I'm fine."

The shield flickered again.

I went to inspect the posts. No leaks. Fuel level nearly full. My mother said they should last about fourteen nights on single fill—so the flickering had to be the interference at play.

"What gorgeous creatures. Such grace, and lovely colours." Jorgep admired the vicious beasts stalking us, both displaying different colour stripes than the first—one emerald green, the other crimson. Keemi's teeth were under wraps again, though Jorgep continued to soothe her. Thankfully, he'd managed to temper her protective instincts and kept her from running out. I could only imagine her rampage if Jorgep had been attacked instead of Sarah.

Numerous incredulous glances sliced his way.

"*That's* what you're thinking about right now, Jorgep?" Sarah said, her tone flat. "Not about how many fucking teeth it has? Or how easily those claws will shred your insides?" She let out a sardonic chuckle. "I don't care how resplendent it looks, I'm still gonna hate it."

"Resplendent," Jorgep replied, tilting his head in approval. "Good word choice."

Sarah just shook her head.

Herc whinnied, his eyes locked on our attacker. I moved to stand beside him, rubbing his nose and neck. "Easy boy. Easy." Though I didn't feel especially calm inside, not in the slightest, I needed to play that role for his sake—needed to keep Herc as calm as possible.

Screams and gunfire continued all around us, and all I could do was hope others had auto-enclosures, too. It saved our lives. However, the device had also effectively trapped us. Unless these creatures moved on, the minute we disengaged it, we'd be fighting. But how many were out there? How did this even happen? Anger over our shitty situation curdled in my gut.

"What are these things?" Vernon bent at the waist to stare into one of the monster's eyes on the other side. It snarled, swiping at the enclosure, and Vernon flinched away. Three more creatures' slunk out from the surrounding bushes, testing the protective field.

Words festered inside me, demanding to be spoken. I sliced a finger toward our snarling prison guards. "I bet *someone* knows all about these beasties… *someone* who sent us into this not-so 'uncharted' place and knew exactly what we were racing into."

A shadow of recognition descended over everyone's expressions.

Tatara's hands balled into fists. "Yeah—uncharted Sweep my ass."

Vernon's shoulders raised. "But again, why would a reputable corporation send a 200-person contingent into a locale they knew was deadly? It just doesn't make sense."

Sarah flung her hands out. "They sent at least one team in here to get slaughtered. Brought poison in even. That shows knowledge and preparation." She clenched all her muscles into an angry spasm. "If they'll do that, those assholes clearly don't give a shit about anything."

Words flew about the enclosure as each racer spoke their mind all at once. Conversely, Lootas simply sat crouched in a far corner, whispering plea after plea as he drew messages in the dirt. "Please Governus, we're surrounded by killer animals. It's an emergency. Send help."

Teensy rolled his eyes in response, but held his tongue.

I'd been standing with my hands on my hips the whole time, seething silently, until a fresh realization hit me. I straightened—letting out a dark chuckle. "*Of course*... They're after something." I paced, mirroring a creature beyond. Griggs and Sarah watched with curiosity.

"What's your theory, Finn?" Vernon asked.

"That has to be it, right? I mean, they sent in who knows how many teams. We assume they used poison to try and kill the creatures. Can't say for sure. Anyway, it went badly. Maybe they didn't get breathers on in time and went loopy, who knows?" I wagged a finger. "But maybe they discovered something they couldn't walk away from. Something worth sacrificing for."

Sarah scowled. "But to sacrifice their own people? *And* us! Who the fuck does that?"

Enek held up his hand and stepped forward. "If that's true, we're just pawns."

I rubbed my tired eyes. "In a game we know nothing about."

"If there's any *game* at all." Lootas glowered from the back of the enclosure. "Nothing's been proven. Governus is probably en-route right now."

I wasn't so confident, but nodded politely anyway.

Dino shrugged. "I guess we'll find out, won't we?"

Our sentry leapt at the enclosure just as it flickered and one of its clawed toes got caught in the beams. It severed the toe with a sizzle, dropping it on our side. Crying out, the creature slunk back to the treeline, licking its injury.

"If this enclosure flickers any worse, those things could still get in. Look how they watch for openings. We're not safe here." Tatara picked up the cauterized toe. She turned it over, running a finger over the razor-sharp hook of the claw. The severed edge was charred black, save for a syrupy ooze of blue seeping through.

Griggs and Jorgep leaned in to look, the former muttering, "Huh, it has blue blood."

I pulled out an empty bag that once contained squished bread rolls. While there, I also grabbed the last carrot and gave it to Herc. He'd earned it. "Here, pass that toe over."

Tatara delivered the appendage with raised brows. "Are you going to *keep* it?"

"Damn straight, I'm keeping it. This is evidence. Better safe than sorry." I held the bag open, exchanging an understanding glance with Griggs—who'd kept the bloody uniform for the same purpose. Tatara dropped it inside with an *I see* look on her face. Closing the bag, I caught a whiff of the toe and my face shrivelled. "Ugh, it stinks. Like sweaty socks and fishy lake water."

Sarah smirked.

I stuffed the sample into my saddle bag, hoping I'd never have to open it ever again. I also really hoped the bag didn't have any holes in it. With pursed lips, I said to nobody in particular, "If I'm lucky enough to get out of this mess, Governus is gonna hear about it."

Sarah released a wry chuckle. "Well now that Finn has the beginnings of a beautiful beast-claw necklace, what do we do next? I say we shoot them to put our minds at ease."

Teensy shook his head, raising a hand. "That might just draw more in."

Dino spoke up. "We can't stay here forever. Eventually, we'll starve to death."

"No, we can't. Finn, how long do we have?" Vernon's brows raised in question.

"She'll last fourteen nights—well, twelve now. That equals six full days."

Vernon looked up at the canopy-obscured sky, then to the shadows lengthening on the ground. "That buys us some time at least. It's getting late in the day. It's definitely not safe to press on, so I suggest we hunker down and strategize for tomorrow. Does that sound good?" When nobody disagreed, Vernon added, "I also propose we schedule a rotating watch. If we're lucky though, the enclosure will hold. Who volunteers to take the first watch?"

Silence.

Faces scrunched up in response. Exhaustion was evident in everybody's heavy eyelids, dragging feet, and sagging postures. I groaned at the thought of forcing myself to stay up late rather than getting a few winks in before taking a turn. But I suppose I would if I had to.

Sarah blurted, "Last one touching their nose goes first!" Her bright orange mech finger was already pressed onto her own. We'd played this silly game all the time on the transport ship enroute to Joya, fighting for things like: the last scoop of non-replicated ice cream, or who had to buy a round of shots at the spacewalk bar. Sarah had learned it from her cousin who was apparently an earth history nut—it was an *old* game.

I snapped my finger onto my nose, and watched Griggs do the same.

It took a minute to sink in, but once it did, all remaining fingers flung toward their corresponding nasal appendages in a desperate bid to get first dibs on sleep.

Everyone except Vernon.

His features twisted in confusion. "What's going on now?"

Sarah pointed with a grin. "Vernon's it! Congratulations, you get first watch, buddy."

CHAPTER 16

The evening was filled with tense conversation.

Faced with this new threat and dreading what might come in the morning, I honestly didn't have much appetite. But I forced myself to eat anyway. I'd need all the energy I could get to fight through the creatures we'd less-than-affectionately named "beasties."

Though the majority forced smiles, trying to crack jokes and shed some light on our various subjects of discussion, I knew everyone had to be struggling with their own internal demons. Whether fear, regret, anger, guilt, or something else. Folks had lives they'd left behind to come here. Families. Businesses. Unresolved shit. I knew their struggle because I was right there with them. Somewhere in the deepest, darkest part of me, a haunting voice whispered I would die tomorrow, and that terrified me. There was so much I hadn't seen or done yet. Dreams unattained. And so much I *had* done that I wished I hadn't. Too many words left unsaid.

Though I detested my father for how he'd treated me, branding me reckless and untrustworthy no matter what I did to atone, withdrawing my inheritance, and wearing his embarrassment on his sleeve, he was still my father. No matter our differences, we were still family. He'd bounced me on his knee, taken me hunting and fishing, and put a roof over my head.

I remember how he used to give the best hugs. He loved me once…

Buried beneath layers of resentment and my own shame, I had clung to hope—that if I could just pay the money back and prove people can change, we could forge a path toward forgiveness. I'd already apologized out my ass for what I did. Now, all I wanted was for him to admit I was not an embarrassment and see me as his daughter again. Perhaps I was just as stubborn as he, but regardless, none of it mattered now. I'd never see my family again.

I looked at Herc, my heart shredding. He had no idea, was only here because I'd brought him. Because of some stupid escapist dream I had to have, and my desperation to keep him in my life. "Dammit, I should've known nobody would give away land for real," I grumbled under my breath. Not only did I curse myself for risking my own safety, but Herc's too—and all because I selfishly couldn't let him go. *He could've been safe in a stable somewhere right now.* But the thought spoiled in my head. Who knows where he could've ended up? Herc could've just as easily landed in an off world auction or snatched up by some black-market parts farm—dead within hours, scared and alone. The muscles in my jaw clenched and unclenched.

Blinking furiously to keep tears at bay, I forced myself to look up. To my left, Lootas rocked back and forth, staring into the fire. The back of the guy's hands had the word "Help" written all over them in soot. Every so often, he'd wave them in front of his eyes. On my right, Sarah sat with her mouth stuffed with marshmallows, an open bag sitting between her feet. She shoved three more in, chewing aggressively. I couldn't help but grin.

Sarah met my gaze and offered the bag. "You want one?"

"No, I'm good. Looks like you need them more than me."

A dejected laugh left her lips. "I've been saving this bag. Was supposed to be my celebration dance. But, fuck it. If this is my last hurrah, I'm going down full of mellows."

Her words made me think. We'd all lost—and stood to lose—in different ways. Sarah owned a hole-in-the-wall repurposing shop on Mexin, one of Earth's colonized planets. She'd learned her skills from her uncle, having lived with him since she was five. One time over drinks on the transport, she confided her parents died in a tragic accident while visiting Crimeoa.

Sarah sighed. "I just wish I could say goodbye to Fuzz. I miss that fuckin' cat."

We shared a smile, one of understanding, resignation, and hidden fears.

"Yeah, alright—" I held out a hand. "Hit me up."

"That's my girl." Sarah plopped two marshmallows into my palm.

Herc's eye had switched from red to green a while ago, clearly believing he was safe behind this flickering enclosure. For how long, I had no clue. He'd devoured his water and the feed I'd set down for him, which was good. He needed it. I couldn't take his tack off, though. I felt bad about that, but if shit hit the fan, Herc needed to be ready to run. From his cramped space beside the bleenad, he kept diligent watch over the beasties stalking our enclosure.

There were even more of them now, recoiling when they challenged the enclosure. They growled, snapped at, and made strange mewling noises to each other, as if coordinating attempts to slip through the auto-enclosure's flickers. Though the rest came and went at random, our toeless friend stayed put, doggedly pacing the perimeter at all times. Watching. Waiting.

"I fear what has occurred is a coordinated mass attack," Vernon said. "The night Finn saw those eyes… perhaps, they didn't want to be seen yet. Our only true hint was the pawprints."

"They were scouting," Griggs said, his words more a statement than a question.

Dino nodded, stroking his broad scaley chin. "Determining if we're predator or prey."

Vernon made a complex whistling noise—a sound no human tongue could produce. "Obviously, they decided we're the latter." He stabbed at the hot coals in our makeshift fire pit.

"Sizing us up. A smart tactic." Teensy's face appeared more impressed than horrified.

It was a sound theory, and from what we'd all seen so far, they were probably right.

"I'm just glad they can be killed," I finally said, my tone flat.

Chuckles wafted from Tatara and Sarah as they chatted quietly beside me, the pair having opted to focus on lighter topics. But their amusement was cut short by a distant shout.

"Everyone who's still alive, sound off!" someone called. Communications like this had been happening periodically. Surviving racers—some alone, some in groups like us—were seeking some semblance of solace. To know they weren't alone in this nightmarish situation.

Dino utilized his booming voice. "We have ten alive over here!"

A roll call of at least twenty other camps responded.

I had to know... "Do you all have auto-enclosures?"

A myriad of "yeses" came back.

It remained quiet for a long time after that. While the fact others survived the attack offered a shred of hope, the reality that the number was so few seeded a sickening ache in my gut. The last remnants of blaster fire had quieted hours ago. At this point, people were either beyond earshot, dead, or laying low in an enclosure until morning.

With my enclosure flickering, all bets were off whether we'd make it that long.

I forced myself not to think about that. But even as I did so, thoughts crept right back in. Damn, I hated my brain right now.

Taking a deep breath, I focused on my marshmallow flaming over the fire. I preferred it charred, which required zero finesse, unlike Griggs, who'd committed to achieving a perfect brown. I laughed at him for that, secretly finding the quirk adorable.

And what about Griggs? Now that we were about to die, should I throw caution to the wind? My jaw clenched as I continued stifling the intrusive thoughts. *No romance. No dying.*

Shrieks carried through the air at regular intervals, and our resident beasties answered.

"I suspect they're doing status checks." Teensy listened with an ear cocked. "The communication and intelligence they're showing is astounding. Such calculated killers."

"You're not exactly instilling much hope for us here," Sarah muttered.

"Sorry…" he said, looking down.

Dino snapped a chunk of deadfall into pieces for burning. "But just because they're smart, doesn't mean they're smarter than *us*. Besides, we have something they don't. Guns."

"That's right." Jorgep's feelers waved enthusiastically. "And Keemi."

"Hear, hear!" Tatara raised her metal mug of granular coffee. "To the bleenad!"

"Who might just save all our asses!" Sarah clinked her mug against Tatara's.

Everyone allowed themselves to smile, even laugh, as we raised our cups to toast.

"So, our plan for tomorrow is to blast and run? Is that the gist of it?" Enek spoke barely above a whisper, and in my head, the nickname Quiet Guy still suited him so perfectly.

Griggs nodded. "Pretty much. We don't have much choice but to fight our way forward. It sounds like the river's not far, and that'll be the rough mid-point of the valley—or the lowest point anyway. We should start climbing back out after we cross it, which means there's no value in turning back now. We might as well continue toward the finish line." Griggs looked around the circle. "Right?"

Collectively, heads bobbed in agreement.

Griggs formed his hands into a diamond shape. "So, if a ton of beasties move in on us—"

"*When*, not if," Sarah interjected matter-of-factly.

Griggs let his hands drop, conceding the point. "*When* the beasties move in—" His fingers formed a diamond again. "—we just keep moving forward in this formation, keeping it as tight as possible. No gaps. No vulnerabilities. It's the safest way for us to travel."

Enek seemed satisfied by the explanation, giving a firm nod.

"And what makes you the authority on tactics?" Dino questioned.

Griggs squared his shoulders. "Martian military, Captain. Do you outrank me?"

Dino returned a grudgingly respectful nod. "Yeah, alright. Fair enough."

"And for goodness sake, make sure you keep your breathers on. Ensure your atmosphere cartridges are fresh." Vernon's eyes darted around the circle, singling a few individuals out. "Chasing rainbows, dancing with imaginary creatures, getting *romantic*, or availing oneself of clothing will not be helpful." His words elicited a chorus of groans.

"You just had to bring it up?" Tatara unconsciously tugged her shirt collar closed. She'd gone streaking, dropping clothes left and right, and poor Jorgep had to tackle her. Though, by the smile on his face when Tatara joined him on the bleenad later, I don't think he'd minded much.

"It was complete insanity." Sarah grinned as she inhaled another marshmellow. "And if we survive this… believe me, I'll have solid dirt on you guys for years to come."

Everyone groaned again while Sarah, Vernon, and Jorgep laughed.

"Don't you dare laugh, Jorgep!" I rebutted quickly. "We got dirt on you, too."

An overly forlorn look crossed his features, but disappeared just as fast. With a flippant wave of the hand, he said, "Oh, I don't embarrass easily, Miss Finn. Spread the dirt all you like. I'm an open book." His round belly shook with laughter once more.

I couldn't help but chuckle. "Jorgep, you're too much."

Griggs caught my gaze and I didn't look away. We shared a smile, our awkwardness far less than it had been earlier. Seconds later, he ran a hand through his dishevelled hair and struck up a conversation with Dino. Peeling the charred outer layer off a marshmallow, I popped the morsel in my mouth, letting it melt on my tongue. Funny, how I'd eaten them before, yet they tasted better than I remembered. I told myself it had nothing to do with our impending doom.

My eyes moved around the circle, soaking in each face glowing in the firelight.

I didn't want anyone to get hurt tomorrow.

***

My hour to keep watch went smoothly, despite the nerve-wracking enclosure glitches. Each flicker only lasted fractions of a second, and the beasties had finally learned not to keep challenging the barrier. Most had filtered away into the trees, not to return. Toeless simply laid down nearby, watching us with those round reflective eyes.

Enek took over the watch after me, whispering, "Sleep well."

"Thank you." I patted his shoulder. "Good luck."

Laying on my bedroll, I stared at the blanket of swaying leaves dimly illuminated overhead. Gosh, I desperately wished the trees would part and show me the stars. I could pretend they were the same ones back home. My eyes had barely closed when a whisper turned my head.

"Do you really think Governus might be after something? What do you think it could be?" Sarah, whose bedding lay beside mine, rolled to face me.

"Sorry if I woke you just now," I said quietly.

"You didn't. I was up—couldn't sleep. Wish I could."

"I hear ya. You should definitely try, though. We can talk about this later."

Sarah's eyelids lowered as she cast a no-nonsense look my way. "Later when? Like *after* we give Governus a good show getting viciously attacked and eaten tomorrow?"

I grimaced. "I'm really trying not to think about that. I just want to sleep."

"Answer the question, Finn." Then Sarah's voice softened. "Please? I want to know."

Letting out a sigh, I leaned closer, whispering, "I really wish I knew. But, if I had to guess I'd say they discovered a precious commodity. Why else go to all this trouble? The race. The land. The implants. Why else risk their reputation? What value would that hold for them?"

"None. Unless they're straight up sadistic sociopaths."

Her words made my lips twitch. "Could be… I agree now with what Tatara said earlier. I think they needed boots on the ground to do the dirty work for them. Expendable boots."

Sarah let out a long, deep breath. "I'm terrified you're right. What could possibly be *that* valuable, though? I mean, couldn't they just level this place and wipe out the beasties?"

I shrugged, picking at the fraying fabric on my blanket. "There has to be a reason behind it all. The shitty part is, I doubt we'll live long enough to figure it out." Pressure formed behind my eyes, then beyond my control, the tears came. Covering my mouth, I bit back a sob and looked away. "Sorry." Dammit, the last thing I wanted was to appear weak.

Sarah's hand reached over, resting on my forearm. She squeezed gently, saying my name until I looked at her again. Her eyes glistened with moisture in the firelight. "Don't be sorry. I didn't expect to never re-open my shop. To never see my cat or my sister again—she just had a baby, you know—my first niece..." She sniffed, her voice quivering. "It looks like we're all in for a fuckin' ride tomorrow, and it's totally okay to *feel* shit."

Wiping my cheeks, I smiled somberly. "'To feel shit.' I love that."

"Another thing to put on a t-shirt someday."

She released my arm and we laughed together. This Sarah wasn't the hard-ass I'd met back on the transport. I hadn't realized then that there was such softness inside. In that moment, I felt a unique kinship with her. A solidifying bond. I'd never had a sister of my own—just a jerk of a brother. I couldn't help but wonder if this was what having one would've been like.

Sarah straightened her face. "Seriously though. All joking aside... I got your back, girl." Her words were earnest, all traces of her trademark sarcasm gone.

Mirroring Sarah's earlier gesture, I placed my hand on her arm, feeling the hard edge of her implanted bio-port beneath her skin. It felt nice to be cared for. To have support. Beyond my mother, nobody in my family—my whole community—seemed to give two shits about me. My voice shook when I replied. "And I've got yours. Now, we really should get some sleep."

"Aye, Aye, *Captain*," she said with a brazen wink.

Groaning, I remembering Pirate-Sarah prying my lips off of Griggs. "Oh, shut up."

She snickered wickedly, then rolled over.

Following suit, I tucked the blanket around my shoulders and closed my eyes. I imagined sitting on the porch back at the ranch, sipping iced tea and staring up at a wide open prairie sky splattered by stars. Then, within a few deep breaths, everything washed away.

***

Morning came fast, carrying with it an all-encompassing sense of dread. This was it.

The beasties must've sensed something was about to happen, pacing back and forth along the perimeter of the auto-enclosure as we all savoured what might possibly be our final breakfast.

Shrieks harkened across the distance separating us from the other surviving racers, which told me the rest were up and moving too. A few of those groups called out to us, advising they were moving forward soon and wished us luck. We replied in kind.

I made sure Herc fuelled up on water and feed, and double checked our gear was tied securely. Fighting the emotions that invaded, I spent several extra minutes stroking his neck and face. Tears threatened to fall whenever the thought of losing him popped in. Herc blew a huff of air against my cheek and lowered his head to rest against my forehead.

"I think you know something's up, don't you?" I whispered. He lifted his muzzle and the peachy-soft hairs tickled my cheek. His ocular implant turned blue as I looked into his good eye, sharing a quiet smile. "I'm so sorry. I don't know what's going to happen today. It might be bad… But no matter what, *I promise* I'll be with you. It's you and me against the world. Okay?"

He nibbled at the brim of my hat and bobbed his head, like he'd understood perfectly.

"I love you, big guy." I fought with everything I had not to break into sobs. I wrapped my arms around his strong neck and placed a kiss there. His coat was stiff with sweat, and I wished I could've removed his tack to give a better brush down. But, not this time.

Stepping back, I dabbed the corners of my eyes, relieved the tears hadn't fallen. Exposing my emotions last night had been enough. Especially now, on the verge of a life-or-death battle, it just felt wrong to cry. No more *fake it 'til you make it*. Today, I had to be tough—for real.

"Is everybody ready?" Vernon motioned for the group to come together. His gaze was steady and gentle, showcasing care for the situation we all found ourselves in. Unknowingly, he'd taken on a bit of a father role to this motley caravan of racers. Not like he was *that* much older than the rest of us—some more than others—but the role suited him well.

We met at the centre of the enclosure, sharing stiff nods and muttered assent.

"Good. Now listen up. We. Can. Do. This." His expression hardened, his hand clenching into a fist. "The last of our vehicles have died, but we've got firepower and strength in numbers. If we stick together and watch each other's backs, I believe we can fend them off."

Dino said, "Just keep shooting and they're bound to thin out!"

A hushed cheer rose in support, none of us wanting to draw excessive attention to ourselves. As it ebbed, we all turned to each other with kind words, handshakes, and other gestures of respect. Not a soul uttered an actual farewell, though. We'd agreed not to acknowledge the finality of goodbye, as though saying the word might jinx the outcome.

Sarah and I squeezed each other's arms, our meaning conveyed without words. I exchanged respectful nods with Vernon, and bopped Jorgep on the shoulder, eliciting a grin. Tatara smiled and slid her palm across mine, a Pembru gesture of respect. I shook the hands of the others, including Dino and finally Enek—who's jaws nervously clenched and unclenched.

I flashed him an extra reassuring smile for good measure.

At last, I faced Griggs, and I didn't know what to do. I really wanted to hug him, but didn't know if that would be okay. He fidgeted with his fingers, staring into my eyes, perhaps warring with the same dilemma. Then he thrust a hand out, which I immediately took into my own. The shake was crisp, and we exchanged tight smiles. But our eyes locked and held.

"I've decided you owe me five more questions." A smile played on his lips.

My brows rose. "Five? Now, that's just excessive. Let's start at three and see how it goes." The moment carried just enough light to shine through the dread-infused gloom.

"Deal. I'm holding you to that."

Then, realizing we'd held onto each other's hands for too long, we let them fall apart. I stepped back and turned away from him, feeling like I'd just swallowed a hot coal.

Patting Herc on the way to my auto-enclosure post, I whispered, "Be brave, boy."

It was go time. Make or break. Time to rock—take your pick of cliché phrases. I knelt beside the post, ready to press the button, then looked back up at Herc. "*Pssst.*" His head swung around to look at me, a layer of grime dulling the metal forming his forehead and cheek. "You have my permission to kick the shit out of any beasty that comes close, okay?"

His eye flipped blue for the barest of seconds, then returned to green.

I took a deep steadying breath, confident I was as ready as I'd ever be.

My finger hovered over the button to deactivate the auto-enclosure. Enek, Dino, and Tatara were poised to collect their designated posts, while the rest aimed to take out Toeless and three other beasties skulking about. Sharing furtive glances, we waited for the final signal. Blaster fire erupted in the distance and Herc's eye turned red. Soon it would shine white.

"Everybody in place?" Griggs asked.

"Yes," came the group-wide mumble.

"We go on the count of 3…"

CHAPTER 17

1...2...3!

Energised pulses sliced and crackled as I deactivated the enclosure. The posts shrunk down and I pulled mine from the ground. The handful of awaiting beasties didn't even have a chance to shriek before they were felled, and we had hoped that might buy us some time.

Toeless sagged lifeless to the ground, blue oozing from broken skin.

I untied Herc, who'd startled from the shooting, and half-jumped into the saddle. Enek, Dino, and Tatara shoved their posts into my saddle bag as I held the flap open, then Griggs and Enek launched themselves into my auto-cart, which still functioned thanks to Herc's bio-linked saddle. Within seconds, we were moving. Sarah and I led. Those whose vehicles died, hoofed it with their packs on their backs or strapped to the sides of my auto-cart. Jorgep brought up the rear, and Tatara sat back-to-back with him again, her guns covering our flank.

We rushed toward the sound of the river, maintaining the fastest pace possible.

A symphony of shouting, screams and weapons fire carried us along. We weren't the only ones pushing through to the finish line—wherever that was. Hopefully close. I also hoped the others battling were putting up a good fight. The better they did, the better we might do. So far, we hadn't seen any more beasties—perhaps they were too occupied elsewhere. Perhaps, we'd been quiet enough that we hadn't called attention to ourselves. Regardless, the more of those *things* the other racers killed, the less might come our way.

I felt thankful we'd strategically trailed the field from the get-go. Hanging back, and then falling an hour behind, likely prevented us from being blindsided by the beasties. Maybe the only thing that kept us alive this long. Especially since the creatures seemed to come from the direction we were headed—which was a whole other concern I tried not to dwell on.

Every little noise had me pointing my rifle side to side. Mercifully, the trees opened up as we travelled, allowing enhanced visibility—but only by a margin. Over the not-so-distant sounds of chaos, the dull roar of the river intensified. I searched, but couldn't see glimpses of water yet. We were getting close, though. If luck was on our side, the creatures wouldn't be able to swim.

It was a long shot, but I grasped onto it anyway.

A creature bounded from a swath of tight bushes to our left, releasing half a shriek before three quick shots sent it skidding nose-first into the mossy dirt. Dino celebrated his kill with a silent fist pump, giving it a foot nudge as we passed by to ensure it was dead.

"One down," I whispered to myself. We'd agreed to travel as stealthily as possible in the hopes of not being detected. No talking, light feet. But our footfalls still crunched over rocks and debris, cracked through rotting deadfall hiding beneath the moss, or made soft sucking noises in the mud. And how in the hell does one tell a bleenad or a horse to tread lightly? You don't.

Rustling leaves and a shrill wailing sound pulled my attention back to the left. Dropping the reins, I utilized heel pressure to keep Herc moving forward. Raising my rifle, I aimed toward the haunting sound. We'd heard similar calls throughout the night—different than their typical shrieks. Teensy figured it was a specific communication. A call to action.

Twigs snapped and approaching paws thudded across the rough terrain.

Another beastie rushed into view, weaving between trees before leaping straight for us, limbs and claws outstretched. Its mouth opened wide, showcasing at least three rows of pointed teeth. Without hesitation, I fired and the round disintegrated its lithe neck muscles. Two more rounds from my cart occupants pelted its side. Herc sidestepped in fear and I reclaimed the reins to keep him from rearing up. The creature dropped to the ground like a weighted blanket.

Enek and I exchanged nods, then more rustling from the opposite direction had us swivelling. This was louder, more chaotic. More sets of paws. Herc pranced, his nostrils flaring, and I knew I'd have to keep firm hold of the reins. I shoved my pulse rifle back into its scabbard behind my leg, and drew a fully charged pulse pistol instead. So far, our guns were unaffected by the interference. Griggs had explained the catalyst element inside every pulse weapon stimulated continuous recharging—thus, it was a self-powered, self-contained process. A stroke of luck.

A beast lunged out at Sarah. She shot it down, mid flight, and its yowling body slid right into her thick metallic feet. To finish it off, she stabbed the flesh of its neck with a blade.

Another jumped at Vernon and Dino, but the two took it down.

The rustling sounds intensified, coming from all directions.

"I'd say they know we're here!" Sarah swept her guns back and forth.

"Here we go!" I shouted.

A beastie lunged from the rear, targeting Keemi. Her broad head swung as she let out a terrifying roar, unequivocally telling her attacker to back off. Surprisingly, it actually flinched, and Tatara's shots made quick work of flattening it.

How many will come?

"Stay tight!" Vernon and Dino stood back-to-back, their rifles covering both sides as they sidestepped towards our goal. "Get into Grigg's formation!"

The racers on foot shifted over. I got Herc in formation best I could, joining the rear with Keemi and angling his kicking legs away from our group members. Herc's eye blazed red while his hooves traversed the forest floor. My head swivelled constantly, watching for threats.

A symphony of shrieks pierced the air. Everything was in motion around us. Branches snapped. Paws thundered. Claws scraped over stone. Shadowy figures wove between trees and whipped behind thickets with each step. I couldn't hear shooting in the distance anymore.

"They're circling us!" Vernon's voice was nearly drowned out by the calamity. His ecto-cannon swung side to side, firing at the shadows as they passed. Beside him, Lootas did the same, though the gun shook violently in his hands—his eyes as round as the buttons on his shirt.

"It's like they're coordinating an attack!" Dino hissed as he aimed; his textured cheek pressed tight against the bulky fabric-wrapped stock of his pulse rifle.

Griggs barked with the authority of a drill sergeant, "Keep moving! Don't stop!"

Two beasties broke free of the bush, surging past a barrage of gunfire by Teensy and Lootas, who stood back-to-back, and knocked them out of the caravan formation. More crashed in from the opposite side. Muzzles blasted and Herc reared up. Griggs and Enek nearly fell out of the cart, but managed to hold on until it levelled out again. As my passengers recovered from being jostled, a creature darted out on the sly, aiming its hooked claws at Griggs.

"Get down!" I shouted. He flattened the best he could and my arm swung back to fire a round between the enemy's cat-like eyes. Blood and tissues sprayed from the wound, splattering Griggs with blue. Wiping his face, he gave a look of thanks. I returned the barest of smiles, before swivelling to fire at more beasties jumping out from up ahead.

"I think they're testing us! Stay alert!" Teensy shouted.

Manoeuvring Herc around natural obstacles and staying in line proved an intricate task. Our forward progress was painstakingly slow, and they just kept coming. A trio of creatures lunged at Keemi, one staying low to snap at her heels, while the others targeted high. Tatara and Jorgep shot two down, but Keemi lurched forward to sink her teeth into the wailing beast at her feet. Her mighty jaws clamped down. Blood spurted from between her teeth as she shook her prey like a ragdoll. The violent motion caused Tatara to lose her seat, and she toppled over the side, landing hard on the ground. She lay on her side, seeming dazed.

Dino broke away from Vernon to go help.

A beastie bee-lined for her as she shook her head, struggling to stand. Dino veered left to avoid the bleenad, firing as he ran. I was busy picking off critters surging in from the opposite side, but between shots I heard the scream. Glancing back, I gasped. An entire wave of beasties had capitalized on Tatara's moment of weakness. Dino clutched her by the arm and pulled while both he and Jorgep drove their attackers back with pulse blasts.

One beasty had snagged Tatara by the foot.

Sinking its teeth in, the creature dragged her out of Dino's grasp with a powerful jump backward. The pain of the bite must've cleared whatever daze lingered from the fall, because Tatara's guns flew up and electrified rounds blazed as the monster pulled her along the ground.

With a violent shudder her assailant sagged lifelessly on top of Tatara's legs, effectively pinning her. She thrashed, fighting to get out from beneath the heavy thing. Dino fired a spray of bullets and rushed up again, hooking his strong forearms under her armpits and yanking. She slid free, and he half-dragged her back into formation under cover fire.

Shit, that was close.

Jorgep dismounted Keemi and slapped her on the rump, letting her loose on the beasties running in. Her terrifying roars reverberated as her great head bit and slammed. Griggs and Enek hadn't stopped firing—desperate to keep the neverending stream of creatures at bay.

Lootas panicked and sprinted away from the caravan, trying to escape.

"Lootas! Get back!" I shouted.

Four creatures lunged before he was even ten feet away, immediately overwhelming his shakily-aimed shots. Me and Griggs fired cover rounds, dropping three of them fast, but more darted from the bush, sacrificing themselves to our shots while other beasties dragged Lootas out of view. A coordinated kill. His screams curdled, each terrorized note piercing my heart.

When the screams melted into gurgles, then faded, I winced, trying to block it out. I didn't know Lootas well, but he didn't deserve a death like that. Then anger flared. *Dammit, why did he run away?* I leaned into the emotion, letting it drown the ache and fuel my fight. I hammered beasties moving in on Sarah who was a blur of action ahead of me. Using swift shoot and stab combinations, she held her own—fending off numerous combatants at a time.

"Fuck, how many are there!?" Sarah shouted.

"We *must* be thinning them out!" I jostled in the saddle as Herc crushed a beasties skull with a powerful side kick. "Just keep moving forward!"

Dappled sunshine seeped through the canopy, highlighting the creatures' jagged tiger-like stripes in shades of amethyst, green, umber, or red—even a few citrine. Sweat rolled down my back from the effort of handling Herc and shooting. My clothes stuck to my skin and the muscles in my neck ached from snapping it around in all directions. A worsening tremble in my shooting arm made aiming difficult. Fatigue was setting in fast, and I imagined the others felt similar.

How long can we hold out like this?

The thought was cut short as Herc kicked out again, sending a vicious creature slamming into a tree. It jostled me forward. The saddle horn dug into my belly, and I cried out in surprise, struggling to stay seated. The guys in the cart held on for dear life.

I'd barely managed to right myself when Herc hoofed another beastie. This time, I lurched too far and one foot loosened from the stirrup. Unable to compensate, my body slipped sideways and I failed to catch a handhold on the way down. My other foot snagged in the stirrup, which slammed my shoulder and back into the ground hard. The breath left my lungs in a rush.

"Finn!" Griggs shouted, hopping over the side of the cart. "Cover me!"

"Got it!" Enek roared, not so quiet anymore. The beasts saw me fall and moved in. Sarah swung and slashed two-fold as a throng of attackers moved toward me. Her laboured breathing huffed through her suit's speaker while she battled to buy me a chance at recovery.

Hanging half under Herc, I rolled away to avoid getting stomped by nervous hooves. My hand still gripped the reins pulled taut over his neck. Griggs' knee drove into the ground beside my torso. One hand grabbed my arm to lift me up, while the other shot at snapping jaws.

With his help, I wrenched my foot free from the stirrup and clambered to right myself. Slipping Herc's reins over his head, I kept a firm grip as I holstered my pistol and yanked my rifle from its scabbard. Saying a silent prayer, I decided to let Herc do all the damage he wanted, and stood tall beside Griggs. "Enek, get out of the cart and give him room to kick!"

Confirming he'd heard, Enek wordlessly abandoned the cart.

Lifting the rifle butt into the crook of my shoulder, I channelled every lesson my father ever taught me about shooting when I was young. Swiping the sweat off my brow, I closed an eye, aiming down the sights. Though my heart jackhammered in my chest, I fought to keep my breathing even, firing round after round at the rush of creatures. But for every one that fell, at least two more appeared. Through the layers of trees and vines surrounding us on all sides, countless shadows gathered and I questioned if we were the last ones left.

Was every predator honing in on us now?

Barely keeping them at bay, we continued sidestepping, pressing onward. Tatara limped on her injured foot, and despite the pain she had to be in, killed critters left and right. She had grit, and I admired her for that.

Herc pulled back on his reins as his powerful metallic legs kicked anything that came close. Beasties flew from the force of his hits, their bodies landing crumpled and limp. Witnessing his fighting spirit only made me love him more. He did his name proud.

While shooting a beast running in on Sarah's backside as she chopped into another, something bright caught my eye. A reflection. About a hundred yards dead ahead, there was a narrow opening in the trees. Blue water glistened as each rippling crest flashed with sunshine.

"There's the river, you guys! Maybe we can lose them in the water!" I bellowed.

The news invigorated the group, renewing our waning energy stores. Eyes brightened and sluggish feet lifted higher. Though we couldn't pick up the pace by much, we moved as fast as we could. Having a tangible target within reach felt like finding an oasis in the desert. Crossing the river represented a possibility for reprieve, even if only for a few minutes as we crossed.

Maybe if we were lucky, these beasts wouldn't exist on the other side.

I clung to any shred of hope, no matter how far fetched.

It was like the beasties sensed our thoughts, though. Shrieks pierced the air and the circling stopped abruptly. They all shifted to one side of us. Adjusting accordingly, our guns trained on the targets as they swarmed in again. Body after sinewy body surged, straight on like a ruthless battalion charging into battle. There were too many in too small a space to keep track of. With my rifle pressed tight to my cheek, my body jerked over and over from the kickback.

Jagged teeth snagged my cargo pants and I kicked to no avail.

"No biting!" Griggs drove a shock knife through the beasties' leathery skull.

"They're coming in too fast!" I shouted, struggling to keep up with the mass of creatures. My rounds sunk into the closest ones, but the space between me and them kept diminishing. Frantic glances at our now haphazard caravan formation revealed nobody else fared any better.

We'd stopped moving forward, now stepping backward to gain time and distance. The throng was too intense. Our energies switched to defensive measures. Keemi's teeth sliced and crunched through bone as she obliterated beasties, but even she was huffing with fatigue.

Wail after haunting wail brought even more swarming in through the trees.

"Where are they all coming from!?" One section of Sarah's frontal shield had steamed up, obscuring the left side of her face, her breath coming hard and fast.

"I don't know!" I shouted back. Fear rose and coagulated in my throat, threatening to strangle me. Herc whinnied in terror behind me, the sound shrill in my ears. A red-striped beast launched off of one of its fallen comrade's lifeless forms, but slipped, its hooked claws sliding into my feet and nearly knocking me over. Firing a quick pulse into its head, a grim realization hit. *There's too many. We can't take them all.*

We were pinned down.

Another wave of creatures rushed in and my burning arms raised my rifle, taking aim. My shots hit two in quick succession while Griggs round exploded the eye of a third. A fourth was on me in the space of a gasp, knocking me backward. My head bounced painfully off one of Herc's legs and he startled, jumping back in reaction. The reins jerked and leather dug into my wrist as I clutched my rifle with both hands, pushing it up to protect my face from snapping teeth. Driving the weapon into the beasties neck, I tried to crush its windpipe—if it even had one. I willed for Herc not to bolt. If he did, he'd yank my arm and my fight would reach a swift end. Although, maybe he should... As I grunted from the effort, muscles straining and head aching, thoughts swirled in my mind. Hope fragmented. *Maybe I'd be better off if death came swiftly.*

The beastie scrambled to get at me. Gooey strains of saliva drizzled on my forehead and cheeks as its claws raked across my shoulder. I screamed, the sound of my flesh tearing echoing in my eardrums. "Help!" I cried. But the gritty sounds of war and death fully enveloped me now, and I knew I was on my own. We'd been overwhelmed and everybody was running on fumes, battling to save their own lives. From somewhere beside me, Griggs shouted my name. I winced and pushed up as hard as I could, turning my head toward his voice, catching a glimpse. He gutted a yellow-striped beast with his knife, his arms and face splattered with blue blood. The creature shuddered and fell, while in my periphery,

Sarah stabbed at one clinging to her leg. She lurched forward as two more jumped onto her back. Shooting over her shoulder and lashing out with her blade, claws raked the protective skin cocooning her body.

"I'm coming, Finn!" Griggs blasted a heavy volley of shots into the horde, his tired eyes meeting mine. "Just hang on!"

Putrid breath steamed against my skin as three gnarled rows of teeth snapped centimetres from my face. A ragged scream rose above the chaos—one of sheer pain and terror. When the horrific sound dissipated into wet sputters moments later, I knew we'd lost someone else.

Herc whinnied, tugging at the reins. My arms trembled as the maw snapped again. I grimaced, turning my head as I tried to flatten into the earth. Teeth clamped down on one of my boots, tugging. My arms sagged by an inch, the rifle digging into my hands and the next bite caught the lobe of my ear. A scream ripped from my lips, the sound devolving into sobs.

Hot moisture slipped from the corners of my eyes. I knew what I had to do.

It was over for me, I understood that now, but I could save someone else. Peeling one finger off of my rifle at a time, I let Herc's reins incrementally slip from my grasp.

"Get out of here, Herc! Run!"

CHAPTER 18

Teeth snapped again, grazing my cheek this time, and I cursed my feeble muscles. I cried out but it didn't matter. Nobody could help me now. Everybody was in the same boat, fighting for their lives. Trembling, I turned my head, stared defiantly at the beast who'd claim my life.

Then a flash of chrome sliced across my vision. A pair of bionic hooves reared and slammed down into the beasties spine. The force of the blow drove the monster flat against my body, and I grunted from the impact. My entire lower left side was pinned by the collapse. But it wasn't dead. It was now well within striking range. However, it snarled up at Herc—distracted.

I capitalized.

My right hand released the rifle and snaked down to yank my pistol from its holster. Wrenching my wrist upward, I fired three quick rounds into the creature's chest hoping I hit something vital. It wailed, snapping at the remaining arm still shielding my face. Razor-like teeth tore into my flesh, but in the next instant, the thing shuddered and went limp. With my arm searing, and every muscle rubbery from overexertion, my entire left side was now trapped.

Herc reared as beasties moved in to finish what its brethren started. I aimed past my new bulky blanket and fired. Herc's flailing hooves reflected in the light overhead, connecting with multiple creatures. Then one of those hoofs slammed down next to my ear. A shout flew from my mouth, head jerking to the side. I knew he was trying to protect me, but a hoof to the face would make for an even worse day. Or maybe not… At least death by hoof would be quick.

A sinewy body dove over me to get at Herc, and it caught one of his legs, teeth clinking against metal while its claws sank into shoulder muscles above his bionic limb. Herc's anguished scream tore at my heart. The monster's hind legs used my blanket as a stepping stone, and an involuntary groan escaped as its weight compressed my chest. It's like the beasties knew I was an easy kill now—a gimme—so they focused on securing the larger meat source. Gasping for air, I forced my rubbery right arm to raise the pistol. I shot straight up, praying I didn't hit Herc.

"Get out of here!" The words rasped like they'd sandblasted my throat on the way out. "RUN, Herc! Please!" If his hooves didn't falter on the rough terrain, I believed he stood a fighting chance to outrun them. I pushed the pistol higher and shot into the creature's lower gut—and continued shooting until the beast finally dropped.

I thrust my head to the side just in time to avoid being suffocated as it flattened my pistol-wielding arm. "Dammit!" I hissed. The immense weight of both beasts compressed my torso, constricting my lungs. Now I had zero mobility, and a rapidly diminishing air supply.

Fighting raged all around me. Helpless to do anything but let the tears pour, I willed for Herc to save himself. Teeth sawed into my ankle, and I let a ragged scream fly.

It's only a matter of time now.

Then a brilliant azure light appeared.

It stained everything within my limited line of sight. The wash of colour caused the leathery striped skin of the beasts blanketing my body to glow. *Is it over? Have I gone to heaven?* Shouting accompanied the glow, though I couldn't understand the words.

A cacophony of shrieks exploded. The tones sounded different, grittier—cutting in and out like they'd lost their voices. The thunder of retreating paws followed. Those strange shrieks faded away, banished to linger in the distance.

"What's going on?" The words released as a breathy whisper. "Help!" My chest heaved and I struggled for air, unable to shout further. Sparkles of light encroached upon my field of vision as an ominous sense of light-headedness washed over me.

Herc's hoof nudged the creature trapping my head and shoulder. He nickered softly as his whiskery muzzle sniffed across my forehead. He hadn't left me.

The glow intensified from nearby, and within seconds, I found myself fully enveloped. My own skin radiated indigo and new fear constricted my chest in a different way.

"Finn!" Male voices shouted. *Oh, thank God.* I smiled as Griggs and Jorgep appeared, hovering overhead. In short order, they rolled a monster off of my upper body. I inhaled a huge lungful of air, then another, before craning my neck to search for the source of the blue glow. My gaze landed on two olive-skinned humanoids, a young man and woman, each dressed in simple, yet beautifully crafted leather clothing. They both had deep royal blue hair, with numerous tribal-looking tattoos marking their arms and legs.

But what captured my full attention was what they held. The pair wielded smooth, wooden staffs around three inches in diameter—their entire lengths embedded with azure stones that appeared to shine from within. The source of the light. Similar stones encircled their necks and ankles, all tied with braided cordage.

I pointed, my mouth agape. "W-who—?"

The woman, whose waist-length hair was braided into multiple strands, waved vigorously. Her brow furrowed, accentuating an expression that oozed impatience.

Griggs, who looked like a blood and sweat-saturated scratch post, said, "They're friendly—we think. They saved us. Just showed up out of nowhere." He grunted, pushing with Jorgep to roll the second beastie off of me. "We're supposed to follow them."

My legs and torso, which tingled, half numb, were finally free. As soon as the weight lifted, I sat up and stretched, grimacing from the pain that caused. The swarm of beasties still wove through the trees, snarling and licking their lips as they circled at a safe distance.

Smiling at my rescuers, I said, "Thank you. I really thought I was done for."

The girl nodded with a tight-lipped smile, keeping an eye on the creatures. She glanced at my torn-up ankle and rushed over, pressing something to it before I could react. The sting intensified from the pressure, and I nearly pushed her away, but then it ebbed. Despite the blood, the joint felt strong enough to use again. The mysterious blue-haired woman retreated, rejoining her partner. They waved at us again, but all I could do was stare at my ankle, speechless.

It looked scarred, like it had been healing for weeks.

Griggs hoisted me to my feet. "I think we were all a few seconds from dead."

"Well, not quite all…" Jorgep bowed his head.

That pulled me out of my bewildered fog. "Who else didn't make it?" I scanned faces, spying Tatara and Dino standing behind the blue-haired pair, whom I had to assume were first peoples to this planet. Sarah held onto a blood-covered Keemi several feet away. Her mech suit was scratched to shit with chunks of orange and pink paint gone. But she was alive.

"Where's Enek? And Teensy?" I didn't see them anywhere.

Griggs sighed heavily. "Teensy didn't make it." He rubbed his face. "And Enek got tackled like you, but they got a bite into his neck. He died quickly."

"Oh no." The news settled like ballast in my stomach. I looked down, knowing that had nearly been my fate, too. Then my head snapped up. "Wait, where's Vernon?" *No, not Vernon.*

"I'm here, Finn. I'm okay." The battered looking man stepped out from behind the wide girth of the bleenad. He smiled, then waved us forward. "I don't know how long these people can hold the beasties back, nor how much patience they have. They seem to want us to follow them, so I suggest we get moving."

Nobody argued. The choice between staying here and getting mangled, or leaving with unknown people who may-or-may-not be friendly, was a no brainer.

Jorgep passed me Herc's reins and I patted my boy's neck, so thankful he'd survived. Everything hurt as I hobbled to meet our new acquaintances. With each breath, my ribs ached. While inconvenient, I could manage that. It was the gouges in my shoulder that hurt like a bitch.

Our rescuers were in motion the moment we fell in line. The woman took the lead, while the man brought up the rear. Both held their staffs out, waving them in slow arcs from side to side as we walked. They shouted to each other, communicating with words our universal translators didn't pick up. At least not fully. Surprisingly, one in every few words came out clear— recognizable, though none of us knew why that would be. For example, one time the woman shouted, and I swore I heard the words "sanctuary", "others", and "heal". How could a newly discovered civilization living on an uncolonized planet have *recognizable* words?

I got a much better look at their features as we walked. The indigenous woman was striking, with long lashes and youthful grey eyes slightly bigger than a human's. Her lips spread wide across her face, while her limbs looked lean and muscular. Up close, her olive skin appeared semi-translucent, with tiny webbed veins showing beneath the surface. Like Vernon's, though his complexion was more weathered, with scars and what I assumed were sunspots. The male was equally handsome, possessing the same grey eyes and blue hair—though his was shorter, falling in waves to his ears. Curious, I wondered if this race was anatomically compatible with humans like Vernon's was, then quickly brushed the thought aside.

A wall of snarling beasties parted as we passed through, all shying away from our rescuer's glowing staffs. Their bitter shrieks pierced the air and they shook stress from their bodies like dogs. One dared to jump forward, snapping, but the blue-haired man swung his staff causing the risk-taker to immediately recoil.

Those blue stones had power.

We came upon the remnants of a camp. Several victims were strewn about with sections of raw flesh exposed. Blood pooled beneath them and stained the grass. Beasties abandoned the tattered bodies they'd been feeding on, slinking away.

I averted my eyes until we passed by, focusing instead on the sound of rushing water ahead, envisioning clear, glistening liquid in my mind. It both symbolised rejuvenation and brightened my spirits. Oh, how I craved washing the dirt, sweat, and blood from my body.

But it wouldn't cleanse the memories. The images. Nothing could remove those.

Minutes later, we reached the water's edge. The stream moved more swiftly than I'd imagined, its current strong as it cascaded over layers of sand and rock. I could see the bottom though, which meant it wasn't too deep. *Good.* I doubted I'd have the strength to swim.

Our female guide turned to speak, pointing at the water. Her bladed hand wound like a worm in the downstream direction. All

I understood was "follow", "careful" and "fast". She made a show of planting her feet firmly on the ground then led us in. My exhausted legs carried me into the water, wading carefully while Herc sloshed by my side. As a group, we crossed the stream to the opposite bank, but didn't get out, merely turned downstream.

The water was cold. But, once the initial shock passed, I welcomed the refreshing chill—a blissful reprieve from the heat. I yearned to dunk my whole body so badly.

"Can you understand what they're saying at all?" I whispered to Griggs just ahead.

Griggs fell into step beside me, stepping cautiously on the slippery rocks. "A few words here and there. You?" He shuddered, his lips forming a tight "o" as the water surpassed his groin.

"Same. But isn't that bizarre?"

He nodded while splashing water over his arms and face. "Very much so."

I watched him wash with a mixture of jealousy and concern. "Ah, Griggs, are you sure the water's safe enough to be splashing it over open wounds?"

He shrugged. "We have wounds on our legs too, and these people are walking in it."

"Yeah, but they're *from* this planet," I rebutted.

"I'll take the risk." Griggs kept splashing.

An internal war raged. I wanted to feel clean so badly, but *really* didn't want to catch some deadly alien parasite either. Sidestepping, I waved at our male guide to the rear. When the man acknowledged me, I pointed to Griggs and mimed the act of washing. "Is the water safe?" Raising my brows in question, I gave a thumbs up. I immediately swallowed a groan. *They likely don't know what a thumbs up is, stupid. This isn't Earth.*

The man's lips curled at the edges, appearing amused. He nodded, speaking a litany of words, from which I caught "wash" and "safe". Then, he returned an awkward thumbs up.

I suppressed a chuckle, confirming I understood by repeating the gesture. "That's good enough for me." The water was waist high and as we walked, I gently bent to submerge my bloodied arms in the cool liquid, feeling the cleansing sting. Purple blotches and a myriad of cuts marred my flesh. I avoided touching the deeper wound in my shoulder, though, not wanting to mess with that until I could inspect it more closely. At least the bleeding had stopped.

Other group members followed suit, the simple act eliciting smiles and joyful moans. I felt sorry for Sarah, who watched with a sour expression behind me. If she opened the front shield of her mech suit, water would rush inside—which wouldn't be ideal. One couldn't exactly hang a mech suit out to dry.

The beasties kept a wide berth of our convoy, hovering along the edges of the stream. Their bright stripes of colour stood out among the ashen bark and deep violet foliage. Some swam in our wake, snapping at us and each other in undeniable frustration. Between feeling their eyes boring into me, and having no clue where I was headed, my nerves were on overdrive.

Griggs dipped his stubbled chin. "How are you holding up?"

I pushed the now misshapen cowboy hat off of my head, splashing water over my face. Chilled rivulets ran down my shirt, feeling both shocking and heavenly. "I'm okay overall, considering. I think. It's all just... a lot, you know?" My foot slipped, the current pulling it out from under me, but Griggs reached out his warm hand to steady me.

"I know what you mean. But at least we're alive." He did a fist pump next to his ear, though the celebration didn't quite reach his eyes.

"For now." My smile felt tight against my teeth. "I just hope these people don't turn out to be dangerous. What if we're just walking into more trouble wherever they're taking us?"

Tatara, who hobbled beside Sarah, had obviously been eavesdropping. She leaned forward to say, "Like roasting us over a pit. Or keeping us as slaves."

"Or tossing us into a volcano to appease their Gods," Sarah quipped sarcastically, joining the conversation. Her heavy metal feet sloshed through the water, almost as loudly as Keemi.

I shook my head at her. "Volcano, really?"

"It's fucking hot enough in this place."

Chuckles rippled through the group—a much-needed distraction from pain and worry. Too bad Enek couldn't be with us now. Despite his quiet ways, he would've laughed at the oddball conversation we were having. He didn't deserve to die. Nobody did.

Our group was down to seven people.

Griggs waved a hand to the side. "I'm sure we won't be slaves, roasted alive, or tossed into *lava*." One eyebrow cocked. "However, that doesn't mean we won't get sent back into the bush to resume dying a horrible death. Ultimately, it'll depend on what these people want."

"Exactly!" I blurted, making Herc twitch. "Why did they save us?"

The stream grew shallower, coming up to mid-thigh instead of the waist. We continued downstream, trailing behind our guide like a gaggle of baby geese.

Dino, who walked ahead of Griggs, swivelled to face me. "Not only that, but if they saved *us*, why didn't they save Governus's people too?"

The man had a point. I frowned.

Vernon, who walked near the head of our gaggle, calmly interjected. "It will serve us well to keep these things in mind throughout our dealings. We can only hope that, if these people *were* selective in who they saved, we don't fall on the wrong side of that." We all unanimously agreed.

The woman leading us turned to look at Vernon briefly, her eyes narrowing.

Had she recognized something he'd said? I leaned forward again, half-whispering, "Um, question. Do you think they can understand us like we can understand them? We should watch what we say, just in case." It only stood to reason—if our universal translators recognized some of their words, maybe some of our words were familiar to them, too. But who's specific words were familiar? All languages were translated via the universal translators in our wrist cuffs or ocular implants. Without either option, someone would only hear raw spoken language.

Vernon replied. "Their language seems oddly familiar to me. Like I should understand it, but yet, don't. Like you, I only understand what the translator picks up."

Hmm, curious.

Leafy vines snaked across the stream to connect with overhanging trees. Gnarled root systems dove into the water through steep, muddy banks. Some of those blue veins of dirt— much thicker now—snaked up on an angle from the stream, vanishing into the forest. For the first time in days, I looked up to see an unfettered sky, thanks to this break in the trees. The bright, purple-tinged atmosphere loomed overhead, with wisps of clouds wafting across it. The faint tips of Joya's double moons teased us with a glimpse.

The chilled stream water, which had felt luxurious at first, now caused my legs to tingle—the sensation bordering on pain. I'd be happy to get out any time. I swatted at a tiny flying insect, realizing I hadn't seen many bugs in the Sweep—a stark contrast to Earth's jungles. Lumpy-beaked birds flitted about, their chirps resumed now that the chaos had ebbed. A furry, monkey-like creature jumped across the branches connecting two trees, and I hoped the little guy didn't lose his balance. With all the beasties below, it wouldn't stand a chance if it fell.

Jorgep, who'd taken up the rear and had been oddly quiet this whole time, spoke. "You know, Mr. Vernon, they do bear a resemblance to you—or you them. Minus your breather and their blue hair, of course." He paused, seeming hesitant, and I had a feeling where he might be going with this. "Perhaps our translators recognize some words because of *your* language."

I gave Jorgep an encouraging nod. "I noticed that too. But is that even possible?"

Vernon's mouth scrunched to one side as he contemplated. Thankfully, he didn't seem offended at all—quite the opposite. He seemed intrigued, stroking his chin like a scholar piecing together a theory. "Hmm… Let me turn off my translator so we can find out for sure. And don't talk to me until I turn it back on, because I won't understand a word you're saying." He chuckled, raising a digiscreen from his cuff and keying in a command.

Vernon stepped out of our two-by-two line and flagged down the female guide. "Excuse me, young miss?" When she didn't reply, he repeated the call, more insistently.

The woman looked over her shoulder, answering in her native tongue. From her expression, I assumed she said something like, *"What do you want?"*

Vernon spoke deliberately, enunciating his words. "First off, thank you for helping us. We are in your debt." He tipped his head respectfully. A solid way to open the conversation. The woman's face morphed into a neutral expression as she listened. Splaying his palms outward, Vernon continued, "Can you understand anything I am saying to you right now?"

I couldn't get a read on her, she controlled her expression so expertly.

"Yes? No?" Vernon's shoulders raised.

The woman glanced ahead to where the stream curved sharply to the left, then her eyes flicked to her male counterpart. Slowly, she nodded to Vernon, speaking. I watched her mouth work, tongue rolling and lips wrapping around each unique sound she produced. The translated words I heard were: "Few…how… language?"

Vernon's eyes widened, shrugging as he held a friendly smile. "I don't know." He looked back at us, adding, "I still understand some of the words without my translator on. How bizarre."

Holy crap. Jorgep's theory was no longer just a theory. Inexplicably, our father-like groupmate was somehow connected to a hidden people living in a deadly creature-filled forest with air that can make people hallucinate and engine-killing interference.

"Do you have any ideas as to how that could be?" I was craving to find out.

"Nothing right now, but I'm thinking." He turned back to our guide. "Thank you."

Our guide shook her head—clearly confused, but dropped the matter, waving us onward. We waded around the sharp bend in the stream, and as we progressed, a hint of light emanated through the tightly knit foliage covering the left bank. Beasties still slithered all around us, but they seemed sluggish now, like they'd lost the will for their chase. They snapped bitterly at each other, fighting amongst themselves. *Sore losers?* That gave me a smug sense of satisfaction.

The dense forest soon thinned on our left, and the bend smoothed out. The source behind that hint of light came into full view. Collectively, we stopped walking. Conversation ceased.

I blinked hard, subconsciously feeling for the breather still perched on my face to ensure this wasn't another hallucination. For good measure, I even pinched my skin. "Holy shit…"

Before me loomed a vision unlike anything I'd ever seen before.

CHAPTER 19

"**Y**es!" Khana shouted, pumping a fist in the air. "Look at that!" Standing, she paced behind her chair, practically vibrating with excitement. She thrust her hands at the screens, which currently presented the view of that odd horse-riding woman. Two blue-haired indigenous people wielding glowing wood staffs were there, having just scared off those vicious Sweep creatures.

"See?" She slapped her brother's shoulder. "I told you this plan would pay off. Look at the glowing stones on those sticks! They're just like the blip of one we saw. *Glowing!*"

Steel rapped his fingertips on the metal desk. "So, obviously these mystery people showed up when our charting mission got attacked, too."

Khana nodded. "They most certainly did. I wish they'd arrived sooner in our case." She frowned for a second, then a grin spread across her lips. "But, lucky for us, they didn't make that same mistake twice. As we speak, they're leading our survivors somewhere. But where? To their home? Out of the Sweep? Are they just another predator fighting for resources? They could've taste-tested *our* team for all we know—damn cameras cutting out."

"Yeah, but at least we learned something. Bio tech is best. That's the new motto." Steel shrugged, pointing at the blue-haired duo. "They don't look deadly to me, but what do I know?"

Khana's eyes sliced into him. "Clearly, not much. The deadliest killers are the ones who can make you believe they're your best friend until the moment they decide to hollow you out."

He scoffed. "Well, you'd know that the best, wouldn't you?"

The air could've turned to ice as the two locked eyes with each other. Then, a wicked smile curled the corners of Khana's mouth. She tilted her head. "Perhaps."

Steel crossed his muscular arms behind his head. "How would you like to handle our colonists? They've been asking questions, concerned with all the gunfire echoing from afar."

"Delicately. For now, we stick to the plan. Tell them about the unfortunate attack. Show concern. Hopefully soon, the racers will lay eyes on our prize, then we'll simply sit back and let the Sweep do the dirty work for us." Khana laughed wickedly. "Oh, our sceptical brothers will have to eat their words now. And the best part? Everything can be done under the guise of innocence and protection. It's perfect." She clapped her hands together.

Steel cocked an eyebrow at Khana. "Did you ever consider the possibility that not all of the racers will die? Then what?"

"They will."

"And if they don't? If we'd just cleared out the Sweep to begin with, we wouldn't be—"

Khana grabbed the back of his chair and spun him around. Wrapping a hand around his sinewy throat, she leaned in. "My dear doubting brother…" Her face twisted into a snarl as she watched his eyes flash wish surprise. "I grow tired of your constant questions. Operations on Joya are well funded by our colonists, and they may not take kindly to us blowing things up. Especially a *whole new race of people*. If they ever caught wind of that, we'd be sunk."

Khana paused to take a calming breath. "As much as I despise the fact—this is a family business, and I swore to our parents before they died that I would keep the peace with you… but, my patience only lasts for so long. You've always been the better brother, Steel. But you are either with me, or against me. What shall it be?"

"With you sister." Steel pulled her fingers from his throat. "Of course."

Khana swiped a few wayward hairs off her face and stepped back. "Good."

"Will you just allow me to say one more thing?"

"No." She pointed to the door. "Go and ready the podium. I need to make a speech to the colonists about how deeply shocked and concerned we are over these *dire developments*—and that we're devising rescue plans as we speak." She forced exaggerated expressions of horror and sorrow onto her face. "Let me know when it's ready."

The muscles in Steel's jaw clenched, eyes narrowing as if considering something very intensely. Then he gave a stiff nod, collected his overcoat, and whisked out the door.

***

An imposing row of thick towering pillars stood at attention maybe thirty feet up from the bank of the stream. The pillars shone a vibrant blue—almost like they glowed from within. Beyond them, nestled in the middle of a sizeable clearing, rested what looked like a rudimentary tropical village sitting atop blue soil. All of those veins we'd seen seemed to converge here.

A sanctuary of glowing stones. At least I hoped it was a sanctuary.

I stared at the countless eyes watching us from beyond the pillars.

"From the frying pan into the fire…" Sarah grumbled in her tinny voice.

"Hope not," I replied, the words merging with a heavy exhale. Stepping onto the shoreline, I shook my tingling feet to help warm them up faster. My attention didn't leave the grand hand-carved pillars, each one standing maybe twenty feet apart, watching over this jungle oasis like steadfast sentries. Our guides waved to the others waiting within the fortress walls. The majority of the blue-haired people gathered near the largest open-air hut at the centre of the little village, keeping their distance. Perhaps they were as afraid of us, as we were of them…

They all shared similar physical characteristics with our guides—blue hair, expressive eyes, and olive translucent skin. They wore clothing combinations made of leather and fabric, some bleached light, or dyed dark, while some showcased dyed patterns. Certain individuals wore head coverings. Others let their hair flow free in various lengths and styles. Some men had shaved heads, revealing scalp tattoos.

"Look at them all…" I whispered.

As we approached, I marvelled at the blue rocks affixed to the pillars. Exactly six generous sized stones had been chipped into a round shape and built into each huge wooden trunk, all arranged in vertical lines down the centre, pointing outward into the jungle. Somewhat gem-like, they glowed strong and steady, their luminous inner cores fragmented by starbursts of light. The colour was reminiscent of the blue sky that blazes as the sun melts below the horizon on Earth—rich, and vibrant, but with hints of night seeping in around the edges. The resultant cumulative glow permeated everything, even the air, casting a faint azure haze.

The pillar stones dwarfed the thumb-sized stones covering our rescuer's staffs, easily the size of a basketball. I made that comparison with certainty because my younger brother, who'd collected antique sports memorabilia since childhood, actually let me bounce one once—a rare experience, considering Earth sports had only been played in holo-arenas for the last 200 years.

As we passed between two of the stone guardians, I inspected the chiselled drawings surrounding their stones. The artistry was incredible, a showcase of swirling waves, detailed shapes, crosshatched lines, dots, and other various patterns. Some were grouped together in a uniform manner, and I wondered whether those markings might be words. They reminded me of the Egyptian hieroglyphics I'd seen on grade school field trips to the Humanities Museum.

A crisscross of vines framing two cowering beasties at the base of one pillar captured my attention. Faces looked down upon the creatures from the top, while over their shoulders loomed the two moons of Joya—clear as day. The pillar next to it was decorated in a similar fashion, but with minor differences. It had different jungle patterns and its vines swirled all the way up, finally giving way to a smattering of chipped holes I assumed represented stars. Amongst them was a flying object in a downward trajectory—perhaps not flying, but falling. The object appeared surprisingly geometric, contrary to everything else I'd seen in this place thus far.

"It looks like a ship, doesn't it?" Vernon said, appearing beside me.

I nodded, having no clue what to make of this influx of input. "It really does."

"And these—" Vernon pointed to the hieroglyphic-like carvings. "—are words." His face was serious, yet his eyes were alight with adventure, glancing between me and the pillars. An expectant look washed over his features as he waited for me to clue in.

I covered my mouth in surprise. "Can you *read* it?"

"Most of the words, yes. It's an archaic form of writing that hasn't been used on my planet for many cycles. It is only studied by historians, or enthusiasts who take a keen interest in languages—like myself." His voice remained low. "That is why your translator can't read it—it's too different. And only some *spoken* words are similar enough to my current language to be deciphered." I blinked, dumbfounded.

Vernon's expression tightened then, and he pressed a finger to his lips. "Until we learn more about our new friends, I want to hold this card close to my chest."

No stranger to poker tactics, I replied, "Understood."

The male guide urged us to keep moving with emphatic finger pointing. Without argument, we did as requested, passing through the pillars to catch up with our caravan.

Vernon's logic made sense. His personal knowledge—however inexplicable—could be leveraged should things go south, and from the way his eyes continuously scanned everything within view, reading and analysing, I trusted he'd use that advantage to the fullest if need be. *Trust...* The concept lingered in my thoughts. It was funny, because when I'd embarked on this journey, I never expected to form friendships, much less trust anyone in direct competition with me. Yet, here I was, counting myself lucky to have connected with this eclectic group of racers.

Up ahead, people of the indigenous community gathered several rows deep, whispering and mingling between the few thatched roof huts. There were no young children in sight, likely hidden away out of caution. Relieved smiles greeted our guides as they returned from battle with us in tow. However, when regarding us, their expressions varied between curiosity, irritation, wariness, and even fear. Many fingers pointed at Herc and Keemi—their interest clearly piqued.

Woven hats, mats, what looked like instruments, and other decorative items hung from support beams in one of the thatched huts, its frame built of debarked wooden beams. However, its side walls looked metallic. *That's odd.* From where I stood, it looked like panels—old, rusty ones. Where would they have gotten those from? Those wrecked Governus hoverbikes were ripe for scavenging. But no, that didn't stack up. These panels had narrow rectangular viewing windows. They had to be some kind of domicile door.

The ship carved into the pillar.

Glancing around, I noticed several other metallic items, including something that looked like a solar panel, and sections of thin sheeting used in conjunction with thatched flora atop each slanted roof. Chimes dangled from low-hanging branches at the outskirts of the clearing, the flute-like cylinders plunking gently to serenade this meeting of the minds.

Hut number two held sharpened stone-tipped weapons, and rows of glowing staffs like the ones our guides carried. What was this place—some kind of staging area? The third hut was taller, with several skinned animal carcasses hanging from the rafters. The gathered people marred my view, but it was still clear from the striped leathers many wore, those were beasties.

I continued gawking at everything as they ushered us forward. The final hut contained what looked like a cooking station, which made sense given its proximity to a smouldering fire pit. Carved forks, and ladles hung from wooden pegs, dishware littering a huge table. Outside, thin strips of powder blue meat hung on slatted ladders over the fire. I was impressed with how industrious and organised these people seemed.

Our guides pointed, telling us to go off to the right. It was only then that I noticed the other collection of life forms tucked away on the other side of the clearing.

A sigh of relief rushed from my lips. Other racers—at least twenty. We weren't the only one's who'd survived. I didn't recognize anyone except Cala, the woman who'd taken off after Raker sabotaged our vehicles. But Tatara and Jorgep waved to a few people they knew. Our comrades stood just inside the pillars, nervously glancing about their new surroundings. Some appeared injured and lay on the ground, shrouded by a semi-circle of protective staff-wielders. An indigenous person held something—I couldn't see what—over their bodies.

Our guides called out and several of their people stepped forward as we reached the others. They motioned for the unharmed to remain at the fringe, and for the rest of us to sit. More staff-wielders amassed, protecting individuals holding blue stones in their hands. *What the—?*

Hesitantly, I complied. Everyone else did too. Except Sarah, who watched anxiously.

Our feminine rescuer approached me and Herc herself, holding out a palm-sized stone. Her eyes were less intense now, rather urging me to trust, not unlike a trainer might approach a skittish horse. I flinched away from her and sucked in a painful breath, remembering the sting of after she'd touched me earlier. Herc snorted and stomped behind me while she inched closer, a string of gentle words rolling off her tongue.

"Let them do it!" The pre-existing racers shouted out.

"Don't be afraid!"

"The stones heal!"

I stopped backing away. Glancing at Griggs, who'd allowed his supposed healer to touch a nasty slice with a stone, my mind whirled. He gave me a resigned *we'll see how this goes* look.

I sighed. "Those racers better be right about this." Then I offered my injured foot.

Griggs gave a nervous chuckle, watching his stone-wielder closely.

My guide laid her stone on my foot, and the same stinging sensation I'd felt before radiated through it. But within a minute, the discomfort faded, and she moved the stone to my shoulder. My chin became three and my eyes crossed trying to see what the stone was doing. Rolling my bitten ankle, the stark lack of pain boggled my mind. It had dark scars before, but now appeared fully healed, as if it had happened ages ago. *How is that possible?*

A new sting swelled in my shoulder, intensifying until my hands clenched from the burn. "Damn, that's zinging pretty good." I gritted my teeth, back muscles straining.

My guide smiled and said something I guessed was meant to be comforting. She paid close attention to my reaction, then her knowing smile widened the moment my frown eased.

"*Ah, baka*," she said, then moved the stone to cover a cut down my arm. If ageing worked the same for this race, I'd put her around my age—a few years younger perhaps—though she seemed so much older. Wiser somehow.

One by one my lacerations sealed, leaving only faded scars behind. My semi-crushed hand, and even the deep claw marks in my shoulder, were healed. I touched it. No pain. It was like nothing I'd ever seen before. "How can a *stone* do this?" The words tumbled from my mouth. Back on Earth, I'd been taught magic wasn't real. There were no warlocks and wizards running about casting spells. Yet, these hidden people—at the edge of explored space—had conjured this incredible ability before my very eyes. The logical part of my brain scrambled to find an explanation. There had to be some kind of science-based reason.

When she moved it to my aching ribcage, the stone glowed even brighter, twice as warm against my skin. I looked at my fellow group members who hissed and groaned as they too felt the healing pain. Jorgep even tried unsuccessfully to communicate with his local resident.

A sudden sting reverberated through my ribs and I clenched my jaw. Locking eyes with the woman at the helm, I focused on anything but the burn in my bones. My mind flashed to the ranch—of running through wheat fields, bottle feeding calves with my mother, and riding Herc for the first time. When my father's face popped up, I winced and blinked the image away.

My healer grasped my trembling hand, holding it as I squirmed. Panting, I tried to swallow the hurt—knowing it was worth it. The last thing I wanted was to be in a weakened state when we finished trekking out of this forest. An involuntary shudder came as the thought of facing those vicious creatures again tied triple knots in my stomach. *Focus on something happy, dammit.* Then Griggs popped into my mind—the way he'd protected me. His smile. That kiss.

As the pain ebbed, the woman leaned in closer to feel my ribs. She smiled. "*Baka.*"

"Baka..." I repeated, still catching my breath. "Thank you."

She held the rock in place another moment for good measure, then stood to approach my horse. He didn't like that much, rearing up in fear, which caused our healer to jump back. I sprung to my feet without pain—miraculously—and settled him down. Herc had nasty claw marks across his chest and shoulders. Streams of dried blood matted the hair down his legs. I invited her forward with a wave. "He's nervous about everything right now. Please, go ahead."

The mysterious woman proceeded to heal Herc, which was a difficult process due to his resistance, but we got through it. Everyone else was stitched back together by the time we were finished, sitting quietly and watching. Our helpful guide tucked the magic rock back into a leather pouch slung over her shoulder, and backed away. She exchanged words with her fellow guide, gave a hand gesture, then her people returned to the other side of the clearing.

I faced my equally dumbfounded companions. "Can you believe that?"

Griggs, Vernon, and Tatara shook their heads. Jorgep and Dino merely blinked.

Sarah rushed over with eyes wide. "Holy fuck, so it's true? You're healed?"

I flexed my arm, legs, and twisted my torso. "Yeah, it's true."

Our caravan melted into the other pre-existing group, everyone a twitter about the healing and eager to exchange battle stories. I stood with Sarah and Griggs near the outskirts, swapping experiences, comparing scars. Herc's eye shone green. I wondered if I'd ever see it blue again.

Meanwhile, the indigenous people remained busy talking amongst themselves at the far end of the sanctuary, sometimes quite heatedly. Their eyes darted over to us; their fingers pointed our way. The woman who'd healed me stomped into the cooking hut, pointing with vigour at the metallic wall panel. Or something near it. Interestingly, our two guides seemed to be at the centre of every discussion. They stood out in front of the group, and had the most visible tattoos out of everyone I could see. *Some kind of status symbol maybe?*

I was desperate to learn why they'd braved those beasts to save our hides.

"I bet they don't know what to do with us," Griggs whispered in my ear.

I flinched at his nearness, heart leaping. A quick laugh covered my knee-jerk reaction, then I discreetly stepped aside and away from him. To a safer distance. "They're probably arguing about what seasoning to use when they chop us up and eat us."

"Ah, well, my mind didn't quite go there. Why would they go through the trouble of saving us just to eat us?" The way Griggs studied my face, I wondered if he'd noticed my tactical movement—if he somehow sensed what fueled it. Part of me— one I loathed right now—felt terrified he might think I didn't like him. While, in truth, I wanted nothing but to hug him. I craved the feel of his strong arms around me again, preferably *without* hallucinogenic prodding. Yet, even if I wished to throw my prior caution to the wind, the very fact we'd nearly died stopped me short. Emotions catalysed vulnerability, the kind that compromised safety. We couldn't afford to do that… not with lives hanging in the balance.

They say near death experiences can give clarity. After today, I agreed with that. Not only did I want to survive, but I wanted those I cared about to survive, too. Distractions seemed likely to get us killed. Whatever existed between Griggs and I had to end. Now. For both our sakes.

I refocused on his question, splaying my hands. "Why? Um, let's see… to fatten us up. To take us as slaves. To put us through torture schemes for their twisted pleasure. To sacrifice us to their Gods like Sarah said—if they have any. C'mon, have you never seen old horror movies?"

"That's kinda morbid, but alright." He flashed a dimpled grin, and I looked away.

Vernon walked past, leaning in to whisper, "Guys. Check this out." He tilted his head toward a pillar, inviting us to follow. Thankful for the reprieve, I jumped at the chance. Tatara, Dino and Jorgep were busy talking with other racers, so we agreed to fill them in later. Sarah, Griggs, and I backed away, crossing the twenty feet to the nearest pillar.

Tucking in beside it, Vernon continued in hushed tones. "I've been reading more."

"Oh?" I crossed my arms, matching his volume. "And?"

Sarah leaned forward. "What are we whispering about?"

"*Shh…* Just listen." I waved for Vernon to continue.

Vernon's thin lips fought a smirk. "Okay. So, reading what's written on the pillars doesn't give me a clear picture, really. From the—"

Griggs sliced a hand through the air between us. "Hold on, did you say *reading?*"

Vernon nodded. "Yes, I can read their writing, but I'm not wanting to broadcast that tidbit of information just yet." Griggs mouth opened to speak, but Vernon pre-empted him. "I have a theory about why, which I'll share soon enough." Griggs opened his lips again but Vernon quickly added, "And no, I still can't fully understand their speech. May I continue?"

Griggs shut his mouth, and I had to swallow a laugh.

"All the pillars I've inspected so far contain fragments of stories. But—" Vernon pointed up. "Like several others, this pillar has a ship on it. But *this* one says something different."

I followed his finger, looking about six feet up the etched wood surface, where a row of glyph-like markings had been written much larger than the rest. "What does it say?"

Vernon's expression filled with wonder as a hushed explanation spilled from his mouth. "It says they came from the stars, settling here after a tragic crash."

Sarah glanced at each of us in quick succession. "And that means…?"

Vernon planted his feet, as though prepping to drop a verbal bomb. "Historically, my people are prolific explorers and scientists. We mapped vast sections of the Galaxium, discovered many new races in our travels. So you see, it's no wonder we were the first civilization to make contact with Earth." He took a long swig from his water flask before continuing.

"Excursions beyond known space always come with risks. There are three recorded missions in Neersoo history that failed to return—deemed lost in space." He pointed at the rusty metal panels forming the cooking hut wall. "I recognize the design of that panel. It is a domicile door from an old Neersoo Deetrex Explorer, one of two sister ships that disappeared nearly six hundred cycles ago." He quickly added, "That's four hundred Earth years, if my math is correct."

"Are you sure?" Sarah asked, failing to contain her shock.

Vernon nodded. "Quite. As a youngling, I helped my father retire those ships."

Four hundred years. My lips formed an "o", letting out a low whistle. "Wow."

"So, they *are* like you…" Griggs mimed his brain exploding with his hands.

"We stem from the same roots, yes. The pieces fit perfectly into place. What a discovery!" Vernon clapped his hands together, then in the next breath, straightened his passionate expression. "But it's clear these people have changed since landing here. We still know nothing about them or what they're capable of, so we must remain on high alert."

I gave Vernon a supportive pat on the shoulder. "Absolutely."

"The Sweep must've knocked out their engines when they flew over trying to scan it. Poor fuckers didn't know what hit 'em. Shit, that would've been a really bad day." Sarah shook her head, then her eyes glanced up, lips pursing. "Hmm—knowing this, I wonder if our translators can be tweaked."

The faint sound of sloshing water reached my ears. I turned to the river, shifting to get a better look. A renewed fervour of shrieks and snapping teeth exploded about the stream. Two forms soon appeared from around the riverbend, wading towards the sanctuary. A short, stocky guide led the way, while a tall, lean frame followed close behind.

Closing my eyes, I groaned.

Raker.

CHAPTER 20

aker was all alone with a single guide. The racer he'd sped off with after sabotaging our vehicles was nowhere to be seen. He passed through the grand pillars, wholly engrossed with scanning this new environment. The man looked as filthy as the rest of us, obviously having faced his own share of battle, yet still, he strutted into the clearing like he owned the place.

"Well, look who's here," I grumbled.

Sarah rolled her eyes. "Oh, of course *he* would've survived."

Griggs glowered at the sour-faced racer unabashedly, yet said, "As much as I dislike him, still, nobody deserves to die here. He was lucky to have been rescued like we were."

Sarah poked a thumb in Griggs' direction. "Look at Mr. Positivity over here. Fair enough, but if he even looks at me the wrong way, I'll flatten him."

"Just make sure I'm present." I smirked, half of me hoping that never came to pass—for Sarah's safety sake, while the other half had already bought tickets to see the show. Our resident tech repurposer was certainly tough. She'd been a fighting machine against the beasties. But was she as capable without the mech suit in the picture? Having seen her softer side, I wondered if her brash talk was a front—bluster to keep people off her back. She'd confided once, after one too many skeetch shots in the transport's lower deck bar, that it hurt being treated as *less than*. I understood that, and I was only human. Crimeons had been exiled from the civilized Galaxium after a failed attempt at war fifty years ago, so it was twice as hard for her, getting called a half-breed by anti-Crimeon purists *and* human trash by the gate haters.

A bloodied Raker strolled up to the conglomeration of racers with a surprisingly friendly smile. Once healed, he melted into the group, his smile faltering when his gaze landed on us.

Sarah opened her face shield briefly to whisper, "Think he's happy to see us?"

Something between a throaty snort and a hiss escaped my mouth. "Um, nope." But a blink later, some new activity happening across the clearing stole my focus. I pointed. "Look."

Two new figures appeared from behind the largest hut, one masculine and one feminine, both fully tattooed—even more so than our guides. Intermittent inked markings stretched down their wrinkled legs, arms, and crept up their shoulders to their necks before fading away at the jawline. However, unlike anyone else, this pair showcased sizable matching tattoos across their upper sternums. It was hard to tell across the distance, but the design looked like something on fire. Again I pondered if the tattoos indicated social status. Or badges of honour. The two walked forward with a distinguished air, their blue hair dusted with white. But then I saw they weren't alone. A step behind them trailed three youths of varying ages—the oldest twelve at most.

We left the pillar and rejoined the rest of the group.

Our guides hugged the children and spoke privately with the elder pair apart from the other community members. The adults pointed in our direction, their four heads nodding at varying intervals, clearly enmeshed in deep conversation. Then the guide who'd healed me touched her mouth, motioning at Vernon.

Several minutes passed before the foursome left the kids behind with caretakers and stepped in our direction, approaching with caution. The younger two took the lead, holding their staffs up in front of their elders.

"Here we go," Tatara mumbled, returning with a smile that did little to veil her nerves. Dino and Jorgep made their way back also. Good. What remained of our caravan was back together. Despite my best efforts to remain race-focused, I'd grown attached to this motley crew, and didn't fancy facing whatever came next without them.

Herc stomped beside me, alert to the approaching dignitaries.

A row of warriors lined up behind the leaders, who stopped maybe thirty feet away. They stared, clearly sizing us up for threats. When nobody on our side made any sudden moves—though plenty of hands hovered over weapons—our guides slowly stepped aside.

The slender, long-haired elder held up a hand and spoke with the authority of a Queen, her fragmented sentences reaching my ears. "...People...safety...why...here?"

Raker of all people stepped forward without hesitation, annoyingly confident as he spoke slowly and methodically. "Thank you for the great kindness you've extended by bringing us here. We wish to be friends and find a way out of this forest."

The leaders' brows furrowed as they whispered amongst themselves.

I turned to my friends. "We'll never be able to communicate clearly like this." Vernon and I exchanged glances with Sarah. "Can our translators really be tweaked like you said?"

The Queen repeated her words much more slowly, as always seemed to be the go-to tactic, despite people knowing that speaking slower doesn't equal comprehension. But the message remained too choppy, too vague. Raker continued speaking for the group since nobody else seemed keen to do so at this point, and he spoke more forcefully with his second attempt.

Sarah nodded. "There's a learning mode. Since Vernon knows the written language, it's a simple matter of comparing dialects and uploading the new pronunciations into the database. It shouldn't be hard, as long as we can get them to do it."

Tatara, Dino, and Jorgep's eyebrows shot up. They spoke over one another, staring at Vernon. "Uh, what?"

"You can read their writing, Mr. Vernon?"

"What did I miss?"

Vernon motioned with a hand flick. "Griggs will fill you guys in. I'm going to try and speak with them before Raker wrecks our chances. Sarah and Finn, come with me."

I pointed at myself. "Um, why me? Sarah's the girl you need to do all the techy stuff."

Vernon's eyes twinkled. "You're approachable, for one. You have strong leadership skills. Lastly, I saw the way our guide fellow looked at you in the stream—when you asked if the water was safe—remember? He is keen on you and I need all the positive influence I can get."

I barked an awkward laugh. "Me, a leader? Are *you* hallucinating now?" My gaze flicked to Griggs whose expression was unreadable, then back to Vernon. "And wait—he's keen? I'm more than a piece of meat you know!" It dawned on me that as Neersoo descendants, these peoples were just as physically compatible with humans. *Do they know that?*

"I assure you I'm very lucid, Finn. Whether you realize your strengths or not, I have. And no, of course you're not a piece of meat, but there is nothing wrong with utilising one's…"

"Assets," Tatara offered bluntly.

"I was going to say *advantages*, but yes. Please consider the greater goal." He straightened his shoulders and cleared his throat. "Now, come on, let's get over there."

I didn't like it, but couldn't deny it made some sense. I shrugged. "Fine."

We made our way to the front of the line. Raker's eyes snaked over us when we appeared beside him, but continued trying to act out his words with awkward arm movements. Worst mime ever. The locals didn't look impressed by his attempt, either. Sadly, no matter how much either party said back and forth, the result didn't change.

Our guides bristled as we took a step toward them—weapons rising in defence. Sarah donned her breather and lowered her face shield to appear less threatening, having refused to take her suit off. If talks went south, she wanted immediate mech power at her disposal.

Vernon interrupted Raker with a loud throat clearing. "Pardon me, Raker. May I try?"

Raker's features pinched into a scowl, then the frown disappeared and he bowed out gracefully. "Of course. Good luck."

That was an oddly polite turn.

Vernon, who had collected a thin stick, took Raker's position at the forefront. Sarah and I flanked him, standing a pace behind.

Vernon waved to the indigenous representatives. Pointing to his eyes, he made sure they watched before bending to one knee. Then, recalling the select words our translators had picked up, he chose one and wrote it really big in the dirt. Vernon pointed to his drawing. "People."

Murmurs rippled through the racers at our backs, clearly baffled by how Vernon had just written in their language.

Griggs made calming motions with his hands, speaking in low tones. "Everyone, I promise you'll get answers soon. For now, please watch quietly."

The guides who'd saved us inched forward, stretching forward to get a better look. The man glanced at me momentarily before refocusing on the drawing. Once they saw what Vernon wrote, their eyes widened. The male pointed to the drawing, spouting a litany of words.

Vernon held his hands up in surrender, quickly pointing to his mouth and giving a firm head shake—essentially saying he didn't speak the language. Then he lowered his stick back to the dirt. He wrote another symbol-like word, saying, "Safety."

The pair of guides shared a confused look, but a hint of excitement brightened their eyes, too. They stepped closer, though their elders expressed discomfort with that action. Ignoring their protests, our feminine guide pointed at the ground, then circled her finger in the air. *Again.*

Vernon understood immediately, drawing a third word. "Here."

The woman found a twig and bent down, drawing a symbol of her own. She invited Vernon to read it, and he stood slowly, shifting incrementally closer to get a good look.

"Home."

Her face scrunched. She tapped the drawing, and said the word herself. "Mee-SAY-ee."

I swiftly turned off my translator. "Say it again, Vernon."

"MEE-saay-lee," he repeated.

"Yep. There's a slight difference." Turning my translator back on, I whispered. "Can you write, explaining who we are and that we mean no harm? That's the best place to start I think."

Vernon nodded, "I agree."

Sarah tapped buttons on her mech's digicuff. "I'll prep for a manual dialect sync."

Raker cut me a glare, but I ignored it. He was the least of my concerns right now.

Vernon wrote a sentence, monologuing aloud as he wrote. "Thank you for saving us. We are trying to reach the other side of the forest. We didn't know you or those creatures lived here. We mean no harm." He sat back on his heels, watching our host's reactions.

They nodded while reading, showing the barest of smiles.

Yes! Progress!

The woman pointed out one of Vernon's words, then curled her fingers like fangs in front of her teeth. "SEE-vers."

He pointed beyond the pillars and made the fangs in front of his own teeth, repeating, "SEE-vers." The guide nodded, and Vernon smiled, swivelling at the hip to share with the group. "The creatures that attacked us are called Seevers." More murmurs rippled.

Vernon wrote, then tapped his chest. "Vernon." He pointed to Sarah and me, stating each of our names in turn.

Unsure what the right greeting protocol was, I simply gave a wave. Sarah gave a lazy salute. Both blue-haired guides smiled in kind, as did the elders lingering behind.

The guide tapped her chest. "Andra." She wrote "Setso" to introduce the man by her side, then the word "brother." With deft strokes in the dirt, she announced the twin-tattoo'd elders as Queen and King. The three children watching from the sidelines were heirs to the throne as well.

Then Andra wrote one last string of words, before sweeping an arm towards the huts.

Vernon translated. "This is our village, Varu. We are the Venanti people."

"Venanti," I whispered to myself, awe-struck by what I was witnessing.

Vernon turned to us again. "Venanti means rebirth in the ancient language. I shall ask them about the dialect sync now. Hopefully soon we will *all* be able to communicate."

"Good luck." I crossed my fingers.

He set to work writing a combination of sentences. Andra and Setso moved in closer. We all watched anxiously as they exchanged missives. Finally, the pair walked back to their rulers to discuss the proposition. Moments later, the King and Queen retreated, leaving the clearing with their youngest children in tow. Andra wrote their reply.

"They've agreed," Vernon said with a beaming smile. He waved me and Sarah forward, and shouted to Griggs. "We are getting to work on the translators immediately. Can you explain to everyone what's going on? That would be wonderful."

"And keep an eye on Herc, please?" I added.

Griggs flipped a thumbs up. "Can do."

Setso must've seen the gesture. He pointed at me specifically, then twisted his hand into that same awkward thumbs up he'd brandished in the stream. The effort was endearing. I bit back a giggle that tickled my throat and returned the hand gesture. *Quirky fellow.*

Vernon, Sarah, and I walked to meet the younger Venanti royalty, stopping at a circle of log stumps resting beneath one of the few shade trees within the clearing. We sat across the circle from each other. Sarah patched into Vernon's cuff and together they raised a digiscreen packed with written words pulled from the universal translator's database. While they set things up, I smiled somewhat awkwardly at Andra and Setso, my hands wringing in my lap. I had no clue what to say—er, *try* to say.

"Vernon, how do I say *you have a lovely home?*"

"I'll write it for you." Vernon did as he said.

The beautiful young woman tilted her head graciously. "Kik-tay-naa."

"Kik-tay-naa…" I repeated, before looking at Vernon.

"It means thank you."

"Ah." I nodded. "Can you write your welcome?"

He scrawled the word, and I pointed to it enthusiastically. Andra smiled.

Setso gave me another thumbs up, which I of course returned. The man's smile shifted slightly, his expressive eyes locking on mine in an oddly hypnotic way. He pointed to one of Vernon's written words, then moved his hands in the air between us, as though running them over the sides of my face.

Setso immediately received a sharp word from Andra. He shot something back, which spurred a sibling glare-off.

I whispered to Vernon, "Uh, what did he say?"

"He pointed to the word *lovely*." Vernon winked.

"Oh." Heat crept into my cheeks as I fell back on the ol' nod and smile manoeuvre. Sarah gave me a nudge, but I refused to acknowledge it.

"I believe we are ready?" Vernon confirmed with Sarah, who gave the okay.

Oh, thank Goodness.

"The process will take a while," Sarah explained, taking a knee. "I've it set to record, so just work your magic and get them to read these words out loud."

Vernon nodded, then communicated this to Andra and Setso. They set to work, taking turns reading the words written on Sarah's digiscreen, methodical in their enunciation. After ten minutes passed, it was clear the tedious process was going to take longer than anybody expected. Twenty minutes after that, my stomach growled obnoxiously, causing Sarah and I to giggle.

"Shh…" Vernon whispered, slapping a finger across his lips. "We're recording."

I mouthed the word *sorry*, shrugging sheepishly.

The digiscreen scrolled slowly, rows of words evaporating once they reached the edge of the translucent page. Absent-mindedly, I rubbed my snarling belly, which might have started eating itself. Herc had to be hungry, too. I glanced at the other racers sitting in circles, chatting or chewing on grub. Herc's head was bowed—his nose in a container, munching happily on something. It couldn't be feed, since my saddle bags were still shock-locked.

My eyes found Raker in the heart of the gathering. He'd sabotaged vehicles without qualm, and he didn't seem to like Herc much. Would he dare poison my horse? But my alliance members were close by. Surely, they wouldn't allow such a thing to happen. Where was Griggs?

As if his ears had been burning, Griggs leaned back from behind Jorgep's broad girth and gave me a wave. I pointed to Herc, miming him eating, and Griggs immediately pointed to himself, mouthing the words *I fed him*. My shoulders relaxed. How thoughtful.

Griggs took a bite of food and popped a questioning thumbs up, seeking validation that what he did was okay. Internally, I groaned. *Another thumbs up*. Never before, had I been so keenly aware of its use. Setso stretched, seemingly antsy from sitting so long in one place, and the movement drew my eye. From his impressive physique, the man didn't seem the type to take it easy for long. In the next blink, his pronounced pectoral muscles flexed rhythmically—as if dancing. I snapped out of my daze, looking up and running right into his amused gaze.

Once again my cheeks flamed. *Oh, great. That's just perfect.*

My eyes flicked back to Griggs, who still needed a reply. Since shouting wasn't possible, I had no other recourse but to return a damn thumbs up.

Note to self… find a new gesture.

CHAPTER 21

Sarah disengaged from Vernon and hooked the cord up to my digicuff, initiating an update. The progress bar slowly filled up on the readout. I'd been ignoring my stomach's now hangry screams for the last half-hour, and I *really* hoped we were nearly done.

Vernon grasped the half-inch wide detachable buddy link located on the outer edge of his cuff and separated the slender ring with a *click*. Every unit had one—a failsafe. Manufacturers designed the feature with its own circuitry, so it would continue to enable communication in the case of malfunction.

Tentatively, Vernon placed the metal bracelet over Setso's wrist. The man stiffened, appearing uncertain, yet allowed it. The buddy link auto-fit to Setso's wrist and seconds later, a pinhole green light lit up. Setso's fingers dug beneath the cuff when it tightened, his words sharp and questioning.

Vernon reached out. "No, don't do that. It takes a minute to configure for new users. Just relax—" Setso recoiled, planting his feet in a fighting stance. Foreign words flew from his mouth and I didn't need a translator to understand he wanted us to stay back. Vernon braced for trouble.

I held out my hands in a calming gesture, speaking softly. "Easy now. It won't hurt you." Taking a tiny step closer, I made a show of disconnecting my own buddy link and attaching it to my other arm. The link auto-fit to my wrist in the exact same way Setso's had. "See?"

Setso's stance relaxed a touch, his head tilting to the side. Recognition crossed his features. "So, what is this thing called?" He asked, casting a wary eye upon the contraption.

A huge smile split my face in two. My cuff's status bar showed the upload was eighty percent finished and climbing. "My cuff isn't even fully updated and I can understand him!"

Setso grinned with amusement. "And I you."

"You can!" I exclaimed, then promptly reeled in my jubilation with an embarrassed laugh. "Sorry. This is just exciting."

Sarah nodded in agreement; her enthusiasm equally high.

Setso waved a hand. "No need to be sorry. This is a momentous achievement. I am pleased to meet all of you, and look forward to figuring out this unique situation we find ourselves in."

"So—" Vernon interjected, pointing at the buddy link. "This works like our translators do… but they can't be more than twenty feet away from their paired unit." He brandished his cuff to highlight his point. "When you want to speak to someone, you can wear their buddy link. But when you're done, you must return it. Make sense?"

Setso dipped his head. "I understand. Thank you."

"Perfect." Vernon gave a broad grin. "Nice to finally talk with you."

I can't believe this is really happening.

Sarah unplugged her cord from my cuff and gave it a pat. "All done, missy. You're good to go. Now, I'm off to update everybody else. Maybe *someday* I'll get to eat something."

"No. You just plop your butt down and start shoving food in your face. You gotta eat. Let them come to you and hook in. You're the one with the goods after all." I winked.

Sarah laughed, already walking away. "Love it. Deal."

"I'm right behind you." I turned back to Vernon and asked if he needed any more help—not that I'd been much help overall. For the most part, I'd just sat there being awkward. At least Setso and his dancing pecs seemed to get a kick out of it. *Piece of meat for the win.*

"Go have lunch," Vernon said, waving me off. He turned back to Setso. "I will need another hour to update all the racer's communicators."

Setso nodded. "A reasonable request." Before I could leave, he addressed both of us. "To ensure wellbeing for all, please ensure your people stay where you have been placed. Exploration is not permitted until the Queen and King extend an invitation. I also cannot guarantee anyone's safety should they leave this protected area."

"That is no problem. We have no desire to cause trouble," Vernon replied.

"I'll tell the others," I said, sharing one last smile before politely excusing myself.

The moment I reached our side of the clearing, I raised a hand and delivered Setso's message, then promptly bypassed everyone with a single focus in mind. After giving Herc a check-over and putting more water out for him, I pulled out two meal rations and ripped into one immediately. Eating was priority one. Sarah was surrounded by a crowd, her cord tethered to a digicuff at all times. With twenty plus people to update, she'd be busy for a while. Yet she didn't seem bothered. Sitting with Tatara, the two chatted flirtatiously. *Geeze, thank goodness the full two-hundred racers aren't here. She'd be updating for weeks.* I winced immediately, chastising myself as I took a seat on the violet-tinged grass. What a terrible thought to have. Two-hundred racers *should've* made it this far. Nobody should've died. This should never have happened.

Griggs, Jorgep, and Dino, whom Sarah had updated first thing, joined me, curiosity plastered on their faces. A few non-alliance racers inched closer, too, clearly wanting to join the conversation. We made room, for they had as much right to know what was going as we did. This wasn't just a race anymore. We were all in this together now.

"So, Miss Finn?" Jorgep blurted.

I proceeded to explain everything I'd witnessed the best I could. Vernon joined us part way through and chimed in here or there. As translators got updated, more and more racers wandered over to hear our takes on the Venanti. Not that we knew much yet. But we shared whatever tidbits of information we'd gleaned. Even Raker meandered closer, listening intently.

Figures. Not so tough now when you need someone else's help.

Before I knew it the Venanti leaders approached our group. They stopped in the same place as before, waiting for us to meet them. Though I still didn't necessarily feel I was the best choice for the job, I stood with Vernon and Sarah once more. Since we'd already spent time creating a rapport with the Venanti, it only made sense for us to continue on.

Sarah stepped out of her mech suit this time. "A show of good faith. Plus I just need a break," she muttered, tying a bandana over her head, looking even more badass than normal.

"And I'll need one more volunteer," Vernon said. "We need four updated buddy links to communicate with them… anyone?"

Raker raised his hand, strutting through the crowd.

Vernon faltered slightly. "Um…" Then he straightened his shoulders. "Thank you Raker, but for reasons I'm sure you clearly understand, I'll have to say no. Is there anyone *else?*"

The Ganglian's eyes narrowed, arms crossing. "I have just as much right as anyone to take part, and I assure you, I am perfectly capable." Curious murmurs swirled amongst the rest of the racers. I could tell by the way Raker's angular jaw clenched that he wasn't pleased.

Vernon cleared his throat, speaking in low tones. "Due to the less than admirable conduct you've exhibited, I prefer someone else to stand beside me as I speak with foreign dignitaries."

"Since when is healthy competition less than admirable? This is obviously *prejudice* against Ganglians. I'm a wealthy and respected businessman on my home planet. This is unacceptable." His eyes swept over the crowd of fellow racers, seeking support. When nobody was willing to join the fray, he turned back, opening his mouth to argue further. "Now you listen—"

Irritated, I stepped forward. "No, *you listen.* Healthy competition has nothing to do with it. We found your gold wrench. Someone who sabotages multiple racer's vehicles to get a leg up in this race shouldn't be speaking in good faith on behalf of the group. It's that simple."

His mouth closed; the movement as sharp as his eyes. I met his gaze, unflinching.

Griggs stepped forward, raising a hand. "I'll come with you guys! That makes four. Let's go." He walked between Raker and I, whispering into my ear, "Just step away."

"Thank you, Griggs, for volunteering." Vernon tilted his head graciously, then addressed the full group. "To confirm, safe passage out of this Sweep is still the main goal, correct?"

Unanimous shouts of affirmation rose up.

"Good then." He smiled. "Wish us luck! We'll fill you in the minute we're back."

Turning, the four of us approached the royal family, leaving Raker fuming in our wake.

Sarah leaned in close. "That was fucking perfect, what you said. Shut him right up. The guy still deserves a haymaker for what he did. I can't believe he had the nerve to question why."

"Yeah, I can't quite figure him out. Is it all an act, or is he really that delusional?" I shook my head, baffled, then broke into a girlish smile, "That *did* feel really good, though."

Both Vernon and Griggs slid me discreet smiles before we came to a stop before the dignitaries. Each of us detached our buddy links and passed them over. Setso took mine.

Andra slipped Griggs's over her wrist. "Vee-kee-tay." *Thank you.*

As soon as her link adjusted, the Queen raised her hand. "Hello race runners. Let us meet officially." She flicked her lightly wrinkled fingers between herself and the king. "We are the King and Queen of the Venanti people. What you see around you is a part of our home, which we protect fiercely." Her eyes levelled on us, pausing for effect.

Point taken.

The woman wore a sleeveless tunic-style leather garment, carrying herself with regal authority and a carefully restrained facial expression. She was definitely not pampered, though. Her hands were heavily callused, which signalled years of hard work. "You're already familiar with my children, Andra and Setso. They are heirs to the throne, and very capable warriors."

The Queen raised her brows. "And you are?"

"Oh, yeah." Sarah placed a hand on her chest. "I'm Sarah. A mechanic of sorts. No fancy title or anything." I loved how unfailingly *Sarah* she was. Following her lead, I gave my name, as did Griggs and Vernon.

"Good, good. Now, there are many things to discuss," the King stated. Despite his age—which looked the equivalent of mid-sixties in human years—I could see defined muscle poking out from the vest-like covering he wore. He sported a braided blue beard on his chin, and his hands were as calloused as his wife's. These royals clearly carried their own weight, regardless of status. He continued with confidence, "Let us start with what you are doing here. You've explained you are part of a race… What kind of race? Are you connected with the others who came before— from the community across the field?"

Griggs and I looked at each other. *The others who came before—Governus.*

Vernon stepped up to the plate. "We're not from that community, but our race started there. The race was held by a company called Governus, who must've believed the planet was vacant when they, uh," he faltered for the right words. "Well, when they claimed this planet as their own. For colonization and resource harvesting."

The royal's eyebrows raised, glancing at each other.

Vernon quickly added, "Like I say, they clearly didn't know you were in here. You see the Sweeps can't be scanned due to some kind of interference. Perhaps you know that already."

"Sorry, the Sweep?" Setso asked.

"Oh, yes, that's what they call this forest," Vernon clarified. "So, in order to win we must reach a new settlement called Novus on the other side. That's why we're here. They didn't know anything about you or the beasties—er, *Seevers.*"

Oh, it was clear they knew, but I kept my thoughts on the matter to myself. Now was not the time for that discussion. Though, more and more, it weighed on my mind. Knowing the people who sent us in here to our deaths might be waiting on the other side didn't sit nicely.

The Queen nodded. "Interesting. And yes, we're well aware of the interference. It causes mechanics to fail. The *Sweeps* as you called them, have a life force all their own—something our people have learned over generations."

Vernon raised his hands. "We are happy to share what little we know with you. I speak on behalf of all the racers present. We mean you no harm. We only want to leave with our lives."

Griggs, Sarah and I nodded in support. I hoped the newly discovered ancestral link lent extra credibility. I hadn't known Vernon for years, but from everything I'd experienced thus far, he seemed a very honourable man.

"I understand," the Queen replied simply. "So does this Governus company own the town we've seen spring up across the field?"

"Yes," I answered, giving Vernon a break. "They own all of Joya."

Andra raised a hand. "What is Joya?"

"I'm so sorry. You must call it something else—of course you would. Joya is the name Governus gave this planet when they discovered and claimed it, again, unaware you were here."

"Discovered. Claimed…" Andra scoffed with her brother, clearly irked. "This planet was inhabited by *our* ancestors hundreds of years ago. It is called *Xola.*"

Andra's tone left little room for discussion, and I wasn't about to argue. After all, the Venanti did arrive before Governus. "Xola. That's a nice name. What does it mean?"

Andra smiled. "Thank you. Yes, it means—"

"Perhaps those details can be discussed later," The Queen interjected brusquely. She turned her gaze back to us. "We assume, since you are not wandering in a stupefied daze, that breathing the air here has not affected you. Is it because of the contraptions you are wearing on your faces? Are they portable filtration devices?"

Andra's eyes lowered momentarily, but returned, perfectly mirroring her mother's business-like nature. Did I sense a hint of tension there? The look the queen gave her daughter was all too familiar to me. My father didn't hide his expressions of displeasure. Perhaps they'd merely had a recent squabble, but regardless I empathized with Andra. I definitely understood dealing with complicated family dynamics.

"They're called breathers," Griggs jumped into the conversation, and demonstrated by pinching the releases on the nose and either side of his lower jaw, removing the appliance.

"See? We were *very* affected by the air, which is why we have to wear these now."

The royal foursome leaned in to inspect the breather.

"The air doesn't affect you?" Sarah asked.

"It did, long ago," the King replied amiably. "The technology our ancestors possessed was far inferior to what you have. Thankfully, our bodies were able to adapt eventually." The Queen's eyes met his and he refrained from explaining further. "We are also curious to learn more about the creatures you keep for riding. What are they?"

Their eyes flitted between Herc and the Bleenad, and I fought to keep my eyes from narrowing. It seemed our mounts had made the list of questions they wanted answers to. But why were they so curious? Remaining friendly, I answered, "The really big one is a bleenad, owned by a racer named Jorgep. The one with the metal legs is a horse, from Earth. He belongs to me."

Setso's brows raised. "Oh, he's yours? Is he a friendly beast? Useful?"

"He's not a beast." I realised my brows had pinched, smoothing them. "But, yes, he is friendly and useful—gets me wherever I need to go. Do you know of Earth at all?"

He nodded. "We have access to a limited amount of records and they do include mentions of Earth, a rudimentary non-contact planet. It's clear that information is outdated. However, there are no notations of horses in our historical information. He is a fascinating creature."

A rudimentary planet. The words rubbed like sandpaper, but I focused on the fact that their information *was* outdated. These people were marooned here a very long time ago. Shifting my feet, I hoped his interest in Herc was innocent. "Thank you."

A painful silence lapsed between both parties. The royals exchanged meaningful glances accompanied by minuscule facial tics, communicating silently as only family members could. It felt odd to be standing there, watching them deliberate our fate. Would they continue to provide solace until we could plan an exit strategy, or cast us out again? I didn't know how some of these rough-around-the-edges racers might take such news. The what ifs were agonizing. We had no way to know if anything we'd said was beneficial to our case or not.

Then, the Queen nodded. She pressed her palms together in front of her chest. "Welcome to our home, race runners. We'd like to propose a deal."

CHAPTER 22

"**A** deal?" Griggs asked. "What did you have in mind?"

The Queen smiled graciously. "There's plenty of time to talk of such things. Let us get to know each other better while we show you around our village. It will be dark soon. I can't imagine your group will wish to press onward, am I right?"

Everyone shook their heads in tandem.

"I didn't think so. We shall provide secure sleeping accommodations."

Sarah and I exchanged dubious looks. The vague promise of a deal after leading us who knows where to sleep made me a touch nervous... I typed a quick message into my digicuff, discreetly presenting the display to her. TRAP?

She tilted her own cuff back towards me. PSYCHO KILLERS?

A deep shiver ran through my body at the thought. But the kindness I'd seen shining in Andra and Setso's eyes—even in the King's, cast doubt on such horrific possibilities. Vernon saw our messages but said nothing, his expression unreadable.

"Please give us a moment to speak with our group. Thank you." Griggs turned, motioning for us to follow with a flick of the wrist. The racers were waiting with rapt attention, crowding around us immediately. Voices mingled and toppled over each other to ask questions.

Vernon waved his hands. "Okay, okay, quiet down." But the din lessened only slightly.

"Be quiet so they can fill us in," one racer said.

Another chirped, "C'mon, listen to the man speak."

Then a shrill whistle sliced the air, and Sarah barked, "Shut up!"

Silence fell and Vernon nodded to Sarah. "Ah, thank you for your assistance…" He turned back to address the rest of the racers. "Now, we had a pleasant conversation. They were polite and wish to show us their home. They have accommodations for us, and expressed a desire to offer a deal, which shows promise. However, they were a bit vague in sharing details—"

Raker stepped forward. "Cut to the chase already. What is this deal they propose?" A few murmurs of assent rose up. I bit my tongue as Vernon cast the unlikeable racer a wry glance.

"Patience Mr. Raker. *As I was about to say…*" he emphasized. "They didn't tell us the details of the deal they're offering. They wish to show us their home and get us settled for the night before we discuss business matters, it seems."

The voice of Cala rang out. "Why wouldn't they say what the deal is?"

More voices chimed in, speaking over one another. "Show us their home *where?*"

"Where are they taking us?"

"Sounds like they're hiding something."

"I don't like it."

Raker crossed his arms. "They certainly aren't putting their best foot forward, are they? I agree with our fellow racers in their concern. These locals—"

"Venanti. They are called the Venanti," I clarified.

My nemesis sneered at me. "Yes, these *Venanti* don't seem trustworthy. We know nothing of their village—*Varu*, is it? It is prudent to consider they may have ulterior motives."

Sarah scoffed. "Well, no shit Sherlock. Only an idiot wouldn't be thinking about that."

Raker's face twisted with simultaneous confusion and irritation. "Sherlock? What are you talking about?" He looked around, and other confused faces stared back at him.

"Sherlock. You know? Like, the treasured mystery detective?" Sarah waved a hand, clearly realizing she was speaking to the wrong crowd. "Never mind."

Raker spat, "Spare me your Earth garbage." He turned his back to face the crowd. "See now, friends, if I had been the one to speak with these leaders, I would have answers! Real tangible information that would allow us to make rational decisions. I propose we return to speak with them again *before* agreeing to anything. Before going anywhere! Again, we know nothing about these people. We must demand proper answers, and I will gladly do what these people failed to do." He pointed at Vernon, Sarah, Griggs and I.

I stepped forward, fists clenched. But an arm stretched out like a bar across my torso. My eyes snapped to Griggs who shook his head, his eyes silently imparting *don't do it*.

"Put your arm down," I whispered, enunciating very clearly.

He leaned closer, whispering back, "It's not the right time, Finn. If we want the Venanti to trust us, starting a brawl is not the way to do it... no matter how justified."

I glanced over at the Venanti gathered at the opposite side of the clearing. Countless pairs of eyes watched us closely. The man had a point. Clenching my teeth, I nodded. "Fine." *But I'm not putting up with much more of his bullshit.* Raker's eyes bore into mine, a gloating smile playing at his thin lips, and I made a point of glaring back. He needed someone to knock him down a peg, and in this moment, I really wanted to be that person.

Vernon raised his hands again. "Listen, we can absolutely go back and talk to them again. But demanding answers is likely not the best tactic. We are at their mercy, and trying to force them to tell us more will only create animosity. Is that what you really think we need right now?" His words rang true, filled with logic. Murmurs swelled and rippled through the group.

"You would have us play nice and be led into some trap?" Raker shot back.

"They might genuinely wish to show us hospitality."

"After all, I bet they don't get many visitors around these parts," Jorgep's jovial tone broke through the tension. "Maybe they want to show off the place." That earned a few chuckles.

I shot Jorgep a smile, thankful for the interruption.

Tatara spoke up, her words crisp and clear. "What other choice do we have but to go along with it? *Really*. Think about it."

"We need their help to get out of this place, and we definitely don't want to get kicked out. Do you want to be out there with those things at night?" I added to the argument. More murmuring ensued. Statements and questions sliced through the air.

"They've got a point."

"Yeah, I don't wanna get kicked out."

"But what if they kill us anyway?"

Raker thrust a hand into the air. "Yes! Exactly. Trusting these people too quickly gives them the upper hand, and we risk losing. I'm not willing to lose. I don't lose."

"They already have the upper hand, Raker!" Griggs shot back. "They had it the moment they saved us." The Ganglian made a show of rolling his eyes, yet didn't argue.

Vernon nodded at Griggs like an approving uncle. "It's true. We don't have much choice but to go along with what they want. If we push back too hard it may offend them. If we don't go with them, it might also offend them. We all know what our chances of survival would be if they cast us out. We can't claim any free land if we're dead… I suggest you keep that in your mind."

A hush fell over the group and I could practically hear the gears turning inside everybody's heads. Then Dino's deep voice blared like a loudspeaker, making me flinch.

"Get your heads in the game. Without the Venanti and their fancy glow sticks, we'd be dead. Plain and simple. So, what do we have to lose?" He stood tall and swept his gaze across the entire group. "I say we take our chances with 'em. Follow their lead. If they don't kill us, then maybe they'll help us get the hell out of this Sweep. Alright?"

The racers looked around at each other, nodding and whispering.

I flashed Dino a smile. As hard as it was to relinquish control in this circumstance, that's exactly what we all had to do. The Venanti held the keys to our survival now. "I agree. Unless anyone else has a miracle solution to get us past the Seevers out there, I think we should be polite and accept the King and Queen's invitation to tour their home."

"Nobody cares what you say, human," Raker declared.

That's it. "Fuck right off, Raker," I hissed. "The Conduit Gates helped a lot of planets too, okay? They've provided reliable and safe travel for many who couldn't before. Your people are just pissy because their piracy and bootlegging got railroaded. Get over it already!"

Raker's eyes opened wide as chuckles rumbled.

"Hear, hear," Sarah patted me on the back, but my focus remained on Raker. On his hands, specifically. His fingers twitched, hovering above the grip of his pistol. *He wouldn't...* If the man had any kind of brain in his head, survival should trump a personal vendetta. But, just to be safe, my hands slid toward the guns strapped to my own hips.

Vernon cleared his throat in an exaggerated manner. "Yes, well, now that the matter has been fully discussed, shall we put it to a vote?"

All heads nodded in unison, and Raker's hand relaxed.

"Good then. Those in favour of accepting the invitation?" Vernon raised a hand. One by one the others followed suit, until it was clear the "Aye's" took the majority. Only a couple of racers withheld their vote, one of those being Raker. Likely only out of spite.

"The Aye's have it. We will accept the invitation. Sit tight until I give the signal—I'll wave when it's safe for all of you to join us." Vernon turned, heading back to the centre of the clearing. Sarah, Griggs, and I followed close behind. It was a relief to walk away.

Griggs waggled his eyebrows up and down at me. "Well said, lady."

I couldn't keep a smile from tugging my lips. "Ugh, I probably just made it worse, though." An odd sensation of déjà vu arose. This was eerily similar to how I'd felt the night I stole Herc—that it was necessary, yet by taking him, my father would only hate me more.

Griggs tilted his head to my ear, whispering, "Naw, Raker deserved it. Whatever happens, Finn, I'm with you, okay?" I didn't have to take any leaps to believe him. The lingering warmth of his breath made my skin tingle, and memories invaded my mind. Vivid images of exploring hands and lips crashing together elicited a very different kind of sensation. *Shit...*

I took a step away, smiling as casually as possible. "Thanks Griggs. It's really nice to know you've got my back." His eyes didn't leave mine fast enough and I resorted to fidgeting with the cuff on my wrist. "Yep, very sweet. And I've got yours, too."

"I know." He smiled, then finally turned away.

The Venanti leaders waited for us. As we strolled up, Setso made a point of grinning at me, his entire vibe oozing charm, and I groaned internally. I just couldn't find any relief.

Once we were within range for the buddy links to work again, Vernon spoke on our behalf. "We're thankful for your kindness and accept the invitation to see your home."

The royal family smiled in response, and the Queen clapped her hands. "Wonderful. The rest of the racers will be coming too, yes?"

"Of course, Queen," Griggs assured.

"Very good. Gather your belongings and come along." With that, the Queen walked away with the King at her side.

Vernon turned and waved to our group. "Come on everyone! Bring your gear."

Jorgep and I looked at each other, his uncertain expression a mirror to my own. What would we do with our mounts? There's no way I'd leave Herc behind. Sarah's digicuff message scrolled back through my brain. *Psycho killers?* If they ate Seevers, what else might they eat?

Andra and Setso lingered until everyone caught up. They remained buddy linked in so they could greet the others. "It is nice to meet all of you," Andra said. "Please follow this way."

I raised my hand. "Excuse me? I don't want to leave my horse here alone. Can I bring him, or is that not allowed?"

Jorgep pointed to his Bleenad, his feelers waving like a flag. "Same for me. Of course, sir and miss—" He bowed his head respectfully to each of them. —"If it is a problem, I am quite happy to stay behind."

Andra and Setso looked at the animals in question, then Setso shrugged. Andra motioned to Herc and Keemi with a hand flick. "The tunnels should accommodate them. They can come."

Wait—tunnels?

Jorgep and I both muttered "Thank you" at the same time, then rushed to collect our mounts. Herc looked exhausted. His head hung low, and the sparkle that usually lit his natural eye was absent, his eyelid drooping. I couldn't wait to peel his tack off, brush him down, and let him rest for the night. He needed it—deserved it after everything we'd been through.

I found myself wondering why he'd stuck by me, even protected me, instead of running. Could he understand obligation in the same way a human could? Was it his way of saying thank you for saving his life after he fell from that cliff?

Herc nibbled at the knotted hair sticking out from beneath my cowboy hat as I collected the reins. He rested his head over my shoulder for a moment and I smiled, patting his neck. *Or maybe it was out of love.* Though I'd never know for sure, I chose to believe it was love.

"I feel the same, boy," I murmured, then led him across the clearing.

"Ready?" Andra asked.

Being filthy and exhausted, nobody argued.

Our royal guides lead us past the shacks to a well-worn path mostly hidden by foliage. After walking about a hundred feet, the pathway opened into a different clearing filled with lush gardens. At the far end of it sat another row of the glowing pillars. Somewhere in the distance a cascade of snarls rang out, and I felt better knowing those pillars protected this place.

What appeared to be a substantial hole bit into the ground up ahead. A collection of uneven stacked stones formed thick walls around it, save for a generous opening on one side. Across the clearing, three stone stacks rose up from the ground, smoke wafting from each one.

Curious.

Nearing the construction, I realized it wasn't just a hole, but a walkway descending gradually into the ground. *They weren't kidding about tunnels.* The walls were supported by sturdy logs and cross-beams, appearing similar to historic mine shafts on Earth. Compared to the self-adjusting metal stent-supports currently used for mining—where you just hit a button and watch them expand to fit—this construction method seemed quite rudimentary. Yet, no less effective. I certainly hoped so, anyway. A collapse would be disastrous.

The walkway, just wide enough to squeeze three abreast, descended via what looked like wide platform-like steps. Each one was made of solid rock slabs and built into the grade going down until pitch darkness marred the view—which was about thirty feet or so in. I assumed they continued the rest of the way, however far that was. A stark sense of unease settled over me. No matter how hard I tried to dispel it, it sat there, heavy and cold like poured cement. And I wasn't alone. As if on cue, the group paused—a myriad of uncertain eyes glancing around.

Setso did a double take between us and the entrance, raising his eyebrows. He then swivelled to address the group. "I assure you it is not dark the whole way down. There is light. You need not be nervous. Our community rests beneath the surface for safety reasons. We sleep much better not hearing the Seever's annoying night time calls." He chuckled, then moved his arm in a sweeping arc, leading us forward. "This way."

CHAPTER 23

The Seever calls faded away in the tunnel, as did all other noise, save for the rhythmic *clopping* of Herc's metallic hooves and Sarah's heavy mech footfalls echoing off the walls.

Setso stayed tethered to me and fell into step by my side. Griggs followed with Andra, while the others formed a comfortable three-by-three train behind. The Queen, King and most of the other Venanti onlookers had disappeared, presumably having descended already.

A shadowy line presented itself where the light fizzled. Only darkness existed beyond that line, with no further sign of illumination. Icy fingers of fear clawed into me as my thoughts whirled unchecked. What if this actually was some kind of trap? Setso had promised light, but what if he'd lied? What if the Venanti could see in the dark, leaving us helpless? All kinds of horrors could await us down there. Based on Vernon's ancestry, our communications, and the fact they'd both saved and healed us, I couldn't truly fathom danger awaiting us below. Yet irritating worries kept popping in anyway. Plus, how would Herc handle the darkness?

A message indicator flashed on my cuff. Discreetly looking, I read a note from Sarah.

THIS IS CREEPY AS HELL. WE'RE TOTALLY GONNA DIE. BEEN NICE KNOWING YA, FINN.

I glanced back at my metal-clad friend and she tipped her head, giving me an overly dramatic salute. Before the darkness swallowed us, I quickly typed back, WE'RE NOT GOING TO DIE. I'M LIKE 95% SURE OF IT.

WHAT ABOUT THE OTHER FIVE PERCENT?

WE'LL BE FINE!

The light slowly asphyxiated like a candle deprived of air.

A swell of panic rose, depositing itself in my throat, thick and unmoving. Herc snorted, his green eye casting a faint glow on the wall beside his head. I cooed softly, "Just relax, buddy. I'm right here. Everything's going to be okay." In the last vestiges of murky shadow, I noticed Setso watching me with curious eyes.

"You speak to your horse like he is human. Like a friend."

I nodded. "Well, that's because he is my friend. He's an amazing animal."

A muted haze of blue appeared just ahead. Rows of wooden boards with hooks lined the walls, and countless Venanti staffs hung from them. Setso deposited his own staff, as did Andra.

I swallowed hard. "Listen, Setso, my horse needs light in order to walk further. I don't want him tripping." Though I tried to hide it, a note of apprehension trembled in my voice.

Setso's eyes widened, then his brows pinched together. He glanced around all of at the barely visible racers. "Race runners, I assure you there will be light!"

"Soon?" I dared ask. By his abrupt tone, I worried he'd been offended. Angering our hosts was the opposite of our group's goal, yet, it was kind of important information to know.

"Soon. Follow me." Setso stepped forward.

I took a deep breath as my right foot crossed the final threshold into darkness. The violet-tinged sky disappeared beneath the upper lip of the tunnel behind us as an Inky black swallowed my leg and arm, then enveloped the rest of me.

Looking back, the remnants of light lingered on the steps like a fading memory. Herc's eye did little to improve the situation.

He snorted again, nonplussed.

"It's okay, boy" I murmured. As we walked deeper, a musty earthen smell crept into my awareness. It reminded me of freshly ploughed fields before seeding back on Earth.

"You think Herc will be alright?" Griggs asked from behind. I heard him try to comfort Herc with a few audible hand pats—a thoughtful gesture.

"I hope so."

The air temperature shifted, cooler with the absence of light. It was a welcome contrast to stifling heat and humidity. Goosebumps actually rose on the exposed skin of my arms.

I couldn't believe how dark it was, but I hadn't stumbled yet. The realization surprised me, and that's when I noticed the next steps down were visible. *What the…?* I couldn't see the hand right in front of my face, yet somehow, I saw exactly where I was walking.

Others noticed too, their murmurs bouncing off of the walls.

I looked at Setso—or at least, in his general direction. I couldn't see him. "How is this possible? Are the steps themselves illuminated?" My eyes scoured the substrate beneath my feet, unable to pinpoint any specific source of illumination. Each platform step glowed blue, the hue similar to that of the Venanti stones. This light was far weaker though—just bright enough to outline the stairway. And oddly enough, the glow shifted like sand when I stepped on it.

"Yes, they are," Setso replied, a smile audible in his tone. "Shall I turn it up?"

Beneath our feet, the stairs burst into life. Light activated on the pathway, growing and intensifying until brightness rivalled that of any top-grade lumen strip. Our moving bodies cast shadows that danced over the sediment and beam-laden ceiling. It was then I realized the stairs were covered in a layer of finely crystalized rock.

Setso appeared serene beside me, like he'd been meditating. He moved his hand up and down, adjusting the brightness level until he felt it was adequate. Then his eyes swung my way, finishing the move with a wink. "I told you there would be light."

Simultaneously shocked and awestruck, I asked, "Did *you* do that?"

Setso's shoulders straightened with pride. "I asked for it to happen, yes. It is the stones that have the power. We just guide it."

"Really? That's incredible." I'd always dreamed of having some kind of superpower. Like unlimited strength, invisibility, or moving things with my mind. Or was this ability more like magic? "Have you always been able to do that?" Enthralled, I leaned in to hear his answer.

Setso mirrored me, also leaning in. "No, our abilities kind of grew. It's a long story—one best told by the King and Queen. I wouldn't want to spoil things by sharing it now."

Griggs cleared his throat, making his presence known behind us. "Sounds like a hell of a story there. Can't wait to hear it." Setso and I leaned away from each other.

But I couldn't curb my enthusiasm. Without thinking, I nudged the prince in a playful way. "Count me in for lessons on how to do that, okay?" He looked a little surprised and I swiftly kicked myself for acting too familiar. I averted my gaze, terrified he'd taken offence.

Then an elbow gently nudged me back. Setso's eyes recaptured mine. "If it were possible, I would love to tutor you." He flashed that charming smile of his.

Oh no, did he think I was flirting before?

Setso continued, "Then perhaps we could—"

A scoff escaped Griggs lips, which he promptly modified into a ragged cough. He pointed to his throat, his face scrunching up. "Something's tickling my throat in this cave. Geez. So, hey, Finn, you want me to take a turn linking up with Setso? Herc's been enjoying the pats I've been giving him, but I bet he'd love yours a whole lot more. Here, I'll switch with you."

I shook my head, irked by his insistence. "I think he's okay. Thanks though."

Setso tapped the buddy link on his wrist. "I enjoy linking with you, Finn."

Griggs took off coughing again and I glared.

Andra caught her brother's attention, speaking a curt word the translator didn't recognize. He shot back a few more mysterious words, then faced me again—his charming smile firmly in place. *Maybe I should switch with Griggs.* I sure hoped Setso wasn't 'keen' on me, as Vernon had put it. I'd already sworn off a romantic *anything* with Griggs during this race, and I wasn't about to hook up with an alien man from a strange forest on an uncharted planet.

I looked over my shoulder to Sarah, whom I desperately wanted to walk beside right about now. Unfortunately, Jorgep and Tatara were keeping her company, the three of them engrossed in quiet conversation. Dino and Vernon had mixed in with the other racers, while Raker walked beside a racer who's name I didn't know yet—one of many. He wasn't far behind Griggs, though. Definitely close enough to overhear our conversation.

"Up ahead! Look!" A shout stole my attention.

A hazy luminescence emanated from down the tunnel. A golden hue flickered like lamplight, the shine highlighting an archway with steps leading through it. The citrine colour intermingled with the ambient blue glow, creating an aura of green light between us and the arch. That must be the bottom. After that last interaction with Setso, I doubted even more that he and his people had insidious plans for us. But for good measure, I'd still keep my head on a swivel.

Within a few minutes, we passed beneath the archway at the base of the stairs and rounded a corner, which opened up into a grand cavern. A network of sturdy looking supports and cross beams bolstered the generous space, additionally braced by tree trunks in several places. At either end of the cavern rested three more tunnels—hallways to somewhere. A long wall sat opposite the entrance, built up with stacked rock and mortar. Three arched fireplaces were spaced evenly across it, each with cooking pots hanging inside. Struck by a deliciously savoury aroma, I inhaled deeply. Whatever they had simmering, I wanted to taste it. I also wondered how they weren't getting smoked out all the way down here. The three rock stacks I saw above ground came to mind, and it made perfect sense. *Smart.*

Continuing my visual inspection, my eyes landed on numerous wooden tables spread throughout the space. Plank benches lined either side; their lengthy tops worn smooth from use.

"This is a dining hall," I said, more to myself than anyone else.

"Correct," Setso replied, then addressed everyone. "Please wait here."

He disappeared with Andra into the watching crowd of Venanti. I continued gawking, inspecting everything within sight. Colourful flowing fabrics that showcased swirling patterns draped across the ceiling, while uplifting hand-painted landscapes hung from the walls. All together, the décor created an inviting atmosphere. This was a bustling community.

My 5% doubt dwindled to zero.

As if on cue, a message pinged from Sarah. *MAYBE NOT PSYCHO KILLERS.*

I grinned back at her, typing, AGREED.

The space was packed with people. In this subterrain village there were elders, teenagers, and young children of all ages. *I wonder what Governus is thinking of all this? Will they get reception this far below ground?* I reminded myself to ask Sarah about that.

However, was them seeing through my eyes even okay at this point? I'd signed a contract consenting to being monitored, but the Venanti hadn't signed any privacy waivers. I wasn't sure I liked the idea of Governus seeing all of this, given their less-than-honest assurances thus far. I mean, they couldn't have known about these people already. With a discovery that huge, surely they'd have said something... Or would they? I wasn't so sure about anything anymore.

All I knew was, I was dying to know what was happening back in Egan. What was Governus doing about this disaster? Had they sent in any rescue crews to extract us yet?

A group of children giggled, pointing and whispering, their focus drawn by Keemi and Herc. Despite the bizarreness of this situation, I slapped a smile on my face and waved to them. The simple action reminded me of when I'd first arrived on Joya. That seemed so long ago.

The kids gasped and giggled, ducking into the crowd. What was it like for them here? Had they ever seen someone of another race before? I was desperate to learn more about the Venanti. My exhausted horse didn't seem to share the same enthusiasm, though. Herc stomped and huffed, and I couldn't blame him for feeling uneasy. Who wouldn't? Tucking the reins under my armpit, I gave his neck several reassuring strokes. It was the best I could do for now.

The King and Queen appeared and made their way to the front of the crowd. People shifted out of their way to let them pass. Andra, Setso, and their three younger siblings, followed close behind. Once they reached us, the royal family stopped, smiling enthusiastically.

Vernon, Tatara, and two other racers provided the oldest four with buddy links.

"I'd like to extend an official welcome to Varu!" the Queen said, her voice strong and confident as her tattooed arms splayed wide. "We, the Venanti people, offer our hospitality by providing you shelter and protection for the night. We also look forward to learning more about one another with the hopes that a mutual friendship can be forged. Is that agreeable?"

Raker strode forward before anybody else could. "Yes, Queen, that sounds wonderful. On behalf of all the racers present, we thank you for your kindness. And I would like to personally offer you and the King *my* time and *wealth* of knowledge. I am at your disposal." He bowed his head, then glanced back at the group with a smug smile on his face.

I sighed, relieved. At least he didn't say anything offensive.

The Queen nodded. "That's lovely. Now, race runners, let us show you the rest of our home, and of course, where you will sleep for the night." With a crisp flick of her hand, she waved for us to follow.

Sleep. I'd never been so happy to hear that word.

CHAPTER 24

Khana stood in front of the holo-conference unit; her arms crossed impatiently as Steel strode into the communications room. His thick boots pounded against the polished tile floor. Having a lower half made of metal components, the man carried extra weight in his walk.

"You summoned me, sister?" His voice was gruff, tired.

"Took you long enough," Khana said, hands dropping to the console's control board. "Good thing it wasn't an emergency." Her fingers punched commands, and within moments, two separate images phased into existence, hovering just above the metallic console. It was their siblings—perfectly photo-real likenesses, though half the size of the true beings themselves.

"Good thing," Steel replied drolly. He sauntered up to the shimmering holograms. "What did I miss?"

"I thought you might wish to be present when I update our brothers about the current *situation* we find ourselves in. Was I wrong to assume?" She raised her brows in challenge, knowing full well he hated speaking with their brothers. Like herself, Steel only put up with their kin because they owned equal shares of Governus. Curse their parents for believing this business could somehow reunite the family they'd systematically eroded through decades of narcissism and abuse. Pitting child against child to win favour. Punishing whoever failed their twisted tests under the guise of pushing them towards greatness. No, their family broke long ago. But maybe their parents knew that, and this was the last inflicted torture upon the offspring they despised.

Steel met her gaze. "Let's just get this over with."

Khana smirked, punched a button and spoke with a clear voice. "Seema, Garido—we're both here. Link in whenever you're ready."

The somewhat tinny voice of Seema emitted from the speakers. "Linking now."

Previously frozen images on the holo-display pixelated while the connection solidified. The signal was much weaker here on Joya, unsurprising given they were thirty days from the nearest colonized planet. They'd been working on getting more integral services arranged. A few Transport Conduit Gates would be useful, which would bring in more regular trade shipments and supplies. Communications beacons could be erected as well, which would dramatically improve lag time and glitching. However, the worst part about new planetary claims was dealing with the Gala-Rights Org. To coin a human phrase, all the *red tape* was a nightmare.

"Hello brothers," Khana said with a polite nod. "Can you see us?" She could see them clearly, both calling in from separate ships.

"We can, sister…. Steel." A twinge of distaste laced Garido's tone saying Steel's name. "So, what news do you have of the race proceedings? Have you found anything of use yet?"

Khana nodded. "That is the reason I called this meeting. We have discovered something quite interesting indeed. The stick with the glowing objects we saw on the charting team's feed—the one that scared off the creatures—well, we've confirmed those objects are in fact stones like we thought. Many stones. And they have power beyond anything we imagined."

Seema stroked his chin. "Hmm, yes, that is interesting. Mineable?"

Steel walked forward. "Everything is mineable. You should know that."

Khana smirked. Garido glared—not a shock. It didn't matter what Steel said—Garido always hated it. Just like Steel would forever blame Garido for causing the supposed accident that took his legs away.

"Fine then. Mine it. Or is there something else?" Seema barked.

Khana took a deep breath, glancing around the room. "There's a slight complication. I've formulated a plan, but as our partnership dictates, you should be kept apprised and allowed an opportunity to weigh in. The situation is very delicate. Our claim is now under threat, especially given the Gala-Rights Org's penchant for muddying the waters by advising parties of their legal rights." She punched a few more buttons on the console, bringing up a third holo beside the other two. Two humanoid forms from one of the racer's live feeds appeared—a male and female each brandishing a staff covered with the blue stones.

Seema and Garido'd eyes widened, both leaning in to get a better look.

Khana waved her hands over the hologram as if she were presenting a prize. "We've discovered an entire indigenous population living within the Sweep. They use the stones to keep the creatures away. I don't yet know all of the uses the stone may have. But I believe they hold great value." Her brothers stared, their expressions a satisfying mixture of shock, awe, and dread. Khana's gaze levelled on them, her smile mirthless. "Gentlemen, meet our complication."

***

As a group, the racers followed behind the royals and a handful of other community members. The Queen requested the majority

257

of her people, including her young children to remain in the common area for the sake of efficiency and space. I felt thankful. Though these inner tunnels were as wide as the one we'd entered through, and just tall enough to let Keemi pass, they still felt confined. Perhaps it was being underground that increased the sense of claustrophobia. Maybe I was simply too used to the wide-open spaces back home.

Tatara walked beside Sarah, who'd lowered her face shield, the two chatting away. Jorgep and Dino lingered in the middle of the pack, discussing something of great interest with two Venanti they'd buddy linked with. Griggs and Setso walked with me, while Andra and Vernon kept up with the Queen and King in the lead. Herc flinched whenever a shadow flitted across the lantern-lit tunnel walls. Probably seeing things. Getting attacked by bloodthirsty Seevers would put anyone on edge. When he wasn't twitching, my horse's head sagged from exhaustion. The mind did funny things when sleep-starved.

That reminded me of the time my ex-boyfriend Reed and I stayed up all night gambling in the local AYOR District—short for *At Your Own Risk*—on Hyka Prime. Being an ice planet, it never stopped snowing there. As usual he counted cards and fed me discreet directives while I played the hands as a distraction. When we'd finally hopped a hover back to our rental, I remember being so tired that every flake looked like a meteor flying at me.

We arrived in another cavern—a slightly smaller one, filled with well-used toys and a multitude of desks. Posters, drawings, and other schoolwork lined the walls. A woven grass mat dyed several different colours acted as a makeshift rug in the centre of the room. I envisioned children sitting cross-legged, listening to their teacher with rapt attention.

"This is our school," The Queen announced, a proud smile beaming on her face. "Learning is very important to us here. Our younglings are the future, after all. I myself enjoy teaching the odd class from time to time. A good leader makes an effort to connect with their people, both young and old."

Vernon nodded. "Impressive, and I'm sure your people adore you for doing so."

The Queen's smile widened.

Well said, Vernon. So far, even without the genetic connection, he'd proven himself a more than adequate emissary. The royals seemed to have a genuine affinity for him.

"Just up ahead is our most treasured common area." The King guided us onward into a moderate-sized room. I stared in awe following him inside. Every wall was slathered with book laden shelves, and each ladder-like structure was built unique from the next. None were straight. They'd been crafted specifically to fit snugly against the contoured walls of the cave. The room was just barely large enough for us all to fit, Herc included. Jorgep wisely kept Keemi in the hall.

"Welcome to the library!" The King announced. "We value learning and reading above all else, and we are forever indebted to our ancestors who had the forethought to preserve these written works. Using a combination of replicated paper and ink, an industrial laser printer, and also paper they made themselves, they transposed every book and historical record into one of these volumes. An invaluable resource. If they had not done so before their ship's power core broke down, the vast data collection stored in its memory banks would've been lost."

"Wow, that must've taken a long time," I mumbled, more to myself than to anybody else.

But Griggs heard. "No kidding." His eyes scanned over the rows of books.

Setso rocked on the balls of his feet. "The project spanned years—the books created whenever there was time. Our way of life might seem simple, but you'd be surprised how busy we stay on a regular basis. It takes a lot of work to keep Varu thriving."

I smiled reassuringly, lest he felt we looked down upon them. "I don't doubt it at all."

The King addressed Vernon. "Since you can read our language, cousin… you are more than welcome to peruse any of these books during your stay."

Vernon's face lit with appreciation. "That is very kind of you. Thank you."

"You're welcome." The King gave Vernon a firm pat on the shoulder, then led his wife by the hand back into the hallway. Their voices echoed down the hall as they explained how other tunnels lead to various private sleeping quarters. The others followed, but I lingered a moment.

I took one last look at the cluttered shelves, feeling my heart ache. How terrified the survivors must have been when they landed here only to realize they'd never leave—wouldn't see their own planet again. Living with limited resources and deadly predators hunting them at all times. I tried to put myself in their shoes and couldn't. I'd been through some trouble in my life— gotten myself into a serious pickle and felt pretty damn low. But it all seemed like child's play compared to what the Venanti must have experienced.

"Finn, are you okay?" Griggs asked from behind.

I looked back at him and spied Setso hovering near the library's entrance. "Yeah, I'm good." Turning, I led Herc out into the hall, his sluggish hooves plodding along. Both men joined me and we trailed the rest of the group strolling through the cave-equivalent of a transport ship's residential deck. An awkward chuckle rumbled past my lips. "All of this is just—a lot to take in."

"I'm right there with you," said Griggs.

"A completely understandable reaction," Setso said to both of us. "I'm certain anyone from here would experience similar feelings if we were to visit your homes."

I smiled. "That's very true."

We rejoined the others, who had stopped outside the opening to another room.

"And here is where you will sleep for tonight," The Queen's words rang out from inside the room I'd been dying to see, bouncing off the walls with a sort of sing-song quality. It was clear she revelled in this unprecedented opportunity to show off her home.

We walked into a cavern about the same size as the library had been. Only this one had several rows of wooden cot-like beds set up in the centre of the room, and two more beds tucked into each alcove.

The King swept an arm across the space. "This is the overflow sleeping quarters built many years ago in anticipation of receiving future visitors." He walked between a row of beds.

They've been expecting future visitors? That's a bit odd.

"If you have wondered why we sleep below ground, it is to provide increased protection," he continued. "Though it is rare, the stone pillars have tragically fallen in the past. But, rest assured, we have secure gates that close when the sleeping hour is upon us. You are safe."

"So, we'll be locked in here?" Raker spoke up after being oddly quiet the whole tour.

"During the time of sleep, yes," The King confirmed. "We also require that our guards remain outside the room at all times. However, if you must use the washroom, they will escort you. I trust this space should suit your needs for tonight?"

Murmurs flew around the room, questioning eyes darting furtively.

"Keeping us prisoner…" Raker grumbled loudly enough to be heard.

The King raised his hands. "I understand being locked *anywhere* is not pleasant. But I assure you all, you are not prisoners.

Consider the situation from our perspective. Our elders and children live here. Until there is trust, we must protect ourselves."

I stepped forward and spoke loud enough for all to hear. "It's no trouble at all, sir. We will respect your wishes." I shot Raker and everyone who still grumbled a pointed look. "The fact that you *saved our lives* and are providing us shelter is greatly appreciated."

Vernon shared an approving glance with me.

Raker glared but didn't argue. Who could? Sure, it sucked to not have freedom to explore. But this was their domain. We were at their mercy, and from everything I'd experienced thus far, if we respected them, I truly believed they'd respect us, too.

We moved in. I chose a bed nearest to a wall where I could easily manage Herc, as did Jorgep. Together, we shifted a few beds over, and used the bedposts to rope off a holding pen. We made quick work of the task, as we were all in desperate need of food and rest.

When I removed Herc's tack, he let out a huge breath. He nudged my shoulder and I ran a soft hand down his nose. "Time to rest, big guy. We've had a crazy day and you did good. Real good." I laid out water and food for him, then grabbed several strips of jerky for myself to nibble on. We both needed to replenish our energy stores, for our trek to freedom wasn't over yet.

Tatara and Sarah claimed two beds in the nearest alcove.

Knowing time was limited, I sat my ass down and sighed as it sank into the thatch mattress. Griggs looked at me from his bed one over, then followed my gaze toward Raker, who rifled through his pack at the far end of the roq. Thankfully, he wasn't close by.

Griggs leaned forward. "Don't worry, he won't hurt you. He'd be a fool to try."

"Fucking right, he would be." Sarah appeared from behind and plopped down on the bed right beside me. "We got your back."

I grinned and bumped fists with her. "Thanks. I'm sure it'll be fine. He has to be as tired as the rest of us. I think sleep will be the priority for everyone at this point. Should be, anyway."

Griggs raised his hands in a halleluiah kind of way. "Amen, sister."

Sister, hmm... Until now I'd been suspecting Griggs might actually be as attracted to me as I was to him. But, maybe not? A sibling-like connection would make things a lot easier, yet a conflicted part of me couldn't help but feel disappointed. To distract myself, I decided to ask Sarah what was going on between her and Tatara, but before I could, the royals clapped their hands to get everybody's attention. Curiosity would have to wait.

"We've planned a bonfire and a hot meal top-side tonight," the Queen said. "There's one more stop on the way up, then the tour will be over. Our community looks forward to enjoying the evening with you around the fire. We will leave soon, so make sure to bring what you need."

Andra pointed to a foot-square metallic panel tethered to the wall, speaking up. "Lastly, please do not touch the button on this panel unless it's urgent. This is an intercom and is used *only* for emergency contact. It is stone powered, so we limit unnecessary usage. If you need anything during the night, call out to the guards and they will assist you." Wires hung from the book-sized metal panel, all of them twisted into a braided cord that ran out the door and down the hall. I'd seen similar cordage running in different directions through the web of corridors.

"That's inventive," I said to Sarah, noticing a blue glow around the button. "So their stones can be used as a power source—perhaps a weak one, but still something. Wow."

"Seems so." She grinned. "These people are right up my alley. I've seen repurposed tech from their ship all over these caves. Solar panels rigged with stones, power grinders in the mess hall. Door and lift gears used to make pulley systems. Old motherboards used to make abstract art. I can't wait to pick their brains about some of it." That certainly wasn't a surprise. This kind of thing was what she did for a living—taking old things and making them useful again.

"But where's their ship? Could they have completely dismantled it?" I asked.

Sarah shrugged. "Seems unlikely. That's a huge undertaking, but what do I know? They've been here a long time. Maybe the last stop on the tour will tell us." She excused herself to gather a few things to take topside. I collected a spare button-down shirt from my saddlebags.

"Miss Finn?" Jorgep leaned on my bedpost.

"What's up?"

His hand motioned towards our animals. "What should we do with them? I don't trust the Venanti enough yet to leave Keemi here all alone."

Brows furrowing together, I stood from the bed and rubbed my stiff neck muscles. While my instincts said the Venanti were trustworthy, I still didn't like the idea of leaving Herc behind. "I could set up my auto enclosure, but there's a strong chance the Sweep has killed it by now. Why don't we just take them up with us and find a place for them to relax?"

Jorgep had already removed Keemi's tack, but he picked up the hefty bridle. "That is exactly what I was pondering, too. Sounds like a plan."

I felt bad putting the bridle back on Herc, but at least he didn't need the saddle. If something went south, heaven forbid, I could easily ride bareback. Once he was ready, I changed my overshirt, leaving the front unbuttoned and my tank top exposed for airflow. Feeling somewhat rejuvenated, I donned my cowboy hat.

The conversations of thirty-five racers layered on top of one another within the room, whispers and murmurs floating about like spectres in a graveyard. I caught snippets here and there. Folks were concerned about their safety at night. Comments like: "They're keeping us locked in this room, yet, we're supposed to trust they'll keep their hands to themselves?" or "They could flip the switch on us any time!" and even, "Sure, they seem nice, but so did Governus, and look what's happened." Raker seemed to revel in all the apprehension.

I offered my two cents. "Give the Venanti a chance. My gut says we can trust them."

Raker sneered. "Who cares about your gut."

"That's enough Raker," Vernon barked. "Listen everyone, to have caution is wise. There are a lot of unknowns we're dealing with. But the Venanti have shown no signs of malice, so why not remain calm and see how the evening goes before passing judgement?" Thankfully, the anxious majority seemed to take a shine to that sentiment, and just in time.

The royal family reappeared, bidding us to follow them to the surface for a hot meal.

I perked up at the prospect of food. *I could definitely eat.* Jorgep and I led our mounts out of the roped pen and towards the exit.

Setso stopped us before we left the room. "You can let them rest here if you'd like. I promise no harm will come to them."

Jorgep and I shared a look, and then, careful to be polite, I replied, "I have no doubt of that, Setso. Thank you. But after a day like today, I know Herc will be way calmer if I'm close by. I prefer it that way."

"My bleenad can be aggressive if I'm not there to temper her, Mr. Setso," said Jorgep. "For everyone's safety it's best she remains within eyesight."

Setso's expression morphed into one of understanding. "Of course, that's perfectly reasonable. Let's head up then." We followed him out, bringing up the rear of the procession.

Maybe twenty feet ahead, a new tunnel veered left. We entered a much wider corridor and soon found ourselves walking uphill, ascending another set of stone-illuminated stairs. So, they had two entrances—another clever play. Always leave yourself an emergency back door.

We climbed for several minutes before a sliver of sky appeared at the end of the tunnel. But there was something else, too. Maybe forty-feet ahead, the walkway glowed brighter in one localised spot. Not just the steps though. The walls glowed too—that familiar cyan blue. Where did it originate from? As we neared, I noticed the walls themselves weren't glowing, but rather, were washed with light. Like when a door opens and illumination pours out.

It was another room.

CHAPTER 25

The Queen ushered us through the doorway ablaze with blue light. A moderate-sized cavern existed beyond the threshold, far less refined than the others. The walls were supported by beams like all the rest, however the space was otherwise barren, save for one thing.

My jaw slackened as I stood with the others in a haphazard semi-circle, every pair of irises glinting azure. Surprised gasps erupted as we viewed the source. There in front of me sat the most incredible gemstone I'd ever seen. It glowed without the aid of any external power, its solid core translucently highlighted by starbursts and fractal patterns just like the lesser versions we'd seen around this community. Like a buried moon, the hulking mass sat at the opposite end of the room, only partially unearthed from the surrounding rocky substrate—which was stained the same royal blue. *So, this is where all those veiny streaks of dirt lead to.*

Its lower half rested on the cavern floor, exposed, while the other half disappeared beyond the roof of the cave. The thing reminded me of an enormous iceberg.

How big was the chunk of stone we couldn't see?

The room held an odd smell, a mixture of wet earth and hot metal, the odour reminiscent of branding irons after pulling them out the fire. However, there was no visible metal aside from two crudely forged pickaxes leaned against the adjacent wall, which explained the chunks chipped away from two sides of the rock.

Remnant granules and finger-sized shards flecked the floor surrounding its generous base like cyan sprinkles. Witnessing this reminded me how much we still had to learn about the Venanti and their mysterious stones.

I yearned to touch the majestic ore to see if it would be as warm as it appeared. Wouldn't anything that created its own light also produce residual heat as well? I thought of stars and the heat of Earth's core. Tearing my eyes away, I glanced at my comrades who appeared equally mesmerized. Raker had inched forward from the group, his eyes scouring every inch of the stone.

Sarah, who'd stopped beside me, cursed under her breath. "Dammit, I took my suit off. I won't get this on my auto-recording. How the hell do I explain *this* to people?"

I raised a hand and tapped my temple in response. "It's likely being watched and recorded by Governus, so—" The words turned sour in my mouth, curdled like overaged milk. Just knowing that a rich and powerful corporation like Governus, who'd proven themselves to be less than earnest for reasons yet to be confirmed, was privy to this sent bad vibes radiating through me. I'd previously suspected maybe they could be after something… what if this was it?

Through tight lips, I whispered, "*Should* they see this, though?"

Sarah matched my conflicted gaze. "It's kinda too late now, isn't it? We're here."

The Queen stood beside the stone and swept her arm in a graceful arc. "This, my new friends, is the home of our Heart Stone. A very sacred place. This is where we obtain the smaller stones you have already seen—each one a gift. Not only do they keep us safe from Seevers, but they also provide light, energy, and healing." Adoration shone in her eyes as she laid a gentle hand against the massive gem and it brightened beneath her touch. Incredible.

"May I ask how you found this stone and learned how to use it?" Griggs asked.

I mouthed the words *good question* to him.

The Queen nodded. "Our story is not a simple one, but I will try to recount it in the clearest way possible. As I'm sure you're already aware, we were not always *Venanti*. Generations ago, our ancestors were Neersoo, a culture of explorers who lived among the stars, travelling in ships and discovering new corners of space. Mr. Vernon here is proof of that lineage—" She motioned toward Vernon. "But over time and with specific experiences we've had on Xola, those ancestors evolved into something different. Once they accepted they would never leave this planet, they bravely forged a new society and culture all their own."

All of the Venanti present murmured their assent, almost reverently.

The Queen crossed the room, hands clasped behind her back. She paused to survey her audience, seemingly reading the mood in the room. Most eyes were pinned on her, absolutely riveted, while a few others, including Raker, maintained stoic expressions as they listened.

"Our ancestors found the Heart Stone quite by accident. Originally, two sister ships had travelled to this corner of space, finding this planet. They had surface scanning capability—though undoubtedly inferior to what likely exists today. However, when neither ship could obtain readings of the forested areas, they descended to investigate. From historical logs and the oral retellings, we know each ship chose a different forest to investigate. Unfortunately, when they made a low pass, the engines failed without explanation, and they fell from the sky. Many died in the crash." The Queen bowed her head, as did her fellow Venanti.

We promptly did so too, out of respect.

The Queen appeared to need a moment to collect herself, so the King took over. "One of the ships crash landed on top of this very Heart Stone, unearthing a small portion that remains visible top-side. The noise and heat of the wreckage also drew the Seevers. They stayed away at first, lurking and studying our ancestors to decide if they were predator or prey."

The eyes in the forest. That confirmed our theories about why they'd slunk around, watching and waiting. Herc had sensed something was out there—he just didn't know what.

The Queen took a steadying breath, then spoke once more. "When the Seevers finally attacked, the Heart Stone was the only thing that saved them. Unfortunately—as you know—the Heart Stone changes the air this deep in the forest. Thanks to inadequate breathers, this affected the survivors, made them giddy and reckless for days. Sadly, too many souls perished as they wandered from the ship's protection. The ship became a safe haven for those that didn't, and the Heart Stone, a blessing."

Raker lifted a hand, the only racer brazen enough to interrupt such an enthralling origin story. "Excuse me, so since the stone changes the air and makes people go mad, how did *any* of the Venanti survive? Is there a way to combat the effects of the stone?" Both valid questions.

The Queen smiled graciously. "Let me step back. In the days following the crash, those who had found shelter inside the ship still went crazy for days. But then the effects eased and they became acclimated to the modified atmosphere—chosen by the stone. The exact time frame is not known, but the ship's logs reported losses from starvation and dehydration due to their lack of common sense to seek out sustenance. Less than a third of the expedition's crew of 142 survived. So, you see, there is no cure but from the stone itself."

"Whoa…" A burly racer murmured from the back of the crowd.

The Queen smiled, acknowledging the man. "Whoa, indeed."

Andra ducked out of the room as a wave of Venanti people travelled up the tunnel. She came back in after speaking to someone carrying a big pot. Catching the Queen's attention, she quietly urged, "Just so you know, the food will be ready at the surface. Carry on."

"Thank you," the Queen said, in a much softer way than earlier in the clearing. A nice thing to see. Perhaps their relationship wasn't as rocky as I'd suspected it was. *Lucky for Andra.* The Queen took a deep breath, walking back across the room. Every pair of eyes followed along.

"To conclude, our lives have since been intertwined with the stone. Over time we have learned to channel its energy and direct the flow. As you can see by our blue hair, it is as much a part of us, as we are of it." She smiled as the King took her hand.

I cleared my throat, nervous to ask a question, yet couldn't stop myself. "So, did your ancestors ever connect with the other ship—the sister ship? What happened to them?"

The King's brows rose. "That is a good question. I can confirm that our forebearers did send search teams into the forest closest to ours, hoping to find survivors. But they didn't return. They never even made it across the plain. They went mad and wandered aimlessly. Anyone who attempted to retrieve them suffered the same effects." A resigned look crossed his face. "You see, whatever genetic changes the stone made to our bodies, it also reversed our otherwise normal breathing capabilities. We cannot leave this forest's unique atmosphere."

Trapped twice—first on the planet, then within the Sweep. *What shitty luck.*

The Queen looked from face to face. "I hope that gives you valuable insight into who we are as a people, and answers questions you may have had. I'm terribly sorry the stories took so long, though. I know you are all tired and hungry." Her smile was one of compassion, and I admired her ability to command respect with kindness.

"No need to be sorry. We're honoured you shared your history." Vernon's tone reassuring.

Raker moved swiftly toward the Heart Stone like an insect drawn helplessly to the light. He raised one arm with anticipation, hand outstretched. A spellbound smile widened his surprisingly elastic mouth, something I'd never witnessed before.

Other racers followed his lead, and I might've too if I didn't have Herc to hold.

Horrified gasps rang out. The stone pulsed brighter.

Venanti surged forward, shouting, "Get back!"

"Don't touch the stone!" Setso commanded.

The racers froze, then stepped backward with whispered apologies. Raker however, turned sharply in surprise. In doing so, his foot tripped up on some rocks and he toppled. He fell forward on an angle, landing hard on his shoulder with his back to us. The detestable man rolled awkwardly, trying to regain his balance. Effulgent shards and crumbles displaced beneath his weight, scattering out in different directions as he moved.

In the space of a breath, Andra, Setso, and two others had a hold of Raker's arms. They hoisted his body off the ground and half-dragged him out of the cavern. The Venanti guard let him go in the tunnel, sporting stern looks of disapproval.

"I didn't mean to cause a stir. It's just so beautiful, I wanted to touch it for myself. Forgive me your highnesses. I meant no offense." Raker bowed his head politely to Andra and Setso, but his words didn't ring authentic to me. *Your highnesses?*

Since when has Raker ever cared about being so polite? He'd shown minimal respect to the Royals when we first arrived, speaking tersely in frustration at times, so why was he putting his best foot forward now? Something stunk, I just couldn't pin down what.

Venanti guards ushered everyone else out of the stone room. Andra and Setso flanked their parents, while the other guards lingered protectively in front of the cavern entrance.

"We accept your apology." The Queen nodded to Raker before turning to the rest of the group, glancing from face to face. "We were remiss to advise your group that only approved Venanti individuals may handle the Heart Stone directly, its fragments included. I should have stated that first thing. As we've said, it is sacred to us, which is why one must be found worthy first. Additionally, we cannot predict what effect it might have on an outsider. I trust you will respect our wishes."

Vernon placed a hand over his chest. "Of course, we will, Queen. I'm sure I can safely speak for the group on that." He looked around at his fellow racers, who unanimously nodded.

Andra responded to her mother's eye contact—another silent familial communication—and clapped her hands. "Shall we head to the surface then?"

Raker lagged behind, still eyeing the stone now protected by a wall of guards. I dropped to a knee, pretending to adjust the clasps on my boots, all the while watching him.

Sarah waited for me, pulling at a hangnail while muttering something about Seevers being on the menu tonight, her expression showing disgust incarnate. "Do you think they're considered delicacies here?"

I hid my smirk. "Delicacies? Doubtful—it's not like they're rare." Herc nudged my back, as if saying 'hurry up'.

Sarah peeked at my perfectly fine boot. "Need help tying your laces or something?"

I shot her a look that said *shush*, my eyes darting toward Raker with intention.

Ah, she mouthed, before turning an invisible key to lock her lips shut.

At the guards urging, Raker continued up the tunnel, and so did we. Intuition told me to keep a closer eye on him. It was only a feeling—but a strong one. The vehicle sabotaging incident flashed through my mind, reminding me the guy seemed to do what he wanted, when he wanted, and didn't mind trampling anyone who got in the way.

After ascending the remaining distance, we breached the surface.

Herc's previously droopy natural eye widened, alertness renewed. I breathed in a deep lungful of fresh evening air—filtered of course—infused by notes of smoke and cooked meat. It felt nice to be out of the tunnels. Being a prairie girl, I didn't appreciate being penned in for too long. I wondered what it might smell like after it rained here, and a trickle of homesickness seeped into my awareness. I used to love stealing quiet moments on the deck after an overnight rain, smelling the aromatic blend of freshly washed earth, wildflowers, and starlight.

Not far off, a fire raged in a grand circular pit lined with stones and singed metal railing sections obviously salvaged from their old ship. Stumps, hand-built benches, and thatch-covered mats spread out around it in no apparent design. Flames danced a flamenco across charred and sizzling hunks of ashen wood. In the failing light, embers floated amidst the wafting smoke and amber flickers slathered everything within reach. A low rumble of voices filled the air. Countless Venanti circled the fire or milled about, carrying children, cups, or plates. Once we emerged from the tunnel; however, all eyes swung in our direction.

Perhaps fifty or sixty feet beyond the bonfire sat a rusted relic of a spaceship, its time-stained shell battered by both the violence of its original crash landing and the elements. Faint firelight stretched across the space to glint off of whatever reflective surfaces still remained attached to the towering structure. It wasn't as robust as most exploration ships in circulation today, but a functional size that would've offered increased agility during flight. The craft had dug deep into the ground when it crashed, leaving a minor crater around it.

Stripped and mangled framework jutted out at odd angles, while unsalvageable panels remained twisted and shredded near the ship's skeletal base. Trees had grown up all around and through it, protecting it from overhead view. Governus wouldn't have been able to see it. However, there was still a core section of the ship that remained relatively intact. The rear loading hatch faced us, sitting open to the air on an angle that exposed only a hint of shadowed corridor. A muted azure glow lingered within its depths, which tempted my curiosity.

Vine-like cordage threaded with Heart Stones fragments decorated the entire area, the lines strung every which way stretching from pit to ship. As darkness fell, the lights looked like floating fireflies. Beds and planters of colourful flowers grew everywhere, and a walkway had been crafted from flat, slate-like stones. Wooden arches wrapped in similar vines covered the path every five feet or so, all the way up to the ship's hatch. Overall, the entire area felt somewhat majestic—fairytale like. I was dying to look inside the ship.

The Queen swept her arms in another grand gesture, the buddy-link circling her wrist glinting in the light. "This is our fireside gathering place. We meet here for fellowship and to honour the vessel that carried our brave ancestors to this planet— our home. Sadly, the ship no longer functions. But it has been preserved as a shrine to our history and all the loved ones we have all lost. It is a time capsule of sorts, and is as sacred to us as the Heart Stone room." While maintaining a polite smile, she levelled a serious gaze at us. "As such, racer runners, I respectfully request that none of you enter it."

I nodded in understanding, yet internally sulked. *Damn, I really wanted to see inside.* What other revelations existed there? I wondered if the section of Heart Stone that the ship crashed onto caused that faint glow, and did it look the same as the chunk below ground?

Griggs appeared by my side, as if out of nowhere. "We should feel honoured that they had even let us see the stone room then, hey?"

"Absolutely," I whispered back. "We need to remember that show of trust."

"You think they would've shown us the ship if Raker hadn't tried to touch the stone?"

I tilted my head towards Griggs. "Geez, I hadn't thought of that. Who knows…?"

The three youngest heirs ran up to the Queen, crushing her in a hug. She gave them a squeeze, laughing, then sent them off to continue playing. The King tugged on her arm and she shared a bright smile with all of us. "Please join the fire, Race Runners. Enjoy yourselves." And with that, the royals wandered away to mingle with their people.

"What's that old saying…when in Rome, do as the Romans do?" Griggs grinned.

"Nice. That's *really* old. Well, let's Roman it up then." I chuckled as we stepped forward, approaching the cozy fireside. At once, we became the centre of attention and curiosity. Despite the jovial atmosphere, the countless Venanti eyes zeroing in on me elicited a sense of unease akin to the one (and only) time I stood on stage during a grade school theatre production.

A gang of kids came bounding by, one of them chirping, "Will you play with us?"

"Come, come. Join us by the fire!" An elderly woman called.

"Who is thirsty?" A fellow inquired with a broad smile.

A woman waved while stirring a steaming pot. "Can we get you something to eat?"

The rapid-fire questions continued to come in a hospitable barrage. Venanti citizens enthusiastically offered their help or companionship, however, without buddy link connections, they couldn't understand our responses. Thankfully a friendly nod or smile went a long way.

A kindly woman ushered Sarah, Tatara, and I over to a pile of well-used thatch mats resting in front of a few benches. It looked plenty comfortable enough, but since Herc was still with me, I told the others to go ahead and save a seat for me.

I led Herc away from the hubbub to a slender tree maybe thirty feet away. *That should do fine.* It was close enough I could keep an eye on him, but far enough he wouldn't be too bothered. I tied the reins around a sturdy branch and smiled as Jorgep joined us, promptly securing Keemi on the opposite side of the tree.

I put down water and the last of the oats I'd been rationing for him to eat, along with an equine EMP. Not as tasty as apples or carrots, but it would have to do. "Time to relax, buddy." After giving him some love, I turned back to the fire. My rumbling stomach was as insistent as my salivary glands. The savoury smell of whatever was stewed in those pots was delectable.

Jorgep fell in step beside me. An almost baffled look crossed the man's face and his feelers rippled beneath his chin. "Miss Finn, could you ever have imagined any of this?"

I shook my head. "Hell no. I figured there'd be critters living in the forest, sure. Not a legion of rainbow-striped, razor-toothed killers the size of tigers, though. I would *not* have guessed hallucinogenic air, and definitely not a hidden society of people with magic rocks."

"Don't forget a filthy corporation who misled two-hundred racers."

"Yeah, that too." I pushed my hat back, letting it dangle by its tether between my shoulders. "We'll need to talk about that more later."

"I wholeheartedly agree, Miss Finn. We will talk later." Jorgep headed off to a bench seat Dino had reserved for him.

I beelined toward my thatch mat. As promised, Sarah patted a spot she'd saved for my tired ass. I sank down into it, groaning with pleasure. It felt so good to sit.

Andra, Tatara, and Cala also shared the blanket. Several Venanti people huddled around, taking turns wearing buddy links. Whoever didn't actively have one translated for the rest listening in. Since Andra was already linked up with Sarah, I promptly passed mine over to a very thankful young woman covered in various body piercings.

A lady walked past and pressed a dented metal cup into my hands. Hot liquid steamed inside, the sweet aroma both floral and fruity at the same time.

"It's tea," Andra said, smiling.

"Kik-tay-naa," I said, remembering their word for thank you. Sara and Tatara clinked their matching cups to mine, then I took a sip. It was sweet with floral notes, yet spicy, too. "Mmm, it's good." I nodded to Andra and the lady who'd served me. She grinned, carrying on.

Smoke billowed into the air, sooty tendrils drenched in light and shadow. Conversations rolled over one another around the fire. Every Venanti seemed voracious for conversation—for knowledge of life beyond Joya. In a way it felt like making first contact. The Neersoo who'd crashed here knew of other species, but the Venanti of today only knew what they'd read.

I played with fraying claw rips in my cargo pants. "I seriously need a tailor."

Andra's brows pinched. "What's a tay-lor?"

"Oh, shoot—sorry. That's an Earth term. A tailor's job is to sew and repair clothing."

Andra's eyes took on an almost wistful look. "I think I would enjoy being a tailor. I create clothes for the children here. Since supplies from our ship dwindled long ago, I reuse old fabrics from those who have passed. Sewing thread is rationed strictly. Adult clothes are mostly made from Seever hides. I also weave things, like baskets, floor mats, or sandals. I like working with my hands."

I smiled, admiring her for that. "Me too. I grew up on a cattle and horse ranch. When I was big enough, I did chores every day. Non-automated stuff like mucking out stalls, moving herds, or grooming and exercising the horses."

"Horses like that one?" Andra pointed to Herc.

I nodded. "Yep—except not many have metallic legs."

"Oh, I see. So he's not an advanced robot... He's bionic."

"Yes, exactly." I sipped my tea, letting it swish in my mouth.

Her head tilted. "May I ask why his one eye changes colour?"

I sipped again. "It's a feature that tells me what he's feeling."

"It's been surprisingly useful as an early warning system," Tatara said.

"And a handy night light." Sarah flashed a wry grin, earning an elbow from me. The jolt knocked her hand away from the retinal monitor disk she'd been fiddling with on her temple.

As Andra glanced around at the Venanti sitting close by, a determined smile graced her lips. "Despite certain challenges on Xola, we are all very proud of our home. However, there are some citizens—like me—who do dream of seeing what lies beyond. Someday, I would very much like to see Earth and its horses for myself. To explore *many* planets."

I placed a friendly hand on her forearm. "That's a great dream."

A young boy handed me a bowl with steaming stew inside.

"Thank you," I replied enthusiastically. His shoulders raised, chin tucking into his chest before he smiled shyly and scurried away. The boy twittered with his friends near the food pot and I chortled. Tatara gave them a wave which really sent them into a tizzy. *Cute kids.* I turned my attention to the hunks of meat and mystery root vegetables saturated with thick, dark gravy. Tatara's bowl already sat empty and I watched Sarah shovel the last huge spoonful into her mouth. She chewed eagerly, motioning for me to try it. Giving it a sniff, my brows shot up.

Damn, that smells good.

Taking a bite, a host of savoury flavours exploded in my mouth and a moan escaped before I could stop it. The meat was melt-in-your-mouth soft, the taste reminiscent of ham. Andra, who'd been watching me, laughed. I pointed into the bowl. "This is really good."

"So good." Tatara crossed her ankles and leaned back on her hands.

"Right?" Sarah nodded enthusiastically, then she leaned in to whisper, "Just don't think about what it is. Seriously, just enjoy it. Pretend it's pork."

Tatara rolled her eyes and met my gaze. Shaping one hand into hooked claws, she bared her teeth, doing her best Seever impression. I laughed and flashed an *of-course-it-is* grin.

A sly smile crossed Tatara's face. "Mmm, Yummy Seever…"

Sarah's hand lashed out and poked Tatara's side. "*Shush!* I don't wanna hear it!"

The two devolved into giggles and I couldn't help but join. Even Andra laughed. *Man, I needed this right now.* It felt nice to set everything aside and simply enjoy a pleasant moment. I'd hoped the entire race experience would be like this—well, not exactly like *this*—but an overall memorable and non-terrifying, or death-inducing, adventure to remember.

Across the fire, I spied Griggs chatting within another group. He'd changed into a fresh shirt, looking quite handsome in green. He laughed at something and his eyes happened to flick my way. Mine immediately snapped down.

"Oh, just jump his bones already. We know you want to," Tatara said flatly.

"What?" A hand flew to my throat in mock-surprise. "Yeah right, I'm not interested in Griggs like that." I motioned for her to keep it down, checking to ensure Griggs hadn't heard.

Sarah scoffed and Tatara furrowed her brows, saying, "Sure, okay."

"What does it mean to 'jump his bones'?" Andra asked, curious.

I cringed a little inside, warmth spreading on my cheeks. Several racers within earshot looked either amused or humorously uncomfortable, except Tatara. What was even the best way to answer a question like that? How did the Venanti regard sex? Was it as sacred as their stones? A chore between betrothed partners? Could speaking about it cause trouble?

Seemingly unconcerned, Tatara said, "It means having sex." Short and sweet.

Andra's lips formed an "O" shape as her eyes widened. "I see." After a slight pause, she added, "We jump bones too once we've found our life mate." She craned her neck to search across the roaring bonfire. "Which one will be your mate, Finn?"

I nearly choked on a hunk of Seever meat. "Mate? Oh, no, no. No mate. I don't want to jump anybody's bones." Shaking my head, I fought the urge to let loose a peel of nervous laughter. Mercifully, Griggs remained enmeshed in conversation, his ears shielded by the crackles and pops of roasting logs. Meanwhile, Sarah suppressed a snicker, and Tatara discreetly pointed a thumb in his direction for Andra's benefit. I promptly shot her a glare.

"Oh, woman up already," Sarah fired back. "You want him. He wants you. So, just make it happen. Griggs is a good shit, you could do a lot worse."

I groaned.

Andra's eyes twinkled with confusion. "What is a good shit?"

"A person who's likeable," Tatara clarified without hesitation.

Andra's mouth made the "O" again. "I'll remember that."

I mashed the last bite of stew between my teeth, entirely unimpressed by the pitiful matchmaking session I'd been thrust into. But then a realization hit. My eyes narrowed and I raised my spoon like a pointer finger. "Wait a sec—Sarah, did you just say *he* wants me?"

A shadow passed over us, blocking the firelight.

I looked up to see Setso's smiling silhouette. He pointed to my digicuff and asked politely to wear the buddy link because he'd like to speak with me. The current wearer handed it over.

Once it acclimated to him, Setso took a knee, looking me in the eyes. "Finn, I would enjoy learning more about Herc. I find him a fascinating creature. Would you mind taking me to meet him?" He extended a strong hand out to me. Andra sent a glare her brother's way.

Tatara and Sarah exchanged amused looks.

I took his hand. "Oh, um—sure, I guess."

CHAPTER 26

"**H**e is magnificent," Setso murmured, looking Herc over. He wore an expression of awe and very slowly inched closer to inspect his ocular implant and facial prosthetic.

"Thanks. He's a one-of-a-kind fella. Don't see too many horses with bionic legs in the Galaxium. At least, not that I know of. Maybe they will now, if word gets out about Herc. Perhaps we'll be trend setters." I chuckled and stroked Herc's neck. My skittish horse had settled down some since resting away from the commotion. Having big, burly Keemi to keep him company likely helped.

"Absolutely," Setso replied. "May I pet him?"

I glanced at Herc, then back to Setso. "Sure. Just hold your hand beneath his nose first—let him smell you." Moving my hand, I modelled what he needed to do. "Like this, see?" Setso followed my lead, holding his hand a couple inches from Herc's fuzzy muzzle.

He looked at me, expectantly. "Now what?"

I smiled. "Give it a minute. Smelling is a horses' way of getting to know a person. Right now, he's deciding if he likes you or not. Don't ask me why, but that's just the way it is."

Setso's mouth formed that same enlightened "O" shape his sisters had earlier by the fire.

Herc sniffed at Setso's palm, his fleshy lips touching it a moment.

Setso grinned, his hand twitching. "He has little hairs on his nose. They tickle." The wonder of discovery was written all over his face. Horses just had this innate ability to get under a person's skin in the best way. It made me think back to my sixth birthday, when my folks bought Misty, our very first riding horse. I still remember the exact moment I felt her muzzle, and after I rode her, I never looked back. My life was forever intertwined with the equine.

"How will I know if he accepts me?"

I shrugged. "Well, he's not biting or trying to run, so I think you can give him a pet."

"He might bite?" Setso's hand pulled back an inch.

I shook my head. "You're fine. Go ahead."

Herc's good eye watched with curiosity as the Venanti prince ran a gentle hand down the line of his long face, then rubbed his peachy nose. Setso's smile widened. "It's incredibly soft."

"Isn't it?" My voice quietened. "Hey…um…I just wanted to say thank you for saving us. We wouldn't be alive right now if not for you and Andra."

He nodded graciously, and I glanced down at my hands, unsure if I should speak the words poised at the edge of my tongue. I had burning questions that begged to be answered. "Can I ask something? When you encountered the first group of foreigners that came into the Sweep from the village across the field… can you tell me about that? What happened to them?"

Setso's smile faltered. His hand lowered to touch one of Herc's metallic legs. His fingers tapped on the contoured plates that housed the inner-workings of that bionic prosthetic. After glancing back, seeing my eager expression, he straightened. "We'd never seen a foreigner in the forest before—weren't expecting it. Their vehicles ran quietly. We hadn't even realized their presence in the forest until the screams and gunfire started. Much like what happened to your people." He let out a heavy sigh, visibly shaken by the memory. He stroked Herc's neck and touched the dishevelled braids in his mane. "They were overwhelmed quickly. When we arrived, only one man was still alive—barely. He died before we could heal him. We were too slow."

I offered a sympathetic smile. "You did the best you could."

"We were late again reaching you. It was so close to nightfall when the Seevers attacked. Even with the aid of our staffs, it's not safe for us to travel at night. We set out at first light... reaching some of you just in time. I wish we could've saved more."

"But you did save some of us, and we appreciate that."

Setso smiled softly. "That's gracious of you, Finn."

His eyes lingered on mine, silence hanging in the air between us. Feeling awkward, I filled it. "So, how many were there? People, I mean. The last time."

"There were ten—all dressed in matching uniforms. They had guns, helmets, and hoverbikes which had stopped working, of course. The Heart Stone chooses to repel the unnatural. We believe it strives to keep the forest pure. Who were they?"

I cleared my throat. "A charting team who worked for a company called Governus."

"I see. And what sort of company is Governus?"

"They're land developers—powerful ones. They built Egan across the field." Then I waved a hand, blurting, "Sorry, did you just say the Heart Stone *chooses*? Do you really believe that it is sentient?"

"We do, yes. In a sense. It doesn't feel pain, yet it can decide and react. We know this because we're connected to it in a very unique way. It's not an easy concept to wrap one's head around." Setso seemed keen to the gears turning in my head and changed the subject before I could tumble down the rabbit hole. "Have you wondered how our ship maintained power for many years after it crashed, while other vehicles stopped working?"

"The thought has crossed my mind."

"Our sister ships were explorer class vessels with experimental bionic interfaces—a cutting edge technology at that time. However, when the ship encountered interference, the bio connections were not strong enough to sustain flight. They were able to keep basic functions running after the crash, though... things like replicators, database operation, and lights. But only if someone stayed linked into it at all times."

I rubbed a hand over my jaw. "At *all* times?"

Setso nodded gravely. "Only commanding class officers had the ports and clearance to bio link. The survivors made great sacrifices to help our people thrive here on Xola. They took shifts on rotation, and did so for years, until the very last of them passed onto the next life."

A sense of heaviness hit my heart. "So that's how your ship ran out of power... it wasn't a core failure or some kind of malfunction. It's because there were no original flight crew left to hook in." I took off my hat and ran a hand through my hair. That's why the Venanti spent years making physical copies of all of the ship's records and book files. They'd been literally working under the pressure of a ticking clock—or more appropriately, beating hearts.

"Yes." Setso swallowed forcefully and looked away.

I touched a comforting hand to his upper arm. "It was heroic for them to dedicate their lives like that. Wow, your people went through so much. I'm so sorry." I dropped my hand.

"With the help of the Heart Stone, our people found a way." He cleared his throat, voice lowering. "Listen, you should know something, Finn. If my parents do decide to help you—it will be a perilous journey. The Seever population has boomed since my ancestors arrived here. We offered an upswing of sustenance that acted like a hot button for reproduction. They hunt us—feed on us—as we do them. But our efforts do little to diminish their numbers. The Queen Seever spawns an incredible number of offspring. They seem to grow more brave and clever all the time. That is why we check our pillars daily and lock the community down at night."

"Gosh, that's a little unsettling. I don't blame you for being extra careful." Glancing back at the fire, I contemplated all the information he'd just shared. My eyes landed on Griggs who watched us closely, and I refocused on Setso. "Do you think your parents will agree to help us?"

Setso lifted his shoulders. "It is not my place to say. But if it were up to me, I would definitely help *you*—with *anything*." He leaned in closer. His hand reached out to touch mine, and I stared at it, as though it moved in slow motion. *Oh, hell no. This can't happen.* I pulled away as our fingers brushed, placing a halting palm against his chest instead. "Um, Setso—"

"Hey guys! Whatcha doing?" A familiar baritone voice interjected. Griggs walked up, hands clasped behind his back and a smile on his face. Setso's eyes flashed with disappointment, or frustration maybe. Yet in the next moment, he was back to his amiable self.

I removed my hand from Setso's chest, stepping back. I was both grateful for the interruption and caught off guard. Why did he have to show up at this exact moment?

A thin smile curled my lips. "Setso wanted to meet Herc."

"Ahhh, I see." Griggs nodded in an exaggerated fashion, then turned to Setso. "So? What do you think of our buddy Herc here?" He stepped between us and gave Herc a few pats. Interestingly, his ocular implant flashed from green to blue for the space of a blink.

Our?

Setso smiled politely. "He is an amazing creature. If we could somehow secure clear paths of travel through the forest, I think the strength and functionality of a horse could serve the Venanti very well. It would certainly make travelling much faster."

"That's true! I'd actually hoped to breed horses here if I won land from this race." There weren't many breeders operating this deep into the Galaxium—if any—which meant I could perhaps corner the market. *Though, I kinda need to survive first.*

I suddenly wondered if the Venanti would even allow land to be parcelled out. Once their presence became known, they'd have rights to the land, could even quash Governus' plans to develop it if they couldn't come to a mutual agreement. Everything had changed. "Land outside of the Sweep, I mean—nothing that might impact you here in the Sweep," I quickly corrected.

Setso didn't seem bothered by the idea. Conversely, his tone grew silken. "Maybe we can work together on making that happen."

The muscle in Griggs jaw clenched and unclenched a few times. "Yeah, that would be super good." He planted one hand on his hip. "You know, Setso, I heard a rumour that you are being *courted* by a few lucky ladies. Geez, I'm jealous. How's that going? Any frontrunners?"

I nearly gasped, shocked he'd ask such a blunt question. However, simultaneous curiosity tilted my head. *Is that how it works here—women court the men? Or is it because he's royal?*

Setso chuckled a little awkwardly, shooting Griggs a barely veiled glare. Griggs on the other hand, simply grinned back like a drinking buddy waiting to hear a juicy tale.

"Yes, certain women have expressed romantic interest in me." Setso turned from Griggs, his focus solely on me. "But I am not promised to anybody."

Griggs looked back and forth between us, his brows raised with bewilderment. "You hear that, Finn? Not promised to anyone yet."

I wanted to drag Griggs aside and find out what the hell he was playing at. By his actions, and remembering what Sarah had said by the fire, I'd say he was jealous. I opted to ignore him entirely. The fact that Setso had taken a shine to me was as far as it went, and I wasn't about to let whatever this was be a barrier to positive communications. We still had to escape this Sweep.

I slapped on an approving smile. "May one of those lucky ladies bring you joy."

Setso's response was far less impassioned. "Thank you, Finn."

Griggs cocked an eyebrow. "You best not dilly dally deciding, either, because believe me, the good girls always get snatched up quick. I speak from experience." He flashed a dimpled grin and before I knew what was happening, he'd hooked an arm around my shoulders.

An uncomfortable look of realization crossed Setso's face. "Of course."

My skin heated like an element turned on HI. However, not wanting to make a scene, I had to settle for hurling mental daggers. Griggs didn't see my glares, though—wouldn't even look at me. My teeth clenched. Did he think I needed his help in some way? To be *saved* by his testosterone-laced bullshit?

Setso took a gulp of air and clapped his hands together. "Well, I better head back to the fire. I believe my parents want to discuss some things and I shouldn't keep them waiting." He dipped his head politely, handed my buddy link back, then strode away.

My farewell wave was friendly, but the moment Setso was gone, I whirled on Griggs, shrugging his arm off my shoulder in the process. I hissed, "What the hell was that all about?"

Herc flinched in reaction to the sharp movement, his head lifting, reins pulling against the tree branch. I laid a soothing hand on his neck, but my glare never left Griggs, replacing the daggers with molten ore.

His adam's apple bobbed up and down as he swallowed. "I worried he might be coming onto you or something. Thought maybe you needed help."

"No, I didn't need help. I was handling things fine, thank you very much."

Griggs rubbed his neck, nose wrinkling. "Truthfully, Finn, it didn't look like you had things handled. The guy was all over you. He was about to hold your damn hand when I walked up. Your hand was on his chest. I just don't think it's a wise idea to get involved with a semi-unknown alien species."

My eyebrows shot up. "That's '*all over me?*' Please! Besides, I'd just pulled away before you barged in—was pushing him back, about to tell him I wasn't interested. Wait—why am I even explaining myself to you right now? Despite what you may think, I'm not some damsel in distress that needs saving, and I will *not* be manipulated into doing or *not doing* anything because a man says so." I'd had more than my fair share of that nightmare before.

Griggs opened his mouth to speak, but I didn't give him a chance.

"And another thing—" I caught myself before my voice could get too loud, keeping it to a seething whisper-shout. I thrust a finger in his direction. "What you just did was really rude." I took a step forward and Griggs stepped back. "Setso's been nothing but kind to us. He saved our lives! And you come over here and make him feel stupid like that? Was that even true—about the women?" I leaned in, the heat of my anger smelting like a flame thrower.

"Well, ah—yes. I *did* overhear whispers about Setso around the fire." Griggs took another step back when I continued advancing. His already quiet voice lowered even more, until it was barely audible. "I figured it was a douche move for him to go after you if he's already got a line of women courting him. I'm sorry, I didn't mean to offend you—or manipulate. I was just worried. I—well, I care about you…" He sucked in a breath between his teeth, raking a hand through his hair. "Er—like a sister, you know? I can't help but feel protective."

Like a sister? Goes to show what Sarah and Tatara know about anything. The confirmation should've come as a relief. His lack of feelings shouldn't have mattered. Yet, it sat heavy in my gut, like ballast weighing down cheaply built hovercrafts. After everything we'd been through together, something barely buried had kept whispering there might be more.

But, very clearly, there was not.

Moisture brimmed in my eyes, spurred on by a perfect mix of anger and embarrassment. I blinked it back before it could betray the tumultuous conflict within, and slammed my hands on my hips. "I already have a brother, and I damn sure don't need another one. Butt out, Griggs. I can handle my own business."

Griggs stopped backing up, watching with a simultaneously sheepish and disconcerted expression. My pointer finger connected with his chest and I gave it a solid poke. "Got it?"

"Yeah, got it." His mouth opened as if to say more, then it closed again.

"Good." With one final glower, I stalked off back to the fire.

CHAPTER 27

Khana whipped around the corner, swinging the heavy monitoring room door shut behind her. "This better be good. I had to end my conversation with the citizen association about race concerns and the hovership we sent around the Sweep to keep up appearances." She'd vowed to her colonists that Governus would do everything in their power to assist the racers encountering *unexpected wildlife* within the forest. She, of course, didn't mention anything about the people.

A vibrant blue light washed over her and she halted, staring between the screens and her brother. Steel stared back with uncharacteristic excitement in his eyes. When the man wasn't angry, he was usually irritatingly calm and cool. In this moment, he practically glowed.

Eyes wide with wonder, she pointed to the luminous imagery. "That's it? Our jackpot?"

Steel nodded. "That's it. A racer named Raker got closest to it. This is his view."

Something frighteningly similar to *happiness* bloomed within her, unfurling and insidiously infiltrating all the dark cavities that permeated her typical countenance. Khana stepped forward, rolling her shoulders and the stress of leadership away for a brief moment. A rudimentary mining cavern loomed before her, one that contained an enormous chunk of blue ore. It emerged from the ceiling, its base resting on the floor—and it was magnificent. It glowed just like the minor stones they'd already seen.

"It's magnificent." Her words seeped out in a sigh.

She stopped beside Steel, taking in his confident stance. Her mind whirled with possibilities. She'd already seen proof of the impressive power these stones held. Khana sat in the nearest chair and typed into the viewing console's communication panel, drafting a secure outgoing message to her wretched siblings. No time for holo-chats. Everything had changed.

The stakes at play for this convoluted situation had just quadrupled. This wasn't just about navigating irritating red tape, or fighting to maintain possession of this land anymore. She couldn't simply execute memory swipes via the retinal monitoring implants like she'd banked on doing should any racers make it out of the Sweep. No, the potential for harvest and usage—not to mention profit—of this stone was incredible. It could be a truly perpetual power source. It healed wounds. Its scan disruption and atmospheric distortion capabilities might be harnessable somehow. And then there was always the idea of weapons.

Governus couldn't risk losing claim to Joya, no matter what.

The Venanti could no longer simply be quietly displaced or integrated. Regardless of whether they knew it or not, they held too much power. Her prior plan had been perfect.... To keep the Venanti nice and compliant until the Gala-rights organization finished their *first contact discovery* investigation, then, afterward, simply capture a few of their most important community members to ensure the rest fell in line. But Khana mentally tossed that out the window.

"Time for a new plan, brother." She finished typing her message, her finger hovering over the send button. One delicate brow arched dramatically. "In light of this recent development, the situation must be rectified in an alternate manner. Your brutish skills may be required after all."

Steel's eyes flashed with excitement. "I see. How excellent."

They shared a smile as Khana hit *send*.

***

The King rose to his feet and lifted his hands, calling for quiet. "Thank you for sharing a fine evening with us, race runners. It is getting late, however, and I can tell from the drooping eyes that sleep is needed. Shall we get down to business? That is, if you are all still open to a deal?" He helped his wife to her feet and beckoned for his children to stand by their sides.

Every single head nodded in unison, no hesitation.

"Of course," replied Vernon, still buddy linked with the King, as he'd been all evening.

The King specifically addressed his people. "I'd like to express our thanks to all of you for extending such generous hospitality to the outsiders. We would like to speak with them in private now, so if you can make your way below ground, that is appreciated. Good night."

The Venanti people departed with a flurry of last-minute chatter, tying up conversational loose ends before disconnecting their buddy links. Only a handful lingered at the royals' request.

"Sit, sit." The Queen motioned to the seats around the fire. "We have a deal to discuss."

With a nod, the King sat back down in his hollowed out throne-like stump and everyone else followed suit. "Firstly, we helped all of you because of our belief in generosity and mercy. Nobody should die in such a gruesome way, and the Seevers do not deserve to win any spoils. As a result of what happened, you are now in dire need of help to get out of this *'Sweep,'* as you call it. I'm happy to report we are willing to further extend our kindness to provide that help."

An audible release of breath rushed out around the bonfire en masse.

But what did they want in return? I recalled how interested Setso had been in horses. What if they wanted Herc in trade? The thought made my throat dry up.

Sarah nudged me. "Think they'll demand our first born?"

I stifled a laugh, elbowing her back. "Shh."

The King and Queen exchanged purposeful looks, then the King forged ahead. "You have something in your possession that would benefit us greatly."

I crossed my fingers behind my back. *Please don't say Herc. Please don't say Herc.*

The Queen walked over to the closest racer, which happened to be Dino. She pointed to the transparent breather covering his lower face. "We are interested in obtaining breathers."

The King gave a business-like smile and steepled his fingers in front of his chest. "Cousins from our sister ship could be living in the neighbouring forest. After too many failed attempts to cross the fields between, having breathers would offer us a real chance for success." A contagious sense of hope radiated from the Venanti as they watched our reactions.

A symphonic celebration filled my head. Breathers, not Herc.

Raker stood. "Respectfully, King, we need our breathers to get out of the Sweep."

"Yes, but—" Vernon interjected quickly, "I have a spare. Perhaps others do too. Regardless, once we're safely free of the Sweep, I'm sure we'd all gladly give them over as payment." He appealed to his fellow racers with an enthusiastic nod. "Right?"

Affirmations rippled around the fire, and the royal family smiled.

"Perhaps we should have a private discussion before any official decision is made, *Vernon*. Or have you forgotten this is a democracy?" Raker's eyes scalded, yet his expression remained carefully neutral. While I didn't like the man, I didn't disagree with him. It was important to make decisions together, for everyone to have a say—whether positive or negative. Though, I really didn't see how there could be a negative side to this deal. Once we broke free of this jungle-like hellhole, we wouldn't need our breathers anymore anyway.

The King and Queen dipped their heads respectfully. "We will give you some time to discuss." They walked towards the sacred remains of their relic ship, and waved off the lingering Venanti guards. Setso had noticeably avoided my gaze the entire time. I sighed. *Great.*

Us racers shifted to form a tighter circle for discussions.

Griggs singled Raker out. "Alright, so what do you want to discuss? The deal seems pretty straightforward to me."

Raker cut an icy look in Griggs' direction before addressing the group in a much kinder and very off-brand tone. "No, I don't see any glaring issues with exchanging breathers for their assistance, but I *do* think it's important to clarify the terms of their *help* before launching back into that forest. I want to be 100% sure what we're signing up for, don't you?" Nobody argued.

Dammit. Yet again, he'd actually said something that made sense. That did need to be asked. As a group of somewhat intelligent individuals, I was fairly confident clarity would've been sought anyway, but, with the stakes being so high, it was best to err on the side of caution.

"We will also need to have a serious discussion about Governus and how we plan to deal with them once we get out of here," said Jorgep.

"*If* we get out of here," Raker sniped back. "Be realistic."

Ah, there's the scathing Raker I know and love. Well—know, anyway.

Jorgep stood a touch taller, meeting Raker's caustic glance with a polite smile. "There's nothing wrong with a little positivity, Mr. Raker. We all hope to get out of here, after all."

If glares could electrify, Jorgep would be nothing but a pile of crumbled char.

"*Anyway…*" Vernon continued, addressing everyone. "It sounds like we're in agreement. To fulfil the deal, we will give over our breathers once we're out of the Sweep. Correct?"

Everybody agreed.

"Good." Vernon crossed his arms. "We will ask some clarifying questions, and if their answers are satisfactory, we'll shake on it. Last chance—does anybody have any other issues?"

Sarah raised her hand. "No issue *per say*, but logistically we will need to figure out how to make the breathers work for them. They use filters and home atmosphere cartridges. The Venanti don't have cartridges for the atmosphere here." Everyone listened, concern showing on their faces, likely wondering the same thing I was. What if we couldn't fulfil the deal?

Cala, who had been fairly unaffable in the past, thrust her hand up. "I have an idea to try. I work with breathers all the time back home—I've had to mod them before."

Another racer raised his hand too. "I'm familiar also. Happy to help."

Vernon nodded. "Let's roll with that then. You two work together. Anyone else have anything to add?" When nobody spoke, he waved to the single Venanti guard posted outside the sacred ship's entrance. She signalled the royal family, who made their way back to the fire.

I lingered near the back of the group to avoid getting roped into linking up with Setso again. I'd had enough awkwardness for one day. Not to mention the fact that Griggs kept looking at me with these wounded-puppy eyes. I was so over it.

Once all buddy links were active, Vernon spoke. "We have some questions we'd like answered before agreeing to your proposed deal. Can you share with us exactly how you plan to help us get out of the Sweep safely?"

"How?" Andra asked. She seemed thrown off guard by the question. "Well, we will accompany you through the Seever nest all the way to the outer edge with our staffs. One of us for every two of you. Our presence should keep the Seevers away." Using some quick mental math, that meant we'd have 17 or 18 guides with us.

"*Should...*" Raker said. "So, you can't guarantee our safety?"

"There is always risk. Certainly, you must be aware of that," Andra answered with diplomacy. "But, rest assured, we will do everything within our power to get you out *alive.*"

Everybody glanced around at each other, murmuring, shrugging, nodding. Dino's deep rumbling timbre carried above the rest when he said, "Seems simple enough. I'm down."

But Vernon had another question. "Can you explain the specific risks? Do they pertain to the Seever nest you referred to?"

Excellent question.

"Every hunt is dangerous and we have had casualties before. It's rare, but when it happens, it's usually because a staff gets dropped somehow, or knocked away. But, the stone itself hurts Seevers—severely. We don't know why. It just does." She lifted her own glowing staff into the air for effect. "If a stone physically *touches* their skin, it scalds like acid. That's why they rarely get close enough to run that risk." Andra ended with a confident nod.

Setso joined in. "We theorize that just as our genetics changed and our bodies absorbed the Heart Stone's gifted essence, the Seevers' genetics rejected it, creating an acute aversion."

Griggs rubbed his jaw. "Huh. The stone is essentially the Seevers' only natural enemy. Well, aside from you guys."

"Exactly," Setso said.

Sarah released the retinal monitor disk she'd been playing with on her temple and crossed her arms, lips pursed. "So, it's like their kryptonite..."

Setso's face scrunched up. "Their krypto-what?"

"Oh, kryptonite—you know, the rock that made Superman weak." Sarah turned, appealing to her fellow racers and received little help as most appeared equally confused. I watched with amusement, knowing exactly what she was talking about, thanks again to my brother's collectibles obsession.

"C'mon, seriously, nobody's heard of *Superman?*"

Setso's confused look only deepened. Sarah shifted uncomfortably.

I threw her a lifeline. "Oh yeah, that superhero who can fly and shoot lasers out of his eyes. You're totally right with the kryptonite reference." I glanced around the group with a casual shrug. "It's an Earth thing. Carry on."

Sarah mouthed the words *thank you*. I winked back.

"Right. Now that we have that covered. Are we ready to strike this deal?" Vernon's thin eyelids hung at half-mast; his movements sluggish. The poor guy was bagged, and I felt his pain. The group gave final assent and he happily faced the royals. "We agree to give you our breathers once we're safely out of the Sweep. But you should be aware, the breathers may not function with your specific atmosphere. We will work on figuring that out." He offered his hand to shake. Vernon, like many peoples around the Galaxium, had adopted this standard Earthian gesture.

The King and Queen beamed. "Wonderful. It is a deal then." In a show of friendship, the King extended his arm out like Vernon had, mimicking the bladed hand position.

Vernon firmly grasped the King's hand and shook it up and down. "This is called a handshake—it's a customary signal of good faith in business."

"Very good," the King replied, releasing his grip.

Everyone present proceeded to circulate, exchanging hearty smiles and handshakes.

Once the commotion died down, Andra invited everyone to follow her back down into the caverns. "We should rest now. It is a big day tomorrow. We leave first thing after breakfast."

I pulled Sarah aside. "Hey, I keep seeing you messing with your retinal monitor. Maybe you should cut that out. If you're not careful, you'll detach it and blind yourself."

Sarah smiled. "Appreciate the concern, but I actually *want* to detach it. I'm trying to figure out the right way to do it. I'm reading through some notes stored in my cuff." Her voice hardened. "Governus shouldn't get to see anything else."

"Oh, okay." I said, surprised. "Wow, I didn't think that was a possibility. Well, let me know if you figure out how." Tatara sauntered by, hips swaying as she headed for the tunnel.

"Will do. See you below." She flashed a smile, then jogged after her flirtation.

Jorgep and I collected Keemi and Herc, bringing up the rear as we descended. Oh, how I looked forward to sleeping—to feel some measure of peace and rejuvenation. Though, with the disquieting reality of tomorrow looming in my thoughts, I doubted I'd be so lucky.

CHAPTER 28

Once Herc was comfortable in his makeshift rope pen beside Keemi, I dragged my sorry behind over to my bed and flopped face first onto it. It wasn't exactly springy, and I hit a little harder than anticipated. But I didn't care. It was a bed. However, I couldn't succumb to blissful slumber yet. There was still business to attend to, talks to be had, headaches to make worse...

Footsteps approached and I pried one eyelid open to peek.

As if he'd read my mind, Jorgep stood there looking at me, urging with his eyes. "Shall we have those discussions we talked about earlier, Miss Finn? Best to do it now."

"Yeah, we should." I pushed my body upright again with a groan.

Jorgep nodded, his feelers calm and unmoving.

The Venanti had closed our cavern door, and their guards now sat somewhere beyond the entrance. Quiet murmuring filled the space while racers prepared to rest their weary bodies. I waved to our alliance members, beckoning them all to join us. I avoided eye contact with Griggs as he walked over, though I wouldn't be able to evade him forever.

Once everyone arrived, Jorgep looked straight at Vernon, who'd taken on a figure-head role within the group. "Want to lead the chat?"

Everyone stared expectantly.

Vernon placed his hands on his hips. "Nope, sorry. I've done my fair share of talking and mediating today. I'm spent. Somebody else can take a turn with this one."

Shoulders slumped en-mass as though air had seeped from a leaky plug. But nobody dared argue. Vernon had worked hard smoothing the waters and shouldering the lion's share of negotiations with the Venanti. Playing the go-between undoubtedly had to be tiring, especially after a near-death encounter with the Seevers. He deserved a break.

Eyes flitted around our circle. Nobody seemed eager to volunteer and everyone looked about as dragged out as I felt. *Twice ridden with a credit left…* My father's old phrase popped into my mind as I curled my lips. It meant a person was bag-tired, but the fun wasn't over yet.

Griggs and I both replied at exactly the same time.

"Fine, I will," Griggs offered at the exact same time I said, "I'll do it, I guess."

We looked at each other. His brows raised.

I shrugged, muttering, "You go ahead."

He half bowed, sweeping an arm toward the middle of the room. "Please, ladies first."

The expression on his face was a mix of apology and graciousness, rather than malicious—like he believed he was doing me a solid. *Does he think letting me talk to this motley bunch will make up for what he did? He better not.*

"Great," I said flatly. I spun around and hopped on top of my bed. Trepidation rose like flood waters at the thought of leading, but I swallowed down the swell. Giving my arms a wave, I cleared my throat and fell back on old tactics. *Fake it 'til you make it.* "Hey everybody!"

The murmuring didn't stop. A few eyes turned my way, but nobody seemed to care. Well, that simply wouldn't do. I placed my thumb and middle finger sideways in my mouth, ready to let fly a shrill whistle—the kind that brought horses in from the pasture—but a hand on my arm stopped me.

"Wait," Sarah said.

I looked down at her, mouthing *what?*

She tapped her temple. "I think I figured it out. We should get these retinal monitors out of our heads before we discuss anything important. They're supposedly visual-only... But I don't trust Governus as far as I can throw them. For all we know they've been listening this entire time."

I bent to her eye level. "You *think* you figured it out, or do you know for sure? We're not doctors, and I'm not keen on being blinded if an error is made." More eyes swung our way from nearby, clearly having overheard snippets of the conversation.

"No doctor is needed." Sarah dug her fingernails beneath the circular external implant that sat snugly atop her temple. "You just do this—" She pulled it out with one swift tug. A barely audible clicking sound accompanied the motion, as did horrified gasps and cringes.

Unfazed, Sarah held out the metallic implant with two thread-sized wires hanging from its flat-bottomed base. I watched her for signs of distress, my heartbeat thumping in my ears. But nothing more than a quick wince and a confident smile crossed her face.

"I'm fine—really. It's just a pinch. All temporary retinal implants have quick-disconnects built in. It's a standard failsafe feature. You just have to pull the exterior appliance out at a certain angle and it'll force a shut down." Sarah tossed it up and down like flipping a coin.

A collective exhale filled the room. She'd claimed everyone's attention. Even Raker's.

Sarah continued with a matter-of-fact voice, "These are very simple models. No frills. If it was a permanent implant, that wouldn't have worked. Of course, we'll have to get the internal connection point removed later, but at least the bio connection is severed."

I slanted a sideways glare at her. "You're damn lucky you didn't go blind just now. What if you'd been wrong?"

She shrugged, pointedly flashing me a wry grin. "I was like 95% sure I'd be fine."

"Nice…" I rolled my eyes at her tease, harkening back to the text I'd sent when we'd first descended into the Venanti cavern. "Cheeky woman." Sarah winked.

"Hey, how'd you do that?" A racer with a fox-like face called out.

"I want to take mine out, too," said another.

One by one, with Sarah's guidance, weary racers removed the discs affixed atop their temples. Only a few hung back from participating, watching with uncertain expressions.

I gripped my own implant, let out a nervous whimper—the same kind I made whenever I got bloodwork done—then pulled it at the angle Sarah had specified. Then, with a tiny pinch, the contraption was out. My relieved, almost giddy laugh followed. Governus was out of my head.

Cala spoke up, her tone hopeful and at odds with the majority of the group. "But are you sure we should disconnect the implants? That's our last link to Governus. If they *are* on their way to rescue us right now, they won't be able to find us. If we just wait for them, we can figure all of this out and still get our land. We're not going to give up the chance for land, are we?"

Her words spurred memories of Lootas and his dogged hopefulness—rest his soul.

Tatara shook her head at Cala. "Hate to burst your bubble, but they're not on their way to save us. Think about it. If they'd brought in the big guns after their charting mission failed, they could've killed the Seevers altogether. Problem solved. No more threat. But they didn't do that. They planned this sham of a race instead, using us as free labour to chart the Sweep—"

"*Expendable* labour!" A racer covered in jaguar-like markings blurted out.

Tatara pointed at him. "Exactly, and I bet it has everything to do with the Venanti stones."

A short, cherub-looking fella spoke up, "If they *had* done a clean sweep for the Seevers, they could've hurt the Venanti, too. That likely explains why they didn't do that." A low whistle hissed between his crooked front teeth. "Harming a first contact civilization is a major offence with the Gala-Rights Commission. There are strict rules about finding original life on claimed planets, and hefty fines to pay if you step out of line."

"Then why not figure out another way to make first contact themselves?" Sarah raised her eyes from the deconstructed retinal implant in her hand. "Smile pretty. Make some deals. La-di-fucking-da, everybody lives happily ever after?" She lowered her voice. "Unless, the Venanti are lying about talking with Governus before meeting us…"

A few racers raised their brows, considering that possibility.

"No, they're not lying," Vernon interjected, his voice confident. "My work requires daily interaction with clientele. I'm well versed in lie detection and they're *not* being disingenuous."

Sarah raised her hands. "Hey, I'm just putting *everything* on the table for discussion."

Since the conversation had taken on a life of its own, I rolled with it. "I agree that the Heart Stones have to be the lure for Governus. They're too precious a resource to ignore."

"It always comes down to money," Dino muttered.

Sarah tugged on my shirt sleeve as a flurry of voices cluttered the room. She motioned with her head for me to follow. I hopped down from the bed and joined her several feet away.

"What's up?"

Sarah opened her palm to reveal her implant and whispered in my ear.

As her words sunk in, I closed my eyes, exhaling a heavy breath. "Oh great. Well, we better tell everyone else." I reclaimed my lofty bed top position and whistled to get everyone's attention. "I know everyone is exhausted. So am I. But there's been a new development."

A few people who'd been lying down sat up to listen.

An elastic-skinned tri-pedal racer spoke from his place beside Raker. "Get on with it then. Say your piece so we can move on with our lives."

I cocked a brow, staring him down. "Well, aren't you a charmer? And your name is?"

"Ryxol-ytxtaaa-klopicazeeyx." The name rasped, rolled, and clicked all at once.

Shit. "Ah, um…"

Clearly exasperated, he saved me from butchering his name. "Ryx is fine."

Oh, thank goodness. "Ryx—very good, then." Looking away, I didn't give him a chance to say anything else. "Sarah found hard evidence that Governus never intended on making good on their promises. She's the best person to explain it." I waved for her to take the floor.

Sarah reached into her suede vest's pocket and pulled out the circular retinal monitoring implant she'd shown me moments earlier, brandishing it like an antique 21ᵗʰ century Canadian loonie. She turned it over and pointed at the flat underside. "Look."

People shifted and leaned forward to get a good look.

"What are we looking for?" Someone asked.

Sarah sighed. "Here." She tapped on one of two tiny compartments that would normally be screwed shut. "There's usually only one compartment in these simple implants, but this one has two. Tell me, are all of yours the same?"

Griggs checked his implant, flipping it over to reveal the same double compartment setup. Voice after voice confirmed that everyone's retinal implants were identical.

Sarah pointed to one section. "I suspected that would be the case. This compartment is the normal one containing typical retinal monitor components. Standard tech. But *this* one—" She tapped the second tiny chamber. "Is pretty fucked."

Dino's eyes flicked up. "Fucked how?"

Sarah pulled an ancient looking multi-tool out of a holster on her belt, and flipped open a narrow set of pliers. Carefully, she plucked out a miniscule circuit unit wrapped in a host of thread-like wires. "This is a portable memory wiper. Black market tech, mainly used by spies and the military. A perfect failsafe. Failed mission? No worries. Just wipe the operative's memory and voila, no intel leaks. They're compact, portable, and plantable."

Tatara took a step back. "Are you serious right now?"

Sarah's lips smacked. "As a heart attack." She closed the compartments. "These babies are usually triggered remotely. But because of the Sweep's interference, its signal beacon was paired with the retinal monitor's bio connectors. So, it's fully functional. Very sneaky business."

Gasps rang out, swears tumbled from mouths, and emotions flared as the cavern was engulfed with verbal flame. I overheard someone say, "So if we didn't die, they would've wiped us?" Another racer growled, "Them assholes were never gonna cough up any free land!"

Griggs fists clenched with white-knuckles. "Those bastards!"

"That's quite a bold tactic. Interesting…" Raker rubbed his chin.

Vernon calmly exchanged nods with Sarah. "Thank you for that vital information."

Nobody could argue Governus didn't have nefarious motives now.

I planted my hands on my hips and channelled my inner loudspeaker. "Whoever hasn't taken out their retinal implant, do it now. They're not coming to help us, and they sure as hell don't deserve to see anything else we do!" My guts twisted. They'd probably seen too much already. We'd unwittingly given Governus a wealth of information they didn't have before.

A chorus of voices rose in agreement. The last functioning implants were discarded.

"One more thing." Griggs raised a finger into the air. "The only thing valuable enough for Governus to go through all of this shit for, is that Heart Stone. It heals—gives power. And, if they're willing to sacrifice us to get their hands on it, what will they do to the Venanti if they don't play along? Guys, we not only have to get our asses out of this Sweep and stick it to Governus somehow, but we need to help protect these people, too."

I gave him a smile for that. Despite my lingering irritation with Griggs, I felt equally thankful and impressed by his caring sentiment. The man had a big heart—a quality that showed more and more, and only intensified my attraction to him. He was one hundred percent right.

Sarah thrust a finger into the air, akin to a eureka moment. "I bet the colonists of Egan would love to meet the Venanti—to have the thrill of discovery, increase tourism, and all that… Unless they know already. I doubt it, though. Bringing an entire colony in on a scheme like this seems impossible to manage." She looked around. "So we could enlighten them."

Jorgep nodded enthusiastically. "I was raised in a business-oriented family and colonizing corporations like Governus rely heavily on their investors and colonists' income. They will have sway. If they're not corrupt and learn Varu exists, it will help force Governus to deal with these matters properly. Legally."

"Or to pay off authorities and make it go away," Raker scoffed.

I couldn't help myself. "Not everyone can be bought, Raker."

"Really? And what Galaxium are you living in, human?" He won a few snickers.

My hands clenched into tight balls. "The name's Finn."

Raker merely looked away.

Griggs clapped his hands. "Alright, so all we need to do is figure out a way to expose Governus to the colonists and ensure everything gets reported to both the Magistrate and Gala-Rights Commission. Anybody got any ideas?"

The room devolved into chaos.

"Listen up!" Sarah jumped onto the nearest bed and waved her arms. "Using my suit, I'm confident I can hack the Governus feeds in Egan, then broadcast my mech's auto-recording to the colony. I've been documenting the whole race. They'll see everything—well mostly. Governus won't be able to feed them any lies about anything. They'll be totally fucked."

"But you can't do that from inside the Sweep, can you?" Tatara asked.

Sarah shook her head. "No. But the minute we get clear of the interference, I can."

I grinned, patting Sarah on the back. "Oooh, I like that. Let's do that."

Vernon's eyes swept around the room, stepping back into his leadership role. "That sounds promising. Does anybody have any issue with this plan of attack?"

"None of it will matter if we don't make it out alive," a sour-faced racer barked.

"That is true," Vernon returned politely. "However, it's best to prepare for anything."

"Pardon me!" Raker's voice boomed, silencing everybody. "Might I suggest an alternative to this hacking and broadcasting option? I'd like to reiterate that what Governus has done is unforgivable, and as such, they shouldn't be allowed to continue colonizing Joya—*which they will.* The GRC will merely be an inconvenience to them. I propose we force Governus to relinquish *all* claims to Joya and send them whimpering with their tails between their legs."

Jorgep meandered closer to Raker. "You're proposing a corporate takeover. We're not prepared for, nor do we have the resources amassed to do something like that."

Raker clucked his tongue. "If you were an *astute* businessman, then you would know that in a successful takeover, the taker inherits the corporation's on-site assets. We'd keep whatever they leave behind. That would allow us to maintain and defend our stake until supplementary support arrives. Efficiency at its best."

"Which is precisely the problem I stated," Jorgep said matter-of-factly. Though he was usually polite to a fault, he glared at Raker now. "Where is this supplementary support going to come from? My family has resources—maybe they could help, but our holdings are too far away. *Everything* is too far away. It would also depend on them even wanting to take a gamble on a planet like Joya. And I know plenty about business, thank you."

"I nominate Raker!" Ryx called out. "He has the resources and the know-how."

Raker's eyes flashed with an emotion I couldn't quite place. Whatever it was, it was intense—and smug. He nodded to Ryx in approval. "Well, I am a *very* wealthy businessman and I'm willing to take that gamble. I opted to come here strategically, to win land and forge new trade alliances, you see. I have plenty of resources and ships at my disposal to keep this planet safeguarded *and* ensure Governus stays away for good. In fact, I already have a ship en-route to pick me up. You know, in case I happened to lose the race. I'm nothing if not pragmatic. Being prepared is an imperative quality for any leader."

Jorgep looked away, briefly meeting my eyes, then Vernon's.

Sarah huffed. "So, *you'd* be the new leader here. That's rich."

"What makes you think we'd all agree to something like that?" I asked. "It sure seems like a whole lot of trouble and risk. Besides, I think with the right pressures, Governus could be persuaded to play nice—to apologize and atone for the wrong they did. I think hacking and reporting them is the safer play."

Raker placed a hand over his chest. "I respectfully disagree."

"Since when does he *respectfully* anything?" Sarah muttered, and I elbowed her.

"Why should we believe you want to help?" Griggs challenged.

Raker's expression morphed into something oddly wistful. "I have a very good reason for wanting to help. On Ganglia, my people live by a sacred code of honour. Part of that code is what we call a sworn life debt. Since the Venanti saved my life, I must now save theirs." He presented a rare smile. "Unless Governus is overthrown, the Venanti will never truly be safe. But with my resources, I can make that happen. And I'll ensure you all get triple the land owed."

The possibility of winning a greater prize inspired a variety of different reactions, including intrigue and skepticism as each racer weighed the pros and cons of both options. I had to hand it to him, his argument was surprisingly convincing. Raker had some people whispering amongst themselves, thinking about the spoils of an overthrow, seriously considering his offer. However, that's precisely what had me worried. It just seemed too convenient.

I didn't buy it. Not from Raker.

Ganglians were best known for deception and cut-throat business tactics, and thus far, Raker hadn't exactly been the most reliable, or upstanding sort of fellow. A corporate takeover sounded right up his alley if he was as well-off as he purported. It would be an opportunistic acquisition, especially with the Heart Stone in the mix, but what's to say he'd hold true to his word? He could end up being no better than Governus. Based on my experience with the guy, he'd be the last person I put my trust into. Too many lives were on the line.

But it wasn't just me deciding. I hoped the majority felt the same.

Vernon stepped forward again, raising his hands in a calming gesture. "Okay everybody, it's late and we're all tired—and *that* is a very big decision to make." He looked from face to haggard face. "So, I suggest we sleep on it, and if we survive the day tomorrow, we'll discuss it again. Does that sound fair?"

Raker didn't look overly impressed, but, being the *oh-so-fair-and-kind* businessman he now touted himself to be, he acquiesced. Nobody else argued either.

"In the meantime, Sarah, start planning to hack the Governus feed." Then, before Raker could object, Vernon clarified, "Even if the hack doesn't happen, it never hurts to be prepared."

Sarah nodded. "I'm on it."

I hopped off my bed, eager to lay on it instead. But there was one more thing to do. For good measure, I dropped my retinal implant and crunched it beneath my boot.

"There. Monitor that."

CHAPTER 29

"The racers disconnected their retinal implants. We don't have any eyes in the Sweep anymore." Steel's voice remained irritatingly even.

"They what?" Khana hissed into her communicator as she stalked down the hallway to her living quarters. The transmission crackled, thanks to the sound proofing material that lined the walls this deep in the heart of Governus's headquarters—one could never be too cautious. One gloved fist shot out and punched the wall. Funny how threats came in surprising forms and from sources you'd least expect sometimes. Her own parents—a menace all their own—had taught her that fine nugget of wisdom.

"We shall discuss it later. I'll be in my domicile. Ensure I am not interrupted," Khana commanded. The elevator doors slid open and she entered it, slamming a button and feeling her insides drop with that familiar hit of inertia as the metallic cubicle rose. Within several short seconds, a single *ping* announced she'd arrived at the top floor—the executive living quarters. She stomped into the kitchen, poured a shot of replicated scotch, and slammed it. Grimacing as the liquid burned down her throat, she wasted no time pouring another. Lather. Rinse. Repeat.

Then she hurled the glass against the ornately scored metal wall, shards rebounding and scattering violently. She paced back and forth across the space. "You little cretons. How dare you! You think you can evade me?"

"Ahem. Sister, you left the channel open," came Steel's monotone voice.

Khana winced, then quickly collected herself. "So, I did. Forgive my error."

An awkward moment of silence persisted over their secure comm channel.

"Understood," Steel said finally, then added, "Are you alright?"

That caught Khana off guard. What was that—kindness? Uncertain how to react, a radiating heat spread through her cheeks and ears. No. That had to be pity. Despite his being the least insufferable brother, she was mortified by the idea he might feel sorry for her.

"Of course," Khana barked. "Mind your own business!" She closed their secure channel and downed another shot. *I will not let these racers ruin everything I've worked for.*

***

The morning had come and it was time to face my fate.

Racers were scattered about, getting ready for the trek in their own ways. Some prayed, meditated, or hid worry with laughter, while others practiced with a variety of weapons alongside the Venanti leading us out. Dino was surprisingly good with a spear.

Cala, and another racer who'd both proven very familiar with how breathers functioned, were busy talking with the royal family about them, and it looked like they were testing out using shards of the Heart Stone in place of atmospheric cartridges.

Everyone would be on foot today, except for me, Sarah, and Jorgep of course. Our Venanti protectors had already buddy-linked with some of the racers. With so many stone-laden staffs in a concentrated area, our hosts felt confident the 'wiley' Seevers would keep their distance. So confident, they allowed Setso and

Andra to accompany us as ambassadors. That didn't come as a shock, though, since the prince and princess were capable warriors as well.

I felt safer knowing they were coming along.

Andra volunteered to buddy-link with me versus Setso, which was a relief. I didn't want to worry about any awkwardness or romantic complexities while trying to stay alive. Yet, when I glanced over at Griggs—despite how angry I still felt—I couldn't deny that a complication had already wormed its way into my heart. I groaned internally, hated myself for letting him get under my skin, and needed to find a way to suppress it.

I went to Herc and ran a hand over the metallic star etched into his forehead. Closing my eyes, I took a deep breath in, then exhaled slowly. Herc nuzzled my shoulder as I stroked his face and neck. Taking more deep breaths, I mentally prepared for the trip.

"If something goes wrong and the Venanti can't get us out, this could be our last ride together," I whispered, blinking to keep the invisible dam holding my tears from bursting. His soft lips nibbled at my shirt collar. I smiled. "I'm not going to say another sappy word after this—I promise… But I love you, Herc. We've been through a lot together, and we make a damn good team, you and I." A single tear slid down my cheek. I swiped it away. There was a lot more riding on this race than he'd ever know. "And I'm sorry for getting you into this mess."

Herc's good eye stared into mine, streams of early morning sunshine glistening in that inky pool. When he let out a gentle huff, in my heart, I believed he understood.

The heavy footsteps of Sarah's Mech suit sounded behind me.

"The posse's getting ready to roll. Are you good to go?"

I blinked away any remnants of moisture, then glanced over my shoulder. "About as good as this girl can hope for right now." A forced smile accompanied my quip.

Sarah lowered her torso shield, her gaze discerning. "You, okay? Seriously?"

"I'm good." I straightened my shoulders. "Seriously."

Her eyebrow arched, but she didn't press it. "Alright then. We're all meeting by the fire."

I walked with her, Herc following along beside me.

"Did Cala figure out the breathers then?" I asked.

Sarah smiled, a look of relief crossing her face. "Yeah. From what she said, since the stone off-gasses or radiates into the air, using shards in place of our standard atmosphere cartridges should work. We won't know for sure until we try it outside of the Sweep, though." She caught herself. "*If* we make it out."

I mirrored her relief. "That's good. Here's hoping for *both*."

Raker's voice caught my attention. He'd bowed his head, addressing the royal couple.

"Your highnesses, I have been considering the safety of every racer here, and wish to respectfully ask that *we* also carry a stone staff for the trip. It would provide double the security and I'm sure I speak for everyone when I say, we would respect the sanctity of your stones at all times." His tone remained honorific throughout, and I wondered if this bizarre politeness he'd been showing the Venanti was all because of the life debt he'd mentioned last night. Maybe it was less about him acting shifty, and more to do with his—dare I even say it—honour?

"While that is a notable sentiment, I'm afraid it is not possible," the King replied. "Only Venanti may possess and wield the stones."

Raker's smile wilted slightly after receiving that polite denial.

The Queen clapped to gain our attention. "It has been our pleasure to meet all of you. We are thankful for the deal we've struck, and wish you the best as you return to your lives beyond this forest. The breathers will be of great benefit as we search for our lost brethren. I also hope we can continue communicating as new friends and neighbours. I humbly request you pass that message on to the village across the field as well. We wish to maintain positive relations." She signalled her husband with a nod.

"We call upon the stone's protection," the King's voice boomed. Every Venanti took a knee and placed a hand flat on the ground, closing their eyes. Andra glanced up and motioned with a few brisk head tilts for us to do the same.

"Oh, yep…" I lowered to one knee and replicated their actions, placing a palm flat against the sandy loam. The other racers followed suit. Sarah tried her best in that bulky mech.

The King continued. "Great Heart Stone! We request your ever present power as your people lead these race runners—new friends—past the Seever nest. May your light shine bright and strong throughout the journey."

The word nest made my skin skitter.

The gathered Venanti repeated the King's words in a chant, then slapped the ground once before regaining their feet, immediately pressing forward. Our guides beamed with positivity as they bid farewell to those who'd gathered to watch our departure. The King and Queen waved as our lengthy caravan ambled forward. Both Andra and Setso arced their staffs in the air in reply.

I leaned over to Sarah and muttered from the side of my mouth, "They're far too chipper to be heading into Seever territory."

Her robust metallic shoulders shifted up and down—the mech equivalent of a shrug. "Hey, their confidence gives me confidence. I'm rolling with it."

I swung into the saddle, easing Herc forward. "I'll go with that, too."

We followed the rest of the line beyond the Venanti's sacred ship, exiting the clearing. We'd barely travelled two minutes on a wide pathway before arriving at another threshold of grand, carved pillars. They loomed before us, signalling we'd reached our point of no return.

It was eerily quiet out, a stark contrast to the cacophony of shrieks we'd heard the entire day prior. Perhaps the beasts had all given up and returned to their so-called 'nest'.

With staffs held out, the guides at the front of the procession pushed forward.

Andra, who walked on foot by my side, smiled reassuringly as we approached the pillars. She gave me a thumbs up, and I flipped her one right back, repeating Sarah's wise words like a mantra in my head. *Their confidence gives me confidence.* "Alright. Here we go."

And through the azure encrusted totems, we went.

CHAPTER 30

The path was hard packed and relatively free of encroaching vines or branches. Though no part of this forested Sweep allowed a person to see clearly for long distances, now and again, there were nice sections like this—where the canopy spread thinner overhead, the underbrush grew low, and the trees were not clumped. Violet light filtered down to the exotic undergrowth.

At least here we'd see the Seevers if they came. Not *if... when*.

As if on cue, somewhere in the near distance a Seever cried out, and a litany of shuddering shrieks followed. I saw no sign of movement, but from all I'd learned about these creatures, the calls meant they were likely planning with each other. Coordinating their attack.

"Do *not* fire upon the Seevers," Setso announced, to the shock of every racer. But before any of us could question his tactics, he added in a firm tone, "Believe me, it will only incense them into a frenzy, which will not be helpful. We are confident they will steer clear of our staffs. Besides, it is a waste of life and meat to fell them unless it's absolutely warranted."

Grumbles wafted throughout the caravan—my own included—but we agreed to respect his wishes. They were the Seever experts, after all. Despite my hatred of these beasties, I had to admit the Venanti's respect for all walks of life, whether friend or foe, was admirable.

"You better be right," Raker hissed, his voice quiet, politeness on pause.

Not everyone would've heard him, but I did. He didn't see my glare though, too busy fiddling with his digicuff. The man held it near his mouth and whispered into it. *Odd.* No outbound signals were available in the Sweep, so what was he doing? *A verbal journal entry?*

The pillars we'd passed through soon vanished, swallowed by the Sweep. Herc's eye glowed the same steady green I'd grown used to seeing. The perma-pit in my stomach knotted and needled, showing no sign of easing as I surveyed our group. It was hard to fathom that, from a field of two hundred competitors, we'd been whittled down to a meagre thirty-five survivors.

A Joyan bird, the same odd-looking kind I saw when we'd first entered the Sweep, flitted down from the canopy and glided between trees to perch on a branch several feet away. Dejavu swept through me. Had that really only been a few days ago? It felt like a lifetime had passed. Images of Herc and me loping headlong into this purple jungle meandered through my mind. I'd been wide-eyed and hungry for the prize—for a new start—and so stupidly trusting.

A chorus of Seever cries shattered my introspection. My eyes snapped up, scanning our surroundings. Though I couldn't see them yet, I heard them coming. Buried maybe fifty-feet into the bush on our left, a ridge had risen up and that's exactly where the sound emanated from. The thudding of paws rushed in, accompanied by rustling foliage and crunching debris.

It wouldn't be long.

"Stay alert! They're close!" Griggs shouted, voice barking like a general.

Our Venanti guides shifted so that an even number of them walked on either side of the caravan. From my vantage point atop Herc's back, the formation created a glowing blue zigzag effect.

Every guide held their staff outward, moving it in practiced arcs. They shouted commands and worked seamlessly as a team. A shred of apprehension ebbed just watching.

We travelled as fast as our slowest legs could manage, staying as tight knit as possible. My thoughts wandered back to the Venanti origin story. How many of their ancestors had wandered off alone after the crash, affected by the air and oblivious to the dangers lurking in the shadows. They would've been sitting ducks, easy pickings for the Seevers.

How close had we come to that same fate? If it hadn't been for Sarah and Vernon, who'd had their own breathing systems in place, we might have all been rendered helpless.

Andra flashed me a reassuring smile, as if sensing my troubled thoughts.

Movement registered in my peripheral vision.

Seevers slipped over the crest of that ridge line and surged towards us. Their shadowed bodies ran together as a pack, their motion intuitive like a school of fish. It was difficult to get an accurate count, but my best guess, there were around twenty-five Seevers inbound.

"There they are! Be ready!" I shouted at the top of my lungs, aiming my sights.

More sounds came from the other direction. More Seevers streamed towards us.

"They're flanking us. Cunning beasts!" Dino growled between gritted teeth.

Setso waved his staff. "Whatever you do, don't stop moving! Stay in the line!"

Griggs military training kicked in as he added, "But if shit gets dicey, form a circle—backs in, then move! Always keep moving!" He and Setso exchanged nods.

In total maybe forty or fifty Seevers rushed in, each one skidding to a halt and wincing away from the Heart Stones, roaring in frustration. Their deep-set eyes focused on the Venanti' staffs, tracking every movement while their sinewy forms paced the length of our line. They moved like caged animals, their bodies from teeth to claws built for speed and ruthless efficiency, all clamouring for their moment to break free.

We pushed onward at a brisk pace, trying our best to appear natural so as not to antagonize them—an impossible task. Herc's eye shone a solid red the entire trek, which was not a shock. Every so often a Seever grew brave enough to dart inward. They swiped their massive paws and snapped their generous jaws, ready to latch onto anything within reach. But that bravery was thwarted time and again by the Venanti's swift staff thrusts. Every time, the monsters screamed and immediately recoiled.

A bulky Seever with jagged caramel stripes running the length of his body—a muted colour in contrast with the bold shades painting other attacker's hides—stared at Herc. Saliva dripped. His leathery skin appeared moist; his head blocky like the rest. I assumed he was male because we'd learned most Seevers were, save for the Queen and her harem of breeding females.

The thing's eyes bore into mine and raked over Herc's meaty form, searching for weaknesses—more than ready to capitalize if given the slightest opportunity. I envisioned those claws slicing towards my jugular and shuddered involuntarily.

"These Seevers are just the sentries," Andra explained, her voice surprisingly calm. "They scout the forest regularly, killing whatever they can, then return to the nest to report their findings. They would've been tasked to keep tabs on Varu. We expected this." She whistled up to Setso, pointing a finger straight up into the sky. Though it was barely visible through the thick canopy of trees, the sun shone bright overhead. "Break soon!"

Setso waved back.

Andra refocused on me. "An emissary will have already been sent to alert the Queen that we've ventured into the forest. We will see more Seevers the further we travel." She nodded to the caramel striped one stalking us. "That big one is a leader, we suspect a mate to the Queen. Or as you say, he has 'jumped her bones'."

I nearly choked on a laugh, then nodded. *I'll have to explain that better.*

Caramel's ears must have been burning, because the Seever ventured closer. A little too close. I opened my mouth, but before I could utter a word of warning, Andra had already thrust her staff towards him, shouting, "Back off!"

It shrank away, the spikey row of hair running down its spine rising as it bared its teeth. If a shark merged with a lion, you'd get something similar to Seever teeth. I cringed, recalling haunting images of those terrifying canines sinking into flesh.

"It didn't like that too much." I tempted fate with a grin.

Andra spun her staff, oozing moxie. "Definitely not."

And so it went for hours as we trekked.

We were one big moving sandwich. Our long caravan squeezed between two shorter, and much noisier lines of Seevers. They whined and roared, the sounds chaotic, constant, and maddening. I'd never wished for anything as hard as I yearned for a simple set of earplugs.

Our group only made two brief pit stops, one for lunch and one for supper.

"You must not stray from the line of our caravan," Setso commanded.

Andra explained, "If you become separated, they'll surround you and overwhelm you, staff or no staff. I assure you our safety is managed, but it is precarious."

Their warnings made perfect sense. Even with guns, if a swarming enemy got in close, you couldn't possibly hit 'em all. While nobody opposed, the strategy certainly made taking "nature" breaks a challenge. We had to get uncomfortably creative—peeing within the draped enclosure of a blanket held aloft by the only person tall enough. I felt so sorry for Sarah. Even more so if a deuce was involved.

The good news was, we'd been walking on a gradual incline for several hours now. We were going the right direction—ascending to the top of the valley. With each step we drew closer to the Sweeps edge, and to escape. I pondered at what point we'd safely be able to remove our breathers. If Grigg's had still had his spyro, would it have started working again by now?

Right about the time my eyes started feeling like half-filled sandbags, is when I began worrying we hadn't made camp yet. The sun had waned overhead. Shadows lengthened, and the details of the trees, leaves, even the Seevers textured skin lacked the crisp clarity of daytime. I was just about to tap Andra on the shoulder and ask, when Setso shouted, "There it is!"

He pointed to an outcropping of rocks up ahead, about as tall as a quonset with a natural concave depression within its sediment layered face. The overhang was plenty big enough to protect both our backs and our heads.

I gave Andra a beaming smile, which morphed into a yawn. It sure would feel good to rest. Herc had worked himself into a lather trekking in this humidity. Not to mention toting weary racers in intervals. My auto cart was fully functional, thanks to it being synched with Herc's custom bio-linked saddle. So when it was needed, we gave rides to weary racers, though I made sure to space out the rides so he didn't get overworked. Yet again, I silently thanked my mother for the cooling breast strap she'd gifted. I doubted Herc would have fared well without it.

"We're making camp in that rock alcove!" Setso shouted. "Everyone, collect whatever firewood you can carry along the way. Don't stray from the line. We won't be venturing out to harvest more wood. Too dangerous. We will need to make do."

Thank goodness it doesn't get very cold here overnight.

I activated the auto-cart. "You can pile some in my cart!"

As the violet Sweep morphed into ashen shadows, our group finally reached the rock outcropping—our safe haven for the night. Several of us tackled fire-making while our guides got to work securing their staffs onto nearby trees to create an outer perimeter. The Seevers climbed over one another beyond the invisible barrier, forming a writhing semi-circle around our rocky shelter. I couldn't help but notice how many more of them there were now. Andra had been right. They were trickling in the further we travelled toward the nest.

My tension doubled, the reality of our situation hitting deeper somehow. Any wrong move and this tenuous notion of safety could get sliced like a katana cut silk. There was no quit in these creatures. They kept pacing, watching, and waiting to rip our throats out the minute we slipped up. At no time could we afford to let our guards down.

"Why are you tying your staffs to trees?" I asked Andra, offering my help.

"Because they can't be knocked down this way. We've learned the hard way not to stake them into the ground," Andra said with a sombre head shake. "Seevers will shove stones and other debris with their paws and knock them over if they're not in deep enough. It's too risky."

"Makes sense. They really are smart, aren't they?" I held her staff in place while she tied the last strap.

She nodded. "Unfortunately, yes."

Seevers shrieked and complained mere feet beyond, probably livid we'd evaded them for an entire day. I scowled at the nearest one as he growled at me—which happened to be Caramel. I sighed, so tired of hearing their sounds.

Andra released her staff and smiled. "Done. Thanks."

A dim cyan glow now flooded the alcove.

"No prob." I walked back to Herc, whom I'd tied to a tree away from the fire making commotion, and promptly dug through a saddlebag. My fingers found my auto-enclosure. While I trusted the power of the Heart Stones, I didn't mind having an extra security blanket in place.

"Whatcha doing?" Sarah asked, now free of her bulky mech suit. She puffed on a whiffer and her slicked back hair was moist with sweat from the trek. A bonfire sparked to life behind her, silhouetting her athletic frame. Damn, it would feel so good to sit around a fire and relax.

I brandished the posts. "Setting up my auto-enclosure. Can't be too careful."

"Agreed. Need help?" She blew out a lazy smoke ring.

"Sure, thanks. I want to cover as much space as possible. Just put 'em exactly opposite mine. Here." I handed her two of the posts, and we split up. We each stuck a post into the ground on either side of the cliff face, then sunk the other posts about four feet shy of the staff barrier, creating a huge rectangle. Folks watched with curiosity as I turned it on. The webbed force field glitched and sputtered, but it *did* light up. It continued flickering like before, but it worked. I smiled, relieved. Honestly, I doubted I'd be alive right now if not for this helpful gadget.

Sarah lingered by the fire while I returned to Herc. I set up his rope pen next to where Jorgep had erected Keemi's while I'd been busy helping Andra. It was finally time to get that sweaty tack off his back. The minute I loosened his cinch, he nickered and nudged my arm.

I grinned. "You're very welcome, buddy."

As I disconnected the coolant breast strap from Herc's saddle, I glimpsed the sturdy silhouette of a man approaching from the direction of a now blazing fire. From the lack of pistols on his hips and the overstuffed cargo pants pockets, I knew it was

Griggs. I shifted backwards, using Herc's broad shoulders to hide behind.

"Hey, Finn. Can we talk a minute?"

Dammit.

CHAPTER 31

"What do you want, Griggs?" My brows pinched as I turned to face him.

He slowed to a halt a few feet away, rubbing the back of his neck. "I just wanted to smooth things over between us. I hope you can believe me when I say I didn't mean to offend you."

With a head shake, I turned to focus on Herc again. I pulled the saddle and moisture wicking cushion off his back. "Yeah, well, you still did." Sending him a sideways glance, I grabbed the brush I'd pulled out. I worked on Herc's matted mess of a coat, brushing his haunches and shoulders. Griggs shoved his hands into his pockets, eyes down, and a pang of sympathy struck. "But… I do understand you didn't mean to." It was the best I could do.

"So, what, you're just going to hate me for the rest of the trip? Is that how this is going to go?" He took a step closer. "Finn, what if we die tomorrow?"

"Then we die, I guess. It's not like any of this will matter at that point anyway." I lied.

Griggs shook his head. "No, that's not true. I can't die knowing you're upset with me. I want to move past this. Our— friendship is important to me." He shrugged in an exhausted kind of way. "I just didn't know what to think when I saw him go for your hand. I got protective."

The heat of my glare could've branded him. "If you'd *trusted* me to handle my own shit, you would've noticed me pull away from him. But no, you came barging in like some white knight I didn't ask for, nor did I need." I removed the brush from Herc's shoulder to work on his back. Flecks of grime and horse hair flew with each bristly stroke.

"But—"

"Look, I'm pretty tired and…" My words trailed off as Griggs took yet another step closer, now only a foot away. My hand paused brushing. Sensing his nearness, a tide of uncertainty swelled. Hesitant, I looked over at him, and as I met his waiting gaze, my resistance buckled. His fingers twitched at his side. His brows raised ever so slightly, eyes looking into mine with an intensity I'd never seen before, something different—something inviting and warm. No, more than warm. Sensual. I felt my anger melting beneath the heat of his attention.

"Finn…" Griggs' hand lifted to sweep a wayward lock of hair behind my ear. His fingers lingered against my cheek and the whisper of his callused skin brushing against mine sent electricity arcing through every nerve ending. *Oh, damn. Step away, Finn. Step away. You're still mad, and rightfully so.*

But I couldn't step away. His eyes—his *everything* held me there.

The corner of his mouth raised, and one stubbly dimple presented itself to clip the last straining shreds of my resolve. Memories of our last 'encounter' galloped through my brain, unbridled and unchecked. My thighs straddling his hips. His hands. His lips. I knew I should've reacted. Should've pulled back and stuck to my guns, steering clear of romantic complications. But no… instead, I swallowed hard and inhaled his outdoorsy scent, waiting for whatever might come next.

Griggs face inched closer and dammit all to hell, my chin tilted up.

His lips caressed my cheek. "Listen, you know I—"

"Hey Finn! Oh, and is that the top of Griggs' head I see? Good!" A voice rang out, accompanied by rapidly approaching footsteps. Barely a second later, Sarah appeared around Herc's front end. "The group wants to talk—" Her words cut off and Griggs' hand dropped from my face. I pinned my gaze back on Herc's coat, and forced my brush to resume its work.

"Oop, I'll come back." Sarah spun on her heels.

I whipped around, so fast Herc flinched. "No, Sarah— everyone wants to talk? That's perfect. Yep, we really should, you know, talk." All business, I glanced back at Griggs, whose slightly pinkened expression seemed a mixture of bashful and irritated. "Let's go."

I needed to get away. He was too dangerous. I clearly couldn't trust myself to be alone around him. Not if he was going to get all soft and kissy on me like that. Besides, what even was that? First, he acts like a jerk and says he cares about me like a sister, then he makes a move to *kiss* me? Nothing like sending mixed messages. Then another thought struck. What if that was just some twisted way to get me to forgive him? To sweep his blunder under the rug and ease his guilty conscience before we hit the nest tomorrow. My temper flared at the notion, and yet, I couldn't embrace it. Not with Griggs. I couldn't imagine *him* doing that.

The firelight beckoned me, and I ushered Griggs and Sarah out of the pen. Herc deserved to rest. I'd already set food and water out for him, so he'd be content for a while.

Griggs pointed at the group of racers gathered around the fire. "What's got everyone all worked up?" Voices layered atop each other in heated discussion. Several racers sliced their hands through the air as they spoke to each other, while in contrast, all of our Venanti guides listened in with a mixture of angry or bewildered looks on their faces.

"You'll see," Sarah said with a rueful glance.

Jorgep perked up as we approached. "There they are. That makes all of us." He gave Raker a pointed look. "*Now* we can make decisions."

Apparently, Raker had wasted no time trying to cut out the human element of the group.

"The party has arrived," Sarah quipped with a hip shake, but her wry grin was rewarded by scowls as discussion continued. Tatara gave her a sultry wink, though.

"So, what did we miss?" I asked.

"Well, Ol' Raker here's been making his case for emperor of Joya," Dino stated bluntly in his usual baritone timbre. Another round of chuckles went up, but not from everybody. Ryx and another racer flanking the Ganglian glared at Dino. Raker's new minions, obviously. Wherever he went he seemed to collect followers, those mindless enough to swallow his garbage. Or perhaps just fellow human haters showing their true colours.

Raker strode forward, splaying his arms wide. "*Emperor*, no. But in light of this horrific discovery—" He tossed his implant into the air, catching it with his other hand. "I believe Governus deserves to lose it all. They need to be run out and left empty handed. And I, my friends, have enough money and influence in the corporate world to make it happen."

I was still suspicious about why such a powerful businessman would even bother entering a race like this. Was his desire to forge new trade alliances a strong enough motivation? Both Vernon and Jorgep had family-run corporations, too. I didn't believe they had concerning motives—though, truth be told, Vernon hadn't said much about why he was racing.

Tatara spoke up. "For one, that's a whole lot of trouble. Two, as race winners and fellow participants in this overthrow you're concocting, would we get our fair share of Joya's claim?" From her tone it seemed like more of a challenge than an earnest inquiry.

"Well, you see, my company would be outputting the resources and taking on all the risk…" Raker replied.

Tatara crossed her arms, nodding in an *oh, I see* kind of way.

Andra, who was buddy linked with Tatara, straightened, holding a hand out. "What claim do you mean?"

Raker cleared his throat awkwardly, appealing to the racers, "Perhaps we should discuss these matters in private."

Andra's eyes flashed. "You will not. My brother and I have been entrusted by the King and Queen to address any issue that may affect our people, which includes Xola—*our* home."

Tatara sliced Raker a look as sharp as the barong blade in her holster. "That's right. The Venanti are technically the first peoples here—they deserve to hear what might happen to it." She turned back to Andra. "To answer your question, because this planet was believed to be uninhabited, according to Galaxium law, an uninhabited planet can be claimed, colonized, and mined by land development corporations. Governus won the bid and did exactly that. Egan is their settlement across the field. They want to build another beyond the Sweep called Novus."

"Yes, Novus. That's where your race ends. I remember that." Andra pursed her lips. "And to be clear, a corporation is like a company—a business, correct?"

"That's right," Tatara said, shifting to sit on a log.

Andra nodded, then looked at Raker. "But *you* want to be in charge of the planet now?" When he nodded, she glanced at Setso briefly. "Governus must be very evil for them to use you all as scouts the way they have. To treat your lives with such little regard. Will this takeover stop them from doing such vicious things?"

Without hesitation, Raker replied, "Yes."

"But!" Vernon interjected. "Not for good, and that is the true dilemma. Takeovers happen all the time, claims usurped by whichever corp—er, *company* is the strongest. Authorities let it play out as long as they stay within certain bounds. The only time they'll intervene is if civilians get hurt or first peoples are abused. So we—or more appropriately Raker, it seems, plans to kick Governus out of Joya and take over their operations… which means *he* will have *claim* on the planet. That said, he assures us this takeover would be done in an ethical manner." Vernon locked eyes with Raker, as if searching for signs of deception within those golden pools.

Raker didn't even flinch. "Of course, it will be. I have an honour debt to repay these fine people. They saved my life. All of our lives. Now I vow to preserve theirs."

"But preserve how?" I contested. "You talk a good talk, but there's way too much vagueness for me to get on board—like, what happens after *you* take over? Will you make an agreement with the Venanti for a shared claim, too? They are indigenous to this planet."

"Technically they are the first to colonize. They came to Joya on a ship. There's a difference," Raker said. "But I would absolutely allow them to live here without qualm."

I shook my head. "No, they've lived here for generations, long enough to have created their own world and way of life. This planet has even changed their bodies. It's theirs."

Raker's eye twitched. "I suppose that's a matter of distinction that would need to be determined." He turned to address everyone. "The fact is, I would ensure the planet is safe."

A racer across the fire shouted, "But, how would we gain true justice from that? Governus will just move on and keep doing the same shit somewhere else!"

"Or come back here with more firepower to take it back," Griggs said.

Jorgep paused his saddle polishing. "That is exactly my concern."

"What do you take me for?" Raker barked. "A weakling? If I take Joya under my protection, it stays mine. Governus won't be taking it back." He raised his hand before anybody could say more, softening his tone. "Involving the authorities only complicates matters. They'll either drag decisions out for years, or Governus will buy them off. As long as they're gone from here, that's what matters. I will ensure nobody on Joya ever has to deal with them again."

Several racers shifted away from Raker, murmuring. His use of "take" and "mine" didn't seem to sit right for everyone. It certainly didn't for me. Something wasn't right there.

Andra and Setso shared communicative looks, speaking with their eyes.

Sarah scoffed as she tossed a couple of logs into the pit. "Nobody on *Joya*. But, I want Governus to stop for good—so that nobody *anywhere* has to deal with their sociopathic shit. They need to get shut down permanently and pay for what they've done. By hacking their feeds and exposing them to the colonists, then to the Gala-Rights Commission, that'll happen."

Many heads bobbed in agreement. At a glance, it looked like the majority. I spoke up again. "It's the principle of the thing, Raker. If we just send them away, they'll be angry and embarrassed, but they'll also have gotten away with it. No, they need to be reported."

"That gets my vote," Vernon said. "The commission will give the Venanti a say."

Raker groaned. "Do you realize the painstaking process taking the legal route will be? And costly, to fund your applications and trials. You have no clue, but I do. I have experience."

"It'll be a nightmare," Ryx said, standing tall at Raker's side.

I shook my head in full disagreement.

Raker glared at me. "There is honour among corporations— a self governed set of rules must be followed. Once ousted, you don't complain or raise a stink. You either accept the loss and move onto another venture, or you return to try and take the claim back. I *guarantee* Governus won't come back. Fast and easy. Believe me, you don't want authorities involved."

"Yeah, well, what if we *do* want that? What if we want to ensure everything is one-hundred percent legal and fair for everyone involved?" Dino asked with raised brows.

"Yeah!" shouted someone from across the fire.

More mutters rippled around the circle. More racers shifted.

Andra and Setso leaned forward, listening and whispering with the other guides. Their expressions didn't look impressed, and I wondered what they truly thought about all of this.

Griggs lifted his chin. "Some people don't mind taking the harder route if it's the right route, Raker. But I'm sure that's not something you understand… Ships conducting legal business don't need black market cloaking devices. Isn't that the tech some of your Ganglian ships have?"

Internally I both cringed and cheered. Raker wouldn't like that, but maybe he needed to hear it. He hated humans for spearheading the Conduit Gate network, which had offered safe and practical travel for all—not just those with the most money and ships at their disposal.

Raker's eyes flashed with rage at the dig, yet he said nothing.

I gave my arms a wave. "Hold on, hold on. Listen, before we keep arguing—I think the Venanti deserve to have a chance to speak. They've been patiently listening and have heard every single point we've made. All of this directly affects them. This is their home."

Jorgep raised a hand. "Not to mention they have the Heart Stones that Governus very clearly wants." Some Venanti heads tilted at the mention of their Heart Stones.

Andra and Setso finally stepped forward. The rest of the guides packed in around them in a show of support. The Venanti prince nodded to his sister and she glanced around the fire.

"Yes, thank you. We have been listening and considering our options as you have been talking. We have suspected that this Governus company might be after the Heart Stone's power. I am not happy to hear you believe this too, but it is good to have it confirmed."

"Well, we don't know for sure," Sarah said. "But it's the only logical explanation."

"Sadly, I agree." Andra took a breath. "For this Governus to do everything you've said, to lie, plant memory wipes, implant you with recording devices, and plan this deadly race—"

"*Fake* race," Tatara blurted bitterly, before biting her lip, contrite. "Sorry. Continue."

Andra waved it off. "I was going to say everything they've done seems outlandish without a strong motivation." She grasped a twig and picked at its spiky leaves. "It is easy to imagine their greed for precious gems and ore. Even easier still to imagine it for ones that can heal."

Everyone nodded.

Vernon's shoulders deflated. "So, you understand the danger your people face. We weren't certain how ruthless Governus had truly been—didn't know how much to say since we were still figuring things out. But, and I can only speak for myself when I say this, I fear they'll do whatever they can to get their hands on your stones." He paused. "I'm sorry we never discussed this with you sooner. We should have."

"He speaks for us all," a racer announced, and a round of hear-hear's rose up.

Vernon nodded, then focused on Andra. "What would *you* like to do?"

"I can run them out of here," Raker countered. "I want to help."

"We understand that," Setso replied, stepping around the fire to pat Raker's shoulder. "And we thank you for that kindness.

However, we also know our parents would not relish exchanging one power for another." If he had any distrust of Raker, he kept it well hidden.

Andra tossed her now leafless twig. "We're confident our parents would say Governus should be stopped for good, not just for right now. Nobody deserves to be treated as they've treated you, and we must ensure the safety of our people, too. They should be punished by the law so they can't continue conducting underhanded and malicious dealings."

Raker took a step closer. "But, what if—"

"Enough already, Raker. Let's just vote so I can get some damn sleep." Tatara looked around the group, ignoring Raker's glare. "Or does anybody need to hear more? I think we've covered the big-ticket items *at length*. But if you've got something to say, say it now."

Raker raised a hand. "I will remind everyone that I have an honour vow to uphold—to save the Venanti because they saved me. If I am not allowed to do what I *know I have the power to do*, then I can never move on. It means a lot for me to do this."

I resisted rolling my eyes. Boy, he was playing the sympathy card hard. It was clear the guy *really* wanted to help. Or… *really* wanted to take over Joya. "How about you explain why we should trust you, Raker, after you unapologetically sabotaged our vehicles on night two." I pointed to the affected racers, then crossed my arms.

Raker's eyes narrowed, then he laughed, as if my words were the most preposterous thing he'd ever heard. "Now, now, I merely created a delay. If I had wanted to sabotage you, your vehicles would never have re-started. Don't forget, we all signed up for a *competitive* race."

I looked from face to face, shaking my head. "Yeah, okay. Whatever."

Tatara's eyelids fought to stay open, yet she thrust a hand up, addressing the group in a take-no-prisoners manner. "Time to vote!"

Vernon walked up to the royal siblings. "As the royal representatives here, will you vote on behalf of your people, or will all of the Venanti present vote?"

Andra replied, "I'd like everyone to vote, racers and Venanti alike."

Without another word, Tatara shouted, "Alright, let's do this! All those in favour of hacking and reporting?" Twenty-eight racers and all eighteen of the Venanti raised their hands in favour. The remaining seven racers supported Raker's honour debt takeover—which was more votes than I thought he'd get.

"The hacking plan has the majority. Vote concluded. Goodnight." Tatara blinked her double lids, gave a finger-flicking wave, and walked straight to her bedroll. She wasn't kidding about wanting sleep. Most followed her lead, only a few lingering to listen in.

Raker's face had anger painted all over it in bold primary red. He muttered under his breath, shook his head—his in-check demeanour evaporating before our eyes. "You bunch of simpletons! You've made the wrong choice." He kicked at the dirt like a disgruntled baseball coach. "You're going to regret this when Governus finds a way to quash your lofty plans. Money talks like guns do…" Hostility twisted his face. He pointed a finger at each racer in succession. "But guns are cheaper."

Dino waved a meaty hand. "That's enough Raker! The vote didn't go your way. Don't be a baby about it."

Griggs crossed his arms. "Yeah, shit happens. Be mature and move on."

Raker barked, "Don't patronize me, human." He gave Griggs a cross-fingered *fuck off* gesture, then spun on his heel, ignoring Sarah's diamond cutting glower as he stormed past.

"And *that's* why nobody wants to work with you," she muttered in a steely tone.

His entire body stiffened in response to her words. But instead of exploding with more threats—or worse, physical violence—he stopped and leaned in close, whispering something. I couldn't make out what he said, but it made Sarah clench her fists.

Her brows crumpled together before she snarled, "Fuck you."

Raker let out a cackle and walked away, claiming a spot on the opposite side of the fire. Good thing he was over there because I didn't want to be anywhere near him. I wanted to sleep in peace. Plain and simple.

Sarah's head shook as she pulled out a whiffer and lit it.

"What did he say to you?" I asked.

She frowned, inhaling long and deep. "He called me a Crimeon mutt. Said we didn't know who we were dealing with." She blew out a stream of smoke. "Fucker."

"Wow." I removed my hat to scratch at my hairline. "That's aggressive."

Griggs had been keeping a respectful distance, so as not to earn more *back off* glares from me. But he stepped closer regardless of what I might think, saying, "I'm sorry he said that to you, Sarah. You're not a *mutt*. That only proves his real character. That man deserves no measure of trust as far as I'm concerned." As if in agreement with what Griggs just said, the perpetually noisy Seevers pacing beyond the barrier exploded with a fresh round of frustrated cries.

Sarah's expression softened. "Thanks, Griggs." Then it hardened again. "I'm thinking we should keep an eye on Raker tonight—*discreetly*—maybe set up a watch, just in case."

I nodded. "That's a wise idea. Maybe just our original crew—keep it small."

"I'm in. I'll go round up the others." Griggs wandered off.

"Hopefully we'll still get some sleep tonight." I yawned.

Because, tomorrow we get the hell out of here.

Because, tomorrow we get the hell out of here.

CHAPTER 32

"**C**itizens of Egan!" Khana announced from her podium, her voice broadcasting across the central square located at the heart of the colony. "We have all heard the distant gunfire echoing from the Sweep, and I know everybody is very concerned. Be advised, the emergency response ship that we sent out to investigate returned with vital news. There might be survivors!"

Gasps and murmurs spread through the crowd of colonists in the early morning light.

She slapped on a practiced expression of concern. "We've confirmed there are predators in the forest, and I'm sorry to report, many of the racers have been killed." She clapped a hand over her heart, shoulders wilting. "Our hearts ache thinking about the hardships those poor people endured. Due to the interference in the Sweep, we had no idea the creatures existed. However, Governus is happy to pledge a support sum to every fallen racer's family."

An explosion of questions rang out.

"What are you doing to fix the problem?"

"How will you rescue the survivors?"

"Will those creatures come here?"

Khana motioned with her hands for calm. "Rest assured, we vow to protect this colony—this planet—from those vicious beasts. We're going back in!" She thrust a fist towards the sky.

"Our hover ship is already refuelled and restocked with the equipment needed to save the survivors. My good colonists, I promise you...whoever is still alive, we will get them out. And once they are safe, we will clear the Sweep of these dangerous predators. So, should you hear more gun fire, do *not* be alarmed. It is a good sign. It means we are completing our mission."

The crowd clapped and whistled in response.

Khana exchanged a knowing glance with Steel, took a deep breath, then engaged her boot thrusters. Rising several feet above the podium, she looked at her following with a determined smile. "Finally, my good colonists—since I am so committed to bringing our racers home, I will be overseeing the mission personally. I assure you this bizarre and unexpected threat will *never* reach our colony. Thank you!" The majority of the people cheered below. Such lovely yet naive souls—so optimistic and supportive. Khana lowered to the ground, striding to the hover ship.

Steel fell in step beside her. Once out of earshot, he muttered, "It'll take about six hours to travel around the Sweep to the other side. It's a *shame* we won't reach the survivors in time."

She spun a polished pistol in her hand, then re-holstered it. "Let's finish this."

***

I sat up with a groaning stretch and dragged my aching limbs into motion. Inky shadows slathered everything, yet birds chirped nearby, signalling a new day had arrived. Hardly anyone was awake yet, but Griggs jumped up from his bedroll the minute I stood, following as I headed towards Herc's pen.

"Hey, Finn, can we continue our conversation from the other night?"

I eyed him warily, not slowing down. "Nope."

"C'mon, I think after what happened yester—"

I halted and spun, my finger raised and ready. Griggs ground to an abrupt halt, nearly running into me. He teetered off balance a moment before planting his feet again. "Yes—what *did* happen? Didn't you say you cared about me like a *sister* before?" With a shake of my head, I continued walking. "You know what, it doesn't even matter. What matters now is getting out of this Sweep and surviving this damn race." I strode at a brisk clip towards Herc's rope pen, ignoring how green his eyes gleamed in the morning light.

Griggs sighed heavily, chasing after me. "Finn, this is getting ridiculous. Yes, I messed up. I apologized for that. And I got flustered before, but I mean, you can't deny that we—"

"*Noooope*. Don't want to hear it," I shot back, my hand slicing through the air. I'd nearly thrown caution to the wind last night, wholly ready to give in to my desire. Even now, the thought of pressing my body against him sent warm tingles into all the right places, but that was exactly the problem. I grit my teeth. "We can't afford to distract each other. Not now. *This*—" I flicked my fingers back and forth between us. "Can't be a thing. I'm sorry."

I didn't look back when his footsteps slowed to a stop. A sudden pang of guilt swept through me. *Shit, maybe I was too harsh.* I nearly turned, but then internally kicked myself in the ass. *No, the angrier, the better. It makes things easier.* Last night, once I'd finished my shift on Raker lookout and should've been sleeping, I'd stayed up thinking. About him. About us. About passing through the Seever nest and what that might mean. Deep down, I knew his 'protectiveness'—no matter how misguided—had been honourable. I'd been around my fair share of questionable characters in my gambling days, and I knew Griggs wasn't one of them. He was a good man, but I couldn't afford to make the same mistake I did years ago—of getting too wrapped up in love. No, I needed to rely on myself. Stay level-headed.

That plan was failing miserably, though. The mere thought of Griggs dying wrung my insides like wet laundry. Once I reached Herc's pen, I braved a glance back. Griggs had returned to the fireside. He rubbed his neck, the toned muscles of his arm flexing. I yearned to shout out to him. To tell him I wasn't mad anymore—that, in fact, I felt quite the opposite.

But I held my tongue. Dug my figurative heels in. *It's easier this way.*

Movement from the corner of my eye caught my attention. Sarah, who had apparently been watching from her cozy spot beside Tatara, waved to get my attention. She glanced pointedly between me and Griggs, her brows raised in severe arches. The look on her face said, *what the hell?* Not in the mood to discuss, I looked away, readying Herc for the final leg.

My digicuff pinged. *DON'T BE AN IDIOT, FINN. THAT MAN IS CRAZY FOR YOU.*

Okay… Clearly, she wasn't going to let it go. With a sigh, I typed in my reply. *HE DOESN'T KNOW WHAT HE WANTS. ONE MINUTE I'M LIKE HIS SISTER, THE NEXT HE'S TRYING TO KISS ME. DOESN'T MATTER. I'M FOCUSING ON STAYING ALIVE.*

Sarah shook her head, her expression surprisingly sombre.

Moments later, my cuff pinged again. *HE'S A GOOD ONE. DON'T FUCK IT UP.*

Now, that was a little blunt. "I'm not in the wrong here," I muttered, irked. I punched in a return message and planted my hands on my hips. *WE MIGHT DIE TODAY, SARAH!!!*

Sarah's eyes narrowed as she lit a whiffer, then raised her arms, the motion shrug-like. Our gazes locked, holding until Tatara stirred. The beautiful woman stretched up to give my friend a kiss on the cheek, and Sarah promptly turned to capture her lips, instead.

I averted my eyes, bending to collect breakfast from a saddlebag. After I'd set down feed for Herc and ripped into a meal-preserve-packet, my digicuff pinged again.

MAYBE. BUT I'D RATHER DIE IN LOVE, THAN ALONE.

I sighed and stared at the message. What if she was right?

***

It was time to move. Despite wolfing down a crack-of-dawn breakfast and packing our gear in record time, nobody seemed overly eager to leave this refuge. Seevers waited beyond the boundary.

Setso and Andra briefed us on what to expect.

"Today will be a shorter but more intense day." Setso pointed into the trees. "Since this side of the ravine isn't as wide, we covered most of our distance yesterday. By around midday we should pass through the Seever nest. Be warned, they will be everywhere."

"And why can't we go around?" A racer asked from the back of the line.

"There's no way around it without adding days to our trek, which is more dangerous than going through the nest. Their cave system spans a vast distance near the edge of the forest."

Setso nodded. "That's right. The Queen is incredibly cunning, too, so be alert at all times. Protect each other's backs and move as a group. Do. Not. Get. Separated."

The nervous energy encapsulating our group was palpable. Herc's ocular implant glowed a steady green, but I knew it wouldn't stay that colour for long.

"We're almost out now." I leaned forward in the saddle to stroke his neck. He turned his head to look at me with his good eye and I whispered, "Let's finish what we started."

The group formed a tighter line, following Setso two-by-two with our guides flanking. The Seevers kept up with us, sandwiching us in just like the day before. Jorgep brought up the rear with Keemi. Herc and I hung out somewhere in the middle, as did Sarah in her mech suit. Folks took turns riding in my auto-cart again while we trekked, thankful for the chance to give their feet a tiny break. The sweltering humidity eased and the flora grew less jungle-like as the day wore on, reminding me of our first day in the Sweep. The cooler air was blissful, and I felt relief on Herc's behalf. He'd worked tirelessly during the race, pulling vehicles out of the mud or over obstacles, carting bags or people around. There was definitely *no quit* in his character.

I doubted we'd even need breathers now, yet I wasn't about to test the theory.

Hours passed.

At one point, Caramel lunged at my foot, but Andra swung her staff, warding him off.

"Thanks." I looked out over the swarm of tiger stripes on either side. Most of their markings showcased shades of amethyst, umber, and red, while the odd few presented orange and more golden tones. The vision reminded me of snakes writhing in a pit. I mumbled to myself, "There's so many more of them now…" New creatures appeared at random through the foliage, joining the growing horde. The Seevers never seemed to tire, doggedly stalking us and testing their boundaries the entire way. Any slight motion we made riled them up.

"We will approach the nest soon!" Andra warned, shouting over the din of snarls.

One frustrated racer shouted back, "And you said the nest will be *worse* than this?"

"It will! So, prepare yourself—all of you!" she replied.

We passed by a collection of mounded boulders merged into solid hunks of stone. Each jutting mass was pale in colour, and both veins of web-like vines and lichens marred the rock's naturally marbled surface. The canopy thinned as the ground swelled with a violet blanket of leafy undergrowth, thriving thanks to the increase in light. Sadly, in our wake, it lay trampled.

Up ahead in the line, a clump of creatures got a little too zealous in their tussling for position. A tangerine striped Seever got tumbled into the guide walking beside Cala. The Venanti man jumped to avoid the creatures swinging legs, nearly falling over. Catching himself, he thrust his staff out to ward off the closest beasts, but a slippery Seever had already darted in from the side. It snagged Cala's pants leg and she screeched, losing her balance.

Gasps and warning shouts erupted from those close by.

"Get back!" While still steadying himself, the guide swung his staff around. The weapon collided with the creature's side before it could drag Cala away. The beast jolted backward and shrieked in pain—the sound piercing, yet ragged like a bear. Where the stones had touched its leathery skin, the flesh turned white and blistered violently, the wound frothing and oozing.

"Thank you, thank you, thank you," Cala said to the guide as we pushed on.

The close call hammered home exactly how precarious our situation was. One wrong move and that could be it. I suspected the others must've felt similarly rattled, because the level of idle chit chat lessened after that, everyone's focus sharpening.

Griggs glanced back from his position two racers ahead of me. I returned a shaky smile, but he looked away. Did he hate me now? The question popped in without warning, bringing with it a gnawing sensation. *But, isn't that what you wanted? Girl, get your head in the game.*

"We've reached the outer edge!" Andra shouted, pointing to another rocky outcropping on our right-hand side. This one had a dark hole carved into its centre. "That is a Seever cave, a small one—just a scout outpost." Andra stabbed her staff at a brazen Seever, forcing it back.

Setso waved, halting the caravan. "We will break here before we make our last push through. It will not be safe to stop after this point."

I seized the opportunity to give Herc some water and handfuls of oats. To maximize our agility from here on out, I disengaged the auto-cart. I downed several generous swigs of aqua, and locked eyes with Caramel—the Seever who'd been by our side from the start of this trek. He bared his teeth, letting out a stuttering growl. I growled back, fingering my pulse pistol's grips. The beast wasn't about to let Herc out of his sight. He certainly earned props for dedication.

"Alright, let's get moving!" Setso shouted, spurring the caravan to press onward.

Climbing back into the saddle, I nudged Herc forward. "Let's do this."

CHAPTER 33

We'd only travelled a few minutes before another cave appeared. Then two more. Then five more. Soon, we were fully surrounded by a cavernous hive. Seevers of all shapes and sizes emerged from their caves, salivating, screeching, and gnashing their teeth at the sight of us. It didn't take long for the horde to triple in size.

"Well, this is fucking terrifying," Sarah muttered.

The Venanti stared down our opponents and swung their staffs back and forth in steady arcs to ensure the creatures didn't get any bold ideas. Our guides hissed and growled at them, like alpha dogs staking claim over their territory. I cringed a little inside. Clearly they understood Seevers much better than we did. Still, the old phrase 'don't poke the bear' came to mind.

Setso called out over the clamour of Seever cries, "Do *not* show them any fear. It only emboldens them! We've passed through the nest before without incident. In smaller groups of course, but the principle remains the same. If we don't give them an opening to attack, I'm confident we will be fine!"

Vernon, who walked beside Setso up front, added, "We are all capable beings—otherwise we wouldn't be here now. Gather your courage for one last push, my friends!"

"Exactly." Griggs pumped a fist. "Stay tight and let's get the hell outta here!"

I ignored the cluster of nerves pervading my insides, shouting, "We can do this!"

Seevers slunk about, taking hail Mary bites at the closest prey. From my perch atop Herc's back, my vantage point offered a grander scope of our opposition. There had to be at least a hundred Seevers within view. Was this even all of them? Adrenaline surged as my heartbeat ran the Kentucky Derby. Cat-like eyes seared into me from all sides, their owners licking long tongues over lips. And the noise was near deafening. The damn things never shut up.

While I watched the number of caves steadily increase, the Venanti thwarted random attacks as we pressed on, jabbing and swinging their weapons with proficiency. The ground rose higher on our right side and the protruding caves formed plateaus with numerous holes sinking into the layers of marbled rock. One plateau stood above the rest, and at its apex sat a rocky ledge and a hole twice as large as any others I'd seen. From its murky depths emerged a distinctly unique-looking Seever. Its navy skin contained jagged aquamarine streaks that ran in haphazard lines down the length of its body. The spiky hair lining its spine was not black like the rest, but rather, matched the teal tone of its stripes. A thick swipe of that colour also marked the centre line of its face, much like a white blaze might run down a horse's nose. The creature strode into the light with purpose, its teeth bared, stopping at the ledge to survey the scene below.

"There, on the right! That's the Queen!" Andra shouted.

The impressive creature let loose a shrill shriek, and every single one of her underlings looked to her, crying out in reply. She screeched again, and all at once the chaotic noise stopped. As if choreographed, countless piercing orbs shifted in tandem back to us. It grew eerily quiet, save for the sound of our own feet moving forward. A pernicious shiver crept up my spine.

The Queen shrieked once more, and the reaction was immediate.

Every Seever moved in for the kill. Andra stabbed at an influx of creatures. Caramel sprung forward with incredible speed, snaking past my protector, his trajectory aimed straight for Herc's neck. I thrust my boot out, heel colliding with his solid jaw. "Incoming!" I shouted to Andra as I aimed my pistols, itching to fire. The blow knocked Caramel back, and right into the path of Andra. She pivoted and swung her staff, connecting with enough force to stop Caramel short. Our stalker whined and shuddered as his skin burned, yet he didn't recoil. Surprisingly, he fought through the pain and swiped his deadly talons at Andra.

Jumping back, she avoided one paw, but the other sliced into her shoulder. Before she could even scream, I fired two pulse rounds into Caramel's head and he dropped.

The Queen wailed, and Herc jumped beneath me, startled by the gunfire—but didn't bolt. I looked up. The Queen Seever glared down at me. I remembered what Andra had told me about Caramel, that he was one of her preferred fellas. *Sorry Queeny, but it was him or us.*

A barrage of gunfire erupted down our line.

"Are you okay?" I asked Andra.

She seemed shaken, but nodded. "Yes, thank you." Soon after, her eyes darkened, their depths molten. "Something has changed. They're not respecting our Heart Stones!" Andra shouted for all to hear, swinging her staff, scalding a younger Seever that pushed forward. "I think there's too many of us—the temptation is too great—the Queen won't let us pass."

A frantic voice shouted, "So, what do we do?"

Andra stabbed at a trio of Seevers. "Do what you must!"

"Fire away!" Sarah's voice blared through her mech suit's speaker.

Pulse blasts sliced through the air, but the beasts grew bolder. The Queen Seever's body contorted, almost writhing, as she let out a guttural bellow, the sound chilling as it echoed.

Monsters darted in while the Queen continued braying her commands. They clambered over themselves to attack. Even though her flock were being shot and stabbed by staffs laden with acidic stone, the Queen didn't relent. Clearly, she'd decided we must die, and that was to be heeded no matter what. Her pack pushed through the pain and continued to fight forward.

My neck was like rubber, turning in all directions to keep tabs on things. It was getting harder to keep track of them, they moved so fast, darting every which way. *The Queen won't let us pass...* Andra's words haunted me, ringing true. We were now at the heart of a feeding frenzy.

Gunfire blazed. Pulse rounds, shock shots, and ectoblasts knocked Seevers back, but more jumped forward over their fallen brethren. I considered popping a shot off at the matriarch, just to shut her up, but I was too busy keeping the nearest claws at bay. Herc pranced in place, his eye glowing a brilliant white, but so far he hadn't reared up. I dropped the reins in favour of my second pistol, and fired at anything lunging in, staying mindful of the friendlies below.

The Venanti were a flurry of agile motion—their fluid prowess with their staffs a wonder to behold. Glancing up the line, I spotted Griggs and Dino fighting back-to-back, felling foes on both sides. Sarah and Tatara battled one place ahead of them, while Vernon remained paired with Setso up front, breaking trail.

"Keep moving!" Griggs bellowed. As a unit, we doggedly shuffled towards the Sweep's edge. So far, every member of our lengthy caravan seemed to be holding their own.

Maybe we stand a chance after all.

The Seever Queen screamed as she watched her pack fail to take us down.

I blasted a steady stream of critters trying to get at Herc's legs, and Andra scalded anything she could lay a staff on. It didn't seem to matter how many we felled. More took their place. Noticing a gap had formed behind me amidst the chaos, I swivelled in the saddle and tagged four Seevers moving in on Herc's flank. "Close the gap!" I ordered Cala and the others, who'd fallen behind.

Two Seevers lunged before they could do so, and on a whim, I slammed my hand on the auto-cart button built into Herc's saddle. It flared to life, as solid as any metal, and it slammed into the creatures, sending them flying backwards. "Ha! Take that!" A wild cackle escaped my lips. "No rump roast for you!"

Griggs shouted, "There's too many. Everybody form a circle! Quick!"

"Move your asses!" Sarah added with gusto.

I holstered one pistol and disengaged the auto-cart, manoeuvring Herc as he pranced and reared, balking at my efforts to form into the circle. It was all I could do to keep him under control. I couldn't blame him for being terrified. At least he hadn't spooked and taken me for a ride. Other horses might've. But not my Herc. He was a true warhorse like his ancestors.

After a string of curse words, I finally got his ass end tucked into the rough circle formation we'd managed to achieve. I couldn't guarantee how long he'd stay there, but we were in. Poor Jorgep fought to get Keemi half-way into the formation, then gave up. His bleenad had murder in her eyes. Blood dripped from Keemi's mouth as her powerful jaws snapped. She caught a Seever by the leg, let out a reverberating grunt, and thrust her muscled neck side to side, thrashing the thing like a toy. I almost felt bad for the Seever as its head slammed into the ground over and over. With terrifying teeth bared, she continued mercilessly ripping into fearful Seevers.

All Jorgep could do at this point was hang on tight and shoot.

"Keep up with Keemi!" I bellowed. She was a force to be reckoned with, and the Seevers had quickly learned to respect her space. We needed to use every advantage we had on tap.

The caravan focused their firepower outward from our circle. Seevers fell in droves, yet we had close call after close call. Progress was slow, but we steadily kept moving forward.

In the next blink, screams rang out and I glanced back to see three caravan members get dragged away and their flailing forms dogpiled by Seevers. Shots rained onto the throng of attackers as those nearest tried to save our people, but it was too late. In seconds, their screams silenced. Two racers and a Venanti guide—lost. I hadn't known them well, but *dammit.*

"I see daylight up ahead! Keep moving forward!" Vernon called.

He was right. There was a clear break in the trees—maybe 150 yards past the last outcroppings of caves we were about to pass. A crisp, pale violet sky awaited. The purple leaves at the Sweep's edge appeared irradiated beneath the sun's brilliant light, marking our exit.

The Queen roared again, her entire sinewy body shaking. The coarse hairs stood on end down her back and her stubby, leaf-shaped ears flattened to her head. From atop her cave's plateau, she'd kept pace with our progress, barking orders at her legion. But, now, she jumped down from her lofty perch and paced along a low-lying outcropping. I'd been sneaking peeks at her amidst the fighting, and I saw when her head snake out to snatch a youngling by the scruff of its neck. The much leaner creature instinctively curled into a ball, and with a powerful flick, the Queen hurled the youngling like a projectile towards our circle.

"Watch out!" But my shout came too late. The rolled-up creature unfurled as it collided and knocked out the legs of Tatara and two others. They toppled like pins in an archaic bowling alley. Gasping, Sarah spun to grasp the offensive intruder with her mech hands, keeping it from doing damage. It was immediately pelted by Venanti staffs and pushed out of the circle. But just as Tatara and the others scrambled to their feet, another balled-up youngling careened in. Before anyone could react this time, it latched onto the nearest racer's foot and bolted. Vernon's foot.

The critter dragged him just enough to allow a mature Seever to latch on and pull.

His shout sliced through the air as he slipped away.

"Vernon!" I screamed, firing like mad. I was terrified I might hit him, but had to take the risk. If he went too far, he'd be swarmed and we'd have no hope of saving him. Someone's shot connected with the mature Seever and the thing dropped to the ground—fifteen feet away.

Vernon's cannon blazed furiously, but the beasts were on him. He screamed in pain.

No… I kept blasting, sharing a look of panic with Griggs. My mind raced, thinking of what I could do. I had to do something— maybe rush out as one big group. But before I could suggest a thing, Griggs bolted into motion, enacting his own haphazard rescue mission.

"Griggs! Oh, shit. More cover fire!" Whoever could, aimed shots to help. But everybody already had their hands full keeping the horde of Seevers off our asses. A critter jumped onto Sarah, raking its razor-sharp claws across her back and face shield, leaving scratches behind. The Queen hurled more younglings in a slick attempt to break our formation. One chomped on Herc's rear leg and he kicked out, hurtling it into a wall of Seevers— narrowly missing Dino in the process. I focused my firepower on covering Griggs and Vernon.

The Queen shrieked louder still, and in response, a new batch of younglings ran towards her. That clever beast had figured out a way to weaken our defences.

"Why didn't you warn us they would do this?" Sarah spat at the nearest Venanti, Setso.

He barked back, "They've never done this before!"

Griggs fired his pearl-handled pistols in all directions as he ran, the rounds ejecting as fast as he could pull the trigger. By some inexplicable miracle, he actually reached Vernon's side. I expelled a breath, momentarily relieved. But it didn't last. Somehow, he still had to get himself and a likely injured Vernon back alive while simultaneously repelling Seevers. That was a tall order. A stab of fear sunk deep—targeting the heart. I couldn't watch him die.

Sarah's text message flashed through my mind. *I'd rather die in love than alone.*

Aiming to misbehave, I bellowed to the others, "Hold the circle!" But it was already falling apart. The Queen tossed continuous offspring, breaking into our formation and splitting our focus. While we shoved the little ones out, the mature legion pushed equally hard to get in. Three more racers and a Venanti guide had already fallen prey to the barrage, getting dragged away and mauled, spreading our firepower even thinner as we tried in vain to save them.

Keemi was the only thing keeping the enemy from flanking and overwhelming us entirely. My fingers tightened on the reins as my pulse blasts knocked more Seevers back from Griggs. I glanced warily at my caravan. *Just hold out a little longer.*

A guttural roar burst from my mouth as I kicked Herc with my heels. We surged forward. In the next breath I hit the auto cart button, adjusted my weight, and pulled on the reins, putting Herc into a slow spin. The cart materialized behind us, crumpling Seevers in its sweeping path.

"Finn, get back!" Tatara shouted, her voice frantic. But I didn't slow down.

Still shooting with one hand, I reined best I could with the other, spinning Herc closer and closer to my targets. The commotion provided just enough distraction, allowing Griggs to hoist a now half-conscious Vernon up, draping an arm over his shoulder.

"Hurry!" Sarah's voice rang out, her cover fire slamming into creatures.

I wasn't far away when a set of claws raked across Griggs leg, slicing fabric and flesh. He released a rasping shout as his free arm snaked out to shoot the offending monster dead.

"Into the cart!" I ordered, slowing Herc's rotation. Griggs unceremoniously tossed Vernon in, rapid-firing as he waited for the cart to come around again. On the second pass, Griggs jumped in too, and quickly righted himself to cover our flank. I straightened Herc out, and aimed him back at our ragged circle of racers. Contorting my body in the saddle, I aimed shots to protect Herc and clear a path for us. Sarah waved and let out an enthusiastic hoot.

After what felt like hours, but was really a matter of moments, I pulled up alongside the formation and Griggs jumped out. Dino broke ranks to help, using his bulk to lift Vernon from the cart. Once they were clear, I swung Herc around again, arcing the cart back and forth to hold back the shrieking horde. With Keemi rampaging on one side, and us swinging on the other, I dared hope it might be enough to get us out of this hellhole.

Then a Seever jumped into the cart.

I couldn't snap my pistol around fast enough. It sank its talons into Herc's flank. He screamed, kicking out with his back legs, but the cumbersome cart hindered the full potential of his blows. The action only made the sanguine-striped beast dig in deeper and bite into my saddlebags with its teeth, refusing to be knocked loose. Herc broke into full bucking mode, splattering blood and eviscerating my ability to aim.

"Finn!" Griggs shouted. "If I shoot I might hit Herc!"

Shit, shit, shit… Then an idea struck.

I shouted a command into my digicuff, "Shock locks, activate! Max power!"

A sharp howl escaped the Seever as rippling jolts of electricity surged through its jaws into its sinewy body. Its teeth released from the saddlebag and it dropped, claws slipping out of Herc's blood-smeared skin. It landed square in the path of Herc's bionic back legs, and my horse hoofed it square in the chest, sending it hurtling into more of its brethren.

Undeterred by his kin's failure, another Seever jumped into the cart with paws raised to swipe. This one avoided touching the saddle bags—*smart*. My sweat slicked skin frosted over as dread settled. We'd just lost an advantage. "Get off!" With Herc's feverish kicking I still couldn't aim worth a lick, but I did manage to slam the butt of my gun onto the auto-cart button.

The cart's translucent support disengaged, toppling our attacker.

Desperate, I tried to get Herc under control. He was hurting and scared, and kept kicking out. One of his hoofs connected, crumpling a Seevers ribcage with a sickening crunch. His strong metal legs impacted over and over, snapping spines and sending Seevers flying like missiles at the enemy—which was good—but as he bucked, we inched farther away from our group. I held on tight. We were so close to reaching that violet sky. I had to get him into formation again.

"C'mon Herc, we gotta get back," I urged, my voice an exhausted rasp. A sharp buck jerked me sideways, but I clung to the saddle horn, mercifully staying aloft. My shots continued firing wild, their accuracy and stopping power far less effective than I needed.

"We need to cover Finn!" I heard Griggs shout, his voice fraught.

Raker's reply echoed, ragged and bitter. "We're barely saving ourselves here!"

Like a shark smelling chum in the water, a Seever jumped at us from the side. The thing latched onto the stirrup and sunk its teeth into my thigh. I screamed, firing a pulse blast into the critter's guts as syrupy blood welled out around its embedded maw. It released and fell limp, however, another attacker skewered Herc's left shoulder, just above his prosthetic leg.

I clung to Herc's neck as he reared, steadying myself enough to shoot it off, which left a gory hole in its head. My horse's legs faltered as the offending Seever went limp and fell away, then exploded into motion, bucking even harder. Distracted by the sucking bite wound scalding my leg, Herc's reaction was more than I could compensate for. My fingers lost grip on the reins and my feet slipped out of the stirrups as Herc's rear bounced me out of the saddle. The world flew by in a weightless blur, and the ground came up quickly. My body hit hard on its side. I squeezed my hand, but the pistol wasn't in it. My breathing echoed as everything spun. Somewhere in the distance, I heard my name.

Pulse blasts flashed overhead. In the periphery of my hazy vision, those rounds pummelled a wall of Seevers that circled me, the volley's barely enough to keep them at bay. *They're trying to help me.* Hot tears pearled in my eyes. *I need to move.*

But my sluggish body didn't agree. Snarling echoed in my ears as pain radiated from the bloody Seever bite in my thigh. I dragged my heavy head upward, watching Herc move away from me, bucking and kicking as if in slow motion. Fear stabbed into my heart. *Fight em' off, Herc. Run for the violet sky.* Blinking hard, I looked beyond him to the caravan's formation, which was getting ripped full of holes as members got toppled, bitten, and dragged off. Seevers swarmed around a rider-less Keemi. Her deafening roars reverberated off nearby outcroppings as she battled with vicious fury. How long could she sustain that? Where was Jorgep?

Numerous mature Seevers loomed on the ledge now—weaponizing their younglings just like their Queen had done. But where was the Queen herself?

With a sickening tear, blinding pain erupted as teeth ripped through my pants. The fangs cleaved into the flesh of my already injured thigh. The excruciation dissipated the fog clouding my mind. Instinctively, my hands reached for my holsters. My second gun was there.

Screams, weapons fire, and shouting mingled with the horde's chaos.

Movement registered—two bodies coming closer. The Seever gnawing on my leg dragged me with a swift tug and another cocoa-striped beast tried biting my arm, but I jerked it away. Its teeth only dragged across my skin without sinking in deep. I opened fire on both.

A gasp ripped from my lips as more creatures appeared overhead, their jaws open and spewing steaming breath so abhorrent, it made my stomach roll. I flicked my gun up, aiming to give them all a third eye hole. Yet, before I pulled the trigger, two leathery heads exploded, a fiery ectro-cannon blast splattering fragments of tissue and bluish goo across my face and neck. A glowing staff shot forward to pierce other Seever chests, their skin sizzling while their bodies jerked, then landed lifeless. I craned my neck to see Griggs and Andra's exhausted faces.

Griggs held out his hand.

I took it and sprung up as fast as my injured leg would allow. "Thank you."

Andra nodded determinedly, her focus locked on the enemy surrounding us.

Griggs sent another blazing arc through the throng. "It was either save you or shoot you." He must've seen my eyes widen, because he flashed a haggard half-smile. "And I could never shoot you." He tossed me one of his pearl-handled pistols. Catching it stretched the scratches on my arm, but the discomfort was tolerable. It could've been worse. He continued searing Seevers with what I recognized was Vernon's ectro cannon. I backed up against Griggs' and Andra's shoulders. Our bodies formed a triangle as we sidestepped back toward the caravan, which had moved much closer with Sarah leading the charge.

Oh, God. Herc… I whistled for him—my eyes searched past the writhing wall of Seevers. My heart turned to lead as we shuffled over bodies of all species littering the ground in various states of gore. *Where was he?*

The shrill equine scream reached my ears before my eyes found him.

I jerked towards the sound, wincing from the pain that caused, then froze in horror at the sight. A razor-toothed creature had sunk its teeth into the crest of Herc's neck, and now clung to him. Not just any Seever… One with distinctive aqua-blue stripes and face.

The Queen.

"Herc!" I screamed, rushing forward. He was maybe thirty feet away.

My brave Herc battled to keep from being dragged down, thrashing and bucking while her claws scored his flesh. His good eye was wild with terror; his nostrils flared as he panted.

No, no, no!

CHAPTER 34

I couldn't shoot her for fear I'd hit Herc. Cursing, I strained for more speed.

"Finn!" Griggs gave chase, arms splayed wide as he unloaded shots at the Seevers impeding our progress. Andra launched after me, too. Vaguely, I heard Jorgep and Sarah shouting from the formation, but their words failed to register. I did see a robust body charging toward us, though—Keemi—who vigorously ripped into Seevers on all sides as she swung in front of us to break trail. She panted heavily, her entire face and torso drenched in gore, blue Seever blood dribbling in her wake. Our foes scattered and cried out, yet more surged forward to block our path like they had a death wish. *They're protecting the Queen.* A tunnel formed in my view, blocking everything out except the vision of Herc's straining body looming ahead.

Despite the risk, I raised my pistol to fire at the Queen. There was no time to waste, and even though missing and hitting Herc would crush me, I'd rather he die by my hand than being torn apart. Seevers dove in front of us, piling atop one another, and at the same time Keemi lurched closer, her swell of predators colliding with ours. I couldn't get a clear shot. "Dammit." Pushing my limping leg into frantic spurts, I kept shooting, trying to create a line of sight.

The Queen jumped up, then let herself drop like dead weight in an attempt to disrupt Herc's balance. His head and neck jerked to the side, a feeble scream ripping from his lips.

My heart lurched in my chest. Maybe fifteen more feet to go.

A violet-striped beast evaded Griggs rapid-fire shots and lunged from the right. With a quick flick of my wrist, I let a point blank round fly into its snarling maw, exploding its throat. On my left, Andra's laboured breath huffed loudly as she stabbed and bashed with her staff.

Loosing a battle cry, I bolted forward. My chewed-up leg burned, held stiff like a stump connected to my hip, but I kept swinging it forward, grunting through each step. Alongside the others, I blasted like a commando to punch a hole and clear a pathway, simultaneously worrying whether my ammo would hold up. Would my guns be able to recharge fast enough to replace all the pulses flying down their barrels? *I hope so.*

"I've got a shot!" Griggs' voice was a forceful rasp. Sweat dripped from his hair.

"Take it!" I sucked in a deep breath, praying his aim would be true.

He fired, but a fresh surge of beasts dove in, and the rounds slammed into them. A feral growl escaped his lips. "Shit! It's like they're sacrificing themselves for her!"

"That's exactly what they're doing," Andra hissed through gritted teeth.

Five feet.

I shoved my spare pistol into a holster and yanked the knife from my belt—ignoring the sting the movement caused. A flash of orange and pink metal glinted off to the side and I knew Sarah was trying to get to us. A quick glance revealed what remained of our caravan rallying to help. The swell thinned in front of us as we broke into the tight Seever barrier circling Herc and the

Queen. Blood sprayed as we pelted the last three Seevers blocking our path. We were in.

I didn't hesitate, limp-hopping forward.

Behind me Griggs and Andra spun on their heels, protecting my back.

The matriarch released her bite on top of Herc's neck, letting her claws rake down his shoulder and chest. She caught sight of us just as her jaws clamped on Herc's throat latch. The Queen shuffled backward within the shadow of his now outstretched head, trying to topple him.

"Get off of him, you Bitch!" I roared, lunging. She shrieked, the noise muffled from Herc's flesh filling her mouth, and the matriarch swiped at me, reefing on Herc further.

One of her claws raked my forearm, but the pain barely registered. I was a grav-train without brakes. Sliding into her, I thrust the blade of my knife into her neck—up to the hilt. She screamed and snapped at me. Freed, Herc's head jerked up and he reared. One of his mighty metallic hooves collided with the Queen's back. Her spine caved with a sharp crack. Griggs scrambled to grasp Herc's reins while Andra remained a whirlwind with her staff.

Gunfire still blazed all around.

I yanked on the knife still sunk into the Queen's flesh, widening the wound. Viscous blue blood spurted and oozed over my knuckles. The Queen jerked away and my blade slipped free. Jumping back, I avoided a feeble swipe as she lurched backward, dragging both legs behind her.

"Oh, no, you don't…" Whipping my gun up, I shot three times in rapid succession. Blood erupted from the craters I'd wrought in the back of her head, splattering my shirt like paint on a Pollock canvas. Ferocious spasms overtook her body and she finally fell into a heap.

The chaos ceased. Every Seever froze, staring at their felled leader.

An eerie silence settled, hushing the forest.

"Go, go, go!" Griggs whisper-shouted, thrusting Herc's reins into my hands.

Without hesitation, I tugged on them and sprinted as fast as my injured leg allowed. My horse's breathing came fast and rasped in my ear as we ran. His neck was slick with blood; semi-circles of ragged wounds marked where the Queen's teeth had been. The opening in the trees wasn't far away though—maybe fifty yards. *We can make it.*

We merged with our fragmented caravan, and Keemi brought up the rear at Jorgep's command. The remaining Venanti guides wielded a staff in each hand now, the extra weapons clearly salvaged from their fallen brethren. Raker had picked one up, too, and swung it with his non gun-bearing hand. Everyone appeared injured in some form or another, however, three members were in particularly rough shape. Sarah carried a bleeding but conscious Jorgep in her arms; two Venanti half-dragged Setso as he limped along; and Dino carried Vernon—fully soporose—over his powerful shoulders. *So that's why Griggs has his cannon.*

Blood trickled down the front of Herc's chest and legs. Scarlet hoofprints stained the ground wherever he stepped, his gait growing slower, sloppier. All I cared about was getting him to safety so I could treat his wound. My wound. *Everyone's* wounds.

I tugged harder. "C'mon, keep moving, buddy."

Seever shrieks catalysed behind us with a renewed vigour that gave way to the sound of thunderous paws slamming into the ground. It became clear our distraction had ended. Their already fervent cries tripled in intensity.

"At least we've thinned out a fair chunk of them," Dino said between puffing breaths, though there were still plenty enough gnashing teeth and razor-sharp claws to do us in.

Andra shouted, "Just get to the edge! They won't follow us out!"

The bites on my leg scalded, and defiant grunts spilled from my mouth with every painful stride. *I'm getting us out of this damn Sweep—period.*

The Seevers caught up, flanking us. Having left the last of their caves behind, it was now a mad dash towards freedom. A smoulder of hope flared within, like a fresh log had been tossed on a bed of coals. Griggs ran alongside Herc firing rapid bursts, while Tatara, Cala, Raker and the other hands-free survivors pelted the enemy on all sides. Andra stuck up front with me.

A robust golden-striped Seever picked up where the Queen left off—leaping onto the nearest outcropping to hurl more younglings. When I caught a glimpse of sea-green, I stole a double glance, thinking my eyes had played tricks on me. But they didn't. An aquamarine stripe had formed on the golden Seever's face. *A new Queen.* With a violent snap of her neck, she fired two more youngling projectiles, but Keemi blocked both with her rugged body. Her broad head whipped around, teeth chomping one of the offender's legs, before flinging it back at the throng. The bleenad let out a reverberating roar, and I worried she might abandon us to fight more of the enemy. But faithful Keemi stayed close to her owner, who didn't look so good.

Jorgep's eyes hung at half-mast, his body listless in Sarah's metal clad arms.

"Fifty more feet!" Someone bellowed.

The sunshine intensified as we neared the Sweep's edge. Blinking and wincing, it shocked me to realize what little sky we'd actually seen these past several days. Ribbons and fluttering patterns of light filtered through the leafy canopy overhead.

A fleet-footed Seever snaked out in front of us and rushed at me. Aiming as best as I could while limping and pulling Herc along, I fired five shots, hoping something might land. If not, at least I had Andra close by. After a wet *thwick* and the creature's resulting screech, it face-planted, skidding across the ground. Unwilling to slow down, I jumped over it. "Watch your step!"

Herc's increasingly sluggish hooves stumbled over the fallen Seever, and he nearly toppled. I pulled hard on the reins, trying to keep his head up. "No, Herc! You gotta keep going! You can do this!"

He managed to right himself, seeming to rally with a slight burst of energy. He picked up his feet, perhaps bolstered by my encouragement.

But it didn't last. Within a handful of strides, his head sagged again—lower—his breath rasping harder as pink-tinged moisture dripped from his nostrils. A hollow ache of dread seized my chest, warring with the fear and determination already claiming space there.

We surpassed thirty-feet, and every single Seever within range launched a last-ditch attack. Waves of snapping teeth and lashing claws encroached from all sides, and it took all of our focus to keep them at bay. Seevers landed in lifeless heaps as we moved, creating continuous obstacles to navigate—a task which grew increasingly difficult for Herc. Agonized screams rang out twice more, and I knew our group lost more members. I glanced back each time to see opportunistic Seevers enveloping their flailing forms. Griggs swung his cannon and blasted, shredding sinewy feline bodies in an attempt to help, but their cries were quickly smothered. There was nothing more we could do. Slowing down meant death, and they were already gone.

A red-striped monster yanked Ryx's foot, and he slammed hard into the ground. Raker reached out for his buddy, but the poor sod got dragged within the space of a yelp. Without flinching, Raker sent a single round into the racer's chest before he vanished into the throng.

I wondered if he'd show me the same kindness if I got pounced.

"Fuck off!" Sarah huffed, slicing Seevers left and right.

Within twenty feet of freedom, the trees thinned even more, allowing waves of glorious sunshine to warm my already sweat-slicked skin. The horde of Seevers doggedly flanking us slowed. They shrieked and trembled while they fell behind, staring us down. It was like an invisible line had been drawn in the hard-packed soil, one our formidable opponents weren't willing to cross. Andra had been right. An elated sob wrenched free of my throat.

"We're nearly there!" Andra bellowed, a weary smile beaming on her face.

Herc's knees buckled and he went down hard.

"No!" I shouted, pulling up with everything I had left, but my horse had no more gas in the tank. He'd lost so much blood. His muzzle dipped—hovering just above the ground like a wounded soldier desperate to stay conscious in enemy territory. Tears flooded my eyes without warning or control. "Please get up!"

The new Queen Seever roared at the sight of us faltering and snatched the closest youngling, rolling it at us with startling speed. The ball of teeth crossed the distance, collided with Keemi and was promptly silenced, but that gave our foe new hope. Another Seever ball came whirling in, then another. It was horrifying how these creatures valued the hunt over their own young. It was also clear they weren't giving up. The throng hesitantly inched forward.

With shaking hands, I holstered my pistol and shrugged out of my overshirt, balled it up and jammed it into Herc's seeping wound. I wrapped the sleeves behind his ears to snug up the makeshift wrap. Then I grasped his breast strap, pulling up and forward. Jolts of electric pain radiated from my injured limbs, but it didn't matter. Herc huffed loudly and he lifted one foreleg as though he might try to stand. Then he wobbled.

"C'mon, Get up!" I commanded.

Griggs latched onto the other side and pulled with me, but Herc continued sagging.

A trickle of hot moisture scalded my cheeks. "Please, Herc!"

Sarah appeared, nodding at me through her cracked and scratched shield. She carefully but swiftly passed Jorgep to Tatara and another haggard Venanti, who slung his arms over their shoulders. "Get him to safety," she said. Then, sliding her mech hands beneath Herc's underbelly—one behind his front legs and one just in front of his rear legs—she lifted. Her hydraulics hummed and clicked as Herc's body raised. Sarah's arms trembled, the suit struggling to maintain the generous weight, but she managed to get Herc's legs beneath him. Barely.

"I don't know how long I can keep him up," Sarah shouted. "We gotta move!" Her wide feet plodded heavily as she assisted Herc across the last twenty feet. With her additional support, his metallic hooves stumbled forward. He hadn't given up.

I shuffled beside him the last several feet. Weapons blasts cut down any rolling projectiles still being hurled our way, but as the caravan crossed the Sweep's outer threshold and emerged into a wide open grassy plain, those assaults stopped. At our backs, cringe-inducing screeches morphed into rageful baying as the Seevers gave in to defeat.

Joya's brilliant sunshine splashed across my blood and grime-encrusted skin with full intensity, a sensation I would've found wonderful under normal circumstances. But right now, all it did was further remind me of the sweltering hell this planet had become. Multi-coloured wild grasses, like those we'd raced through as we left Egan, painted the fields this side of the Sweep. Several hundred yards of rolling hills stretched out from the forest's edge. Sparse trees dotted the plain, and a winding river claimed the base of a shallow valley not far off. One metallic shack. Besides that, there wasn't much to look at. There was no race signage or celebratory fanfare.

Several clumps of craggy rock outcroppings lay maybe fifteen feet ahead—the burrowless kind, thank goodness. They were just tall enough to create shade.

We surged towards them.

Sarah's hydraulics whined and shuddered in complaint. "I can't hold him," she hissed, rushing to the nearest rocky clump before releasing her hold on Herc. When she did, his knees buckled and his body collapsed. Sarah managed to help guide his battered form to the ground. I applied pressure to the wrap I'd fashioned around his throat the whole way down, kneeling beside him. He didn't look good at all. *He's suffering.*

I couldn't stand to watch it. "Dammit, I should never have brought him here." At once, my pulse pistol weighed a tonne on my hip. My shaking hand enclosed around the textured grip, the steel trigger guard cool beneath my fingers. Herc's breathing came short and shallow. He looked up at me with his natural eye, his blinks sluggish. I lifted my saturated shirt to check his still-bleeding wound, then reapplied pressure. If I couldn't stop the flow, I'd have to shoot him. He didn't deserve to suffer.

"Sarah, you better start hacking," Griggs muttered from somewhere behind me, but a quick glance revealed Sarah's head already down, her fingers typing on a projected digiscreen.

"On it." Sarah cast a concerned look my way before lowering her face shield to receive an elated kiss from Tatara. The two exchanged a few quiet words. Sarah also tossed her breather to the nearest Venanti, reminding her to insert the shard of stone their royals had told them to bring into the filter cartridge slot. Cala, Andra, and Setso directed the other survivors to do the same. Last thing we needed was for the Venanti to go loopy.

Griggs sank to the ground beside me. "What can I do to help?"

I nodded towards the saddle. "Can you get my med kit? I need to stop the bleeding." Herc's ocular implant still glowed white, reflecting against the flattened grass, but it was fading. "Please don't die. Please don't die," I whispered like a mantra as I ran a hand gently over his face, trying my best to soothe him. Injured group members received similar care from anyone in fair enough shape to help. Racers packed wounds, stapled lacerations, and sprayed healing salves. Our Venanti guides healed each other first, then fanned out in mass to apply their stones to our bloodied flesh, too. They focused on getting us to a functional level for now.

Whoever wasn't engaged in triage, took a moment to celebrate our escape. Folks embraced, hooted victoriously, or collapsed with exhausted smiles. I couldn't blame them, of course. Despite the horrors we'd seen and the lives lost, we were still breathing. We'd made it.

But I was in no mood to join.

Tatara and several others moved to keep a watchful eye on the forest, while Raker stood apart, whispering into his digicuff again. I glanced at Jorgep and Vernon receiving Venanti care, hoping they'd be okay. Jorgep was conscious at least, moaning about pain in his shoulder. But Vernon looked like death—his complexion pallid, and breaths as shallow as Herc's.

Griggs returned with the med kit and pulled out an item. "Cauterizing laser?"

"Yes, perfect." I jutted my chin toward the kit. "I need a fresh compress, too." Griggs promptly dug into the kit, brandishing the wrap. Herc's breathing was so faint now.

I swallowed a sob. "Hang in there, buddy. Don't leave me…" One ebony ear twitched in response to my voice. His muscles quivered—perhaps from shock. Removing my sopping shirt, I pushed the new compress onto his grievous wound, applying steady pressure. Griggs readied the cauterizer for me. I gripped it in my hand when Andra knelt beside me and stilled it. She placed the flat circular Heart Stone that was usually tethered around her neck over Herc's wound. She closed her eyes, brows pinching with focus.

I was speechless, overwhelmed by her thoughtfulness and care. Herc was pretty damn special to me, and she knew it. I wiped the moisture from my cheeks using the back of my filthy, blood encrusted hands. "Thank you, Andra."

She met my gaze, and it felt like she was seeing into my soul. "Your horse is a hero. I only hope we're not too late." She closed her eyes again and silent sobs wracked my body.

From the shade of another outcropping, came a weak moan. A weary and blood-stained form dragged himself into a sitting position—his more alert face a welcome sight.

"Vernon, you live!" Tatara said with a huge smile. "Thank goodness. I was worried."

Vernon chuckled, the sound quiet and broken. "As was I."

"They're coming." Raker said, his attention focused off in the distance to our right. Everyone froze, their gazes sweeping our surroundings. Dino and Griggs looked ready to kill.

Tatara's gun trained on the forest, panning left and right. "Where?"

Raker flashed an annoyed glare. "Not from the forest!" He pointed sharply to the right, tight to Sweep's tree line. "Over there." Gazes followed his finger to where a sleek Governus hover ship approached. Looks of dread and uncertainty made their rounds within the group.

"Sarah… how's it coming?" Griggs asked.

"Still working on it." Her fingers punched in code with acute dexterity.

Though I heard everything going on around me, my attention remained focused on Herc. He wasn't looking any better yet—his breaths still shallow. Was the stone even working?

Griggs placed a hand on my shoulder.

"We've come too far to give up now, Herc," I whispered. "We were going to build a new life on Joya, remember?" Gently, my hands ran down his face and massaged the undamaged part of his neck. The dried grime covering his matted coat was crispy beneath my touch. Moisture glistened in his good eye as a pitiful whine escaped his lips. I swallowed hard, murmuring a steady stream of encouraging words.

The light of his ocular implant flickered. I'd never seen it flicker before.

A heavy sigh escaped Andra's lips. The Venanti princess's sombre gaze met my own and she shook her head. "It won't be long now. The stone will help him pass peacefully."

Tears swelled anew. *No.* Blinking furiously, I felt so helpless. My lip quivered as I whispered, "I'm here with you, Herc…" Guilt tore at my insides. This was my fault. I'd brought him here—failed him. I'd failed my family. I'd been so stupid. Caressing his face, all I could do was provide as much comfort as possible. I bent to kiss his thick cheek. "I'm right here..."

Then the shallow rise and fall of his chest stopped.

CHAPTER 35

"**B**oss, there's movement up ahead," the pilot announced from behind his console.

Khana peered through the viewing portal set into the front wall of the hover ship's nav deck, and spied several tiny dots along the tree line in the distance. "Magnify."

The viewpoint pixelated in a flash, then refocused with greater clarity.

Khana sat back in her high-backed captain's seat, counting out loud. "Looks like eleven of our racers made it out. And… ten of the locals. Ah—" She grinned, leaning forward. "I see they have their glowing spears with them, too. How perfect. Goodness, they've made it easy for me, haven't they?"

"For us," Steel corrected. He stood from his seat nearby, smoothing his vest.

Khana waved a hand. "Right, whatever." She inspected the group of survivors more closely. The butt end of a bleenad poked out behind a rock face. There was an oddly familiar Ganglian, a striking Pembru woman, someone in an orange mech, and several other generic forms all blending together. But then a familiar cowboy hat caught her eye. "Well, I'll be…"

"What?" Steel asked, his face a dead pan.

"It's that girl—you know, the human with the *horse*."

"So? What about her?"

Khana shrugged, her expression bewildered. "I'm just surprised she survived, I guess. She looked so fragile and *simple*. And that animal—a bizarre choice. So rudimentary. It's unsurprising, it didn't make it." She donned her signature bowler hat, tilting it just so, then straightened the silk tie knotted perfectly in the apex of her high-neck collar. Khana stood with a determined smile. "I suppose it is time to get ready. Shall we?"

Steel gave a half bow, waving an arm for her to go ahead. "Ladies first."

***

Andra left her Heart Stone resting on Herc's neck so she could reach out for my hands. Grasping and squeezing them, her lips pressed into a thin line. "I'm so sorry, Finn. Sadly, his injuries were too great. The stone didn't have enough time to work." She let out a high-pitched giggle, then bit it back—her eyes shining with apology.

I disconnected my breather, realizing that within the flurry of the situation, she hadn't received one yet. She had her prepared stone shard at the ready while I clipped it onto her lower face. Once the atmospheric cartridge was filled, I squeezed Andra's hands in return, giving a shaky smile. "Thank you for trying." The words came out a whisper. I pushed myself to stand and sidestepped Griggs, who hadn't left me. Sniffing, I ran a hand over my face, feeling the puffy skin around my eyes. *I can't deal with this right now.*

"I'm so sorry," he said as I passed by, sombreness darkening his eyes.

"Me too." With a brisk nod, I strode away from the group. I glanced at the Governus hover ship rapidly approaching and sighed heavily. All I wanted to do was curl into a ball and weep unabashedly, but I couldn't. There was unfinished business yet to attend to. Rolling my shoulders, I cleared my throat and blew out a forceful breath.

When I sensed Griggs presence inch up beside me, I pulled his pearl handled pistol from my left holster and handed it over. He took the weapon back and holstered it, silent. His eyes darted my way furtively every few seconds.

I knocked my hat back, letting it fall between my shoulder blades. I ran a hand through the rat's nest on top of my head and decided to change the subject. "Listen, thanks for the help back there." My voice was hoarse. "Honestly, I don't think we—er, *I* would've made it without you." As my eyes flicked back to Herc, I winced involuntarily.

Griggs hand found mine. "I needed you to make it."

The sound of the hovership's wind turbines reached my ears.

"Sarah, how's the hacking coming?" Tatara called out. "They'll be here soon."

"Nearly there. Just one more bypass—" Her fingers deftly swiped icons and typed commands with proficiency. Then with flair, she pounded her finger on one last button. "Done! We're patched into the colony's video feed and the signal's strong enough for us to broadcast."

"Perfect." Tatara blew an air kiss Sarah's way, the two sharing a grin. "So, we're ready to make their lives miserable if Governus doesn't play ball. Love it."

Raker laughed bitterly, rolling his eyes. "*If* Governus doesn't play ball. Do you really think they're going to care what a few insignificant racers—*who they already tried to kill*—plan to say or do?" He leaned on the Venanti staff he'd commandeered. "Unlikely."

"Yeah, well, we have to try," I shot back.

Raker cocked an eyebrow, donning the hood of his cloak. "I don't think *we* need to do anything you say. What makes you the leader of this little group of ours? You look weak with your face all splotchy from crying after losing your precious little pet. I think it's best to let a seasoned businessman negotiate on our behalf." He flashed a smug smile.

A searing heat broiled inside. *Precious little pet?* I lunged for him, but Griggs grabbed me by the waist, holding me back. "You can go straight to hell, Raker!"

He sneered. "You think your fictitious human hell is a threat?"

Vernon groaned woefully as he stepped into the fray, clearly a bit stiff from his mostly healed injuries. He cast me an *I've got this* look, then cut Raker a steely glare. "Seasoned businessman you say? Well, yes, actually that makes perfect sense. I am quite seasoned. Good suggestion. I'd be happy to talk for the group."

Raker shook his head, shouting, "No, that's not what I meant."

"Nobody wants your leadership! Give it up." Vernon shouted back, as blunt as I'd ever heard him be. While the intensifying hum of the approaching hover ship necessitated raised voices, truth be told, there might've been shouting regardless.

Raker hissed through his teeth. "You're out of your depth here old man! Step aside!"

"You're a saboteur—one whose presence has been barely tolerated. Anybody *but you* would be fit to speak on our behalf!" Vernon's ears flushed and Raker's hands clenched. Several other racers and Venanti, moved towards us, poised to intervene.

As much as I wanted to let this play out and watch Vernon verbally flay Raker, we didn't have time for it. I sliced a hand through the air. "Look, nobody is anyone's *leader*. We already agreed we'd all be present talking to Governus. So, let's just drop it."

A throat cleared loudly. "Excuse me?" Setso interjected calmly, his hand raised as he walked over to us—his injuries freshly healed. Our heated eyes swung his way, and I noticed

Raker ever so casually manoeuvre his salvaged Heart Stone staff behind his body.

"I hate to interrupt," Setso continued apologetically, adjusting the breather on his face, which was clearly functioning as it should—a relief. Though he maintained a tightly collected expression, I could see fragments of sadness layered there. As a warrior and a leader, he masked his pain well... he'd experienced many losses today. His head dipped. "I'm sorry for how this journey played out. We've never experienced the Seevers that riled up. We failed to predict."

Vernon smiled graciously. "What happened is nobody's fault. We are sorry, too."

"Thank you." Setso nodded, his mouth a tight line. Then he turned to address Raker directly, holding out an open palm. "I'll take that staff back now, Raker. You wielded it with great skill during battle and your help will never be forgotten. But it must be returned."

Gusts of dusty air kicked up, causing dirt devils to spin beyond the interspersed rocky outcroppings surrounding us. The hover ship prepared to land maybe fifty-feet away, the great metallic propellers that lined each side of the craft tilting on an angle to slow its speed. It was a streamlined conveyance, shining with chrome-like panels and an obnoxious Governus symbol perched on the angled nose, which the nav deck windows rested just above.

"They're almost here, guys!" Dino called out. "Two-minute warning."

From beneath his hood, Raker's eyes flashed with something dark—an emotion I couldn't nail down. He didn't move, fingers gripped tighter on the wooden pole. Then his mouth curled into an almost creepily amiable smile. "Of course. Forgive me, I got distracted." He presented the staff to the prince.

"You're forgiven," Setso said, gripping the staff in his hand. "It is understandable why you were distracted—why we are all distracted." He looked around at everybody's haggard faces. "We have just been through something intense and tragic… far too many souls have been lost. We will mourn, but we must also remember to be thankful. They gave their lives so that we could live. Cherish that gift."

Our group nodded respectfully in response to his wise words. I found myself thinking he'd make a good king, someday. Setso then excused himself to fellowship with his people. They stood in small groups near the rocks, and some spoke with Andra who still lingered near Herc. I grimaced and looked away, unable to face seeing his lifeless body right now.

The hover ship's engines thrummed and whirred as the landing gear lowered.

I cleared my throat. "Looks like it's go-time. Everyone ready?"

Griggs shrugged, letting out a dry chuckle. "Not like we have a choice."

Jorgep left Keemi tied to a scraggly tree behind an outcropping, joining us.

Sarah exchanged a look with Tatara, then hammer curled a fist, saying with determination, "I don't care what their excuse is. Let's take those fuckers down."

"Hear, hear!" Tatara chirped. A chorus of hearty "yeah's" followed.

Raker let out an amused huff, but kept his mouth shut. Thank goodness for that, too, because after everything we'd just been through, and the hurtful words he'd already uttered, I had very little patience left. None, in fact.

Vernon spoke up again, ever the voice of reason. "They need to atone for their actions, certainly, but we must be thorough and careful in this matter. Let us see what they have to say, then go from there. Keep your anger in check." He turned to our Venanti counterparts. "I want you all to hang back for safety as we handle this negotiation, but remain alert just in case."

Setso waved his people back, but stepped forward himself. "I will stand with you to represent the Venanti in these matters." His expression was resolute.

Respect glinted in Vernon's eyes. "As you wish."

We stepped out, forming a rough line between the two closest rock formations. We'd agreed to present a united front before Governus. What they did was deplorable and they needed to be stood up to, no matter what kind of clout they might try to throw around. No matter what, I aimed to stick to my guns—demand they fess up, and take their lumps. My own regrets aside, their actions killed my horse.

Griggs stood to my left. Vernon, Cala, and two other racers whose names I didn't know stood beyond him. Tatara stood on my right, with Raker, Jorgep, Dino, and Setso beside her.

"You stay behind us, Sarah," Vernon said. "Your suit's transmitting capabilities need to remain intact and fully functional until these dealings are complete."

Sarah didn't look too happy about having to linger behind, but she complied.

Looking down the line, it really hit home that only eleven of us had made it out alive. My mind reeled, thinking back on the two-hundred racers who'd entered the Sweep just days ago.

Only ten Venanti had survived.

The hover ship swung its ass end around and set down. Windswept grasses thrashed violently, powerless against the turbulent air. The landing gear shifted and clunked as it stabilized on the ground. The multi-propeller system disengaged—the engine's high-pitched whine ebbing.

I straightened my shoulders and adjusted the hat back atop my dishevelled hair, biting the inside of my cheek to keep the raw, churning emotions at bay. No easy feat, but a necessary one. We had to present strength as we spoke to Governus, or else, like Raker said, they'd undoubtedly write us off as weaklings. As much as I despised the man, he hadn't been wrong on that. Such a powerful corporation might simply laugh at our demands. Or maybe we'll find out we gave the colony too much credit, and they were in on this ploy from the start. Who knows? Threatening to expose them could turn out to be entirely useless. *No. Don't start second guessing things.*

Giving my head a quick shake, I refocused on the hover ship.

A dark seam appeared in the smooth hull and a heavy metal door lowered. Two thick hydraulic arms revealed themselves, each flanking a wide treaded walkway. Backlit by amber light, numerous figures became visible in the loading dock beyond the hatch. As soon as the ramp reached the ground, ten individuals walked forward into full view. They formed a line mirroring ours about forty feet away. In the centre stood the same two Governus CEOs I'd seen at the start line—each dressed in dapper fashion, their looks completed by fancy hats and guns on their hips. Security personnel wearing matching grey uniforms fanned out to flank them on either side, eight in all. They wore flak vests and black, skull-wrapping helmets, ammo-filled belts, and held pulse rifles in the low ready position.

"What's with the armed posse?" A wary Tatara muttered.

"I don't like it. Be ready for anything," Griggs replied, his eyes hard as steel.

"Agreed." My fingers inched toward the hilt of my surviving pistol, wishing I'd grabbed my rifle. Warning bells blared inside my head. Did they bring armed backup because they were expecting trouble? Were they concerned we'd attack them in cold blood? I checked myself. That actually seemed like a very reasonable worry for Governus to have—considering what they did to us. "Perhaps they're expecting Seever trouble..."

"Or perhaps they're going into the Sweep next," Jorgep chimed in.

Griggs shook his head. "They'd have way bigger guns if they were going in there."

Jorgep conceded that point. "Yes, I suppose you're correct Mr. Griggs."

"Don't worry, I'm recording everything." Sarah tapped the chest panel housing her suit's camera components.

One of Governus's grey-skinned CEOs stepped forward—Khana, if I'd read her name tag correctly back in Egan. Dressed in a silken navy pant suit, crisp tie, and an over-the-shoulder holster harness similar to what Griggs wore, her tall, curvy form cast a formidable shadow. The male CEO—Steel—stood at her side, appearing equally impressive in his cravat and tailored suit, which had been artfully tapered to showcase his metallic leg prosthetics. I noted the long-barrelled pulse pistols on his hips as he eyed us with thinly-veiled disinterest—one brow raised; mouth set in a hard line.

Before anybody could speak a word, Khana tossed a tawny leather duffel bag into the space between us. Her all-business expression was in stark contrast with the friendly, smiling façade she'd presented before the race commenced. She hooked her thumbs through the straps of her holsters, her posture stiff, poised.

"There's more than enough money in that bag to set you all up for life. If you sign a contract to keep your mouths shut and discreetly move on from Joya, it's yours." The CEO gave the barest of nods. Sunlight gleamed off the metallic insignia sewn into her ebony bowler hat.

We all looked between each other, baffled.

"Is she serious?" Cala whispered from the end of our line, taking the words right out of my mouth. Similarly incredulous murmurs followed, building steam like a ball rolling downhill, until Raker burst into laughter, slapping his knee. The sound was harsh and grating, yet it caught like fire in the wind. Incredulous chuckles erupted. My neck and cheeks grew hot. How typical for a big corporation to use money to throw their weight around.

How dare they? They aren't even denying they tried to kill us.

I half-expected Raker to blurt something typically offensive, but he didn't. It was Griggs who spoke up first. He shook his head and raised a hand. "Now, what makes you think we would ever do that? We know what you did. We're the ones holding the cards."

I couldn't contain myself. "What you need to do before anything else is apologize. That's the least you can do, and then *maybe* we can talk about resolution."

Khana's thin brows raised. She exchanged a glance with her metal-legged partner who merely shrugged, then looked down at her row of security crew. A few adjusted their stances, their feet spreading further apart. Steel's fingers rapped against the butt end of his pistols. The already uneasy sensation in my gut doubled.

Khana's lips pursed, her piercing gaze returning to fall upon us. Once more she pointed to the bag and a tense silence hung in the air before she spoke. "You must've caught me on a good day, because I'm offering you a lifeline here. I'm not going to say this again, so consider my words *very* carefully. Take. The. Damn. Money. And walk away."

"We don't want your dirty money!" Tatara shot back with her trademark sass.

"Have it your way." The CEO's right hand moved in a blur.

In the space of a twitch, something warm and wet splattered my face. The world seemed to move in slow motion as my eyes snapped sideways to watch Tatara's body shudder beside me, then wobble, before toppling forward face first into the ground. The impact caused whorls of dust to kick up into the air, and I jerked back in delayed reaction, horrified. Thick syrupy blood poured from a ragged hole in her forehead.

Sarah screamed as more barrels flashed across the field.

Griggs yanked my hand. "Everyone down!"

CHAPTER 36

"**F**olks dove in a flurry of motion. Griggs grunted as he dragged me behind the nearest rock outcropping. I'd drawn my gun in a knee-jerk reaction and fired haphazard rounds in Governus's general direction. But as soon as my back slammed against the craggy rock face, I froze in near catatonic shock. With shaky hands, I wiped Tatara's blood off of my cheek and neck, staring at my stained fingers as though they might burst into flames.

"Tatara…" I breathed, touching my forehead. That just as easily could've been me.

Grigg reached over and gripped my shoulders, giving them a shake. "Snap out of it! Fight now—freak out later!" The words seared through my frazzled emotions like a branding iron.

"Right." I blinked hard several times. "You're right." I crawled the few feet between me and Herc's lifeless body—which had been behind shelter, thankfully—and yanked my pulse rifle free of the saddle's sheath. Andra, who had returned to Herc's side, held one of his rear legs, a strange shimmer covering them both. Having zero time to wonder, I darted back to my previous position and raised the rifle to my shoulder, firing alongside Vernon, Griggs, and Cala. I stole a glance across the way, relieved to see Dino and Jorgep had landed behind the opposite rock face. Jorgep soothed Keemi, while the others jerked in and out from behind their shelter to fire.

Not everyone made it into cover though. Aside from losing Tatara, two Venanti guides had also been caught in the attack before they could seek shelter, their healing staffs proving useless in the face of such advanced weaponry. Another one of our racing ranks fell too, and I felt awful I hadn't even learned his name yet. Each of them lay still in the grass, lifeless.

I glanced at the wide-eyed Venanti people sheltering behind the same outcroppings we were. *What the…?* Just like Andra, their skin appeared to shimmer with… something.

"They're walking forward!" someone bellowed—sounded like Dino.

I spun around again to help knock them back. My teeth clenched, a fresh sizzle of white-hot wrath engulfing me. *Not today, assholes.*

Gunfire blazed between parties across the field, countless rounds pinging off rock and searing into the earth. Jorgep took a shot to the shoulder, which caused an embattled Keemi to go into a rage—her body bucking against the tether holding her in place. And in the midst of it all stood Sarah. She hadn't taken cover. Instead she'd stood defiant, facing off with the enemy.

Governus's rounds ricocheted off the metal as she unloaded her own blasters in return, yet her shots seemed bizarrely ineffectual. In fact, *all* of our rounds seemed to miss.

"Sarah, get back!" I shouted. Her rage-infused screams filled the air, overpowering my fervent plea. Either she didn't hear me or didn't care. Rounds continued hammering off of her suit and I worried how long it could hold out. Was she still recording? Could she still transmit?

Sarah took a knee in front of Tatara's listless form and her motives for lingering in the danger zone became clear. I stopped shouting. Sarah slipped her arms beneath Tatara's back and knees, then lifted the fallen woman off of the ground, cradling her lifeless body as she turned and fell back to take shelter behind my outcropping.

"What the fuck?" Sarah growled after gently setting Tatara down on the ground. She straightened, eyes glistening, her mech's hands punching down. "How are they not dying? I'm going back out there!" She sprinted back into the field before I could disagree.

Sarah pelted them with rapid-fire shots, roaring like a warrior on the charge. But an unflinching Governus focused all of their firepower on her. Pulses criss-crossed back and forth forging a supercharged net of mayhem, until one of Sarah's hands flew up to guard her face shield. She spun on her heel and rushed back to cover.

The clear octagonal barrier protecting her upper body and face had spiderwebbed. Fragmented sections broke loose, crumbling into the grass.

"Well, that's that, I guess." Sarah swung the less-than-protective shield open and pressed a button to disengage the part entirely. The metal-rimmed barrier dropped with a *clunk* and she kicked it out of the way. She was now as vulnerable as the rest of us. Her brows pinched tight before adding, "They must have some kind of special shielding."

Vernon pointed at her scarred suit. "Right, but can you still transmit?"

Sarah nodded. "My suit's internal functions are still operational."

"You're lucky." He looked like he might scold her for her devil-may-care antics, then glanced at Tatara, swallowing hard. He simply tapped his chest. "Then you know what to do."

Both Griggs and I, and everyone within earshot nodded.

Governus pressed forward, walking slow and methodical—like an insidious shadow infiltrating hallowed ground. It's like they weren't afraid of us in the slightest. Several similar rock outcroppings available to them, yet not a single one sought cover.

Only one of their ranks had fallen limp after taking a hit to the bicep. I leaned out just far enough to aim my crosshairs at Khana's pretty smoke-coloured face, then squeezed the trigger, watching closely. The tiniest spark fizzled a blink before the round should've destroyed her nose. *Should've.* The pulse had been absorbed. I gritted my teeth. "You're right Sarah. They have shields!"

Griggs let out a growl, but for a different reason altogether. He'd leaned out too far and got himself shot. Blood poured from a hole in his thigh just above the knee.

"Oh, shit." I holstered my pistol and covered the wound with my hands, pressing as hard as I could. Crimson seeped out between my fingers. Icy fingers of fear gripped my heart, causing it to shudder in reaction.

"Thanks. Keep holding it." He ripped the sleeves off of his shirt and tied hasty knots in the fabric, forming a makeshift tourniquet. Wincing, he wasted no time tying it around his thigh and twisting it tight with a stick he'd grabbed to stem the blood. "There. Should hold."

"Are you going to be alright?" I released his thigh, grasping his hand and squeezing. I didn't like seeing him in pain, simultaneously thanking the stars above that shot hadn't hit his chest. To lose him now after we'd battled so hard seemed worse somehow. The thought of losing him at all caused my breath to quicken. A thought claimed space in my already saturated mind, one that had been building strength slowly, and couldn't be pushed aside any longer.

I couldn't imagine what life might look like without Griggs in it.

He nodded stiffly. "Yeah, I'll live." He rested against the rock for a moment, taking a few deep breaths to compose himself. He let out a breathy laugh. "Ahh, chicks dig scars, right?"

"They do." I squeezed his hand again, giving a shaky smile, nearly adding *I do*. But I released Griggs hand instead, and snuck a darting peek beyond the rock. Now wasn't the time.

Griggs brandished his pistols once more and recaptured my gaze. "We have to figure out what kind of shields they've got and fast."

I drew my gun. "Whatever they're using, it's absorbing our rounds."

"Sink shields…" Sarah muttered, contemplative. "I bet that's exactly what the fuck they have. We'll need to disengage the devices somehow, but who knows what they look like."

I'd heard rumours of sink shields before—expensive cutting edge black-market tech, supposedly used by high-profile smugglers and assassins. The name had sounded ridiculous to me before, but now I realized it was actually quite appropriate. Any damage seemed to sink into the invisible barrier and vanish.

"They're getting closer!" Raker shouted.

From the corner of my eye, I spied Andra waving to get my attention, however, she'd have to wait a minute. Popping off several more shots, I inspected the body of the dead Governus soldier, searching for evidence of any kind of shielding device. The enemy had already crossed half the distance between us. If we couldn't find a way to fight back, we'd be done for.

That's when the faintest magenta glow caught my eye. It emanated from a barely noticeable circular disk attached to Steel's right bicep. His movements hid it most of the time, but when his arms splayed to fire wide, there it was. I glanced back at their fallen comrade, and saw a similar disk affixed in the same spot—though his had been shattered. Fragmented remnants jutted out at odd angles from the contraption.

I looked down the Governus line confirming they all wore one. "Sarah, check out the disk on the bionic guy's bicep!"

My friend's eyes narrowed as she peeked around the edge of the rock. Seconds later, her eyes swung back, ablaze with the flicker of hope. "Good eyes Finn."

I grinned, shouting just loud enough for our people to hear, "Everyone, aim for the little reddish disks on their upper arms! No disk, no dice!" And with renewed vigour, that's precisely what everyone did. The hopelessly one-sided battle took on new life.

Three Governus soldiers collapsed into heaps. Another face planted.

"It's working!" I roared, cackling wildly. "Keep shooting!"

The two CEO's faltered, looking down at their dead comrades.

Steel barked something I couldn't quite make out over the gunfire, but at once, the remaining Governus people clasped their hands over the shield units attached to their bodies. In the next second, the disks were gone—relocated over their shoulders.

Governus surged forward once again.

"Dammit!" Griggs spat, his eyes meeting mine. "Now what?"

I looked at Sarah, raising my hands, palms up. "What else can we do?!" If anyone could find a way to disable their shields, it was her.

A look of helplessness shadowed her expression. "I don't know enough about the tech. I'm sorry."

Nobody within earshot said a word, but everyone's shoulders deflated a little. Including mine. How could we combat this? But then I gave myself a mental kick in the ass. *Hell no.* I'd survived some pretty hairy incidents before. No way was I about to go out cowering now.

"Don't give up. We can find a way!" I shouted, bolstering everybody onward. *The fight's not over until my heart stops beating.* As a group, we fired everything we had at Governus. But still, they just kept on coming. In less than twenty feet, they'd be upon us.

They took their time, too, smiling smugly with each step forward, as if enjoying a leisurely stroll in the park.

Raker growled, setting his gun down to punch furious keystrokes into his digicuff. He glanced into the sky intermittently and his eyes scored across each surviving face. "You all should've listened to me—should've played this *my way*. Stubborn simpletons, the bunch of you." He bent his head and muttered something unintelligible into his cuff.

Andra waved at me again, this time shouting my name.

I shot a few more rounds, then met her gaze. "You need to get outta here. All of you. They'll kill you if you stay. Go warn the others Governus will be coming!" *No more Venanti should die because of this vicious race.* And yet, I couldn't shake the deep-seated fear that Khana and Steel would simply clear the Sweep of any opposition once the loose ends—meaning us—were tied up. What's worse, they'd be able to tell their colonists anything they wanted with zero accountability. Nobody would ever know the truth.

I refused to look at Herc lying beside Andra, keeping my gaze pinned on her. She shook her head vehemently. Moisture blurred the edges of my vision. "I'm sorry we failed to help you."

Andra sliced her hand through the air and raised her staff. "You haven't failed. Now, I've been trying to tell you there is something we can try." She cast a pointed look at Setso and the remainder of her guides, tapping her staff on the ground three times. The others followed her lead. All of their Heart Stones brightened. The Venanti chanted something quietly, and that pale shimmering effect I'd seen covering Andra's skin earlier, returned—then intensified three-fold. Andra's skin sparkled effervescently as though made of diamond glitter. They all glittered.

I widened my eyes, staring with an equal measure of shock and confusion.

"What the hell is happening right now?" Sarah whispered between shots.

Andra and Setso nodded to each other before stretching their staffs out to us. The rest of the Venanti did the same, every pair of eyes alight with defiant intensity.

"This power requires a great deal of energy and concentration—which keeps us from using it when on the move in the forest—but, with enough focus, the stone lets us channel forcefields. We can't maintain them for long, though." Andra's eyes glinted with determination. "We've never tried this with outsiders. But, these Governus people must be stopped, so it is worth the risk. We may not have guns, but we have our stones."

"Touch our staffs and let us help you," Setso urged.

Given everything we'd been through together, I trusted them. As pulse fire ricocheted off of rock, pinged off metal, and scorched the earth, I tentatively reached out my fingers. Mild heat radiated off the stones onto my skin. Beyond our outcropping, Governus's footsteps increased in speed, swishing through the wild grasses at a jog—as if they'd sensed something was amiss.

"They're coming!" Dino bellowed.

My grimy fingers shot forward and pressed against the geometric edges of the nearest stone. A familiar tingle wove its way through my body—like when Andra had healed my wounds—and it intensified until it bordered on discomfort. A brilliant shimmer crept up my arm, over my torso, and in the space of a gasp, I was fully engulfed in sparkles. Glancing left and right, all of my fellow racers appeared the same. Even sour-faced Raker glittered.

The Venanti raised their staffs defensively.

I spun just as the line of Governus soldiers rushed between our outcroppings. Their muzzles swept from target to target, firing point blank rounds, clearing the way for the CEO's to stride in. Before I could get a shot off at Khana, she fired a round into my abdomen. The projectile collided with my shimmering veneer; the impact akin to getting walloped by a haymaker. I doubled over, terror permeating my thoughts. Had the shield not worked?

All around me, my friends groaned, collapsing. *Please, no.* My fingers touched the site of impact, checking for blood and torn flesh. But there was nothing there. *The shield held…*

"Finish them off," Steel commanded, his face smug as he shot Griggs in the chest.

"*Veshelda,* now!" Andra commanded. Our guides squeezed their eyes shut, their bodies trembling, then drove the butt end of their staffs into the ground. A blue snake of energy shot between each of them, connecting their stones. A powerful concussion wave exploded outward.

They directed the luminous tsunami toward our attackers and the magnitude of the wave knocked every Governus member clean off their feet. Thrust back several yards, the soldiers scrambled to regain their footing. Khana shook her head, appearing stunned.

"Keep shooting!" Steel barked.

"Holy shit…" Griggs whispered, still patting his perfectly uninjured chest.

I stood and flashed a thankful look at Andra. Then, raising my pulse rifle, I took a deep breath and pulled the trigger. The round evaporated into Khana's shield. *Damn. It's still active.* Her eyes widened with confusion and she fired another round square between my eyes. A grunt ripped from my lips as the impact snapped my head back, but I didn't go down.

The previous confidence on Khana's face withered.

"Come on guys," I said, my lips curling. Griggs and Sarah flanked me, followed by Vernon, Jorgep, and Dino. One by one the rest joined ranks, and we advanced. Together, our shimmering line charged, flipping the switch on Governus. *Let's see how they like it.*

Now a force to be reckoned with, we unloaded on them.

Beneath the barrage of gunfire, Khana snapped her weapon between the lot of us—cracking off rounds. She glared at me and sent two more into my chest. With each impact, my body jolted from the pain, but it didn't slow me down. My glittering skin lustred in the sunshine and I grinned wickedly back at her. I couldn't let myself get too cocky, though. We still needed to get rid of their shields before ours ran out.

"We need to get behind them," Griggs said.

Sensing the shift in power, our remaining uniformed foes turned tail.

"Don't you dare run away!" Khana roared, but her command went ignored.

Without hesitation, we targeted the newly exposed magenta disks perched between all of the fleeing militants' shoulder blades. In rapid succession, the last three fell to the ground.

That left Khana and Steel.

As we advanced, Sarah and Raker volunteered to deal with two wounded soldiers. Raker plugged a quick round between his quarry's eyes, offering no mercy, while Sarah disarmed hers.

"Stay the hell down if you know what's good for you," she warned.

However, the instant Sarah turned away, Raker shot that soldier, too.

"What the fuck?" She spat. "That woman was unarmed!"

"Allow no weakness." He sneered. "You're part Crimeon— act like it."

Sarah disconnected an arm from her mech faster than I knew was possible. As she brushed past him, her fist shot out, connecting with his jaw. He stumbled back a few steps, straightening his hood. Sarah rejoined our line, seemingly unfazed by Raker's eye daggers.

Oh man, I bet that felt good.

We spread out to flank Khana and Steel, who now found themselves very much alone on the battlefield. They stood back-to-back, inching their way closer to the hover ship. Protecting their shield devices. Smart play.

"Give it up, now before anyone else has to get hurt!" I shouted.

"Oh, this is far from over, cowgirl," Khana retorted, her voice caustic.

Steel craned his neck, twisting to check how close they were to the ship, exposing his back for the briefest of moments to half of the racers surrounding the Governus pair.

Dino fired two shots in rapid succession from his angle.

They landed.

The first pulverized Steel's disk, shattering it, while the second sunk into the meat of Steel's back. The CEO gasped, clutching the right side of his chest where the round had exited, but didn't go down. Khana flinched in reaction, then promptly sidestepped in front of him.

Behind us, the Venanti had begun chanting, their layered voices laboured.

"Hurry!" Andra shouted. "We can't hold it much longer!"

Griggs whispered to me from the side of his mouth, "Okay, listen, here's the plan. I'll provide a distraction, while you and the others pull the bionic dude away." Utilizing his military experience, he motioned with crisp hand gestures for our crew to spread out on either side.

"No time for a distraction," I shot back, shaking my head. "Let's just rush them. Tackle them. Hog tie them. Whatever works, but *no killing*. We need them alive. At least one, anyway."

Steel didn't look so great, lumbering and swaying. His black blood painted billowing wisps of wild grass as he shuffled. Griggs nodded in concession, spreading word to the others.

As we moved forward, the bionic man collapsed to his knees.

"Steel?" Khana knelt, still protecting her back. The man's breathing came fast and harsh. A glaze of sweat layered his sallow skin. She supported his back, keeping one gun trained on us. "Get your pathetic ass up. We can still make it to the hover ship."

Steel attempted a laugh, coughing instead. Inky blood splattered from his lips as he spoke. "I'm not going anywhere, sister."

Ah, sister… That made sense. In any other situation, I might've felt sorry for her.

"Damn you, Steel," Khana hissed. Her brother's head lolled atop his shoulders, his back sagging against her. She shifted to accommodate his weight, her eyes flitting between him and us as we spread out. Steel's hand caressed her face and her jaw clenched, her gaze now uncertain.

"I'm sorry, Khana," he whispered, then coughed violently.

"Hurry!" Andra shouted again. The Venanti guides shook from the strain.

"Surrender," Raker commanded. "You're outnumbered. Don't make this difficult."

"Difficult?" she spat venomously. Khana fired a shot at him, however, when he failed to drop dead, she swore and tossed her pistol. Her eyes returned to her brother's face. He coughed, blood gargling in his throat. Snaking one arm over her shoulder, the CEO plucked the glowing disk off of her back. Khana held it out for all to see, then with a pronounced movement, threw it away, too. "There. Happy?"

"Quite. Yes," Raker replied.

Our glittering skin vanished. Groans of relief rang out from the Venanti.

Khana had another pistol strapped to her hip, and who knows what other weapons hidden on her person. I stepped forward, my gun trained on her. "I'll be taking your weapons now."

Circling behind her, I pressed the muzzle of my gun to the back of her head. She eyed me viciously, but didn't move. Griggs, Jorgep, Cala, and Dino moved in closer with weapons at the ready. Sadly, I had to shove my hand between Khana and her brother in order to yank her other pistol free. I discarded it, then searched her belt and removed a multi-tool and a laser knife. Once the search was complete, I moved to the side and kept my sights trained on her temple.

Khana glowered up at me while cradling her ailing brother. "So? Take the shot already. End our misery." Her sharpened gaze pierced mine, challenging. "I know you want to. Be a woman and do it!" Steel's breathing grew more ragged by the second. In stark contrast with her frigid facial expression, the CEO's hand warmly caressed her brother's sweat-slicked skin.

"Don't tempt me." I envisioned myself pulling the trigger and revelling in it. The terrible thought sat heavy and foreign in the darkest corner of my consciousness, yet at the same time, it brought vindication. Here and now, I could obtain justice for Herc—for everyone who should never have died. Neither Steel or Khana deserved to walk away from this after what they'd done.

My fingers gripped the pistol tighter.

An eye for an eye, right?

CHAPTER 37

"**F**inn…" Griggs voice broke into my fuming state of consciousness. A heavy note of warning permeated the single word, conveying a very specific message. *You can't shoot her.* He'd angled himself to face me, his eyes imploring for me to hear him. I grimaced, fighting against a festering desire that yearned to be satiated. And yet, at the core of me, I also knew he was right. I'd never forgive myself if I shot someone in cold blood—no matter how evil.

I lowered my gun. Griggs' shoulders relaxed.

Everybody moved closer, forming a semi-circle around the newly disarmed Governus CEO. Since so many guns were trained on Khana, I shifted to face her head on. Gurgling, choking noises filled the air as Steel struggled to breathe and I could only assume the shot had pierced his lung. It was hard to watch. I glanced back at Andra and Setso, seriously considering asking them to bring a stone to try and heal the man. If he lived, he'd get to face the same consequences as his sister for their actions. But I didn't get the chance to finish deciding.

The unsettling sounds stopped.

Khana cried out—a pained emanation somewhere between a strangled moan and a scream. "You killed him!" She ran a hand over his face, onyx blood smearing beneath her fingertips. She closed her eyes briefly, then laid his body down, slipping out from beneath. Launching to her feet, Khana's eyes scorched into whatever face they set upon. The formidable woman squared off in a fighting stance, hands balled into fists, chest heaving. "Why didn't you all die like you were supposed to!?"

"So, you admit it!" I rebutted, then abruptly realized I had no clue if our plan was fully viable. Had Sarah been able to do what we needed her to? I glanced over at her to check and observed the jovial spitfire of a woman I'd come to know wrought with rage. Her jaw clenched and nostrils flared as she looked at Khana. As if sensing my attention, she looked my way.

I discreetly tapped my chest like Vernon had before, raising my brows.

Sarah nodded and touched her camera panel in return. *Oh, thank goodness.*

"Time for you to talk!" Griggs ordered.

Khana glowered. "I don't have to say anything to you." Her stance straightened to reflect the regal bearing we'd all witnessed back at the start line. "And if you know what's good for you, every single one of you will stand down. Now. You have no idea what I'm capable of, and what kind of power I wield."

Raker scoffed loudly at that.

Sarah jumped out of her Mech and sprinted forward. But instead of punching Khana like I thought she might, she pushed Khana onto her knees beside Steel's lifeless body. She loomed over the bested CEO. "We know first-hand what kind of murderous power you wield. That's exactly what we're going to stop—for good. You're going to answer to the Magistrate."

I found myself impressed by Sarah's restraint.

The CEO laughed, the sound low and sour. She craned her neck to meet Sarah's gaze. "Right. Well, good luck with that. I'll never admit to any wrongdoing, and I've covered my tracks flawlessly. In a perfect world, we would have wiped your memories and quietly moved you off planet. Simple. But you had to spoil it all by removing your implants. YOU sealed your own death warrants." Her eyes scanned the rest of us. "And… if you manage to get off of this planet—which you won't—I'll pay off any officials you go crying to. Who do you think they'll believe? A bunch of lowlife racers stupid enough to think they can get land for free, or me, the CEO of a wealthy and very well-respected corporation?"

The smugness in her voice made my blood simmer.

"Hmm… It sure seems like you've thought of everything," Sarah said. Then she walked back to her mech suit, pointing a finger at the chest plate concealing the recording system. "But you haven't. I've been recording everything from day one. *Everything.*"

Khana looked back with indifference. "Ah yes, most mechs have bio links these days. But that's still useless. The minute you return to Egan, my remaining security team will arrest you and seize your suit. Once the colonists learn how you mercilessly attacked us after we so kindly came out here to rescue you from that horde of killing machines in there, you'll be ruined. Just give up now, and maybe I'll be lenient."

"*Maybe* you'll be lenient…" Griggs muttered. "I don't think *maybe* will cut it. You're not quite understanding what she's telling you." Griggs motioned to Sarah with his head, encouraging her to finish breaking the good news.

"Your colonists already know everything. I hacked your feeds and they're all watching as we speak. *We're* not the ones who are ruined." Sarah smiled with victorious satisfaction, getting back inside her mech. Khana's hard-edged expression wavered, but only for a moment.

I took a knee several feet in front of Khana. "See, we weren't going to broadcast anything at first—we only wanted to have leverage to ensure you'd own up to your actions, honour our winnings, and recognize the Venanti's claim on Joya. We wanted you to go to court. But then you decided to open fire—killing even *more* of us! Yeah, that kind of changed things—"

Sarah aimed a cannon at Khana, her lip quivering. "How could you!?"

"Sarah, back off," I warned, though I knew exactly where she was coming from. *Nobody gets to shoot this bitch today.* Glancing at Jorgep, I jerked my chin towards our anguished friend. He seemed to understand, turning to Sarah in an attempt to calm her down.

Khana faltered for words as her eyes darted side to side. Her mind had to be racing. "How could you manage that? We have top-notch safeguards. You're lying."

Sarah shook her head. "Nope. I'm kind of a wiz. Didn't bank on *that*, did you?"

Khana's gaze bore into me. "So, what do you want from me?" *Ah, there we go.*

I looked at Vernon, but he waved a hand, wordlessly saying *carry on.*

Taking a deep breath, I forged ahead. "We will report Governus to the Gala-Rights Commission and you'll face whatever consequences the Interplanetary Magistrate deems appropriate. You will still give a homesteading start-up sum to the winners—aka *survivors*—but it will be to keep as restitution for the pain and suffering you've caused. Not a loan. You'll relinquish all claims on Joya to the Venanti. The GRC will mediate the rest. If you own up to your actions and agree to those terms, then we'll stop the feed and let you live."

Khana let out a stuttering chuckle. "Hell, that doesn't sound like much of a negotiation. Listen, I think we can still find an amicable solution here. Besides, if you kill me, my brothers—*the other* CEOs of Governus—will gather our resources and come here to reign hell down on you. Magistrate or not, whether they shut us down or not, if you kill me, you're finished. You should know that before any decisions are made here."

"She's bluffing to gain power back," Dino grumbled.

"She's not," Raker said matter-of-factly, stalking up to Khana and slamming the butt of his gun into her head. My arms shot out, pushing him away, but Raker recovered fast.

His mouth twisted in disgust. "Don't believe she will honour any negotiation. She'll do whatever it takes to get what she wants. She'll play nice and then stab you in the back the minute you take your eyes off of her. I know her kind well. As I said before, the only way to truly deal with this situation is to overthrow and push them out according to standard takeover practices. I remain your key to making that happen."

"That's not what we agreed on, Raker," Vernon spoke up. "The matter is closed."

"And it doesn't even make sense," Griggs added. "I've been thinking about your *plan*, and if what you've said is true, the 'standard takeover practices' have already been violated. Haven't they?" He appealed to the other racers present. "Innocent civilians have been hurt. The only way for the Gala-Rights Commission to *not* get involved now is to cover everything up. Which, I bet you'd do if you took over Joya… wouldn't you?"

"You're all fools!" Raker snarled, almost spasming in his temper tantrum. The cloak of his hood fell to his shoulders.

"Listen, I will honour any agreement that doesn't involve tanking my own company," Khana said, capitalizing on the discord. "I'm willing to cooperate. I'll do *most* of what you ask—even leave the Venanti alone if they simply give up the mineral rights. I just want that one measly thing. They can keep anything else. Let's make a deal."

"Mineral rights. See? She can't be trusted!" Raker spat.

Khana glared at Raker, then a spark of recognition flashed in her eyes. Her head tilted like a curious puppy. "Don't I know you from somewhere?"

Raker rubbed a hand over his hoodless head. "No. You must have confused me with someone else." He pulled the hood back up.

"I never forget a face. Hmm, it'll come to me," Khana murmured.

Raker actually looked uncomfortable, fidgeting. That piqued my interest. What did we not know?

"So, will you accept our terms?" Vernon pressed the CEO, his voice firm.

Khana shook her head and crossed her arms. "Your terms are too strict. There has to be some wiggle room. I'll scratch your back if you scratch mine. I'll give you five times the land you would've won. I'll leave the Venanti alone and they can have every damn Sweep on this planet if they want, even half of the regular land, as long as Governus can mine for the local ore we've seen. We'll sign a privacy agreement. Business can continue as usual. Nobody needs to get embroiled in a bunch of legal matters. That's a fair compromise. I suggest you take it."

The group glanced around at each other. *Five times the winnings.*

Setso shook his head, his expression disgruntled. "You can't mine the ore."

Griggs cocked his head to the side. "You're in no position to suggest terms. We told you what we want and you either take it or you don't. It's your choice."

Khana pulled her shoulders back straighter. "I'll also pay each of you an extra 100,000 additional credits for your trouble. *Not* a loan."

That caught everyone's attention. Eyes opened wider, but still, nobody broke—sticking to what we'd all agreed upon. I glanced at Setso, assuring him with a nod that it would be okay.

"300,000 extra credits." She upped the ante.

Whispers flitted like ghostly hummingbirds behind me. Griggs cast me a sidelong glance—a *holy shit* kind of look. I couldn't deny

I felt the same. That kind of money could go a long way. It would buy me the Friesian mare I'd been dreaming about, build me a house, a barn, and pay off my full debts to the ranch. But at what cost? I spied a lot of introspective people now. Dino paced, clearly feeling the lure. Cala's face was contorted with confusion. Then I looked back to the Venanti people and Setso. What would become of them? This was their home.

"500,000 credits each. C'mon, you all seem like smart people. Let's do this." Khana extended a hand to shake, smiling with a hopeful sincerity I didn't believe was authentic. She was no dummy. Khana was working us as hard as she could.

"Um, maybe we should talk a minute," Dino said with a timidity I'd never seen before.

"Yeah sure, let's huddle up," I agreed, then pointed to Raker. "We already know what you want to do, Raker, so why don't you just keep our prisoner in check while we talk. Make sure she doesn't do anything stupid." He didn't argue, which was both a pleasant change and an oddity at the same time. He'd just taken an order from a human… and said nothing. As I walked the twenty or so paces to meet with the others away from Khana's prying ears, I typed a message into my digicuff and sent it to my original core alliance: KEEP AN EYE ON RAKER.

Sarah, Jorgep, and Griggs checked their wrists, nodding back at me.

"That's a hell of a lot of money," Dino said, shrugging apologetically. "I'm not trying to cause trouble, but I have kids to feed back home. Those kind of credits would mean *everything* for us. I'm all for justice and all, but I gotta look out for my own, too."

"I think we should let all of the Venanti vote on this, to be fair," Vernon suggested.

I nodded. "I agree with that. They have a vested interest." Almost everyone nodded in agreement, even Dino, but Cala didn't seem overly enthusiastic. I glanced her way. "Cala?"

She crossed her arms. "I say we make *our* best deal and let the Venanti make theirs."

"Are you serious?" Sarah countered.

Jorgep shook his head. "Miss Cala, making multiple deals is bound to cause conflict."

"The Venanti don't have the leverage we do," I said. "They'll get railroaded and we can't let that happen. Not after they saved our lives. We owe them." I couldn't deny that the credits Khana offered hadn't given me pause too. *Not* getting a prize out of this whole race nightmare affected more people than just me. My folks wouldn't get repaid. It could affect the ranch. But regardless, I still had to do the right thing. After paying the emotional price for the *not-right* things I did in my past, I couldn't live with myself if I didn't help the Venanti now.

All eyes landed on Cala, watching her closely, expectant.

The woman merely rolled her eyes and shrugged.

Vernon waved for the Venanti to join us. Setso walked over, along with the others, but Andra hung back. I hoped she hadn't been hurt in the gunfight somehow. Worried, I made a mental note to check in on her as soon as I could.

With everyone still buddy-linked, we proceeded to provide a full update.

"I don't think we should take her deal," I said in low tones. "Yes, the money is tempting, but she has a proven track record for lying and killing to achieve a goal. I don't trust she'll stick to whatever deal she makes. Raker's right in that regard. But I don't trust him either. Governus just needs to be held accountable and face the law." I watched my fellow racers' reactions, hoping they'd still feel the same, or at least similar enough to fight for the ethical choice.

Griggs raised a hand. "I agree with what Finn said. Governus is shifty as hell. If we let anything slide now, it only reinforces they can do whatever they want and get away with it. I don't like how she's flashing cash and expecting us to roll over." Griggs planted his hands on his hips, levelling his gaze at everyone. "I know money's a concern, but I'm sure the Magistrate will see reason and ensure we're compensated fairly for all the trauma."

I glanced at Raker, who still stood cooly, keeping a gun on Khana.

Dino's eyebrows furrowed as he appeared to contemplate that. "I do really want that money… but I want those bastards to face the consequences even more." He ran a hand over his lower jaw, his baritone voice gruff as he added, "Can't we just be good with the fact she admitted fault for now, and figure the rest out once we've gotten some sleep?"

"And a shower," Cala chimed in. "For the record, I still say we take her deal."

Sarah glared balefully. "I don't care about the money—all I want is to see Governus suffer long and hard for what they did. For who they've *killed*."

"If I may say, I think every life lost will be disrespected if we take their bribe and walk away." Jorgep's feelers hung motionless as he spoke. His eyes flicked to Raker, then back.

"Well said," I replied and most heads nodded in agreement.

"What do the Venanti think? Setso?" Vernon looked to the prince.

Setso stood tall. "We will not grant mining rights. We must protect the Heart Stone. We want our fair claim to this world, but we would be willing to share it with respectful partners."

I nodded crisply. "That settles it, then. We can't accept her deal. Or should we vote?" I was impatient to be done with this. I needed to be alone, to process and grieve. "Are we good?"

Everyone present nodded, even Cala, though grudgingly.

"Great. Let's break the news and get back to negotiations."

Setso bowed his head. "On behalf of my people, I thank you for your kindness."

Vernon clapped a hand on the prince's shoulder, and the two shared a smile.

We walked back to face Khana as a united front. She was busy trying to smooth talk Raker, which, to my surprise, seemed to be about as easy as drawing blood from a hunk of meteorite. His hooded visage was as stoic as a statue. I half-suspected a slippery guy like him would have tried to cut his own deal on the sly while we weren't listening. But I'd been keeping a close eye on him during our meeting, and that certainly didn't seem to be the case.

Everyone looked around at each other, uncertain who should act as spokesperson this time. Vernon took a deep breath and stepped forward, as he'd done so often in the Sweep. "We have decided there must be accountability. We're sticking with our original terms. You will face both the Gala-rights commission and the Interplanetary Magistrate for your crimes."

"And if I don't agree, you'll kill me, right? That's what you said?" Khana glanced up at Raker, whose gun was trained on her. "Well, then do it, I guess. I'd rather die than do what you ask. If I give in to you and doom my company, my brothers will kill me anyway." She glanced down to Steel lying in the grass. "He was the only one I gave a damn about. So just shoot."

One of Raker's brows arched. "You heard the woman. Should I get this over with?" He pressed his gun against Khana's skull.

All of us jerked forward, shouting, "NO!"

Raker rolled his eyes, relaxing his arm again. "Cowards."

Khana gave a dry smile, her brows pinched tight. "I didn't think you'd follow through. You're going to have a lot of trouble on your hands getting all of this to work for you. Be advised, I will throw around every ounce of weight I have. You're going to be sorry you messed with Governus. *With me.*" Then her eyes widened, and her gaze snapped up to Raker. "Now I remember you. You're the CEO of the Geeneglian Clan, right? You vied for Joy—"

The energized crack of a pulse pistol rang out.

A singed hole marred the side of Khana's smooth forehead. She froze in place for a breath, black blood trickling from the wound in her skull while her unseeing eyes stared ahead. Then her body sagged forward, flopping like a rag doll next to her brother in the wildgrass.

Stricken gasps rang out, everyone realizing too late what happened. Raker holstered his weapon and casually pulled out a hanky to wipe the blood splatters from his neck and arm.

Sarah shouted, "What the fuck did you just do!?"

CHAPTER 38

"You're a corporate spy!" Jorgep spat, his feelers crimping.

Raker brushed his hands together, as if removing unwanted dirt. "Regardless of my reasons for being here, I just solved your problems. Governus would never have capitulated long-term. They would've wormed their way out of being *held accountable*. We all know that. You're just too naïve to acknowledge it." He slanted a challenging look at each of us, and I wanted to smack it off his face. With a nod and a hand flourish, he continued. "This is the best solution. My honour debt to save the Venanti has been repaid. They're alive and so are we, and I'll ensure this planet is well taken care of. Governus won't be a worry. So… you're welcome."

"Best solution? You just put a huge target on our backs!" I roared.

"You ruined everything." Griggs, the closest to Raker, rushed forward and punched him.

Raker shuffled back from the blow, then growled and lunged at Griggs—the two trading blows like they'd been dying to do ever since our argument around Tatara's campfire. As the men grappled, a few others slipped in to the scrum. A surviving racer I didn't know well threw dust into Raker's face, while Cala—whom I suddenly liked a little bit more—swept an agile leg low to the ground, knocking Raker's feet out from under him.

Dino capitalized by grabbing the back of Raker's cloak, holding him up straight for Griggs to take undeterred shots. "Bust him up, Griggs."

Raker kicked out at Griggs with one foot and flailed wildly, landing a solid elbow into Dino's rib area, doubling the man over. He twisted at the waist and slammed another elbow backward into Dino's ear, which knocked the burly guy back a few feet.

Sarah disengaged from her bio connectors and bounded down from her mech as Griggs wound up for a hell of right hook. I felt a pang of jealousy, even considered joining in. But then an odd glint caught my eye. It came from one of Raker's right front pockets—just a sliver of illumination… something glowing blue.

Our resident spy, now free of Dino's iron grip, ducked left, narrowly avoiding Griggs' punch. In doing so, his face ran right into Sarah's upthrusting knee. He stumbled back a step, dazed by the blow. She shifted slightly, then drove another knee into Raker's manly bits—handily located in roughly the same place as a human's. Those present, who could relate to such an injury, winced.

Groaning in pain, Raker shuffled backward while furiously punching commands into his digicuff. I exchanged worried glances with Vernon, then eyed the liar's glowing pocket again.

"Who're you sending messages to? Crying to your mamma?" Sarah cackled devilishly, readying herself for another go around.

Vernon waved his arms. "Come on now, fighting isn't the way to solve this!"

Our ranks slowed up, giving Raker the barest semblance of space. Sarah huffed with irritation. Griggs wiped a smear of blood from beneath his split eyebrow, breathing heavy as he stared down his foe. The Ganglian continued backing away, now murmuring unintelligible words into his cuff. Seriously, who was he sending messages to?

A ship. He mentioned having a ship waiting for him. The blue light…

"No more," I said, my voice low and insistent. "Everyone, back off!" I stepped forward as our foe hastily retreated. My eyes narrowed, examining Raker's pants more closely. The sharp edge of something blue now protruded from the top of the pocket, dislodged by all the fighting. Only a sliver of the fragment was visible—but that was all I needed to identify the Heart Stone he harboured. One he shouldn't have.

Where did he get that? How? When? I thought of the staff Setso took back from him. No, the shard in his pocket wasn't as big as those. Images of him falling in the Heart Stone cavern flitted through my mind. He'd landed right on top of a bunch of stone pieces. Raker could've easily snagged one then. I glanced at Setso, but he'd taken his people aside to talk.

He didn't know.

What should I do? Raker couldn't be allowed to keep a stone.

My mind whirred on fast forward. No wonder he hadn't wanted to return the staff to Setso before. It all made sense now. Khana just exposed the fact Raker's corporation had vied for the claim on Joya and he shot her for it, but I suspected he might've shot her no matter what. He wanted those stones as much as Governus did. That snake must've had suspicions Governus found something lucrative here… why else risk entering the race?

With no time to consider tactics, I kicked into a sprint, intent on steamrolling his lying ass. I heard my name being called, but ignored it. If I could just knock him down, it might be a distraction enough to let me reach into his pocket and—heaven help me— steal back that shard.

But Raker darted back before I could get close enough, raising his gun.

Then everyone's guns were up.

I skidded to a halt, pointing. "Setso! Andra! He's got a chunk of Heart Stone in his pocket!" Setso's head snapped toward me at the sound of his name, but confusion twisted his expression. Of course, they were beyond buddy link range. "Someone go get Setso."

Cala took off toward the group of Venanti.

Raker's eyes flashed with an equal mix of anger and surprise. He glanced down quick, then used a bony finger to shove the exposed rock securely back into his pocket. "Hm. You weren't supposed to see that," he muttered, chasing it with a tired snicker.

"So, is your *honour vow* even real?" I challenged, doubtful.

Griggs shook his head, his expression incredulous. "You're no damn better than Governus. This was always about making a play for Joya, wasn't it?"

"And I tried to play nice." Raker glanced into the sky, then back down, his face saturated with annoyance. "Whatever was interesting enough for them to concoct this bizarrely elaborate scheme—as if nobody would get suspicious—was enough to pique my interest. Holding a race for free land through an uncharted forest? *Free land? Uncharted?* Come on…" He drew his mouth into a thin line. "Only, I didn't expect to nearly die. That was an unfortunate turn of events."

Setso came running, an outstretched hand at the ready. His eyes were hard and insistent. "Hand over the stone. It does not belong with you." Cala and the guides stopped behind him.

"It doesn't belong with you either," Raker retorted. "Your people crash landed on this damn planet. You found that big rock, just like I found this little one. Finders keepers."

Setso didn't like hearing that. His hands flexed and he walked forward with purpose. Griggs moved with tactical awareness, discreetly veering to flank the enemy.

Raker backed away from everyone, maintaining distance as he eyed his encroaching attackers. A muted *beep* emanated from his digicuff and a faint whooshing sound permeated the air. I recognized that sound—the distant roar of a powerful engine. Raker spared another glance into the sky and my gaze followed.

There, looming in the hazy upper atmosphere like a ghostly apparition was a Ganglian ship. A stealthy one, keeping safely away from the Sweep.

A cheshire grin spread as Raker raised the cuff to his lips, muttering a single word loud enough for everyone to hear. "Activate." His waiting ship's Vector beam showered his body in what could only be described as a pixelated waterfall.

"No!" I shouted in tandem with several others. As a group, we surged forward, but there was nothing to be done. Raker was too far away for any of us to catch in time.

Setso's hand shot forward, his eyes wide and intense.

"Kreelero pa!" An urgent shout—Andra's—echoed from behind us.

"Pa!" The word barked from his lips while the muscles in his back and outstretched arm strained. A blink later, the shard glowed like blue fire and jerked above the quivering lip of Raker's pocket. The Ganglian must've felt the motion, because he quickly clasped a hand over it.

The Vector beam intensified and Raker's body rapidly diffused.

"Pa!" Setso growled, beckoning the shard with his fingers.

I couldn't believe what I was seeing. A lump of anticipation caught in my throat.

The shard forcibly pushed its way between Raker's fading fingers, but before it could fly free of the beam, our betrayer's lanky form dematerialized into nothingness. He was gone.

Setso stared at his empty hand a moment, breathing heavily, jaw clenched. Then he snapped his fingers shut into a white-knuckle fist and stalked away.

"What the hell are we going to do now?" Cala blurted, looking into the sky. "Do you think Raker will be back?" A crush of colourful curse words erupted from many-a-mouth.

Griggs ran both his hands through his hair. "What will he do with that stone?"

"Did Egan see *all* of that?" Vernon asked Sarah, striding over to her suit, which she'd left standing up and pointed in the general direction of all the action when she jumped out of it.

She let out a long breath, walking to join him. "Should've, if it was in frame."

The Venanti huddled near the rocks, and I could only imagine their discussion.

Dino rubbed his chin. "Was Khana telling the truth about her brothers coming here?"

"I hope she was bluffing," another surviving racer answered. "But I doubt it."

Jorgep spoke over the chatter. "Miss Sarah, did your transmission work *for sure?*"

She lit a whiffer, nodding. "It definitely went through. I just hope the quality was good."

I looked at Griggs, quietly muttering, "Setso moved that stone with his mind. Since when can they do that?" *First the healing, then the shields, that power wave, and now this...* How much more did we not yet know about the Venanti and their stones?

Griggs merely shrugged. "I don't know. I'm still pissed I couldn't get to Raker in time."

"None of us could." I patted him on the shoulder, then slipped away to be on my own—had to. I just needed a moment to detox from the chaotic mess that just transpired. How could so many things go wrong? So many people had died. My Herc died. The race was fake. A jerk stole a stone. So, now what? What came next? Looking out across the rolling hills, I took a few deep breaths. The more I looked at it, the more that gentle valley with the creek running through it seemed like a nice spot. Peaceful. Sure, the trees were sparse, but more could be planted.

That's the land I would've chosen to be mine.

I imagined a perfect world where Herc and I had ridden triumphantly out of the Sweep and made a mad dash to claim that dream-worthy parcel. We would've built a homestead and Herc would come running for a carrot whenever I returned from town. But it hadn't happened like that. Moisture gathered in my eyes. Herc was gone. That dream wasn't meant to be.

"Well, at least we saved the Venanti from being abused or worse. That's something," I called over my shoulder, not particularly caring if anyone heard me or not. "We should try to focus on the positives… First and foremost, we're alive." Sad part was, I had no clue how to ensure we all *stayed* saved at this point. If Khana spoke the truth, Governus would be headed our way in short order—a terrifying thought. But I had to try not to dwell on that. Not right now.

"I'm with you." Griggs appeared beside me, sharing a tentative smile. Then he addressed everyone, counting off using his fingers. "We survived killer Seevers, avoided memory swipes, thwarted an evil corporation and an asshole corporate spy… I mean, that's celebration worthy."

I glanced over my shoulder at Sarah's sombre face, her eyes downcast and dull.

"Yes, we've lost many, but keep in mind, they will be remembered in this victory, too," Vernon said, loud and clear, placing a hand over his chest. "By our continued efforts, we shall ensure their deaths were not in vain. Plus, all of Egan now knows the entire sordid truth thanks to Sarah. Such a thing can only help our cause. Friends, we will continue to prevail."

Friends. That sounded nice. Yes, that's what these people had become.

"Prevail. I like that, Vernon." Sarah sniffed and butted out her whiffer before climbing back into her mech suit. "Fucking right we prevailed. We stopped Governus from getting away with this fucked up race and killing people. And everyone who died helped, which makes them fucking heroes." Metal-clad once more, she headed back towards the rocky outcroppings, presumably to collect Tatara's body. Poor Tatara. I returned my gaze to the hills, still unable to bear seeing Herc lying there. Yes, I knew I'd have to eventually. I couldn't just leave him there. He deserved more than that. But the thought of dealing with his body—of burying him—made it too real. I tried to imagine him the way he was before, beautiful and healthy. Sadness coiled inside, twisting and tightening. A fresh sob caught in my throat, threatening to break free.

As muted chatter wafted through the air behind me, a hand took hold of my own. Griggs warm fingers hesitated a moment, then laced in between mine. I didn't pull away.

A tear slipped down my cheek. "I think Herc would've liked it here," I said, then released a sardonic chuckle. "You know, if everything were normal and the race had been real and all."

He squeezed my hand. "I'm so sorry about Herc."

I looked into his eyes, my lower lip quivering. "Thanks."

"Excuse me, Finn?" Andra said quietly from behind.

I didn't turn around—tried to blink the moisture from my eyes first. "Mm hmm?"

"I'm sorry to interrupt, but I wanted to let you know the Venanti people have pledged to help your group in any way we can. Our resources are limited, but they are at your disposal." I could hear the sincerity in her voice when she added, "We're not just allies, but friends now… and hopefully, you'll help us forge good relations with Egan, too."

There was that 'friends' word again. I don't think I'd ever had so many friends.

I finally turned and reached out to squeeze her arm. "Of course, Andra. Thank you so much for…" The rest of the sentence fizzled on my lips. My expression froze in place.

A familiar whinny rang out, and in the space of a gasp, I lost it—tears poured.

Herc. Was I seeing a ghost?

CHAPTER 39

y hands flew to cover my face. "He's alive!"

My beautiful boy sat upright in the grass, and whinnied again as he watched us.

Andra's eyes sparkled as she gestured a sweeping arm toward Herc. "I wanted to deliver this good news personally." She replaced her Heart Stone necklace back where it belonged. "He's a fighter. I thought we'd lost him, but when I left my stone sitting on his chest, *the stone* chose to save him… just as my people were saved all those years ago. He is a lucky horse."

I sputtered, unable to verbalize emotions exploding from my heart. Careless of whether she'd be okay with it or not, I pulled Andra in for a huge hug. "Thank you!" Then I ran to Herc.

Collapsing to my knees beside him, I ran my hand down his nose, over his neck. "Damn, it's good to see you," I murmured, leaning in to wrap my arms around his neck. I still couldn't believe he was breathing. The wound on his throat had knitted back together nicely. There'd be a nasty scar of course, but at least the flesh itself had healed. Despite his natural eye looking groggy and the fact his body was a little battle worn, he was as handsome as ever.

Herc's long blue tail swished as he nickered, happy to see me. *Wait—what? Blue?*

Most of the braids I'd tied into his tangled mane had fallen out, each wayward and unmistakably blue wisp catching light and highlighting the change. I closely inspected it, felt it. The texture felt entirely normal, yet Herc's mane and tail were far from it. The entirety of his coal-black hair had morphed into a deep royal blue—only slightly darker than the Venanti.

The stone chose to save him. Andra's words echoed in my mind. Was he now connected with the Heart Stone just as the Venanti were? "Will he need a breather out here?" I asked Andra, who'd just walked up behind me.

She shrugged. "I don't know. This is uncharted territory. He might." She ran a hand over Herc's mane, lowering her voice to a whisper. "We'll watch him. If he shows any concerning signs, I will entrust a stone to your care for his breather." She stared into my eyes. "I trust you."

I smiled shakily, more moisture welling up. "Thank you."

Herc huffed against my face, rubbing his peachy muzzle against my cheek. It was in that exact moment, all the shattered pieces of my heart fused back together.

My horse's resurrection garnered attention. Folks watched with elated smiles, and I beamed back. Even Sarah, despite her own sadness, made a point of giving me enthusiastic fist pumps when she passed by holding Tatara. She was headed toward the hover ship, and though her care was nothing if not sincere, I now felt bad for showing blatant glee over getting Herc back. So many others wouldn't get their loved ones back. I was insanely lucky— my mother would say blessed—but I should be more respectful. Shouldn't flaunt it. My smile ebbed.

"It's okay to feel happy, Finn." Griggs walked up, standing beside Andra.

His perceptive words hit home. *I must've been telegraphing my emotions.*

He swept his hand in a wide arc, indicating our surviving caravan. "We're all happy alongside you. It's absolutely amazing he's alive."

Andra smiled encouragingly. "It truly is. Now, Herc is still quite weak. He'll need plenty of rest for a few days, but after that, he should be fine. I expect he'll be able to stand soon."

I stood and crushed her in another hug. "Again, thank you."

She softly patted my back. "I'm glad I could help."

Vernon, who walked over to join us, raised his hands in jubilation. "I am so happy for you Finn. It's good to have Herc back with us." Then his smile dimmed. He pointed to the hover ship. "But before we return to Egan, we all really need to discuss and solidify exactly how we will deal with this *situation*. Things have changed a bit."

"They've changed a lot," Dino said, having also made his way over. The rest of our meagre group meandered our direction as well, clearly ready to talk.

Jorgep, who'd collected Keemi from her spot behind the rocks, stopped to chat. An uncertain, yet somewhat intrigued look shone on his face. "My esteemed racers," he said in his endearingly polite way. "Since, what just transpired would technically be considered a corporate takeover—even though we didn't mean to do that—we are left to deal with the fall out. Standard takeover rules weren't followed and people got hurt, but none of that was our fault. The GRC will see that. So, with that said—and just take a moment to let this sink in…" He paused for dramatic effect. "If we want to, we can take over Governus' claim and all their assets here."

Equally exhausted and mentally wiped, everybody just stared between each other.

"You mean, whatever claim remains *after* the GRC finishes investigating, right? Because all of Joya might get handed over to the Venanti," Cala was quick to point out, despite her earlier qualms.

"Yes, true, Miss Cala," Jorgep nodded. "But it will take a while before we know that. We are in the middle of nowhere, remember? Someone needs to safeguard this place until authorities can arrive, investigate, and make those official decisions. Otherwise, what's to stop Raker from swooping back in and using his influence to bury these injustices like Governus planned to?"

I sighed. "Or any other greedy corporation once word gets out that Governus was overthrown." *Providing Khana's brothers don't get here first…*

Griggs crossed his arms. "We'll definitely need to report this asap once we get into Egan." Then, falling back on comedy as a crutch, he quipped, "Hey, I asked Santa for a pony, but I guess a planet will do." I couldn't help but smirk, giving him a playful poke in the side.

Andra cocked an eyebrow. "Who is Santa?"

"Oh, ah—yeah, he was this ancient Saint on pre-contact Earth. He gave toys to kids who were good. Lumps of coal to kids who were—" Griggs stopped when Andra's brows furrowed. He waved a hand. "Never mind, it's another Human thing. Not important."

"Whatever we do, we need to protect the Sweeps," I said. "We've exposed Governus to the colonists already, and we will report them to the Magistrate. But as Jorgep said, *someone* still needs to maintain day-to-day operations and keep the colony running." Such official-sounding words felt strange leaving my mouth, yet oddly welcome, too.

"Sure, as long as Egan believes we've acted in good faith and doesn't revolt," Dino said matter-of-factly. Grumbles rippled at that, nobody keen on the idea of facing more opposition.

Jorgep looked into the sky as if that stone-stealing snake might drop back down any second. "We will need to deal with the remaining Governus employees in Egan, too, among other things. I have some ideas on the matter." He tucked Keemi's reins under his thick armpit.

"Maybe they'll work for us instead?" Cala offered, leaning into Jorgep's brainchild.

Sarah had returned from the hover, rejoining our ranks with an arched brow already in place. "Wait—work for *us*? What did I miss?"

Griggs shook his head. "Oh… just that we're taking over a *planet*—"

Andra, who'd been quietly listening, cast a disapproving glance his way.

"—Temporarily, anyway," Griggs quickly added. "We're hashing shit out."

The Venanti princess's expression softened again.

Sarah gave a slow nod, her lips forming an "O".

I cast a sidelong glance Griggs way, noticing how the sunshine made his green eyes pop. Then, catching my thoughts wandering, I forced myself to refocus. "Are you still broadcasting now, Sarah?" I looked past her and Andra to the other Venanti survivors congregating by the outcroppings, all huddled together, engaged in deep discussions with Setso.

She shook her head. "No, I stopped the feed right after Raker buggered off."

I let out a relieved sigh. "Okay, that's good. The colony probably doesn't need to hear us discussing all of this stuff at this point. Keeping an element of surprise on our side is good, I think." I motioned for Jorgep to continue. "So, what are your ideas?"

All eyes swung back to Jorgep. Keemi snorted near his head, making the man flinch. "Right—yes…" Jorgep keyed in something on his digicuff to activate a projected digi-screen no larger than my cowboy hat. It was a 2D folder containing a business certificate and a handful of charts. The image was translucent, the hard edges outlined by a typical greyish glow.

The feelers beneath Jorgep's rounded jaw raised and lowered. "I am a part-owner of a thriving family business—but we don't deal in claiming or developing planets. We prefer quieter business. Trade, product sales, and some real estate acquisitions."

With a flick of the fingers, he displayed his credentials one by one. "This is my business name and operating license. These are charts to show my company's growth and our general standing in terms of investments. Perhaps Vernon might consider joining in on this, too, being a fellow business owner… but what I propose is we form our own corporation to show a strong front to other opportunistic developers who might come looking. We would have a close partnership with my company—who could provide guidance and backing—and keep Joya safe until the Magistrate and the GRC arrive. Perhaps even keep some claim thereafter, depending how the investigations and agreements play out." He looked from face to face trying to judge reactions, but everybody seemed too stunned or lost in thought to offer any tangible feedback.

Andra remained quiet, clearly taking everything in.

Vernon nodded contemplatively. "Interesting indeed. I can likely assist in this venture. Of course, I'd have to confirm with my partners, but I feel confident they'd agree. I've invested in philanthropic ventures before, and this is a worthy one."

Once again, I was reminded I didn't really know what Vernon's motivations to race had been—he clearly didn't need the money—and it had me curious. I made a mental note to ask him about it sometime.

Jorgep's feelers waved like a flag. "I'd be happy to do business with you."

"Are you both serious?" Sarah asked, sparking up another whiffer.

The two men nodded.

"Hmm. The prospect is definitely interesting," Griggs said, clucking his tongue.

Setso, who'd approached quietly at some point, spoke up. "So, since you've done away with the Governus leaders, you now plan to *claim* Xola for yourselves?"

Jorgep calmly nodded in response. "Well, in a sense, yes. But with different intent. We would preserve rather than harm."

"And what would that mean for our people? Would official treaties be signed to ensure our rights and lands are protected?" Andra asked, no nonsense. "What if we want to claim Xola ourselves—entirely? After all, we discovered this planet originally, and have lived here long before anyone else arrived. Technically, this is rightfully our world."

Vernon nodded eagerly. "Absolutely. That is precisely what will get straightened by reporting Governus's crimes to the Interplanetary Magistrate and the Gala-Rights Commission. An investigation will be opened, and claims on the planet will be hashed out. I suppose you could assert your full claim *now* already, but I will give you a word of caution… Given you are somewhat landlocked to the Sweep, you are at greater risk. I suggest our groups work together as partners until these things are settled. We can provide you and Egan increased protection from outside dangers." Vernon took a deep breath and continued, "The Galaxium isn't the same as when your ancestors crash landed. The data records you've learned from are far out of date. Money rules everything now. Corporations buy up everything, create monopolies. To truly get ahead, you need power, credits, and sadly, weapons at your disposal. And once a planet is discovered, it can't be *undiscovered*. Especially for Joya. Once word gets out about Governus being overthrown and the Heart Stone's power, others will come wanting what you have."

"You'll need to be able to defend it," Griggs said.

"It might be dicey until my ships and the authorities arrive here," Jorgep said with a nod. "Joya will be vulnerable for a while. But I think with the infrastructure and supplies Governus will undoubtedly have stockpiled here, we stand a chance."

Vernon nodded. "I have a ship I could send for as well."

I gave an encouraging smile to Andra. "You have major power with those stones, which is amazing, but it also makes you a bigger target. It's something to seriously consider."

"Also, setting the temporary aspect aside, I think it's also important to say that to *keep* a hold of Joya for the long term, I think you'll still need external help even after the GRC's investigation is complete. Ships. Guns," Griggs said bluntly.

Sarah nodded. "Yeah, combining resources is the play that makes the most sense."

I looked at Andra and Setso, who listened with non-committal looks on their faces. "Overall, this could be a great opportunity for you and us," I said. "You get to keep your land and protect the Heart Stone. We get to help you, and hopefully, depending how things work out, make a living here on Joya, too. Together, we could even make this into a thriving planet everyone would want to visit." I took in the royals relatively controlled expressions, having no clue what they were thinking. "Or not, of course. I mean, that's just one possibility."

Vernon gave his hands a wave. "This is a lot right now, I know. But it's a necessary discussion to have. You simply don't have the funds or the sway to do it all yourselves. That's the main issue." His tone was both clear and respectful. He steepled his fingers, leaning forward slightly. "We all want the Venanti to have Joya—I know I do—but once the GRC and the Magistrate finish their work, they won't support you in perpetuity. They offer short term assistance only. Even with a full claim on Joya, you'll still need allies to keep it."

The muscle of Setso's jaw clenched. "We don't care if it becomes a hot spot for visitors. We just want to live here in peace. The rest of the Galaxium can do whatever they please. We would, of course, allow the colonists of Egan to stay. They've already made homes here."

A myriad of expressions crossed Andra's face swifter than I could read them. "Certain further development might be agreeable as well. We would need to speak to the King and Queen about those things. But, having access to functioning starships would be beneficial. I've always dreamed of seeing the stars, as have many of our people," Andra murmured to her brother.

She was an adventurer at heart. I could tell by the wistful look that crossed her face. "By partnering with us, you won't have to stay locked to this planet. You can see the stars and more."

Andra's head tilted in serious consideration, while Setso nodded thoughtfully.

Vernon levelled his gaze on the Venanti royalty. "Please trust us when we say there are others as ruthless as Governus out there. We've seen what lengths some might go to in order to get their hands on your Heart Stones. One of them is still out there. If we're lucky Raker's left, but I suspect he hasn't." He shook his head, eyes pleading for the Venanti royals to agree.

Setso pulled Andra aside for a moment and they discussed in hushed tones. The rest of us chatted idly, watching and waiting for their decision. I wondered if they wished the King and Queen were here right about now. I know I would, if I were in their shoes.

For myself, I wasn't exactly confident with the idea of being part owner of a whole damn planet—I hadn't signed up for that… But at the same time, this opportunity to help and do something bigger with my life held a unique draw. My mother always used to say, "Everything happens for a reason, Finn." I never really took much stock in all of that fate garbage—believing I made my own fate—but who knows, maybe there was something to the theory after all.

The royal pair returned to join our group.

Setso sighed. "With our parents not being here, we must make the best decision we can in their place." He looked at Andra in wordless sibling communication, then carried on. "Andra and I both believe your knowledge of the current way of life and technology is an invaluable asset. We can learn much from you, and since you have proven trustworthy, a mutually beneficial partnership can be negotiated. But we need more time to talk it over."

"Absolutely. As do we. This is all very sudden." Vernon turned to address everyone. "First thing, we should take the time to bury our dead and mourn for those we've lost. After that, we will all load our haggard selves into the hover ship, get out of the sun, and get some much needed rest before reconvening to discuss further. Sound fair?" He glanced around the circle.

Everyone unanimously agreed.

Folks set to work digging out makeshift graves for the fallen, which stood to take a lot longer than anyone realized. Jorgep got the bright idea to use the hovership's blaster gun. He and Sarah disappeared into the ship and shot holes into the dirt while the rest of us steered clear.

The blasts worked well enough, creating gouges about three feet deep. Next, we laid all of our dead, Venanti and racer alike, to rest. The group gathered around each one afterward, paying respects and sharing a few honorific words. Sarah had planned to bring Tatara's body back to Egan to bury, but given the uncertainties of what we'd face upon our return there, she changed her mind. Tears slipped down her cheeks as she said farewell to her lover.

Once that somber task was complete, the lot of us headed into the hover ship.

By that time, Herc had regained his feet and was moving around—though his head still hung low. Like me, and everyone else, my poor horse was in desperate need of a place to sleep and recuperate. I went to him, giving his neck and shoulders a good rub down. So far, he'd shown no signs of going loopy. Andra and I theorized the Heart Stone simply saves life however it needs to. Herc's lungs wouldn't have needed any alteration outside of the Sweep. Hopefully, that was true. I tugged gently on his reins. "C'mon. A ration of oats is calling your name."

The group, including the Venanti, moved like a heel-dragging wave toward the hover ship's loading ramp. While we walked, Jorgep and Griggs played an old-timey hand game called rock-paper-scissors to see who'd operate the hover ship. Both had experience, apparently.

Jorgep's paper-like hand covered Griggs rock-like fist. "Ha! I win."

"Fine," Griggs muttered, grudgingly conceding the loss.

We ascended the ramp into the loading area. On the left rested a huge open doorway marked cargo hold. Jorgep and Keemi had already gone ahead. I followed suit—the ache in my muscles intensifying with every second. It was like my body sensed blissful rest was at hand, and had already begun shutting down in anticipation.

"Hey, do you need any help?" Griggs waited for me outside the door.

I smiled, moving past him. "Not really, but you can keep us company."

"Sounds good." His dimples made an appearance and my heart did a flip flop.

The sound of Herc's hooves clopping on the metal floor panels echoed as we walked into the hold. Sarah passed by, giving a tight smile. She must've just dropped off her suit. Without saying a word, I caught her arm and pulled her into a hug. She wilted like a flower against me, her breathing ragged and halting as she struggled not to cry.

"I'm so sorry, Sarah. Tatara was lovely." What else could I say? I squeezed tighter.

"Yeah, she was." Sarah buried her chin in my neck for a moment before pulling back. She mouthed the words *thank you*, then straightened her shoulders, exchanged a heartfelt nod with Griggs, and strode out of the hold.

I wiped a tear from my eye as Griggs and I carried on.

We entered the modest cargo hold. The space was half-full of equipment crates and Sarah's suit, which left a cramped area for Keemi and Herc to hang out. It was a tight fit, but it would do until we got back to Egan. Jorgep had already roped off half of the available space for Keemi, now readying feed for her. Griggs and I set to work roping off the other half for Herc.

Once we'd tightened the final knots, I loosened Herc's cinch and coolant breast strap, then pulled off his saddle. I tucked the liberally scuffed up tack on top of a wide crate, out of the way so Herc wouldn't get tripped up. Next, I removed his bridle. "There, that's better, hey?"

"Do you need anything else?" Griggs asked.

I pointed to the saddle. "In the square saddlebag behind the bedroll, there's a red halter. Looks kinda like a bridle, but not leather. Can you grab it for me?" The faster we got Herc fed and settled, the faster we could relax ourselves.

"Sure." He knelt beside the saddle, opening the compartment in question.

Jorgep gave Keemi a final scratch under the chin and turned to head out. "See you on the Nav Deck." He waved on the way by, then added in a gloating tone, "I bet she'll handle like a dream." Griggs gave him an eye roll, and Jorgep burst into hearty guffaws as he exited.

My next words tumbled from my mouth. "I just can't believe how few of us survived…"

Griggs appeared beside me, handed over the halter. "Yeah, it's terrible. But at least we did survive. It could've just as easily been us that didn't make it out. We got lucky." He let out a sullen laugh. "I still can't get the Seever shrieks out of my head."

"Me too… Between you and me, I'm a little nervous about what's yet to come. Of course, I'm trying to stay positive. I mean, when I came here all I wanted was to win some land, square my debts, and make a fresh start. Then all of *this* happened. I wasn't exactly expecting to 'take over' anything, you know?" My quiet chuckle gave way to a heavy sigh.

"Yeah, I know."

"Despite it all, I do believe we did the right thing, though. I keep reminding myself of that." Securing the halter over Herc's head, I whispered a solemn promise to return and properly groom him once we'd both rested up a bit. Next, I collected some food and water for him.

Griggs leaned against a stack of crates tethered by a cargo net to the wall. "Without a doubt, we did the right thing. We couldn't let the Heart Stone fall into Governus's hands—into *any* profit-hungry corp's hands. Plus, if we walk away now, they'll be lined up to steal Joya."

I let out a sigh. "I sure hope Raker's tiny chunk winds up being useless."

Griggs crossed his fingers. "Maybe the stones won't work outside the Sweep."

"Here's hoping." I set down the bowls in front of Herc. His head dipped immediately to indulge. Dusting my filthy hands off on my equally filthy cargo pants, I faced Griggs. "But seriously, I do think we'll need to play things close to the chest until we know these Egan colonists better. Like, are they innocent bystanders caught up in Governus's bullshit, or were they in on it too? This is all new territory and I *really* don't want to get blindsided again."

Griggs nodded. "Agreed. No blindsiding." He straightened from the crates.

I sensed the mood shift as his eyes gazed into mine. Fidgeting with the frayed hem on my tank top, I said quietly, "Um. Thanks again for saving me back in the Sweep. I would've died for sure if you hadn't. The fact you did that for me—and Herc—means the world."

A tender look crossed his face and a corner of his mouth curled up. He moved closer. "I should say the same to you. You and Herc saved my ass back there." Griggs rubbed the back of his neck, his cheeks flushing like a nervous schoolboy. "Listen, I should explain something else, too. I didn't actually *mean* what I said before—you know, when I said I cared about you like a sister. I mean, I do care—but not like that. I think you're amazing. You're smart, funny, and attractive, and, ah, I just panicked. And you were *so* mad at me. I got flustered, and—"

I grasped two fistfuls of shirt and pulled him in, stopping his rambling with a kiss.

The feel of his lips on mine, being fully lucid this time, sent a thrill through me. Heedless to the mild scratch his stubble caused, I revelled in the softness of his mouth. Griggs' warm hands found my waist before encircling me completely. I slid my arms about his shoulders, running my fingers through the hair at the nape of his neck. The faintest groan escaped his throat when I pressed closer and invited the touch of his tongue. As our hands explored and mouths slanted over and over, we melted into each other, straining for more.

Then I pulled back. "Ah, we should really check in at the Nav Deck, you know, before we find a spot to catch some Z's." Looking at his dimples, I fought the urge to kiss him again.

"We should?" His hand caressed my jawline, eliciting flutters.

I bit my lip, then nodded, my cheeks smouldering like embers. "We wouldn't want to miss anything important." I straightened my shirt and smoothed my hair.

"We wouldn't?" Griggs asked—his eyes still hungry for more.

It took all my willpower to resist hurtling myself back into his arms.

When he realized I wasn't going to cave, Griggs grudgingly stepped back with a nod. "You're right. There's bigger fish to fry." He let out a mock-anguished groan, then darted in to steal a quick peck. "Okay, let's go." He ducked under the rope pen and headed to the exit.

I couldn't help but grin. "Just give me a second." Though Herc was happily chewing on oats, I sidled up to give him one more rub on his muzzle. His ocular implant shone a nice calm shade of blue—a welcome sight. He leaned his head against my shoulder, giving me a nudge.

"You saved a lot of lives in the Sweep, Herc. You saved *my* life. I'm really glad you're still with me. Life wouldn't be the same without you." I wiped a tear from my eye before it could fall, blinking a few times fast to clear the residual moisture. "Thanks for carrying me through."

Giving him one more pat, I turned and rejoined Griggs in the corridor.

"Ready?" He reached out a hand. His fingers threaded between mine and we shared a smile. I gave him a nod, feeling oddly confident that whatever unknown future awaited, we'd be able to face it together. Not just Griggs and I—but all of us. My new alliance.

"As ready as I'll ever be."

ACKNOWLEDGEMENTS

First off, I want to thank my husband Steve who read my novel and has been my sounding board all the way along, and to my kids, Eithan and Austin, who have such imaginative minds, and gave stellar name suggestions for cities and planets. I couldn't have written Race to Novus without their unfailing love and support, their willingness to let me type away in the office for hours now and then, and of course, for all of their cheerleading behind the scenes. They embolden me to chase my dreams, and are the most priceless heart stones in this lucky gal's sweep.

A huge thank you to Andrew Ferrell of Cloaked Press LLC for believing in both me and this novel, to the cover designer Carmilla Mayes, and anyone else with the publishing company who helped to make this book the very best it can be.

Thanks to God for blessing me with words to wield, and for guiding my path—even while giving obstacles to overcome—for it all provided valuable life experience, grit, and ultimately led me to what I was meant to be doing... writing and illustrating.

I'd like to give my humble thanks to all of the other wonderful people who've helped get this book out into the world, some of which might be part of multiple groups listed below. But for the sake of ink and paper preservation, I'll minimize duplicate mentions, and refer to the group or tasks each person helped the most. To start things off, I'll say thanks to the incredible crew of beta readers that gave of their time to read the full novel and share their feedback with me: Karlynn Sievers, Sue Cook, Chad Klein, Lisa Flower, Connie Chang, and Rosa Rawlings. Adding to that, I should also mention Andrea Goyan and Amethyst Loscocco, who both read a few versions of my first chapters.

I'm equally grateful for the WAB beta reading group, who so diligently read every chapter of my novel over many months: Sharon Boyle, Deanna West, Perla Camacho, Mark

Kramarzewski, Allison Hickman, Devis Contrato, Becky Grenfell, Chrissie Rohrman, and Talia Camozzi.

I want to give a special shout out to Josie Thwaites-Queen (my accountability partner), Karlynn Seivers, Sue Cook, and Holly Rae Garcia for being encouraging and esteemed writing/publishing buddies. I'll give a nod to Lisa Short here as well, for she read the original Race to Novus short story and encouraged me to keep writing, saying it had a great hook.

Thank you to the folks in the WAB Query Group: Kim Hart, Janna Miller, Haley Hwang, Shelby Van Pelt, Lydia Collins, Cayce Osborne, Sean Fallon, Trey Dowell, who were kind enough to read my query letters, synopses, and first chapters by them several times when I was in the querying trenches with this book. Katie Jordan also kindly helped to this end.

Thanks to Write Around the Block (WAB), which has been safe spaces for me to hang out, make valuable writing friends, and hone my craft. Thank you to my local Portage la Prairie writing group The Night Writers, who welcomed and uplifted me at monthly meetings while this novel was going through drafts of edits. And of course, I must thank my street team, the Launchables, who've given support and helped spread the word about my books.

Thanks to my good friends Kerri and Mel and the gals I lovingly know as the Bitch Club, who've always been encouraging.

Thanks to Theresa Green and her team at The Writer's Workout for holding the Writer's Games and running the world building event that spurred me to create the short story that inspired this novel.

Thank you to the two Futurescapes crews I've had the pleasure of workshopping this novel with, the first being: Gabriel Salmeron, John Newsom, Roni Stinger, Felicia Martinez, Regis Geoffroy, and Angela Day. A special nod goes out to literary agent Kimberley Cameron (our lead faculty) who's encouragement and kind Futurescapes Award nomination spurred me to complete the novel. The second is: Susan Sechrist, Angie Abdelmonem, Kenny Falconer, Kristie Wang, Samantha Paine, and Neil Flinchbaugh, and of course our lead faculty Sarah Younger (literary agent), who went above and beyond with giving feedback, and was quite frankly, a joy to be in sessions with. Everyone's constructive feedback was very helpful.

Thank you to my high school English teacher, Mrs. Paulette Buizer, who kindly gave her time to encourage me to keep writing. I have no idea where life might have carried her, but I'll never forget that.

Lastly, thank you to my father Jerry Rempel, who doesn't read much of my work, but did read an early draft of this book. He gave some helpful feedback, and said it was alright—that it read like a real book. In his own low-key way, that meant he enjoyed it, which means a lot.

I hope I haven't missed naming anyone else who's given their assistance in some way, whether big or small. If I have, I am very sorry, and please just know how incredibly grateful I am for you, too.

It truly does take a village to bring a book baby into the world, and I feel so blessed to have the supportive community I do. From the bottom of my heart, thank you.

R.A. Clarke

ABOUT THE AUTHOR

R.A. Clarke is a former police officer turned stay-at-home mom living with her family in Portage la Prairie, Manitoba. Besides raising two rambunctious boys, soaking in lake time, and acting in community theatre, R.A.'s spare time is spent plotting fantastical novels and multi-genre short fiction. Her tales have been featured in various publications, and have won international writing contests, such as Red Penguin Books' humour contest, the Writer's Weekly 24-hour contest, The Writer's Workout: Writer's Games, and the 2023 Write Fighters 3-Day Novella Challenge. She was also a finalist for both the 2021 Futurescapes Award and the 2022 Dark Sire Awards.

R.A. Clarke writes and illustrates a children's chapter book series for ages 7-10 as Rachael Clarke as well. The first book in that series, The Big Ol' Bike—a story about a smaller than average kid with a huge heart—was named a Females of Fiction Award finalist by Hindi's Libraries in 2021. To learn more, please visit: www.rachaelclarkewrites.com.

Social Media:
Facebook: https://www.facebook.com/raclarkeauthor
Twitter: https://www.twitter.com/raclarkewrites
Instagram: https://www.instagram.com/rachaelclarkewrites
Website: https://www.rachaelclarkewrites.com/
Linktr.ee: https://linktr.ee/raclarkewrites